TEMPTING *The* EARL

Books by Rachael Miles

Tempting the Earl

Chasing the Heiress

Jilting the Duke

Published by Kensington Publishing Corporation

TEMPTING *The* EARL

RACHAEL MILES

ZEBRA BOOKS
KENSINGTON PUBLISHING CORP.
http://www.kensingtonbooks.com

ZEBRA BOOKS are published by

Kensington Publishing Corp.
119 West 40th Street
New York, NY 10018

All Kensington titles, imprints, and distributed lines are available at special quantity discounts for bulk purchases for sales promotion, premiums, fund-raising, educational, or institutional use.

Special book excerpts or customized printings can also be created to fit specific needs. For details, write or phone the office of the Kensington Sales Manager: Attn.: Sales Department. Kensington Publishing Corp., 119 West 40th Street, New York, NY 10018. Phone: 1-800-221-2647.

Zebra and the Z logo Reg. U.S. Pat. & TM Off.

First Printing: November 2016
ISBN-13: 978-1-4201-4090-3
ISBN-10: 1-4201-4090-6

eISBN-13: 978-1-4201-4091-0
eISBN-10: 1-4201-4091-4

10 9 8 7 6 5 4 3 2 1

Printed in the United States of America

To Mary W. Hawkins, a clever woman

ACKNOWLEDGMENTS

In a difficult year, I have met with exceptional patience, generosity, and kindness.

When I couldn't think or write, Courtney Miller-Callihan at Handspun Literary, my agent, and Esi Sogah, my editor, helped me do both. Esi miraculously created time where there was none, and when I could do no more, she made a path. Her thoughtful decisions and the helpful commentary of Tory Groshong, my more-than-copyeditor, turned my ingredients into a book. Whatever is good in these pages comes from their intervention.

At Kensington, I remain grateful for Janice Rossi's cover design, Anthony Russo's illustration of it, and Erin Nelsen Parekh's cover blurb, as well as Ross Plotkin's kind management of the book's production. I remain indebted to Kimberly Richardson, Lauren Jernigan, and Jane Nutter for their helpful advice and savvy promotions. Outside of Kensington, Jodi Thomas and Cathy Maxwell offered priceless support, while the Handspinners (my agency-mates) offer a welcome (and welcoming) community.

Cathy Blackwell, Celia Bonaduce, Leigh Bonds, Michelle Carlin, Ann Donahue, Stephanie Eckroth, Erick Kelemen, Emily Donnerberg Rowin, Ashley Stovall, and Kathrine Varnes were always available for support or laughter. Maria Hasbany and Allison Whitney offered light in a dark time, while Lynn, Ward, and Cal Rushton always manage to make me laugh.

My deepest thanks as always is to Miles, who makes everything better.

Soon she was receiving correspondence from across the land, asking for her help—or rather An Honest Gentleman's help—in revealing this or that wrong. From one informant in the London hells, she now had more than twenty across Britain. She'd become—according to Tories—the greatest threat to a peaceable England since Napoleon. But no one expected a short, softly rounded woman with a middle-class accent to wield the pen that caused MPs to shudder. She—and her old employers—had believed anonymity would protect her. Now, she was not so sure.

She looked ahead, dismayed by the remaining distance to the carriage. The women stood outside the bookshop, their heads bowed in conversation. *Keep talking*, she willed them. But they moved forward, where a waiting footman handed each one up a three-stepped stool, into the carriage.

She glanced at the nearest window. He still followed. She tamped down on her welling panic. What would she do if he caught her? Him, of all people? It was crucial that An Honest Gentleman's next essay appear before the upcoming Parliamentary session. One of her trusted correspondents had written that a bill widely supported by the conservative MPs was financed by a group of powerful criminals. But he'd refused to send the name through the mail. If she missed their first meeting, her correspondent might never agree to another.

Before her, the door to the carriage remained open, the footman still waiting. Olivia's heart rose. Someone else was in the shop!

Instinctively she quickened her pace, then slowed. But it was too late; he had increased his pace as well. With each long step, he narrowed the distance between them. But he had not yet crossed to her side of the street. The carriage would hide her escape.

Only four more shops and she'd be there.

The footman opened the shop door again, and a young

woman with a brightly colored feather in her hat moved slowly toward the open carriage door. At the carriage, the younger woman stopped before the steps, then held out her hand. The postilion placed it on his shoulder, and the woman raised her right foot slowly to the first step, bringing her left up to meet it, then repeated the deliberate action. Another time Olivia would have wondered at the young woman's slow movements, but not today. No, all that mattered was reaching the shop. And she was almost there.

The footman opened the shop door once more, stepping back to let yet another woman out of the shop. Olivia's eyes met his, pleading, and he held the door another fraction of a second, long enough for her to leap into the bookstore. As the door shut behind her, she heard the coachman call out to the postilion to lash the steps on tight. For another moment or two, the carriage would hide her escape.

To the right of the entrance, two kind-faced women stood at a counter, one an aristocrat, the other a shopkeeper.

"I need . . ." She saw the carriage begin to pull away from the sidewalk, and just past it, the man crossing the street to the shop. She turned back to the women, who waited expectantly. "A man is following me. Can you help?"

Neither woman looked startled. The shopkeeper spoke quickly. "Follow me."

The aristocrat turned confident gray eyes to Olivia. "I'll give you time. Go."

Olivia obeyed without thinking.

"This whole row of buildings backs up to a marsh." The bookseller spoke softly, as they hurried toward the back of the shop. "No back exit."

Olivia felt her stomach tighten. He would find her. If

she had time, she could hide the instructions in a book. But which one?

"The roof, however, connects this row of buildings almost to the tollbooth beyond the marsh."

"The roof?" Olivia felt her throat tighten. He'd found her on a roof once before. She pushed the memory away. He'd been angry enough then. This time he had more cause.

"If you are afraid of the roof, lock the attic door behind you and hide until I return."

"I'm not afraid."

"Good. On the roof, you'll find a path of sorts. Stay near the back of the buildings. That way, no one will see you from the street. At the end, climb down a series of lower roofs and balconies until you reach the ground—the descent is protected from view by the curve of the buildings. From there, you can slip into the street unnoticed. It isn't too hard." The woman smiled, then added, "If you have a bit of a tomboy in you."

The shop doorbell rang. Olivia looked toward the salesroom, the woman following her eyes. "I have more than a bit. Where do I start?"

The bookseller motioned to Olivia's right. A piece of heavy brocade pinned with dozens of broadsides covered the wall between two bookcases. The bookseller pushed against it. Not a wall. A door. The woman stepped into a small office, and Olivia, with a last quick glance over her shoulder, closed the office door behind them.

"He's here. I hear his voice."

"Go up three flights. My rooms, then the attic, then the roof." The bookseller opened a smaller door leading to a stairway, then held out a key. "Lock the door behind you. Leave the key on the hook beside the door."

"How will you retrieve it?"

"I have a second key. You must hurry."

The bookseller paused, searching Olivia's face.

"If you need help again, you will find it. The African's Daughter turns no one away. Now, you must go."

Olivia clasped the woman's hand gratefully, then ran up the stairs.

Sophia Gardiner, Lady Wilmot, prepared to be a distraction.

The shop formed a long rectangle, with the bookseller's counter at the front right, and bookcases down the outer walls. Large tables covered with the latest books filled the front quarter of the shop. Beyond that, tables ran down the middle of the store, flanked on either side by additional bookcases.

Sophia positioned herself at the table displaying her own just-published book, *Mrs. Teachwell's Guide to Botany for Young Ladies and Girls*. From her position, she could observe visitors through the mirrors at the tops of the walls, and she could easily intercept anyone who started down any of the rows.

Seeing a figure approach the door, she pretended to tidy stacks of her book. She made sure not to look toward the door, not even when the bell rang, signaling someone's entry.

A tall man stepped to the far left, looking down each row of shelves as he moved back toward the middle. Sophia watched him warily in the mirrors, until she realized she knew him and knew him well. It was Harrison Levesford, Lord Walgrave, a friend of her late husband's.

"Walgrave! How lovely to see you!" She welcomed him with a friendly embrace. "You've come to buy my book! I had no idea you were interested in botany."

Harrison looked startled, then recovered quickly. Admirably, in fact, Sophia thought.

"I hoped to support your efforts, my lady, both as an author and as a patron of this bookstore." He looked around the shop a second time. "But, I must admit, I've never considered that a bookstore might need a patron."

"Isn't it lovely? If my patronage can bring Miss Equiano's bookshop better trade, then I'm happy she approached me." She smiled broadly, hoping he would not notice the bookseller's absence. "Can I show you my books? I'm so pleased with the options John Murray, the publisher, has provided."

Lady Wilmot held her hand over the different piles of books, describing each one. "They come in a range of bindings—paper, canvas, or leather—and the engravings come either colored or not. Some copies, though they cost a bit more, come with a pretty purple ribbon to mark your place."

Sophia showed him the ribbon, giving the frightened woman more time to escape. Even so, she found it difficult to believe that any woman could be frightened of thorough, sober Walgrave. "As you can see, the print quality is quite fine, and the engravings—I'm especially pleased with their detail, such delicate lines." She turned to an engraving of a rose, alluding to the plot that had recently threatened her life, one that Walgrave had helped thwart. It was a further distraction, intended to draw Walgrave's attention from the dark-haired woman.

The bell rang to admit another customer, but Walgrave did not look to see who had entered. Instead he took the book from Sophia's hand. "A rose." He shook his head at the allusion. "I'm not sure how Forster manages you, my lady."

"I never try," a deep voice spoke from over Harrison's shoulder. Aidan Somerville, Lord Forster, extended his arms in brotherly welcome. As the two men embraced,

Constance Equiano silently took a place across the table from Lady Wilmot.

"Walgrave, it's fine of you to come." Aidan patted Walgrave's shoulder. "How many of my fiancée's books are you buying? I hear they make fine presents for younger cousins."

"Just one . . . for me. My cousins are unfortunately too old for Lady Walgrave's book."

As Walgrave and Aidan's conversation turned from books to more pressing parliamentary concerns, the men moved away from Lady Wilmot's table. Without speaking, Constance met Lady Wilmot's eyes, then looked out the large display window. Across the street at the corner, a well-dressed man talked with a severe-looking woman. As Sophia watched, the man shifted his position, clearly watching the shop. Sophia nodded her understanding to Constance. The woman could have been fleeing the man still waiting outside, and not Walgrave at all.

"I disagree, Forster. The immediate problem is the legislation," Walgrave said. "The Tories wish to make any public meeting with more than fifty participants illegal. They contend that the reform societies are fomenting sedition among the lower classes."

"But Walgrave, it is not the meetings that endanger English peace, but idleness and hunger. Idleness allows men to *attend* the meetings; hunger encourages them to *believe* any bad doctrine or to join any mad experiment that might alleviate their misery."

"Bravo, darling." Lady Wilmot joined them, twining her hand around Forster's elbow. "I'm sure Walgrave appreciates your skill at debate, but the poor man must have other errands before we meet at the theater." She turned to Walgrave. "Kean himself is on the playbill."

Looking out the window, Walgrave ran his hand through his thick blond hair. He needed an excuse to remain in the bookshop a little longer. "Actually, your ladyship, I wished to acquire some books." He patted his waistcoat at the pockets. "Yet I seem to have misplaced my list."

The bookseller intervened. "If you would send me your list, I can gather the books and deliver them."

"I'd prefer to wander the shelves, see if anything jogs my memory." Walgrave looked over his shoulder into the long row stretching back behind him and ending in darkness. "Do you have literature in Greek? I misplaced my old copy of Homer's *Odyssey*. I'd also be interested in books on navigation or seafaring."

"Thinking of returning to the navy, Walgrave?" Aidan lounged comfortably against the table of Lady Wilmot's books.

"Only when I need an escape from parliamentary controversy. More often, it's simply an abiding interest that I satisfy from my armchair."

"Then Constance, you must point out your father's book." Lady Wilmot put her hand on the bookseller's shoulder. "Surely, Walgrave, you know *The Interesting Narrative of the Life of Olaudah Equiano*?"

"Ah, yes." Walgrave gave Constance a more considered look. "The name of your bookshop, the African's Daughter—it makes sense now. I've always intended to read Mr. Equiano's autobiography, if you have a copy."

"I'm happy to show you." Constance beckoned him to follow her into the dark depths of the store. It was the sort of bookshop one could happily get lost in: long aisles of books, punctuated by a table or a comfortable chair. But he couldn't risk being drawn to the allure of the books—he had to keep his wits about him.

The bookseller seemed intent on remaining with him, so he expressed interest in one field after another.

Periodically—seeing a book he recognized from a positive notice in the *Monthly Review*—he would add it to the growing stack in the bookseller's arms. By the time he and the bookseller reached the far back corner, he had more than twenty titles.

"My stack has grown almost too tall for you to carry." He looked longingly at the next shelf. "Perhaps I could continue looking, while you determine how much I owe you."

Constance gave a quick sidelong glance to the middle of the right wall—where broadsides and other papers covered a wide brocaded cloth.

Her eyes returned to his, the hope in them unmistakable. "*All* of these?" The set of her shoulders was tense. She clearly expected him to decide against his purchases.

True, he had intended only to buy at most three of the books, but he was unwilling to disappoint her.

"All."

A smile tugged at the corners of her mouth, then spread broadly. "Of course, your lordship. I will have the total at the desk." She hurried to the front, balancing his stack of books on her hip.

Once she was out of sight, he slipped away quietly to investigate. The brocade covered a wooden door, behind which a tiny room housed a desk, a chair, piles of books, and a stairwell up to the bookseller's lodgings. No outdoor exit on this level.

"Walgrave!" Forster's voice resounded down the aisle.

Harrison pulled the brocaded door shut, using the flat of his hand to control the sound of the door clicking against the jamb. He pulled a book from the nearest shelf.

"Ah, there you are." Forster read the sign over the rack of shelves Walgrave stood before. "In household management?"

Walgrave held up a battered edition of Susanna MacIver's *Cookery and Pastry*. "My cook deserves a gift."

Forster barked a laugh. "She must, to put up with you. But no matter. We are going. Do you wish for a ride back to Mayfair?"

Walgrave considered his options. "Would Whitehall put you out of your way?"

Chapter Two

"You are late, my dear, very late. The curtain opens in an hour," chided Mrs. Helena Wells, the star of the night's main play and editor of the *World*. "Come in. Tell me what you discovered."

But when Olivia stepped into the light of the dressing room, Mrs. Wells and Meg, the wardrobe maid, both gasped.

"My girl, look at your dress. With those tears, it's fit only for the workhouse! And you are covered, head to feet, in dirt." Mrs. Wells wet a towel with water from the basin. "Meg, bring Miss Olivia's costume here. She can dress with me."

Olivia waited until the maid left before speaking.

"It's soot. I was followed from my meeting with Mentor, and my only escape was by rooftop." Olivia scrubbed her hands and face with the towel. Her hands trembled with the aftereffects of fear and desperation. "The descent wasn't meant for a dress."

"I don't like this. It was much safer when we received all our information by correspondence at the *World*. Then the only risk came in confirming that what our various writers told us was true. But this new set of informants, insisting on meeting in person, making you skulk about in alleys or taverns, and escape by rooftop! It's not safe, Olivia. The tips I've taught you on how to alter your appearance are little good against a knife or a pistol or a strong man intent to overpower you. And the number of meetings . . . how many this week?"

"Only three. This afternoon, tonight, and tomorrow. I agree: The risk is greater, but the information is invaluable. This afternoon, I was simply stupid—stupid and reckless." Olivia felt frustration tighten at the back of her throat. "I could have altered my height, or my gait, or used paints to appear old or misshapen. But I did none of it. I only hope Mentor was not also seen."

"I imagine you thought it was foolish to put on one set of paints only to come here and put on another." Mrs. Wells patted Olivia's arm consolingly. "Yet we should have anticipated someone would try to unmask our Gentleman by unsavory means. Not a day goes by without another letter demanding to know who An Honest Gentleman is, and not a week without another speech in Parliament decrying our Gentleman's investigations. I thought your sex would protect you from suspicion, but I was wrong."

"No, I should have been circumspect." Olivia refused to be mollified, not when the stakes were so high. "But I was lucky to have seen him following me, lucky to have found strangers willing to help me, lucky even that the bookseller's building was so suited for escape. Just think—if I hadn't seen him I would have led him straight to you."

"But, my dear, how many times have you been in London—in *that part* of London—and never been followed?" Mrs. Wells shook her head disapprovingly. "The next time you are in town, we will expand your repertoire of costumes before you have any more meetings. We will talk to the property-master—thicker soles on your walking shoes would make you taller, and wigs . . . we can do surprising things with wigs. Perhaps he'll even let us borrow that marvelous one you wear in the interlude."

A sharp tap at the door silenced the pair, and Meg entered, followed by the wardrobe mistress. The pair placed Olivia's costume on an empty chair.

The wardrobe mistress, Mrs. Price, a stern old woman who had been an actress in her youth and still played any hag or witch in the repertoire, examined Olivia. "There's no salvage for that dress. Soot, you say?"

Olivia nodded.

Mrs. Price held out a gnarled finger to Meg. "Get one of the burlap bags. It won't do to get soot on Mrs. Wells's feathers. And you"—she pointed Olivia to behind the dressing screen—"I'll help you contain the mess."

At Mrs. Price's direction, Olivia unbuttoned her walking dress to the waist, then folded the bodice down over the skirt to the point where Mrs. Price held up the skirt by its hem. The pair then rolled the material from Olivia's hips to the floor. Even so, the dress tucked into the burlap bag with a dark puff.

"Price, dear, can you find something Olivia can wear home?" Mrs. Wells called from the other side of the screen.

"She can take the blue muslin walking dress she's wearing at the end of the afterpiece—but it has to be returned tomorrow by noon."

"That's excellent," Mrs. Wells cooed. "Of course it will be back in time."

Mrs. Price pressed a key into Olivia's hand, whispering, "My son Horace will watch over you." Price picked up the soot-filled bag and left the room, calling Meg to follow.

Olivia, dressed in only her chemise and drawers, stepped from behind the dressing screen. Holding out the key, she asked, "What did you tell her?"

"You are meeting with an old lover." Mrs. Wells, seated at her mirror, applied white powder to heighten the contrast between her skin and her paints. "He has refused to accept the end of your liaison and might be belligerent. Horace will intervene on the word *stop*."

Olivia stepped back behind the screen to don her costume for the evening. When she finished, she watched as Mrs. Wells rubbed lampblack on her eyelids to define her eyes, then, using a pot of artist's pigment, painted her lips and cheeks.

"Can you help me with this, my dear?" Wells picked up a flamboyant hat dyed a rather startling shade of orange with an ostrich feather stuck upright at the back. When she moved her head, the ostrich feather moved with her, creating the effect that the feather shared her every opinion.

Olivia held the hat straight as Wells pinned it into place. Olivia had come to admire Wells, as an actress, editor, and even an adviser, but with her the story always came first, and Olivia had secrets.

Should she tell Wells that she knew the man who had been following her? Suddenly, and without warning, she remembered the last time he had held her. The weight of his body on hers as he'd pressed her into the wall. She felt again the warmth of his breath against her neck, the caress of his lips moving in a line from her jaw, down her neck, across her chest, slowly, maddeningly, until he'd taken the soft center of her breast into his mouth, and teased it until her whole body ached with need and desire.

"Olivia! My dear! You are flushed." The actress searched Olivia's face for signs of illness or fatigue. "Are you well?"

Olivia returned to the present moment with a start. "It's only a bit of stage fright, that's all."

"But there's no need for nerves. I knew from the moment I heard you sing that you had to perform the gypsy's role in my benefit. Even if you couldn't act that voice would mesmerize them. But then when you took the stage— oh, you are made for it! Once they hear you tonight, my benefit will be the talk of the town—and talk sells newspapers, dear!"

"Well, you will be pleased with your ticket sales for tonight's benefit. The stage manager says they sold more than four hundred advance tickets." The thought of that many faces watching her sing made Olivia's throat go dry. "That should provide a nice income for you and the other actors during the off-season."

"That it will, my dear, that it will." Mrs. Wells preened, pulling on long gloves dyed the same garish orange as her headdress. "Oh, dear, you look green. But once you are on stage, you'll feel right at home. Besides, there's no one to replace you at this late hour. Mrs. Farley sent a note only half an hour ago that she will not be performing tonight. The old diva has fallen ill—or rather drunk—for the third time this week, and the understudy Julia is taking her place." The ostrich feather conveyed Mrs. Wells's disapproval. "Can you hand me my wrap, dear?"

Olivia picked up the gossamer shawl, a rich violet, to complete Wells's costume, but her thoughts were far away. How had Harrison found her? The neighborhood was far from his typical haunts. If he was in that part of London during the day, he had likely been sent there, but by whom? And for what purpose? She had seen him only after she and her informant had parted ways. Still, Harrison may have seen the meeting. Would he recognize the man who had offered her his arm to cross a muddy stretch of boardwalk?

As she considered whether the entire situation could have been simple chance, Olivia tried to shake off the niggling fear that she had been betrayed. She would have to warn Mentor. It would be risky, even dangerous, to meet again so soon, but she had little choice. Not warning him could be disastrous.

"Of course, you must be careful." Mrs. Wells hadn't

noticed that Olivia was lost in her own thoughts, and Olivia struggled to put together the pieces of Wells's lost conversation. "Would you recognize him if you were to see him again? Did he have any distinguishing features or marks?"

"Tall, quite tall. Lithe, but with a strong set to the jaw and shoulders. A deliberate walk, firm with long strides." Olivia closed her eyes, remembering the surprisingly graceful way Harrison moved.

"My word, girl. How he walks is nearly useless if he comes to the *World* looking for you. What of his hair color? His eyes? His clothing?"

"You won't need to recognize him. I know his name. It's Harrison Levesford, Lord Walgrave. He was once my husband."

Mrs. Wells fell backwards dramatically in her chair. "Your *husband*? I thought you were a widow."

"I am, in a way. But it's a long and not very interesting story." She leaned over to buss the older actress's cheek. "And it's far less important at this moment than getting into my costume and paints. You've given me this chance, and I don't want to disappoint you. I promise: I will tell you all tomorrow."

Mrs. Wells sat brooding as Olivia picked up her costume. Part shepherdess, part gypsy, the dress was designed to tease the audience. The blousy cotton bodice scooped low enough to reveal the soft mounds of her breasts, while the colorful skirt split on one side to reveal glimpses of her calf and knee. Olivia knew Wells was deciding how much to push her, so she kept her silence as she dressed.

When Wells eventually spoke, it was with resignation. "I haven't time to find out the whole story *and* help with your face, so I will let it go . . . for now." She picked up her pots of paint. "Sit. It's time to transform you from mouse to temptress."

Half an hour later, having described each step, Mrs. Wells handed Olivia a hand mirror. "Your own mother wouldn't recognize you tonight."

Olivia regarded herself with surprise. Wells had thickened and darkened her brows, brightened her cheeks with more rouge, filled out her lips with a deep red pigment, and applied a dark beauty mark under her lower lip at the corner. "*I* don't even recognize myself."

Wells tucked Olivia's shoulder-length brown hair under a thick wig of heavy red tresses that reached almost to Olivia's waist, then stepped back, clearly pleased with her work. "Now let me see the rest of you."

Olivia stood, smoothing her skirts, then lifted her chin and held her shoulders back.

"Turn." Mrs. Wells waved her hand in a circle. "But as you will on stage. Use your body, your clothes, to captivate me."

Olivia paused and closed her eyes. Imagining herself in her part as a seductive gypsy, she stretched out her arms shoulder level, then began to undulate her hips and arms slowly as she turned.

"You will drive the rakes mad." Mrs. Wells held out a fan. "Now what signals are you to use for this meeting with your informant?"

Olivia removed her instructions from her reticule. "To refuse the meeting, I open my fan but snap it shut against the palm of my right hand. But I'm not going to refuse."

"You have no idea what might happen between now and the end of the play. It's best to keep your instructions in mind, in case something unanticipated happens. Tell me the rest."

Olivia sighed, knowing Mrs. Wells was right. Too much that they had not anticipated had already happened. "To accept the meeting, I open the fan with my left hand and draw it down my jawline. The meeting itself will take place in the prop room beside the old lion cages, immediately following my performance."

Mrs. Wells placed her hand on Olivia's arm. "My dear, are you certain you wish to risk this meeting? My gut tells me this man is dangerous. Surely writing another novel would involve fewer dangers."

"You simply don't like his pen name." Olivia tried to keep her tone light.

"Cerberus. Guardian of the gates of hell. Now why would such a name give me pause?" Mrs. Wells's ostrich feather turned down, disapprovingly.

"There's more at stake than my safety, Helena. We need Cerberus's information." Olivia put her hand on top of the older woman's. "But I'll be safe. We planned it this way. The theater will be full. Horace will be watching to protect me if I need him. This is the safest possible place to take this man's measure."

Mrs. Wells embraced her unexpectedly. "Be wary, Livvy. I'd rather lose the most scandalous information than see my best correspondent harmed."

Olivia tied a loosely knit shawl at her hip and tucked the fan in at her waist. She held up her reticule. "When I go onstage, might I leave this here?"

Mrs. Wells began to reply, but a loud voice from the corridor called, "Mrs. Wells. You are needed on the stage. Mrs. Wells."

"I must go, dear. I promised to show Julia the changes we made yesterday to the fourth act. She dies then, you know, and very prettily." The actress took one last look in the mirror, then headed to the door, answering with only partial attention. "You may remain here until your performance. And leave anything you like, dear, anything at all."

Chapter Three

"Drinking without me, gentlemen?" Harrison asked his two oldest friends as he entered his study.

Henry, Lord Capersby and John, Lord Palmersfield, were collapsed in the two most comfortable chairs, legs extended, cravats untied, each holding a full glass of wine.

"I see you've found my best claret." Harrison loosened his cravat while glancing at the clock. He had more than enough time to share a drink with his friends, change clothes, and meet Forster and Lady Wilmot at the theater.

"Join us, Walgrave. We've left you the couch." Capersby gestured broadly, or as broadly as he could from the depths of his chair. "We're discussing the newest rage of a novel. Francis Jeffrey, the editor of the *Edinburgh Review*, calls it 'immoral, corrupt, and improper for women.'"

"Listen to this one." Palmersfield held up the *Monthly Review*. "'The plot is instructive, encouraging dissolute young nobles to value their estates and family ties, particularly their faithful and long-suffering wives. But we cannot laud the story itself. Beginning with war and espionage, the narrative progresses through every gothic abomination imagined by Horace Walpole or Monk Lewis.

Murdered corpses rot in the ancient manor walls, long-lost heirs are identified by bloody birthmarks, unearthly music fills the manor at night, and ghosts walk from paintings. Rape, shocking incest, and other sins lead our noble protagonist—we cannot call him a hero—to a cruel and bloody end, justified by his dereliction and deceit. How much better would the novel have been, both for public morals and private instruction, if the lady proclaimed as its author had relied more heavily on the model of Mrs. Radcliffe?'"

Walgrave settled onto the couch, stretching his long legs out across the opposite bolster. "No redeeming qualities?"

"None whatsoever," Capersby declared. "I've already subscribed to the author's next book."

"Does this paragon of literary skill have a title?" Walgrave swirled his wine, watching it move against the glass.

"The Deserted Wife," the two men said in near unison.

"Or? There must be an *or*. Perhaps *the perils of virtue*? or *the reward of infamy*." The tightness in his lower back began to loosen. It had been too long since he'd relaxed like this.

"*The lap of luxury. The hounds of hell*," Capersby chimed in from the depth of his chair. "Subtitles are better when they alliterate."

"*The louts of London*. Present company included." Palmersfield raised a challenging eyebrow. "The title is *The Deserted Wife*. Nothing more."

In mock umbrage, Capersby sat upright. "Duels! There must be duels. Palmersfield has called us louts. You, Parliament's greatest orator. And me, London's brightest legal mind." With a flourish, he brought his hand to his chest, raising his chin in a mock theatrical pose. "Brighter even than Palmersfield."

"I'm sure your bright legal mind, even pickled as it is

now, can recall when you've behaved as an ill-mannered clown," Palmersfield scoffed.

"I'm being one, even now." Capersby grinned winningly, and Palmersfield shook his head with mock dismay.

"Palmersfield, how did you come to pick up such a book?" Walgrave turned the conversation deftly in another direction. "Have you traded your dratted ornithology books for gothic novels?"

"Capersby dared me to read it," Palmersfield confessed.

Walgrave raised one eyebrow. "But it must have included birds for you to *finish* it."

Palmersfield brushed back the wave of bronze hair that had fallen forward over his left eye. "Three, in fact—all birds of prey, tearing the flesh of the deserting husband. All quite accurate in the descriptions. I wonder if the anonymous *lady* author is one of us."

"One of us?"

"A Cambridge man," Capersby explained. "I know a dozen men who write novels under women's names because women's novels are priced higher and sell better. But the Latin epigraphs are exact—that's not something a woman would do correctly."

"And the science is top-notch." Palmersfield pulled out the loosened cork from a bottle of claret on the floor.

"Top-notch science in a gothic novel." Harrison watched Palmersfield pour another glass. "What's this world coming to?"

"It's quite a good read." Capersby waved his fingers for the bottle. "Jeffrey is right. There's not a moral in it."

"Unless," Palmersfield interjected, "you count the observation that women, like men, are capable of strategic revenge."

"Nothing new there." Walgrave breathed in the aroma

of the claret, then drank. "The wars taught us that, if we didn't know it before."

"I'll send the three volumes over tomorrow. You might even like it. Besides, you can't be hopelessly out of fashion all the time." Capersby passed Walgrave the half-empty bottle.

"To avoid the sin of being out of fashion and with the recommendation of two such . . . discriminating . . . readers, I'll read it between parliamentary reports."

"Or perhaps you could simply read it," Palmersfield chided. "Take an afternoon. Get your terrible cook to make you some cakes, and *read*. Parliament will still be there when you finish, and you might find yourself refreshed. Lately when we see you . . ."

"*If* we see you," Capersby corrected.

"If we see you, you look a cross between, well, cross and beleaguered."

"Yes, man, we've had to invade your study and wait for your return." Capersby counted the empty bottles strewn around their chairs. "We've drunk four bottles."

Harrison emptied the remaining wine into his goblet. "Make that five."

"We even drank slowly," Palmersfield said only half apologetically.

The men grew silent, waiting for Harrison's reply. He had been fast friends with Palmersfield and Capersby since Eton and before any of the three had attained a lordship. Palmersfield, a first son, had taken his father's title shortly after Walgrave had gone to sea, while Capersby had been granted an extinct title for his war service.

But recently Harrison's secret work for the Home Office had consumed him. He told himself his sacrifice was necessary. Dangerous times required men of conviction and ability to be ever vigilant. He had even convinced himself that he was temperamentally better suited to the job than other men. Then a mission had failed, and that failure had almost cost a friend his life. Since then, he'd realized the unflattering truth: He served his country because he was restless. He wasn't a country squire to dote on his prize hogs or write articles for the *Agricultural Magazine* on how to make pond mud into compost. The Home Office challenged his heart and mind, but for a healthful life, he had to find a middle path, one between boredom and danger, friendship and duty.

He looked at his friends, sprawled unbecomingly in front of his fire. As distant as he had become, they had never deserted him. A deep affection warmed the center of his chest. "You are right: I have been a terrible companion. Though I cannot promise to amend my ways completely, I can at least try."

"Hear! Hear!" Capersby and Palmersfield both drained their glasses, and Palmersfield opened a sixth bottle of wine.

Reform was clearly going to be expensive.

"Speaking of sending things over . . . your butler placed a letter on your desk." Palmersfield poured himself another goblet.

"Is it urgent?" Walgrave looked at his desk without rising.

"Urgent?" Palmersfield growled. "How would I know? I only open your mail when directed to do so."

"Walgrave merely wants to know if the letter can wait or if he must unfold that giant frame of his from the comfort of his couch."

"Yes, man, you could have told me before I settled in." Walgrave rested against the cushions for another moment, the events of the day still heavy on his mind. "But I should retrieve it. Grant indicates what needs my immediate attention by the room he places it in. Things that can wait until tomorrow go to the office; things sent here . . . well, I must get up." Walgrave pulled himself up from his comfortable recline and strode to the desk.

"Always surprises me that a man of your height can move that smoothly. Reminds me of that line from Coleridge, something about 'a thousand thousand, slimy things.'"

"Funny, John." He read the address. "Either of you know Traister, Belanger, and Bidwell, solicitors?"

Palmersfield and Capersby grunted negatives.

Harrison read silently. Still holding the letter, he returned to his couch and stared at the hearth.

The logs cracked on the fire. One spilled over beyond the marble hearth, its embers burning the edge of the ornate wool carpet. Capersby jumped to intervene, using the brush and shovel to return the log to the fireplace.

Harrison didn't move.

Finally Palmersfield broke the lengthening silence. "What is it? Good news or bad?"

He examined the letter once more. "Apparently I'm being sued."

"For what?" Palmersfield and Capersby spoke in unison and with equal levels of outrage.

Harrison looked back over the papers. "My dutiful wife desires a separation." He picked up a favorite piece of polished tiger's-eye from a bowl on the table and rubbed it between his fingers.

At length Capersby pulled himself upright and leaned forward, facing Harrison. "I've told you to at least answer her letters. One a week, like clockwork, for six years. Any woman would grow tired of being so completely ignored." Capersby spoke softly, as if Harrison might break with his words.

"Yes, Walgrave, any woman could reasonably expect

that an arranged marriage meant children." Palmersfield's voice was gentle. "You've left her on that estate with no communication since your wedding."

"That's not true. Each week we communicate about the estate accounts."

"Through your agent," Capersby corrected.

"You'd think you hated each other, as carefully as you buffer your communication," Palmersfield observed.

"I don't hate her. I barely know her," Harrison lied, not wanting to admit how he'd devoured her letters over the years—or how many nights he'd dreamt of her kisses. "I simply didn't want her. I didn't want to be married."

"As a result, you're punishing your dead father by refusing to communicate with the woman he coerced you into marrying." Capersby let the goblet hang loose between his fingers.

"It's not that simple."

"It *is* that simple," Palmersfield objected. "If it weren't that simple, then why haven't you at least written her, or better yet visited that blasted estate of yours?"

"My wife manages the estate quite well on her own, and I've left it to her. It's been my gift, to make up for my absence. She gets to be mistress of all she surveys—at least to the edge of the property. And I haven't abandoned her. When she wishes for my opinion, I'm certainly available to offer my advice."

"Through your agent . . ." Capersby refused to be mollified.

Palmersfield leaned forward. "So be truthful, Harrison. When *was* the last time you visited your estate?"

Harrison offered only a dark stare.

Capersby answered, "Unless Walgrave's been deceiving us, he hasn't set foot on the place since he married."

The men grew silent again. After some time, Palmersfield spoke. "May I see the letter?"

Harrison held out the pages, distracted by memories and long-buried emotions.

"The documents appear to be in order. She's asking for a small maintenance, a sum you can easily afford. But this is strange. I expected her to claim a sort of abandonment. But she offers no reasons to justify her request, other than a letter from a clergyman who indicates her reasons are sound and preclude a reconciliation." Palmersfield scratched his forehead. "This could play poorly."

"What do you mean?" Harrison shook off the memories of Olivia's deep eyes and full lips.

"You have a bit of a reputation as a rake and a scoundrel."

"That's from before the wars."

"True. But clergy are supposed to counsel, except in dire circumstances, that married persons *remain* married." Palmersfield looked distant. "You didn't beat her on your wedding night, did you?"

In an instant, Harrison remembered his wife's limbs pale against the bedclothes, her skin flushed with pleasure. He shook himself from memories he had long suppressed. "I believe the lady was quite satisfied with our wedding night."

"Actually, he could have beaten her on their wedding night and been within his rights," Capersby observed. "Let me see it."

Palmersfield handed the letter to Capersby who, donning spectacles, tilted the page to the light of the fire to read.

"Hmm. Who's your solicitor?" Capersby asked absently.

"Aldine at Leverill and Cort."

"Aldine's a good man. If either of you had read to the second page, you'd see she doesn't provide reasons because she isn't asking for a separation or an annulment. She wishes to have the marriage declared invalid." Capersby adjusted his spectacles.

"How, since the marriage was consummated?"

Palmersfield harrumphed. "You've likely consummated your relationship with your mistress more often than with your wife."

"I don't have a mistress. Besides, which side are you on?"

"I always thought you'd come to your senses about Olivia. Instead she's come to hers." Palmersfield ignored Harrison's response.

"I. Didn't. Want. A. Wife." Harrison enunciated each word with crisp clarity.

"If Olivia's right, you've never had one." Capersby looked back at the second page.

"But annulment . . ."

"Not an annulment. Let's see. She quotes a recent book on legal marriages: 'If the parties neglect the forms required to be observed, the state of such persons does not form a matrimonial, but a "meretricious union." In such cases the sentence of the Ecclesiastical Court does not *dissolve* the marriage, because no *lawful* marriage can have taken place. It merely *declares the fact* of marriage to be a nullity.' Well, that seems straightforward."

"Straightforward?" Harrison's brain felt thick, as resistant as a peat bog giving up its dead.

"If she's correct that the forms of the marriage weren't legal, then she could have a case for it being declared a nullity."

"But it's been more than six years." Harrison tried to imagine never having been married. It was easier than thinking that Olivia didn't want him. But whether she wanted him or not, what woman didn't want to be a countess?

"If I understand her claims, 'neither time nor cohabitation' will matter." Capersby's voice drifted into silence.

Palmersfield harrumphed again at the word *cohabitation*. "She's asking for a settlement *and* a declaration of nullity?"

Capersby turned back to the papers. "Appears so."

"That's only fair." Palmersfield poured another drink. "She'll be considered damaged goods on the marriage market. With money, at least, she can attract a husband from among the fortune hunters. It will be a juicy scandal."

Harrison's stomach clenched at the thought of Olivia in another man's bed. But he said nothing, merely let his friends debate his future as if he weren't present.

"Damn fine woman. Never understood why you didn't want her." Palmersfield leaned forward. "In fact, if the marriage is invalid . . . and if you are happy to be free of her, then perhaps I could court her. I have an estate of my own she could manage and . . ."

Harrison looked up, his eyes cold. "How would you know she's a fine woman, Palmersfield?"

Palmersfield looked at the floor, and Capersby shifted in his chair. Guiltily.

"What do I not know?" Harrison felt the muscles along his jaw tighten.

"We thought the two of you would eventually reconcile." Palmersfield held out his hands, palms up.

"What did you do?" Harrison pushed as if he were interrogating a criminal.

"You have to understand: Olivia is a lovely woman, charming, intelligent." Palmersfield rubbed his forehead.

"Don't forget elegant. Not a woman in the ton has better bearing." Capersby seemed to be enjoying the awkwardness of it all.

Harrison noted their use of his wife's first name and forced himself to appear calm, even though he felt like throttling them first and asking for explanations later. "You are discussing my wife as if you are old friends."

"Well, if truth be known . . ." Palmersfield paused and met eyes with Capersby.

"I prefer the truth." Harrison stared until they shifted uncomfortably in their comfortable chairs. His two oldest friends, men he had trusted with his life, fell silent. He felt gutted. "Gentlemen, I'm waiting for your explanation."

Capersby started first. "Olivia . . . I mean Lady Walgrave . . . in the past sometimes came to town. When we discovered it, we . . ."

"Kept it from her husband." Harrison was unwilling to offer any generosity to his two traitors.

"No. I mean, yes. But it wasn't like that." Palmersfield turned red around the ears as he had when embarrassed as a boy.

"Like what?" Harrison pushed.

Capersby, always the less flappable, explained. "You were still on the Continent. Anyone would expect her to come to London occasionally. The best modistes are here. You can't have expected her never to leave that blasted estate. You yourself took every opportunity to escape."

"Of course, you're right." Harrison felt as if he was listening to the conversation from a long distance. He knew that it was reasonable for his wife to come to London, but it had never occurred to him that she had—or that she would without informing him. "I suppose I've always thought of her as a homebird, enjoying the quiet pleasures of rural life. She's a good woman, the modest, practical sort of woman my father preferred for his wayward son."

Harrison ignored the glances his friends shared. As the clock chimed the hour, Harrison forced himself out of his chair. "As much as I would like to remain and discuss my failed marriage . . ."

"Not a marriage, Walgrave." Capersby waved one finger half-chidingly. "Never a marriage."

"Then my failed . . . I haven't a word for it."

"No, it's an unusual circumstance, to be sure." Palmersfield poured himself more wine. "Your best strategy will be to trust your solicitor."

"Yes, Walgrave, this is your opportunity to be free, if you want to be."

Walgrave shook off the interruption, not knowing how he felt. The idea that Olivia was not his wife produced no pleasure and some unexpected pain. "As I was saying, gentlemen, I have plans for the theater tonight with Forster and his fiancée. I must take my leave of you to change."

Capersby lifted his glass. "We'll be here when you return."

Chapter Four

At precisely half-past the hour, Flute tucked his watch into his waistcoat pocket. Time to interrupt a meeting. Charters, Flute's business partner, never met with any new clients unless Flute or one of their bodyguards was available to intervene in case the meeting turned bloody. It was one of the problems of doing business with criminals: No one could be trusted. Only last month, one of their clients had tried to murder another, though luckily Flute had intervened in time. He shook his head at the memory. Charters had said he wouldn't have minded the murder, except that the client had intended to point the blame at their firm.

Flute rapped hard on the office door, then entered. Charters sat behind a large desk, while three clients—two men and a woman—sat in the chairs before his desk.

"Ah, Flute, come in! We have just concluded our business." Charters held out his hand, palm up, thumb tucked across. A signal that at least one of the clients had behaved unpredictably.

Charters rose, and the two men followed suit, giving Flute a chance to assess them. Wiry and dirty, the smaller man hung back, keeping one hand out of sight. Flute considered what weapon he might be carrying, then examined the older, taller man who was clearly the group's leader. The leader was smartly dressed in the Continental style, but his smooth manners barely hid a cunning ruthlessness. The man offered his hand to help the woman up.

Charters caught Flute's eye, directing his attention to the woman. Her bearing was elegant, and her features were regular in the way British lords found captivating. But the lines around her mouth spoke of disdain, even malice, and her dark gray walking dress was several seasons out of date.

The well-dressed man led the woman out, followed by the wiry man, then Flute. At the end of the hall, clients could turn right for the gambling hell or left for the street. Flute made a show of stopping before reaching this crossroads. He pulled a piece of wood from his pocket and began carving a small animal. The ruse always did the trick, making him appear no more than an inattentive flunkey. If clients were inclined to whisper about their meeting, they would do so before reaching the doorkeeper.

Flute was not disappointed. The trio stopped at the juncture. The wiry man turned left. Watching him go, the woman pulled her arm away from the well-dressed man. Her patience had apparently reached its end.

"I still don't see why we must hire those criminals. I've already proved I can discover the names as easily as they can." Her voice was brittle and angry.

"You have a remarkable ability to ferret out secrets, Calista." The man spoke in a calming voice. "But you tend to be more bloodthirsty than necessary. After the incident at St. Bride's, I prefer a different course."

"It's my life that was ruined then put on display, Archer, not yours." Looking suddenly like the most dangerous of the three, the woman stabbed a narrow finger at the man's chest. "I'll do what needs to be done. I'll get my revenge . . . on them all."

Archer said nothing, simply waited impassively for the storm to end.

Growling, Calista pushed past, calling for the doorkeeper to let her out.

Archer stood quietly, as if making a decision, then he turned back toward the gambling hell.

Flute carved until their client was out of sight and returned to the office.

"Ah, Flute. I have business tonight at Drury Lane." Charters looked up from his pen.

"Is it that pretty miss from last week? I was surprised you let her come up . . . but then I heard how much pleasure you took in her company."

Charters ignored Flute's jibe. "Remember that interest we own in an unlicensed theater across the river? The miss you saw came fresh from the country hoping to become the next Dora Jordan. I told her that if she wished to play breeches parts, I would need to evaluate her legs in breeches."

"And out of them, from what I heard."

"I can be charming when I wish, Flute." Charters smiled. "I simply don't wish it very often."

"How were the miss's legs?" Flute leaned back on the doorjamb, enjoying having the upper hand, even if it happened only rarely.

"Entirely satisfactory. I'm sure she will find her way into a leading role quickly." Charters paused. "She is very . . . agile."

"I'm sure she is." Flute snickered. "Fresh from the country, you say? Did you check your pockets before you let her go?"

"My pockets had nothing in them to steal. Nor did I offer her any payment for my entertainment. I would hate for her to think me crass."

"Then she's a fool."

"Precisely." Charters smiled. "But as to our business tonight. I have tickets to Mrs. Wells's benefit. Kean is performing. Do you wish to accompany me? Your orange girl likes to haunt the intermission, doesn't she?"

"She does." Flute dragged his favorite chair to the desk. "How should I dress?"

"As a man of means. As for me, I will be disguised as a Mr. Blaine, the newest associate in a successful shipping venture."

"How will this Blaine fellow look?"

"A study in black and white and beige. A follower of Beau Brummel, but with none of his flair or taste. Tonight he will be buying one set of information and giving away another."

"I prefer selling to buying and giving."

"Ah, but these will advance our interests in shipping. One of my parliamentary committees has proposed expansion to the canals and docks, and we already have opposition. I'm buying information that will encourage our detractors to be more . . . amenable."

Flute picked up one of Charters's pieces of pumice and rubbed it against his fingernail. Grimacing at the sensation, he replaced it in its dish. "We made a fine profit on our last cargo."

"True, and by selling our goods at a discount to the local gangs, we've encouraged them to become part of our trade network."

"Encouraged? So, that's your word for it? I suppose you'll call it convenient that some of our competition happened to end up dead with your mark cut into their chests."

Flute leaned back, putting his feet on the edge of the desk. "No, you're already the most feared man in five hells."

"Not me, Flute. Never forget. They fear our imaginary employer and his vast criminal network."

Flute shook his head in admiration. "I still can't believe it worked. Tell people you work for a master criminal with fingers in every pie in the land, and soon they begin acting as if you do."

"People like to believe in a conspiracy." Charters tested the ink on his document—a list—and found it dry. "You and I together are not nearly as frightening as a nameless vicious mastermind who directs all our efforts."

"A bugbear to frighten them."

"Yes, isn't it grand?" Charters began drawing stars, daggers, and arrows in front of the items.

"As for the theater, are we going for the full performance, or just the second half?"

"I prefer to arrive early and remain until the end to watch for any complications or surprises."

"Pit or gallery?" Flute began to carve another stick of wood.

"Mr. Blaine has an aunt who loans him her box whenever he comes to town."

"He does, does he? Does this old lady have a name?"

"I wrote it down when I bought the season." Charters consulted a ledger at his right. "Ah yes, Hortensia Scrubb."

"Scrubb?"

"I wasn't feeling particularly clever. But Aunt Hortensia is a fine upstanding Scot, with a penchant for broad comedy and oratorios. She has returned to Aberdeen and has left us—I mean Mr. Blaine—in possession of the key, for which Blaine is deeply grateful." Charters, picking up his penknife, trimmed his pen in three sharp cuts. "My first rendezvous—to buy the shipping information—

will be during the intermission. My second will follow the afterpiece."

"Your second?"

"The second is related to our new clients."

"I was wondering when you would tell me their business."

"Ah, but Flute, I enjoy predicting how long you are willing to wait." Charters set the document aside to dry. "Remember that I told you I used to pass information to a client abroad using the London *Times*?"

"I remember. You placed an advertisement with the information in code."

"Correct. About that time, I decided to test other ways to use the periodical press to my advantage. Whitehall had collected some scandalous information about some peers, and I incorporated the juiciest bits into a series of essays I wrote under various names. To keep the controversies alive, I even rebutted my own essays, using different pseudonyms. The experiment was an unquestioned success. But growing tired of writing the essays myself, I began sending information to those regular correspondents who had large popular audiences."

"You fed them information when it could benefit us."

"Of course. Because my information could always be confirmed, several correspondents now trust me. Tonight I meet with the most eloquent: An Honest Gentleman."

"If communicating by letter has been successful, why change now?" Flute crossed his arms over his chest and stared at Charters.

Charters pulled a black satin bag out of his top desk drawer and tossed it at Flute. A necklace studded with diamonds, emeralds, and sapphires tumbled out of the bag into Flute's hands. "Our new clients have given us that pretty piece simply to retain our services. If we provide the information they want, our fee will be substantial."

Flute bounced the necklace in his palm. "Heavy enough. Real or paste?"

"Real."

Flute whistled in appreciation and bounced the necklace again. "What do we have to do?"

"Our new clients wish to know the true identities of ten newspaper or magazine correspondents." Charters floated the list across the table. "Of the ten, four are names I used. We'll report those as dead or missing. Three have been vocal in favor of reform, and I'm not certain about the others."

Flute looked over the list. "What do they intend to do once they have the names?"

"As long as we are paid for our efforts, that is of little concern to us."

"It's a shame. I like this one: Prosperity Once More." Flute pointed to a name on the list, then shrugged. "But you know best."

Charters shook light sand over the document to absorb the excess ink. "Flute, we are partners. If you wish not to investigate someone on that list, we won't. Or if you want to hold back information, we can do that too. The jewels are a retainer. That's all."

Flute grew more cheerful with Charters's expression of confidence. "If it's not us, it will be someone else, and if there's money to be had, I'd rather it line our pockets."

"With your agreement, then, we will proceed. I've devised a little plan to flush out the first three writers on the list."

"Let's see. An Honest Gentleman, A Pursuer of Peace, and Hannibal?"

"Yes. Those three have been most active in supporting the rights of reform groups to hold public meetings. Though they have avoided direct accusation, all three have implied that the government is actively suppressing reformers."

"Direct accusation can get you hung."

"Certainly, one can understand their reticence. But this list will fuel their outrage. It proves—or pretends to prove—that the government is acting to limit the rights of man. See these symbols. These identify public meetings likely to be dispersed by magistrates or His Majesty's guard."

"How do *you* know? Did you discover it in one of your parliamentary meetings?"

"I have no solid information whatsoever. The groups I've marked publicize their meetings. If they meet with government suppression, then my information will have been good. If the groups don't, I can praise the correspondents for successfully curbing the government's willingness to act."

"We win either way." Flute nodded appreciatively. "But I don't understand how this will flush the writers out. If they write under pen names already, they must be cautious of their privacy."

"But I am a trusted informant. Yesterday, I wrote that my newest information is so sensitive that I fear it might fall into the wrong hands."

"If they refuse to meet, the information might go to another newspaper."

"Along with the sales that information would bring the newspaper," Charters said. "At the same time, the correspondents might still send an agent to avoid meeting with us themselves. But we will follow whoever meets us, watching until we know exactly who is writing what and for whom."

"This only works if someone agrees to meet with us. Why can't we just bribe a magazine's proprietor or the editor?"

"Our new clients suggested they have already tried bribes

and even some stronger measures. I fear they might be responsible for the fire last month in Fleet Street."

"The one called Archer mentioned something to the woman Calista about St. Bride's." Flute shook his head. "Twenty newspapermen died in that fire."

"Ah, Flute, eavesdropping again." Charters patted the large man on the shoulder. "Our methods will be less . . . conspicuous. Our client claims they wish to know *who* the authors are, I assume to stop them. But new writers will always emerge. *We* want to know who the writers are so we can shape the content of the articles. Some writers might even be willing to accommodate us to avoid our clients."

"A bit of blackmail?"

"That might prove quite fun."

"So this is all about playing the Machiavel."

"If playing the Machiavel gains us a diversion for our other businesses, then yes." Charters picked up his coat. "But set Timmons to investigate those three. Archer and Calista are not the names they gave me at our meeting, which leads me to suspect that they intend to double cross us. And you know how much I dislike that sort of thing. By the way, after tonight, I'll be gone for a week. I wish to settle the disposition of some lands we acquired at the Blue Heron."

"Will you be staying at the same place as before, if you are needed?"

"Ah, yes, my pretty rural retreat with free food and lodging and unmatched conversation . . . all available to me at my leisure for another six months. But you won't need me, Flute. I have no one I trust with our ventures more than you."

"You have no one you trust, other than me."

"But that's a compliment in itself."

Chapter Five

"Walgrave! Over here!" The duke stood at the doorway of his box, the lovely Lady Wilmot on his arm, both surrounded by a group of gesticulating Whigs. The circle opened to include Walgrave, and immediately he was barraged with questions from all sides.

"What have you planned, Walgrave, for the next session?"

"None of us could predict that turn in your last argument."

"We'll need your voice to defeat this threat."

"There isn't another man—save for Forster—who can quell the Tories so thoroughly."

He groaned inwardly. After his surprising marital news, he had little energy for another debate on the need for reform, not even with such congenial company as Forster's guests.

Forster read his face in an instant. "Walgrave, your seat is on the front row. In the corner to the right. Don't frown—your long legs will fit there better than in any other seat."

"Forgive me; my frown is related to other business. The corner seat will certainly offer me all the pleasures the theater and good company can afford."

"Always the diplomat." Lady Wilmot placed her hand on Harrison's arm. "Would you escort me to our seats and entertain me until Aidan joins us?"

"Of course." Harrison bowed slightly.

Sophia kissed Forster's cheek. "Darling, I expect you by my side long before the curtain rises."

Forster gave him a look that clearly meant *take care of my fiancée*, and Harrison nodded his reassurance.

Taking Walgrave's arm, Lady Wilmot leaned into his side conspiratorially. "I know you have enough of these debates at Whitehall, so I thought you wouldn't mind being stolen away."

"You are right, as always, Lady Wilmot."

She searched his face for a moment. "Yet you are saving me more than I am saving you. With my blackmailer not yet found, I feel wary of being in the box alone."

Harrison felt chastened to his depths. "Ah, my lady, I had forgotten you were threatened here. Forgive me."

"Yes, tonight is my first time back. But I have determined to be brave, and I refuse to let a theater box defeat me." She poked fun at her fears with characteristic good grace. "These seats are ours. Behind us will be my sisters-in-law and some of Aidan's brothers, though I'm not sure which ones—and on the back row, the MPs now colluding in the corridor." She motioned for him to precede her to his corner chair. Forster's box was the second from the stage, situated on the proscenium itself in the space before the curtain, but behind the orchestra. The box was separated from the stage only by the short wall at the front, making its guests both observers and observed.

As Harrison tucked himself into the corner, he found that as Forster promised, the angle of the box offered ample space for his legs. The position suited him in other ways as well. Lady Wilmot was an attentive observer, wishing only to converse between pieces or acts, but not during them. Once Forster joined them, she neither expected nor desired entertainment. Harrison, then, could pretend to be absorbed in the plays, when in actuality he was lost in his own thoughts.

The first play was a comedy, a story of thwarted love, chosen to showcase Mrs. Wells's talent for portraying voluble women. Harrison found little to admire in Wells's theatrical gifts. Her voice was too loud, even in a theater built to seat three thousand, and her gestures too broad.

Since the play seemed predictable, Harrison had ample time to consider how he'd come to be married and unmarried, and what he would do with his newfound freedoms.

To call his marriage *arranged* was too benign. No, *forced* was the better word. One night, he'd gone to bed at his lodgings in London, and he'd awoken, head throbbing, at his family estate, locked in his tower bedroom with his father sitting by his side. The old man—ever jovial—had patted his arm, declaring, "I've found your perfect wife." Though he'd tried to object, his father had left no room for objection. He'd arranged it all: Harrison would marry, and marry by the week's end. Realizing he could not escape, Harrison had rammed his fist into the oak door over and over, until his knuckles were bruised and bloody.

He'd met his father's happy accomplice later that day: a plain woman in drab colors, her hair pulled back into a severe bun. Olivia had everything to gain: trading the dismal life of a governess for the rank and wealth of a countess. Even now, he could not blame her. Who would not have done what she had? He only wished some other lord had been the sacrifice. Beneath her demure exterior, she had been well-spoken, well-read, thoughtful in her opinions, perceptive in her observations, and even kind, though his behavior had hardly warranted it. But she was neither adventurous nor daring. Olivia was a swan when he had wanted a hawk.

Yet he'd still felt drawn to her. Like the sirens, she tempted him to give up his plans for adventure and glory and remain in her arms forever. He remembered the feel of her hair, thick and luxuriant. But though he could recall each kiss, each sigh, every moment that he had buried himself in her, he could only remember her face in pieces. Her eyes were bottomless, her brow honest, her cheekbones firm, her jaw strong, her ears a sweet labyrinth. But knowing how many kisses it took to travel to her chin from her ear offered little help in recognizing her in a crowd.

The wailing of Mrs. Wells's heroine brought Harrison back to the present. He looked over the stage. Mrs. Wells was kneeling, holding a young woman's body across her lap. Her cries resembled the honking of a goose in flight. Lord, what a sound! And this play was a comedy?

He fought the urge to run from the box and seek solace in the relative quiet of a gambling hell. But he was surprised to find the audience—men and women alike—brushing tears away. Even Lady Wilmot raised her handkerchief to blot her eyes. Harrison looked back at the stage. Perhaps had he been paying attention, he would have found the scene affecting as well, but he doubted it.

On stage, a young man, weeping, sat beside Mrs. Wells and took the dead girl in his arms. "Our parents, united in their hatred of each other's family, refused our love. Though God had already heard our vows, they rejected our marriage and chose for us other wives and husbands. But you, my sweet Jennie, have thwarted their plots, and shown me the path to avoid the foul marriage my parents have forced upon me." The actor gently brushed the hair from the dead girl's face, while Mrs. Wells wept some more, a horrible peacock feather swaying dramatically before her face.

I am not a good audience for this play, Harrison thought, but he forced himself to pay some attention. A good guest should at least know how the confounded thing ended.

The boy-lover raised a vial that had fallen to the floor, and ignoring Mrs. Wells's protest, drank it dramatically, declaiming to the girl's corpse, "Life without you is a dark vale, promising nothing but sorrow. But I can die, my sweet wife, and dying join you in paradise."

Soon, *thank God*, the young man slumped over as well. From the corners of the stage, pallbearers entered bearing coffins. They lifted the bodies into them and hammered the lids shut. The coffins were left on the stage side by side, as the lamps dimmed for a change of scene.

He unfolded the playbill he had slipped into his waist-coat. Thomas Middleton's *A Chaste Maid in Cheapside,* in a new version, adapted for the modern stage by "Dr. Busby." He hated not knowing who to blame for this bas-tard *Romeo and Juliet*. He should have stayed with Palmersfield and Capersby and drunk another bottle of claret.

A collective gasp from the audience drew Harrison's attention back to the performers. While the priest looked on, workmen were prying the lids from the coffins. *What have I missed now?* Standing between the coffins, the priest called for the lovers to arise.

The parents—led by a joyful Mrs. Wells and her equally joyful feather—embraced their living children, and the lovers entered the church accompanied by the sound of wedding bells. *Drivel, pure and simple*. But the crowd's applause was thunderous.

"What do you think, Walgrave?" Lady Wilmot watched him with all-too-perceptive eyes. "Can two lovers, sepa-rated by prejudice, be reunited by the power of love?"

Forster leaned forward to comment. "Be careful how you answer, Walgrave. Sophia believes in the strength of love to overcome all obstacles."

"I am too jaded to believe in fairy tales." Harrison

accompanied his answer with what he hoped was a winning smile.

"Why, Walgrave, I do believe you have never been in love," Lady Wilmot chided.

"I merely know love's limitations. In my experience, a dead lover tends to remain dead, and she certainly doesn't spring to life on the church steps."

"Beware, Sophia." Forster shook his head. "In Parliament, he's famous for chipping at an opponent's position until he has dismantled the whole."

"There are *arguments*, and there is *truth*. When you love someone, it is a truth that admits no argument," Lady Wilmot pronounced firmly.

"I agree, your ladyship. Many a fool who has set his cap on love refuses to hear any argument."

"I fear you will not approve of the afterpiece—in it, a case of mistaken identities leads to true love," Lady Wilmot teased.

He read the title on the playbill. "Ah, I know this piece. It's silly."

"Silly?" Lady Wilmot raised an eyebrow. "Another might call it sweet, even charming."

"Let's review the plot, shall we, my lady?" Harrison pronounced with a wink. "Two young persons, unacquainted with one another, are betrothed by their fathers. The young man is sent to visit his fiancée, but disguises himself as a cowherd in order to discover her true character. The young woman, like-minded, disguises herself as a gypsy, hoping to intercept her betrothed and observe his character at the market. Cowherd meets gypsy. She sings a provocative love song, and they fall immediately, irrevocably, and passionately in love."

"Do you find love at first sight so impossible to believe?" Sophia tucked her hand around Forster's elbow.

In his mind's eye, Harrison saw Olivia, standing on the

battlements, the starlight behind her, her soft body calling to him despite his anger. He pushed away the memory. "Oh, no, Lady Wilmot, I'm sure someone somewhere has loved truly and well from the first moments of a chance acquaintance. But whenever I hear such a story, I always wonder if it is love or indigestion."

"You devil." She shook her head in mock dismay. "Someday, Walgrave, you will fall in love, and I will be the first to send you flowers."

"Whiskey, my lady. If you ever discover I am besotted, whiskey will be the cure. It is unfortunate that after this evening's performance, half of the unmarried audience will believe that arranged marriages between perfect strangers lead to true love."

Forster leaned forward to quiz Harrison. "And the other half?"

"They will be intent on taking advantage of each believer's gullibility. No, don't roll your eyes at me, Forster. I wear my skepticism proudly."

"Even if you find the plot foolish, you will likely admire the quality of the musical performances." Forster wrapped his hand around Lady Wilmot's. "Apparently the actress who plays the gypsy sings with the voice of an angel."

"Look, the curtain is being drawn already." Lady Wilmot turned silent, her attention fully on the stage.

Harrison shifted his legs and settled in for another inane performance. But he would survive another hour, especially if it meant he could avoid making a decision about his failed marriage. It was his fault that Olivia had come to question the validity of their marriage. He had known from her letters that she was growing restive, but he had done nothing to increase her happiness.

Yet all thoughts of his failed marriage disappeared when the actress who played the gypsy-heiress took the stage. Harrison's seat in the corner of Forster's box was closest to the stage, not five feet from the spot where the gypsy stood. Her hair, a brilliant red, fell down her back in long tresses, tied back loosely by a brightly colored ribbon. Her mouth was a red wound, begging to be kissed into health.

Her clothing was intended to capture the interest of the male portion of the audience. The cut of her bodice rested low on her breasts, revealing almost everything a man might wish to see, particularly when she leaned forward provocatively. The material of her skirt was split from knee to hip along the side of one leg, and as she walked, she pulled one edge forward, then back, tempting the audience with a soft knee or a slender thigh.

Harrison leaned forward, mesmerized, and the gypsy turned to look at him. When their eyes met, he felt a depth of connection that caught his breath. He had no doubt she had felt the electricity between them; the look on her face appeared both startled and wary. No woman had captured his attention in years, and he could not pinpoint why the gypsy did.

Before he could even begin to tease out the answer, she turned away, flirting with other members of the audience. He felt bereft. Eventually however, her eyes returned to his, and she began to sing in a rich mezzo-soprano. Her low tones were close to tenor, while her upper notes soared expressively. It was an earthy voice, the kind that made men think of naked flesh and welcoming bodies. A voice made for sex, Harrison thought, then wished he hadn't. Thoughts of sex inevitably made him think of his wife, of warm nights spent in her arms, and all the cold ones without her.

Only once in his life had Harrison felt the dangerous pull of love, and that it had been for Olivia was . . . unexpected.

Olivia, his dutiful and practical wife. His father had

declared Olivia to be the woman Harrison would "love until divided by death." The problem came—Harrison realized years later—in the way his father had phrased it. If his father had said instead *You will love with so great a passion that the joy of it wakes you up in the morning and eases you to sleep at night*, Harrison might not have bolted. But he'd already lost so much to death; he couldn't give up on his dreams of adventure to watch time slip away on a country estate. The wars were his excuse to leave, and though he'd returned to England, he'd never come home to the estate or to Olivia.

He gave the gypsy a long, assessing stare. She was luscious, all shapely legs and generous curves. Each note of her song was filled with longing and heartbreak, making him want nothing more than to pull her against him in a firm embrace. He imagined kissing her neck in a line to her breasts and pushing up her skirt to reveal more of that tantalizing thigh. Hers was a siren song dizzying in its intensity, making him want to forsake home and hearth to follow her anywhere.

If he were truly not married, he could take a mistress. Who better than this woman who heated his blood with a glance and the curve of a beckoning finger? His bed had been too long empty. He had been faithful to Olivia, but if he was free he could return to sea, join one of the expeditions to the Arctic, take a mistress or choose a wife—anything he wished. While he might still dream of Olivia, he could—with the right distraction—forget.

He'd spent his adult life focusing on his career. But perhaps he should not hold himself apart, but allow himself to become entangled. What if he chose a woman who could capture his body but never hold his heart? He looked at the gypsy once more, at her shapely leg and her ample bosom. She moved with the grace of a dancer and the elegance of a duchess. Surely an actress would do. She would be unlikely to challenge his mind, however well she satisfied his body.

He willed the gypsy to look at him again, but her gaze avoided his. Even so he never stopped watching her. Disappointment, anger, manipulation, suspicion, affection, desire, love, all played on her face with a sincerity unequalled by the other actors. She played the role so effortlessly that it seemed that she wasn't acting at all, that this temptress was her natural self.

As he watched her movements, he wondered if he had seen *her* on the street, not Olivia at all. If she were as alluring in life as she was on stage, and if she possessed at least half a brain, then perhaps he might take a mistress to begin his unmarried life.

When the final curtain fell, he excused himself and hurried from the box, intent on intercepting her before she left the theater. But a slow river of playgoers filled the corridors, blocking his way. He looked over his shoulder at Forster's box. How easily could he climb over the short wall and onto the stage? But that would attract more attention than he wished to garner.

There was another way, if Forster would agree.

Chapter Six

"Well, this is a surprise." The man standing in the half-light by the lion cages motioned his hand at her costume. "That performance was stunning, my dear. The brothel keepers will see an increase in business tonight. But *you* as the Honest Gentleman—that's an even more impressive performance."

She gave her best confused look. "Patrons are not allowed in this part of the theater. You need to go back." Knowing Horace was hiding in the shadows, she decided to test Mrs. Wells's belief that Cerberus was dangerous.

"Oh, yes, I forget the formalities. Let's see: I ask 'Can you direct me to Canterbury Cathedral?'"

"I said patrons are not allowed here." She stiffened her back and pointed her finger to the door. When he stepped forward into the light, she would be able to see his face.

The man looked confused. "Oh, yes, certainly. My mistake." He began to back away, stepping farther from the light.

"What would be your business at the cathedral?" she called after him, waiting to see his reaction.

The man immediately resumed the agreed-upon dialogue.

"King Henry sends me to murder the archbishop." His voice sounded annoyed, but not angry.

"Then murder him you must." She kept her hand hidden in the folds of her skirt, her grip on the penknife steady and firm. "I am the emissary of An Honest Gentleman. I take him your information; he chooses what to use and what to discard. Are you Cerberus?"

"I am, and as such, I prefer to deal with the gentleman himself. I like to know the character of those I work with."

"And yet the lantern over your left shoulder reveals traces of paint on your collar." She waited. Most men would look over their shoulder at the lantern, giving her an opportunity to see his face in the lantern's light, but he did not. "Perhaps you only prefer to deal with those you can deceive."

Cerberus paused for a moment, then shrugged. "What if I confided that I have a disfiguring skin disease?"

"I wouldn't believe you."

"And you shouldn't, my dear." He leaned into the space between them, moving only his upper body, but never passing beyond the line of heavy shadow on the floor. "Ah, this will be fun. I haven't had a worthy op . . . collaborator, for some time."

"And yet, you almost called me a worthy opponent." The old surge of excitement warmed her veins. "I will warn HG to treat your information with care."

"Ah! HG, so those *are* the writer's initials."

"They are. HG stands for Honest Gentleman. I think, good sir, that you wish to know who HG is more than you wish to help him shed light on injustice."

"Can I not wish for both?" Clearly enjoying the repartee, he stepped toward her, into the half-light. She could almost make out his features. "I prefer to make my bed with those who share my agendas."

"Stay away." She held open her palm to reveal her

penknife. "We will not be bedfellows. I am simply a messenger. And do not underestimate my penknife. It may be small, but a well-placed stab can be just as fatal as that of a larger knife."

"I rarely underestimate a blade . . . or a woman."

"Tell me what you wish HG to know." She resisted the urge to step farther away from him, to create a safer distance between them. She would not show fear.

"Ah, I've written it down. It's in my pocket here. It's not quite the information I promised, but it's valuable all the same." He patted the outside of his coat, then held his hands out to his sides. "I have no interest in harming you, my dear gypsy. You are my only method for communicating with your HG."

"Set your information on the box to your right, then leave."

Extending his hand into the half-light, but keeping his face obscured, he showed her his forefinger and thumb, and slowly—theatrically even—reached into his pocket and pulled out a fat packet of papers. His hand came fully into the light as he placed them slowly on the box. A thick raised scar marred the back of his hand. "What if I wish to give HG more information in the future?"

"Do as you did before. Send HG a letter at the *World*. He will decide if he wishes me or one of his other messengers to meet with you. This time you were allowed to determine the time and place, but from henceforth, HG will decide when and if he wishes to meet you."

"A wise man as well as honest." He backed further into the darkness. "This has been a pleasure, *HG*, a pleasure."

Horace emerged from the shadows.

"Make sure he is gone, please." She felt the energy of the moment drain away. She was certain his final "HG" was simply an attempt to rattle her, but she couldn't stop feeling that she'd been exposed.

The hulking man turned toward the exit without a word.

She opened the packet. A list of various reform societies and their planned meetings. Nothing she couldn't find by reading the *Times* or half a dozen other periodicals. She suspected that it was a ruse to discover An Honest Gentleman's identity, but surely there was more to it.

She turned through the pages again, noticing that many of the meetings were marked in the left margin. Daggers, asterisks, crosses. Some meetings were identified with one mark, some with all three. At the bottom of the last page, she found a legend. Dagger meant the group had a member who was a government agent; asterisk meant the group had been targeted for suppression by whatever means; crosses meant a member or members had been killed.

She read back through the list, focusing on the daggers. Westminster, Stockport, Oldham, Blackburn, Halifax, Birmingham. All meetings that had been suppressed, sometimes violently, by the government. More than a dozen meetings that hadn't yet happened were also marked for suppression.

She stood still in disbelief. If this information were true, then the government's role went far beyond maintaining the public good. No, it had actively been targeting and eliminating reformers and planning its suppression of peaceable public meetings far in advance of the events themselves. Her hand, still holding the papers, fell to her side. To publish this—to accuse the government of corruption—that would be treason. But to let the suppression, the violence, go on without check would be immoral. Cerberus certainly merited his nickname.

It was good she was separating herself from Harrison. The game she was playing could turn bad so easily, and while she had little to lose, he was a rising star in Parliament.

"'E's gone, miss. I saw 'is back as 'e walked down the

corridor. Then I locked the door, so 'e won't be returning that way wit'out a key."

"Thank you, Horace." She forced herself to appear calm as she pressed a half crown coin into his hand.

Horace's smile turned broad, almost giddy. "Me bride will be 'appy to see this, miss. Enough to pay the bills for better than a month. I'll be waitin' by the stage door to escort ye home."

"I'll need a little time. Perhaps a quarter of an hour or a little longer?"

He bounced the coin in the air, smiling. "Take yer time, miss. Mrs. Wells will 'ave plenty for me to do. Find me in 'er room when ye wish to go."

Her ruined—and now discarded—walking dress held a pocket in the inner lining. A few whip stitches to sew up the opening and any document she collected from a correspondent was safely hidden. But with the dress gone, her only option was the more obvious place: her reticule. She folded Cerberus's list, then tucked it into the small space beside her pocket pistol.

She sat to remove her makeup, but before she could begin, a voice called to her from the other side of the door.

"Flowers, miss. For your performance."

"How lovely. Bring them in."

But the man who entered carried no flowers. As he pushed the door closed behind him, she pulled her penknife from her reticule and hid it behind her as she stood. Even so, she wasn't prepared for the man's speed or the sharp pain as his fist struck her jaw, knocking her back against the dressing table. She reached for her reticule—less to use her pocket-pistol than to hit her assailant in the head with the bag—but it fell to the floor.

"That's yer warning. Now y' listen."

* * *

"Do you still have that key?" Harrison pulled Forster to the side of the box, speaking low so that none of the other guests, particularly not Lady Wilmot, would hear their conversation. He nodded toward a door at the end of the hall, painted to match the walls.

"The key to the prop room?" Forster asked in his regular speaking voice.

"Yes," Harrison whispered, pulling Forster farther into the corner, away from the rest of the group. He didn't wish to cause a rupture between Forster and Lady Wilmot by revealing Forster's former liaisons.

"Sophia has it."

"Your fiancée knows that you once had a mistress in the chorus? No wonder she keeps the key to the dressing rooms." Harrison shook his head in dismay. "I suppose the two of you aren't as reconciled as I imagined."

A broad smile stretched across Forster's face. "I can't imagine being more reconciled. You forget, when Sophia was threatened, we escaped through the prop room. I thought having the key tonight might give her an extra measure of security."

"Might I borrow it?"

Forster stared at Harrison with shock, then amusement. "I never thought I'd see the day. Walgrave—steady, constant, unswerving Walgrave—moved by a pretty face. Or was it a leg? There were some very fine legs tonight."

Harrison said nothing, trying to look bored. Forster searched his face, then continued, even more amused. "Let's see here. My bet is on the gypsy. Pretty face, pretty legs, and a dance designed to set a man's imagination on fire. Edmund is in town. He might know her if you wish for an introduction."

"I don't need your brother to introduce me."

"Not the gypsy? Hmm." Forster could not have looked less convinced. "Then what is it?"

"One of the actresses looked familiar. That's all. An old acquaintance I haven't seen in years. I would like to see if she's returned to London."

"I still think it's the gypsy. But I'll get you the key." Forster made his way to the other side of the box. Whispering in Lady Wilmot's ear, he pointed to Harrison. Lady Wilmot's knowing smile made Harrison wish the ground would open up and swallow him as if he were Doctor Faustus. He could imagine no greater hell than the look of bemused interest on Lady Wilmot's face as she watched Forster return, key in hand.

"I must admit, Forster, I'm imagining a hundred ways to kill you. What did you tell her?"

"Who, Sophia?" Forster shrugged. "Just that you recognized an old friend in the chorus."

"Then why is she smiling at me like that?"

"I'll offer you one piece of advice, Walgrave: Never underestimate a smart woman." Forster grinned brilliantly at Lady Wilmot. "We leave for Lady Wilmot's estate in the morning, so return the key to its place above the door."

As Harrison made his way backstage and through the prop room, an old woman glared at him, as if she knew his purpose. But of course she knew. For what other reason did well-dressed men from the boxes take this path? If he was not married and the gypsy was willing, where would the injury lie?

But in his heart, he could not escape the feeling—however irrational—that he was somehow betraying his wife. He had believed himself married for so long that it would take some time to think of himself otherwise. Perhaps it would be best to continue behaving as if he were married, at least until this business with Olivia was concluded. He thought of the gypsy and her dulcet tones, which seemed even sweeter in memory. No, he was tired of being circumspect.

At the gypsy's dressing room door, he paused. He had no flowers, no gifts, only a sincere appreciation of her tantalizingly erotic performance. If he met her, he might find she was only an actress creating an illusion with paints, powder, and talent. Her seductive tones might be replaced by a jarring lower-class accent, and her skin might reveal a hint of the pox. That might be for the best.

Though the door was only pushed to the jamb, leaving a gap wide enough see a bit of her dressing room, he did not enter. Instead, he paused outside the door, wondering if he should knock, or if he should just go home.

Beyond the door, he heard muffled voices, one low and ominous sounded threatening. The other, the woman's voice, was pitched to sound brave.

He pushed the knob, and the door swung open. The voices came from around the corner.

"I have nothing to hide," the woman asserted.

"Everyone's got somewhat to hide, you more than others. But for a bit of money . . ."

"I want you to leave."

"Ah, lovey, that's not a good idea. My master, he is a very determined man."

"Tell your master that I do as I wish."

"I think you will change your mind, miss. I really do."

Harrison stepped into the room from the corridor. From his position he could see the blackmailer—short and wiry—lean toward the gypsy.

Suddenly the actress moved, grinding her heel into the man's instep, until he howled in pain. While he was off balance, she shoved him back, angling him toward the door. "Tell your master, if he wishes to blackmail me, he should do it himself."

When she pushed the man far enough away, she could

see Harrison filling the doorway. She stopped. She looked from the small, wiry man to Harrison, and her face revealed a sudden fear. She felt comfortable handling one man, Harrison realized, but two would be too much for her. He felt obligated to assure her of his good intentions.

Stepping farther into the room, Harrison grabbed the blackmailer by his lapels and swung him through the open doorway into the corridor. "You, sir, mind the lady's desires. If she wants you gone, you should be gone." To keep the man out, he pushed the door shut with a single, hard shove.

He turned back toward the gypsy, expecting to see relief or even gratitude on her face. Instead she held a penknife before her, defensively, her hand gripping the shaft. Her body was taut and ready for battle.

The actress pointed an accusing finger at his chest. "I was doing quite well, thank you."

"Then allow me to apologize. I thought you might wish for some help. But you are right: You managed that churl quite well."

"Why would I want your help?" She refused the compliment bluntly, tossing her deep red hair over her shoulder. Her voice sounded calm, but the blue vein in her neck still pulsed hard. "I don't know you—for all I know, you could be that man's accomplice."

"I must apologize. I am Walgrave, Harrison Walgrave." For some reason, he chose to elide his title. "I came to commend you on a brilliant performance."

"Oh." She lowered the knife, but did not set it aside. The pulse still pounded hard in her neck. "What pretty compliments have you to offer?" He was surprised at the disinterest in her voice.

"Your voice was exceptional, and your rapport with the audience was the greatest of any this evening. I'm surprised Mrs. Wells allowed such a stellar performance at her benefit."

"I owe Mrs. Wells a great deal. Few actresses would allow an untried singer so large a part." Her eyes never left his. She was still wearing her final costume from the afterpiece, a demure blue muslin walking dress, appropriate to her role as a country squire's daughter. He noticed again the way the bodice skimmed her breasts and waist before falling gracefully over her hips to the floor.

"After that performance, she should ask you to perform in all her benefits. It will improve ticket sales." Somehow he was trapped spouting inanities about audiences and tickets, when what he wanted to say was that he felt like he had fallen into the depths of her brown eyes.

"With Wells and Kean on the playbill, the sales were robust enough." The gypsy placed her penknife on the dressing table. "Audiences know actors rely on the profits from the benefits to survive in the months when the theaters are closed."

There it was: his opening. He took it, then held his breath. "How will you survive?"

"My reserves are adequate, if not ample."

At the word *ample*, without thinking he looked at her breasts, then as quickly looked away. He wasn't some randy schoolboy visiting his first prostitute. The silence grew between them. Harrison was afraid to look anywhere but at his shoes. How had he lost all his skill at making fine speeches? The Walgrave who swayed Parliament seemed to have gotten lost somewhere between Forster's box and the gypsy's dressing room.

He glanced at the door. Would it be wisest simply to retreat? But he didn't wish to go, not yet at least, not while he still felt inexplicably drawn to her. "Perhaps I could escort you to dinner at my club. The chef is very fine." He looked up to watch her response.

"Why?" She raised a single eyebrow, then wrapped the colorful gypsy shawl around her shoulders, as if she were cold.

"I would like to know you better. You say you are an untried actress, but you showed a mastery of the stage that takes others years to perfect." He pointed to her shawl. "You wear the gypsy's shawl over the squire's daughter's dress. You play them both so well, I'm left to wonder which role suits you better—the flamboyant gypsy, or the demure squire's daughter? Or is it more complicated? Are you a gypsy with a hint of reserve, or a proper lady with a desire for adventure?"

"Those are roles, nothing more. If I blacken my teeth and hook my nose with putty, will you wonder if I have a penchant for casting spells in my garden?" She sat on the well-worn ottoman before her dressing table and folded her hands primly in her lap. Long, slender hands. He wondered what it would feel like to take one of her hands in his. "How exactly do you wish to know me better? Intellectually or carnally?"

Harrison choked and coughed. How could one small actress steal all his words while making his palms damp and his heart race? He should have expected such directness; any actress of her skill would have to juggle propositions of all kinds, from the merely friendly to the erotic. He'd already seen how she managed threats.

He nodded toward the shut door. "I thought my name might offer you some protection."

She stared at him for a moment, as if she had expected him to say something else. Then she shook her head. "I can manage on my own, even without the protection of your name."

"But that man . . ."

She raised her hand to cut him off. "That man is another matter entirely and none of your concern." Her voice was chiding. She might be amused or angry, he could not tell. "Are you always so clumsy when talking to women you wish to . . . know better?"

"I appear to be out of practice talking to beautiful women at all."

"That sentence is better, but still not quite good enough to merit my continued attention. Give me one good reason not to send you on your way."

She was rejecting him out of hand. He hadn't considered how that might feel. But now he knew. It felt like he'd been pummeled in the stomach. Without thinking, he confessed a piece of information he had not intended to reveal. "You remind me of someone I lost long ago."

"If that was intended to gain my sympathy, I find it falls flat." She grew silent for a moment. "I am not interested in being wanted for my resemblance to another person. If we were to begin a liaison, you would always be watching for glimpses of that other person, and you would never see me. No, I prefer to be known for myself."

She turned to face the ruined mirror before her dressing table. The reflective mercury was pocked and clouded, and he could see her face only imperfectly. "But not all of my fellow thespians are as scrupulous as I am. Beatrice next door has been interviewing possible protectors, but hasn't made her final decision. If you hurry, you can likely gain her undying devotion before she leaves the theater." She pointed to the door, and his heart fell to his feet.

"I assure you I saw no one but you on stage all evening."

The gypsy rolled her eyes. "Beatrice won't care if you didn't notice her, as long as you offer her carte blanche. Compliment her legs. She hopes to make a name for herself in breeches roles." She turned her back to him, leaving him to marvel at the line of her neck and the set of her shoulders.

"I must explain. All evening, I felt this tension between

us, an attraction, a connection. When you ended the song, you looked at me. Tell me you did not feel it as well."

"What do you want me to say, your lordship? That our eyes met and I felt the earth tremble beneath my feet, that the stars seemed to dim in the heavens, that my world will be incomplete until I hold you in my arms?" She waited for his answer, and he found himself unable to respond. "I thought so. Ignoring any connection between us, why did you choose me to approach? Because I perform provocative songs on the stage? Because my flirting with the audience suggested I will be as free with my favors in life as the character I play on stage? No, your lordship, I am not the woman you think I am. Besides, men like you rarely marry actresses, unless of course we have the wit and beauty of the Countess of Derby. And I am not interested in being any man's mistress, stealing his minutes from his family and his wife."

"I've recently discovered I'm not married." For all his vaunted skill at convincing the inconvincible in Parliament, he was floundering for any excuse to stay in her room.

Her laugh was almost a bark as she pulled back in surprise. "That's a strange discovery. How does it happen?" She leaned forward conspiratorially and said in a half whisper, "Did you have your wife murdered? Has she been lost at sea?"

"No. Apparently our banns weren't read. If they weren't read, we are not married."

"You are serious." She sat back, regarding him anew. "Why are you telling me this?"

"For years, I've felt constrained by my marriage, but now if my marriage is a fraud, then I may do as I please. Admire a tempting actress, dine with a lovely woman, take a mistress, go back to sea, whatever I wish." He stopped, suddenly realizing what else it meant: that Olivia would be gone from his life as surely as if she had died. But he pushed the thought away. For Olivia to have taken this step meant she was already gone.

"Are you well, sir?" The actress's voice turned soft, even kind. "Your face for a moment was quite blanched."

"What? Oh, yes, I am well."

"Are you certain you didn't kill your wife?" Her words were skeptical, but her face wasn't wary. It seemed only sad.

"As far as I know, she is well, perhaps even happy. She is suited to the country and a quiet life. I am not."

"And you have come to me to inaugurate your new-found freedom. Have you made a list of things you wish to do? Number one: take a mistress. But surely you've had mistresses before. No, your list should include only those things you have never done."

"Then number one stands. I never wanted my wife, but I didn't wish to hurt her either." He never spoke so openly with strangers; perhaps it was the arc of energy that still, he believed, passed between them. "But I must admit, I haven't filled in the other numbers on my list."

"Might I give you some advice, your lordship?"

"If I let you advise me, will you come to my club for dinner?"

She shook her head, this time with clear sympathy. "You have recently discovered that the world you thought you knew doesn't exist. You chose me for a mistress because I remind you of a woman from your past. You claim you are free to do anything you want, but you can't even fill in number two on your list."

"Take you to dinner," he announced triumphantly. "That's number two."

"If dinner is a prelude to seduction, then it's simply part of number one. You will never be happy until you reconcile with your past."

Picking up her reticule, she rose and walked toward

the door. "As for me, I have a rendezvous with a special gentleman, and I do not wish to keep him waiting."

He caught her arm, unwilling to let her go. "Might I write to you as I sort these things out? If you found my letters interesting, you could write me in return?" He watched as she turned the idea over.

"When you have discovered what you need to know, you may write to me here in care of Mrs. Wells."

"To whom should I address the letter? I must admit, I've lost my playbill."

She thought for another moment, then smiling, answered, "You were once a sailor?"

"In His Majesty's fleet."

"Then address the letter to Circe."

He laughed. "Am I in danger of being turned into a pig?"

"That, sir, depends on what you write."

"Then, Circe, I look forward to our correspondence." He raised her hand to his lips and offered a chivalrous kiss, then he let her go.

Harrison stood alone in the gypsy's dressing room. To the right of her dressing table, a rack held the cast's costumes from the first play and the first part of the afterpiece. Mrs. Wells's infuriating headdress was perched next to the gypsy's blousy shirt and slit skirt.

He stepped to the rack and let his hand caress the material. The shift was as soft as he had imagined from the way it had clung to her curves on stage. But it held no hint to her identity.

Circe. He smiled. The sorceress whose song tempted Odysseus to abandon his wife and land, and who turned into animals all those who displeased her. An unexpectedly literate answer.

He started to leave, but stopped when he saw an envelope on the floor beneath the costumes. What could it be? A love note? Instructions for an assignation? Or something more mundane, like pages from a script? If he were lucky, the letter would be hers, and it would reveal her true name and her address.

There was no address on the outside of the packet, only the recipient—An Honest Gentleman—lettered in a bold, flamboyant hand.

Interesting.

For the last year, the Gentleman had been making quite a stir in Parliament. In fact, at the last parliamentary committee Harrison had attended, one of the Tories had waved a copy of the *World* and declaimed loudly: "Rights and reform! Haven't we seen where such complaints lead? To the Bastille! To the execution of Louis XVI! To the end of peace and order for a dozen years! No, sirs, the best thing we can do for our nation is to find, try, and if necessary execute this Dis-Honest Gentleman."

Over the last several months, Harrison had read all the Gentleman's essays carefully. He'd been impressed with the thoughtful and convincing arguments. Few men were as well-informed as the Gentleman, and of those, even fewer took such care to be rational and balanced. Recently, however, the Gentleman's letters had grown more provocative. None of it was too dangerous . . . yet, and Harrison had grown increasingly interested in finding out who in the government was passing sensitive information, and to what end.

Clearly it was a letter from an informant to An Honest Gentleman. He turned it over. An address, but no postmark and no frank. Had the informant come to the theater to deliver the letter to Mrs. Wells? Or had Mrs. Wells received the letter at the *World* and brought it to one of her fellow thespians?

He surveyed the gypsy's dressing room with new eyes. The odious man who had confronted the gypsy earlier had insisted that she had secrets; he had even thought that keeping her secrets mattered enough that she would pay. Was she keeping secrets for An Honest Gentleman?

Looking to see that the dressing room door was shut, he unfolded the packet and began to review the pages. Dread curled with cold fingers around his heart. He knew that the Prince Regent had instructed the Home Office to watch the reform societies, but to his knowledge all they had done was watch. But whoever had written this list made it appear that the government's role was far more active, and that the societies and their members were being actively targeted and suppressed. If true, the list was a damning indictment of the government's policies. Of course, he didn't believe it, but Harrison knew—and suspected the writer did as well—that truth didn't matter. It simply had to be believable, and then it would spread on wings of outrage. What laborer with too little bread wouldn't embrace the information as an excuse for his discontent? The people's confidence in the government—already low—would be shattered.

This document was more dangerous than any he had seen before from An Honest Gentleman. But who had written it, and who was intended to receive it? Mrs. Wells? The gypsy, or some other cast member? Because the person who wrote this list was either a traitor or consorted with one. He needed to find out who—and soon.

Chapter Seven

Mistress! Olivia pulled her large valise from the boarding house wardrobe and set it roughly on the table in the middle of the room. The first conversation she'd had with her husband since he'd left for the wars, and he'd thought her a whore. When would she learn?

Olivia stopped packing and leaned back against the wall, covering her face with her hands. But she had no tears. She'd spent them all long ago, when she still hoped they might make a marriage work. In the early years of their marriage, she'd dreamed that Harrison could come to love her, that he would recognize all the ways he and Olivia were suited for one another. But in the end, Harrison's longing for adventure never disappeared, and Olivia was left alone.

Without thinking, she slid down the wall until she was curled up in the small space beside the wardrobe. The tight quarters felt safe, protected.

She brought her knees to her chest and folded her arms on top of them. But as soon as she laid her head on her arms, she pulled back. He had touched her hand and left behind the faintest hint of his cologne, a distinctive musk made from green lemon and pinewood. It was the same one he had always worn, and she remembered how catching hints of it unexpectedly had pained her for months after he'd left. Then one day she realized every trace of it was gone, and she'd wept for hours.

She caressed the spot on her hand where he had kissed her, imagining that the warmth of his lips still burned her flesh. He was more handsome than he had been when they'd parted, and he had been handsome enough then. The rich blue of his eyes, the strong line of his jaw, the broadness of his shoulders narrowing to the flat plane of his stomach, all left her breathless. She felt the ache of missing him.

It was good that she would be leaving the estate. She might never learn how not to want him, but she already knew how to live without him.

She remembered her first day at Mrs. Jeraldine Flint's School for Exceptional Girls. She had felt homesick, abandoned. She had curled into a corner in just this same way, and Mrs. Flint—kind and brusque and wise and impatient all at once—had come and sat on the floor beside her. Since then, when she felt overwhelmed, she would imagine what Mrs. Flint would tell her. Today Mrs. Flint's voice came easily.

Now, listen to me, girl. He will never, ever want you. As much as you want him, as much as you long to feel his lips in a kiss, or his hand holding yours, you must stop being a fool. Even now he isn't trying to convince you to marry him again. No, he had your letter for less than a day and started interviewing mistresses—and making a mess of it, I might add. But did you expect anything less? It was unlucky that you were the actress who caught his eye, but eventually Beatrice or one of the others will be happy to catch a rich lord and his ample income. But that won't be enough for you. You won't be satisfied with anything less than his

*heart. Now get up and build yourself another life . . . a
life worth living . . . a life where your actions matter.*

She pulled herself up from the boarding-house floor, not
because she wanted to move, but because it was foolish to
remain there. She straightened her skirts, then wrenched
open the door of the wardrobe and began pulling out the
makings of her various costumes. When Olivia wasn't in
town, the materials remained in a trunk in the attic, ready
for her next visit. As she packed, she began to plan how
her new life would proceed.

Her obligations at the estate required that she be back
no later than Wednesday morning. She would leave the day
after tomorrow. Until then, she would fill her time with
writing and meetings with her informants. Based on the information she had gained from Cerberus, she would draft
another essay for the *World*, and deliver it to Mrs. Wells for
printing. Then, if she had time, she would meet once more
with Mentor. After that, she would return to the estate for
the last time and begin the work of letting him go.

"Ouch!" Harrison pulled the straight pin out of his
thumb and watched the blood pool. Strange how much a
small wound could hurt. But at least the pain drew his
mind back to the present task, away from the questions
about his wife, the gypsy, and An Honest Gentleman that
had kept him restless half the night.

"The great spy felled by a pin." Joseph Pasten, the ad-
jutant for a secret division of the Home Office, grinned. To
keep track of the division's various operations, Joe had
created what he called the mission table: a map of England
glued to a heavy linen backing and laid out under the only
natural light in the basement room, a row of windows
running along the top of the walls. Joe's good humor accompanied a stalwart and courageous heart. During the

Battle of Waterloo, Joe had saved the life of Mr. James, his superior officer and now the director of their division. Cut by bayonets and then trampled by a terrified horse, Mr. James would have died on the field had Joe not dragged his body to safety, then spent months nursing his broken body back to health. Few doctors would have even attempted what Joe accomplished.

"Walgrave's been cursing for the better part of an hour." Adam Montclair looked up from his desk. "But now that he's wounded himself, we should all be wary. I predict a bloody overthrow of our map of England."

"In my years abroad, I acquired several hand gestures to indicate displeasure." Harrison rubbed the blood off with his other fingers, but it quickly pooled again. A deep one then. "But I have held off using them—out of respect for Joe and his belief that this damned board is vital to our planning."

"If hand gestures are all you acquired abroad, you should count yourself lucky." Adam threw a scrap of linen at Harrison, who wrapped it around his thumb. "But Walgrave's right, Joe. We'd have burned that damn table years ago, if you didn't spend half your time mollifying us."

"A dozen groups, both at home and abroad, threaten the peace of the nation, but my task is to pamper battle-hardened men wounded by straight pins." Joe lifted his face and hands as if supplicating Heaven. "The table stays, pins and all. It's my mnemonic. Each time one of you dolts forgets something vital, I simply gesture at the table."

Harrison cleaned his blood from the head of the pin with the linen. "I submit to the judgment of my betters—and by my betters I mean Joe."

"Your words have wounded me." Adam spoke dryly, returning to his papers. "How ever shall I go on?"

Harrison returned to his task of pushing pins into the map. Joe had carefully painted each pin a different color, and each one represented some aspect of an operation in motion. The blue pins indicated groups or individuals engaged in suspicious, but perhaps not illegal, activities. The green pins signified an agent of the Home Office, either a trusted local or an officer—whether in disguise or not—dispatched to watch over the area. The black pins—well, Harrison tried to make sure there were never too many of those—but sometimes agents died, and there was not one damn thing you could do about it. He pushed the next pin—a black one—into the map with more force than necessary. A woman. Missing in the north of England for weeks, her body had just been found in the mountains. None of them knew how or why she had died.

Harrison stared at the pin. When he had first come back from the seas, his seat in Parliament had been enough to satisfy his restless spirit. He'd used his skills as an orator to argue for improvements to the lives of all English citizens, and his reputation grew with each speech. He'd relied on arguments appealing to each man's self-interest, knowing that at the end of the day what mattered most to the other lords was a full stomach and a full wallet. But he'd always believed in justice, and he'd always hoped that by beginning with *me*, his listeners would be enlightened enough to end with *us*. One day, however, he'd realized that for many, the questions "What is best for me?" and "What is just for all?" were answered by a single sentence: What is best for me is just for all. On that day, he'd drunk himself to oblivion.

The day after—still feeling his disgust in the roiling pit of his stomach and his disappointment in the aching throb of his head—he had made his way back to Whitehall. But instead of heading up to the parliamentary rooms, he'd descended to the basement, through a maze of offices to a secret suite that housed an equally secret branch of the Home Office. Harrison had thought his life as a spy had ended with the wars and that a life as a public servant would be satisfying enough. But when Joe Pasten had opened the door and, smiling, led him in, Harrison had felt like he'd found his way home.

His secret work for the Home Office had made his life useful, even meaningful. But recently he had been unable to overcome a growing sense of emptiness. Sure, he could remind himself of all the threats he'd averted or how many people he'd helped, but more and more often, it didn't seem to matter.

Joe put his hand on Harrison's shoulder and looked at the black pin. "It never gets easier. You'd think after the wars we'd be inured to death, but each one still catches me off guard. What was her name?"

"Mrs. Louise Gail. She was a good correspondent, observant, timely. She was watching the northern reform societies for evidence of rebellion. A cottager found her body at the base of a ravine."

"Do you think it was related to the information she was gathering?" Joe touched the pin reverently.

"My gut tells me yes, but I have no proof." Harrison picked up a letter and handed it to Joe. Anger simmered at the edges of his control, but he forced his voice to sound dispassionate. "Only days before she disappeared she wrote that she was investigating a new threat."

Joe read the letter slowly, then chewed the end of his pencil for a few minutes. "Was she a graduate of Mrs. Flint's school?"

Montclair joined the two men, looking regretfully over the table. "No, she wasn't one of Flint's. She was a widow who moved to the north when she inherited a cottage. I met her at one of the reform society meetings, and she welcomed the chance to be of use."

Joe pointed to one of the new green pins somewhat nearby. "Who's that?"

"The new governess to that American industrialist who wants to buy up all of our tin mines." Harrison tapped the top of the pin. "In Jeraldine Flint's words, Miss Blackwell can 'unsnivel a pack of sniveling children' and pick a lock in fifteen seconds."

Joe chuckled. "I'm not sure which will be the more useful skill. Which one was she?"

"Fresh-faced, blond." Adam grimaced.

"Ah, yes, a winsome smile. She should discover her employer's secrets easily. As I remember, she offered a striking demonstration of her ability to read a handwritten document upside down." Joe read over Harrison's list of new pins. "A skill I've always wanted to cultivate."

"I expected you to say you enjoyed it best when Blackwell threw Adam—a man double her size—over her hip to the floor."

"Well, it does suggest she can hold her own with the rakes and roués common to country house parties." Joe tapped the list. "I see you are almost finished."

"With this and with all the other reports and correspondence on my desk. I was hoping to shift my attention to some new inquiries."

"That's our Walgrave: never able to give a big messy pile of documents to the next man. No, everything must always be tied up with a neat bow before it can be passed along." Adam laughed wryly and returned to his desk. "You know, Walgrave, that some of the newer fellows would be grateful for a mess of their own to sort out."

"At least this way, I know who to blame when something falls apart." Walgrave without thinking touched a black pin to the east of England—Princess Marietta, a minor Hapsburg princess, killed by highwaymen. Another death on his watch. He would never confess to Adam, or any of the other men, that he worked so hard to atone for all the agents he'd lost.

"You can't always predict all the possible outcomes." Adam shook his head ruefully. "Sometimes situations change in the middle, and the best you can do is adapt. And you adapt better than any of us."

"You've been on edge all morning." Joe noticed the black pin and laid his hand on Harrison's shoulder. "Is there something amiss? I mean other than the loss of a correspondent."

Harrison held his hands out to his sides, pushing down the bone-deep loneliness that he'd battled for months. "I believe I saw my wife yesterday walking down Bond Street. Same build, same hair. I followed her, but somehow she eluded me."

"She eluded you?" Adam's head bobbed up from his papers. "A mere woman escaped our best spy. I believe Shakespeare would say, 'There is a mystery.'"

Joe shook his head at Adam, as if to say *not now*, and Adam mouthed *Troilus and Cressida*, then returned to his work.

Joe looked at Walgrave, his face filled with concern. "If you were certain yesterday, why are you not certain today?"

"Last night at the theater I saw an actress similar to my wife in build and height. I could have seen her on the street instead."

"You mistook an actress for your wife?" Joe's face clouded. "When did you last visit your estate?"

"Joe! Must you even ask? Walgrave cannot tell the difference between a woman on the street, *an actress*, and his wife," Adam interjected. "He has been away too long."

Walgrave chose his words carefully, knowing he could not avoid looking like a lout. "My work keeps me often in town, and Lady Walgrave is an exceptionally competent manager." He was not yet ready to reveal the rest; he would sound an even bigger fool. What woman would willingly give up the rank of countess to become a nobody? It was

unimaginable, and, though Adam had been joking, many
would lay the fault firmly at Walgrave's feet.

Joe patted his arm in commiseration. "You probably did
see her ladyship—on the street, that is. Before his death,
your father asked the previous head of this division to keep
a watch on Lady Walgrave until your return. She came to
town quite frequently. From what I understand, she was
quite fond of the maritime plays at Sadler's Wells."

"How is it that everyone has seen my wife in London
save for me?" Walgrave saw the noose tightening. He could
hear the jibes now. Instead of being described as thorough,
candid, and frank, he would be found dispassionate, feeling-
less, and cold.

"Luck?" Adam suggested wryly.

Joe cuffed the junior officer in the arm. "He's not in
jest, Adam."

"Nor am I," Adam said. "He has made no secret of his
disinterest in his marriage. I would have thought he'd be
pleased to know his wife has come and gone for years without his being troubled in the slightest by her presence."

At the back of the main office, Joe and Mr. James, their
superior, had their own separate rooms. Joe never used his;
Mr. James always did. The door to Mr. James's private
office opened, and the three men grew silent.

A stocky man carrying a coat and a worn leather lawyer's
briefcase left Mr. James's office and pulled the door shut
behind him. Once an agent of the office himself, William
Aldine left the division to join one of the Inns of Court, but
he had kept up his association with the men and often ad-
vised them on the legalities of their various activities. He
was also Harrison's personal solicitor. Though Aldine
always looked a bit rumpled around the edges, he moved
with the agility of a dancer. Aldine nodded his greeting.

Harrison held up a pin and his thumb wrapped in linen.

"'Look you, his thumb is stuck full of pins.'" Aldine pointed at Harrison theatrically. He held the pose for a moment, then transformed back into a rumpled solicitor. "Webster's *White Devil*: I'm expanding my repertoire, but in the original play, it's his codpiece that's stuck with pins."

"I'll note that in my book of memory," Joe joined in. *"Henry VI, Part 1."*

Aldine joined them at the mission table. "What do you think, gentlemen? From the severity of Walgrave's injury, I'm sure he will die. Should I draw up his will before I leave?"

"Walgrave, if Aldine is writing your will, then 'forsake thy fortune; Bequeath thy land to me,'" Adam teased. "Gentlemen, that's a happy mutilation of a line from *King John*."

All three men turned to Harrison, waiting. But he merely held up his thumb once more. "I must decline to participate. This current craze for Shakespeare will eventually pass. As a seafaring man, I prefer *The Iliad*, *The Odyssey*, *The Aeneid*—those are the texts that will last for all time. But, Aldine, have you had a chance to review that piece of . . . estate business we've received?"

"I have." The stocky solicitor shifted his coat to the hand not carrying his briefcase. "Joe, may we use the meeting room at the end of the corridor?"

"Certainly, certainly." Joe drew a key from a box on his desk. "Just return the key when you are finished."

Chapter Eight

"I have reviewed the packet of documents sent yesterday from her ladyship's solicitors, enough to get a sense of the issue. However, a more precise answer will take some time." Aldine set his briefcase on the table and opened it to reveal a cramped mass of papers, with a tight roll of newspapers crushed onto the top of them all. He pulled out the newspapers and set them to the side, then rummaged through his papers until he found the sheet he wanted. "I brought some preliminary questions with me."

Aldine fostered the appearance of rumpled incompetence, but Harrison—like all the other men in the division—knew the clothes hid an exceptionally incisive mind.

"I have my own questions as well. Am I married or not?"

"It would be for the courts to decide. But if your wife's recollection of events is correct, then legal defects in the marriage likely render it invalid."

"She has taken a long time to raise these objections." Harrison tried to sound impartial, but even he could hear the edge of strain.

"She might not have realized the status of your marriage until recently. A number of new books have discussed void and voidable marriages. Besides, if the marriage is not valid, the amount of time that passed is irrelevant. An invalid contract is invalid, regardless of whether the persons involved have believed it to be valid."

"What do we do?" Harrison steepled his fingers before his face.

"What do you *wish* to do?" Aldine paused. "As I see it, it all hinges on whether or not you wish to be married. If you wish to be free, we accept her set of irregularities as accurate and petition the court to have the marriage declared null. If, however, you wish to be married, then we need to convince the courts that her claims are erroneous by showing that the marriage conforms to the requirements of the statute."

"What are the irregularities?" Harrison tapped his fingertips together, uncertain whether he was angry or relieved.

"She claims that your banns were not read on three occasions preceding the marriage. Nor was the ceremony performed in a church or public chapel." Aldine looked up hopefully, as if Harrison might have a record of the church banns or the marriage in his pocket. "Was it a special license?"

Harrison shifted in his seat, unwilling to reveal to Aldine the full circumstances of his marriage. In an instant, he could see his father's face again, laughing, a full glass of whiskey in his hand, as he pronounced with glee, *Don't worry, boy, I've taken care of all the details. I have friends in the bishop's office, got the special license right here*—he'd patted his waistcoat—*even got permission for you to marry here in the chapel, in the hall of your ancestors, surrounded by your past and looking to your future.*

Harrison pushed the memory away. "It was a special license, I'm sure of it."

"Then, I will see if we can discover a record of it." Aldine read over the documents. "The marriage was in your family chapel, but there's no one living there. Do you remember the minister's name or from what village he came?"

"I only know that my father knew him well." He remembered nothing of the minister, but everything about Olivia. Standing at the front of the nearly empty chapel, he'd grimaced to see his father in the first row of pews, but then, looking up, he had seen Olivia waiting at the back of the chapel. Her hands had been clasped beneath a bouquet of daisies. Her eyes—full of hope—had met his, and his heart had expanded in his chest. Remembering, he felt it once more, the sense of possibility coupled with the heat of desire.

"Walgrave?" Aldine asked quietly.

Harrison, returning to the present, ran a hand through his hair. "I was trying to remember the name of the minister. Can you repeat that last question?"

"The witnesses. Who witnessed the ceremony?"

"My father; his valet, Baxter; and the housekeeper, Baxter's wife. But all are dead. Wouldn't the parish record or the license have the signatures of the witnesses?"

"Unfortunately, the church in the village closest to your estate burned several years ago, and its records were lost. If the minister was a friend to your father, he may have come from a nearby parish, and I might find some information in that way. If there is no special license and no village register, we will have trouble refuting her claims. But even if we could, we will have trouble disproving her final two claims: She indicates that she did not provide her true baptismal name and that she knew your father was not observing the legalities of the statute."

"Doesn't that constitute a fraud?" Harrison felt the hurt twist in his chest. A fraud with his father at the heart of it. His old anger, long cold, began to simmer anew.

"She claims that your father assured her that he acted

according to the bishop's advice. She has realized he was in error—whether he intended the mistake or not." Aldine after a slight pause continued. "All this leads us back to the question I posed at the beginning. What do you wish to do? Either path will cost you somewhat, but her requested settlement is quite reasonable."

"I don't care about the money." He pushed the papers away.

"What do you care about, Walgrave?" Aldine's voice was gentle. "What do you want?"

"Strangely, Aldine, you are the second person to ask me that, and I don't yet have an answer."

"I only need to know how to proceed." Aldine folded his list back into his briefcase. He picked up the roll of newspapers, then pushed them toward Walgrave. "I'll leave these for you—or whoever might like them. Tell me, Walgrave, what do you want—married or free?"

Harrison thought for a long time before he spoke. "I want to know why. I married on my father's insistence and recommendation. He presented Olivia as the impoverished child of an old friend, and I believed him. But if her name is a lie, then what other lies did she or my father tell?" He felt his heart grow brittle like a piece of flint struck too many times. "Find the truth—her name, her background, all of it. I'll pay whatever it costs."

"Certainly, my lord." Aldine snapped the lock shut, then hesitated. "Of course, there is a third route, less public than the courts. But given the thoroughness of Lady Walgrave's proposal, I hesitate to suggest it."

"I would like to know all my options, even if they are disagreeable."

"If your marriage is not valid but you wish to be married to her ladyship, all you would have to do is marry again. I could arrange for the license, make sure everything is done correctly this time. Given your reputation as an orator, surely you could convince her ladyship to marry you again." Aldine touched Harrison's shoulder as he rose, and when his client did not respond, Aldine placed the key on top of the newspapers and slipped out.

Harrison sat in the conference room for a long time. The question of what course the remainder of his life would take had been plaguing him for some time. But before the letter from Olivia, his plans had been inchoate and inarticulate. For years, he'd found friendship and solace in the company of Mr. James and Joe Pasten. All three men worked late into the night, reading reports from their informants across the country in order to see patterns and intervene. But recently Mr. James had developed a persistent cough, and Joe, blaming the damp of their basement office, had been insistent that Mr. James spend his evenings in the apartment given him by the Prince Regent—another hidden space, but one with a rooftop view of the city. Though he could not resent the loss of the two men's company, he felt their absence deeply.

Each night, when the last man in the division lifted his hat off the rack and turned his feet toward home, Harrison felt the question of his life laid bare. Other men would take to the bottle; Harrison took to work, more and more and more work. With the blessing of Mr. James and the gratitude of Joe Pasten, he'd begun to supervise their agents. He was clearly being groomed to take over the office when Mr. James's health demanded retirement. But if his life were to change, did he want to be the great spy, or did he want something else? All his adult life, he'd felt constrained by his father's choices for him. But if he could begin again, if he could make whatever choices he wanted, what would he choose?

He'd made the first step in setting Aldine on the path to discover Olivia's real name. While he had not wished to marry, having a wife had often proved convenient, and sometimes even comforting. No marriage-minded mamas paid attention to a wedded man. His estate was well managed and prosperous, all without his having to offer it the least attention or worry, a situation that provided him with a warm sense of satisfaction. He had not wished to give Olivia a greater place in his life, but sometimes he had found the idea of her a comforting possibility. Whenever his life grew too frustrating, he could imagine returning home and being welcomed as lord of the manor, even if he never made that journey. Or on days when he found himself plagued by a sense of nostalgia for family—brought on usually by visiting with those in his circle with happy families—he reminded himself that someday, if he wished, he could return to the estate, to his wife, and begin his own happy family. But if Olivia were not the honest, biddable wife he had believed her to be, then those comforting thoughts were merely more lies to count against her reckoning. Even so, he found himself angry with her for displacing them. If Olivia was other than he had been led to believe, she would never see another penny of his funds. It wouldn't matter how reasonable her request for a settlement was.

He rose, setting his hand on the key and the newspapers Aldine had left. On top, a copy of the *World* was folded open to An Honest Gentleman's most recent letter. Perhaps as he waited for Aldine's inquiries to come to fruition, he might find some solace in doing his duty—and the letter he'd found in the gypsy's dressing room suggested his duty involved identifying An Honest Gentleman.

"He can see you now." Joe nodded his head back toward the closed door of Mr. James's office. "But you might want to make it brief. The Manchester debacle has kept him in meetings for the last three days, and he's worn thin."

Joe brushed his hand through the waves of his thick black hair, a characteristic gesture when Joe was worried or dismayed. "Are you sure it won't wait until tomorrow?"

"I'll be brief." Harrison folded the newspaper he had been pretending to read. As much as he cared about his commander's health, he knew that Mr. James would want to know if there were traitors in England, and he would also want Harrison to investigate wherever that might lead. "I'm considering doing some traveling this week."

"To your estate?" Joe's eyebrow raised suspiciously.

"I haven't decided my destination." But traveling to his estate might be the perfect excuse to justify his need to be gone from the office.

"Well, it's about time," Adam muttered from his desk.

"Why does everyone say that?" Harrison knew he sounded petulant.

"Is that a rhetorical question?" Adam countered. "Or do you actually wish to know?"

"It's not as if I've been needed at home." He gestured toward his desk. "My work here is too important to neglect."

"Don't blame us. Mr. James has suggested you go home a dozen times or more."

"Not this year." Harrison glared, then growled. "I don't wish to justify my decisions."

Joe turned back to the paperwork on his desk. "You never do. But someday you are going to wish you had paid more attention when you had the chance." He looked at the clock above the door to Mr. James's office. "You have five minutes. Use it well."

Harrison crossed the room in three long strides. Tapping once, he pushed the door open and stepped through. Mr. James's office resembled what Harrison imagined a rabbit hole might look like if the rabbit had a taste for books. Hundreds of them, on shelves, in piles, and making—for part of the room—a short wall on which other papers, maps, and engravings were laid haphazardly. For all the disarray, however, Harrison knew that Mr. James could lay his hand on any piece of paper he wished to find, or recall any detail at the snap of his fingers.

"You know, it's the women killed at Peterloo who haunt me. Mary, thrown in a cellar, and Martha trampled by cavalry." Mr. James shook his head. "The old soldiers knew what the costs might be. But those two . . . it was supposed to be a parade." The head of the division folded the map of the countryside he'd been examining. "Joe says you have something important to discuss, something that can't wait."

Harrison slid a copy of the *World* in front of Mr. James. "Have you read this?"

"Only under duress." Mr. James barked a laugh. "Why?"

"I suspect that someone is using periodicals like this one to send confidential information to our enemies abroad. Worse, I believe someone in Whitehall is providing at least some of that information, but whether for idealism or for a price, I don't know."

"That rag? The *World* will make up any accusation to sell a paper." Mr. James looked uninterested. "Most of the time their writers merely rehash the parliamentary reports printed in the *Times* and serve them up as scandal."

"I don't think so. Something else is going on, and I want to find out."

"Why do you think so?"

"This." Harrison folded the newspaper open to An Honest Gentleman's latest letter.

"That?" Mr. James didn't take the paper, but instead leaned back in his chair. The scar that disfigured one half of his face remained visible behind his steepled fingers. "Joe investigated An Honest Gentleman months ago. He's just an eccentric with a banner to wave. Besides, aren't you a Whig? Don't you want someone like An Honest Gentleman promoting the cause of reform?"

"I want reform. Universal suffrage, freedom of the press, freedom of assembly—all those are good and necessary, and I hope to see them flourish in my lifetime. But ranting letters that point up every failing of the House of Lords and the Prince Regent harm more than they help."

Mr. James turned to pull some papers from a pile to his right. "Does An Honest Gentleman rant?"

"That's a tricky question. He appears more reasonable than the others, but he always includes information that isn't widely known outside of Whitehall."

Mr. James shook his head. "He's simply well connected— one can find out almost anything with the right circle of friends."

"No, my gut tells me that someone in government— perhaps in this very office—is using An Honest Gentleman's position to rabble-rouse." Harrison leaned forward confidentially, his elbows resting on his knees. "A hint here, a nudge there, and suddenly a peaceable reform society transforms into an angry mob. And certainly that would suit the purposes of our enemies abroad."

"I'm not convinced. It's a letter in a newspaper—how much influence does he really have over the worker or the shopkeeper? And is the circulation of these papers abroad timely enough to aid some plot in Prussia?"

"Well, here's an example. Yesterday, An Honest Gentleman praised Richard Carlile, the newspaperman, as a sort of folk hero forced to flee the podium when the Manchester rally turned bloody. Here's what he said: 'The question of whether the government can hold publishers liable for the contents of the books they publish is an important one. But is Carlile being tried for republishing Thomas Paine's *Age of Reason*, or for being a champion of the people, of reform, and of freedom of the press?'" Harrison pushed the paper toward Mr. James. "And today at Carlile's trial, three hundred constables were required to keep the peace. So, yes, I'd say that these correspondents have tremendous influence over the common man, and I'd like to investigate."

Mr. James picked up the *World*, folding it back into its original shape. "Your attention is needed elsewhere."

"Lately, my attention has been too many elsewheres. At least in the field, if I miss a threat, I put only myself at risk."

"Ah, so that's what this is about: Princess Marietta's death and my brother Colin's injury when trying to protect her." Mr. James turned his full attention to Harrison, speaking kindly but firmly. "You might be our best, but you are not our *only* analyst, Harrison. None of us saw anything that predicted the attack. But what matters is how you responded. Though the princess didn't survive the birth, you intervened admirably to deliver her child to his relatives and to ensure that my brother's wound had time to mend. So, 'forget, forgive, conclude and be agreed,' as Shakespeare would say. 'I find you empty of that fault.'"

"Not you as well." Harrison sighed heavily, fearing that he had somewhere lost the battle. "'I am thoroughly weary' of this Shakespeare game."

"And yet you quote *Cymbeline* in your weariness." Mr. James smiled, his grin crooked as a clown's, before his face returned to its sober mask. "Besides, I have something pressing that needs a good man."

"Whatever it is, give it to one of the new men. Quarles or McFadden would do well." Harrison felt his frustration harden. "Only you and Joe have been in this office longer than I have. That's what it will take to root this out: someone with a long memory."

Mr. James picked up the periodical he had pushed to the side and scanned the table of contents. "I must disagree.

The *World* is more likely to provide a biography of—let's see here—Edward, 'The Corpulent Baker of Malden' than to offer astute political commentary."

"We shouldn't ignore this. The Tories are already talking of limiting civil liberties in the upcoming special session. If it looks like the rabble are rising, then we Whigs will have little hope of stemming the tide of repression."

"It might already be too late to stem that tide. The Prince Regent fears that common Englishmen are primed to become a revolutionary mob." Mr. James turned away from him. "As for the *World*, you've been working night and day for months, and it's leading you to see conspiracies and traitors where I see only foolishness and clowns."

At other times, Harrison would have argued, pressed his point with conviction and zeal, until Mr. James allowed him to follow his instincts. But Joseph was right: Mr. James looked worn. Though still physically strong, his body had been broken in the wars and the pain of it still troubled him. "Then if you wouldn't mind, I'd like to take a week, perhaps two, and return to my estate. Some business there requires my attention." Walgrave picked up the copy of the *World* and tucked it under his arm. His instincts insisted that An Honest Gentleman led to a larger plot, but he would gain nothing by insisting Mr. James was wrong.

"That's an excellent idea." From a cubbyhole to his right, Mr. James retrieved a map of the counties between London and Harrison's country estate and examined it. "We haven't yet fully contained the highwaymen on that route. When do you intend to leave?"

"Tomorrow before noon. I'd like to arrive before dark."

"Good idea. I'd hate for that doe-eyed brunette of yours to worry over your safety."

"How do you know what my wife looks like?"

For a moment Mr. James looked stricken, then a lop-sided smile spread across his face. When it met the corner of his mouth, it intersected with a thick scar that ran across his cheek and caused his eye to droop at the corner. Lesser men would have quaked at the sight, but Harrison had long grown accustomed to it, and he preferred it when Mr. James had something to smile about. "I am a master of spies. What in the realm do I not know?" The ruined face turned serious again. "As for the *World*, I can assure you, An Honest Gentleman poses no danger to the crown."

Mr. James rose with difficulty and set a friendly hand on Walgrave's shoulder. "I'll send the file I need you to review to your estate."

Joe leaned back, stretching from the work before him. Walgrave had left after his meeting with Mr. James, and Adam soon followed. In the unusual quiet of the office, Joe had set himself to work. His large desk was covered with reports. In one pile to his right sat a series of documents related to the—yet unbroken—code sent back to England by the late Lord Wilmot. Wilmot had been murdered for his service to the Home Office, and his wife threatened.

"Any luck?"

Joe looked up to where his superior officer stood in profile. From this angle, with only one half of his face visible, Benjamin Somerville looked every whit the handsome officer, waves of blond hair thick around his face, eyes of the clearest blue. For a moment, Joe caught a glimpse of the man Benjamin had been before the wars: strong, lively, sociable. Were it not for Benjamin's hand on a cane, Joe could imagine him once more as the kind upperclassman he had met his first day as a charity student at Harrow.

But then Benjamin turned, and the illusion disappeared. It wasn't vanity that led Benjamin to avoid mirrors. Instead, it was a way to forget the horrors of a war that had left him disfigured. Joe had long ago steeled himself to the change: the foot dragging uselessly behind, the twisted arm, and the hopelessly damaged face with one long scar from temple to chin and the upper part of the ear missing entirely.

Benjamin had lost even his name: the first in line to be the Duke of Forster, he'd told the Prince Regent that he had no desire to be on display, scaring children and causing women to hide their faces. He'd asked that his service be rewarded with a death as another casualty of Waterloo whose body was never found. And knowing the good Benjamin did directing his spies, the Prince Regent allowed him his solution. Now Benjamin hid in the shadows, dead to all but the Prince Regent and the small number of men who worked in their most secret of government offices. Only Joe—and occasionally Walgrave who had known him since childhood—still called him Benjamin. The rest of the men called him Mr. James.

"I thought I'd try my hand at the code Lady Wilmot found in the proofs to her late husband's final book. I have been trying to find a pattern." Joe shook his head. "But I'm at as much of a loss as the others. You and Walgrave are the only ones who haven't tried it."

"That's not unexpected. Walgrave and I both hate to fail." Benjamin scratched his head. "Before his death, Wilmot suggested this code was somewhat urgent, but he's been dead for more than a year, and we still have nothing."

"Well, not nothing. Two months ago, we didn't even have the code." Joe pushed the pages across the desk to a clear spot in front of an empty chair. "You knew Wilmot best. Perhaps you will see something the others have missed."

"I will look them over." Benjamin lowered himself slowly into the chair. "But first, we are going to have a problem in Sussex."

"Sussex? Should we send Walgrave? That's his home county."

"Yes, but the problem *is* Walgrave. He approached me to investigate An Honest Gentleman, believing that some of the information in his essays is coming from someone in Whitehall."

"Well, he's not wrong about that." Joe looked concerned. "But if he goes to Sussex, it makes it more likely that he will find out the whole of it—and not just that his wife is a spy. And that threatens the whole enterprise."

"Yes. That's exactly what I'm afraid of. He can be very unforgiving."

"Should we tell her? She knows he worked for the Home Office during the wars, but she thinks it ended then."

"Is she still leaving him?"

"Yes."

"Then no. There's no reason for her to know about his work, unless it becomes necessary. Just as there's no reason for him to know about hers." Benjamin picked up the coded list. Slowly, his look of concern changed into a sort of grin, one side of his face brightening while the other remained immobile. He began to pack all of the sheets into a pile. "We have copies of all this, correct?"

"Correct. Those in fact are copies."

"Excellent. Perhaps we can come up with a little game to keep Walgrave's attention divided."

Chapter Nine

The next morning Olivia made her way to a small coffee shop near St. Bride's to meet Mentor. She'd visited the offices of the *World* the previous afternoon and come away with not only a new assignment but some disturbing news as well—the kind only Mentor could help her evaluate.

"I was concerned I might attract attention by drinking coffee with a beautiful lady," the older man teased. "I see my fears were . . . toothless."

"It's black wax—easy to take off, but convincing from a distance. A trick I learned from Wells."

"I am afraid to ask where you found those clothes."

"A secret is a secret." Olivia relaxed in his company. Mentor had interviewed her for her first position as a governess when she'd graduated from Mrs. Flint's school, and he'd been her most trusted associate since then.

"Those clothes carry only one secret: How long had their former owner been dead before you stole them?" The man leaned far back in his seat. "But with that stench, we won't have to worry about eavesdroppers. Don't you worry about lice?"

"All part of the illusion, Mentor, dear. I created that

'stench' from the scent gland of a dead skunk, a bit of eel ink, some sardine oil, and . . .'"

He raised his hand. "Please stop. I begin to wonder if you are one of the witches in *Macbeth*."

"Toil, toil, boil a trouble." She raised an eyebrow and leaned in conspiratorially.

He rolled his eyes. "'Double, double toil and trouble.' I'd ask if you've ever read a book, but I know the answer."

"Why, Mentor, you flatter me." She pushed a packet of letters across the table.

"Still, it might have been wiser to meet at our regular spot and on our regular schedule." Mentor looked down the corridor. "You might not be recognizable, but if the wrong person were to see me . . . chatting . . . with so lovely a lady as yourself . . ."

"They will think you have the clap, and no woman but a whore will keep you company."

"Remind me why I continue to employ you." He untied the twine holding the letters together.

"How many reasons do you need?" Olivia leaned back in her chair and crossed her arms over her chest. "I can think of two offhand: I am the only person who can do what you need, and I am the best student ever to graduate from your little school for spies."

"School for Exceptional Girls," Mentor chided. "We don't like the word *spies*. You've left out the most important reason: You were bored, running that little estate. You had reached the limit of your endurance. If you hadn't, you never would have come back to us."

"It's not a little estate." She picked up the twine and twisted it around her fingers. "But the rest is true. These are threatening letters An Honest Gentleman has been receiving at the *World*."

Mentor looked startled. "Threatening? In what way?"

"The ways one would expect." She shrugged. "An Old

Sea Captain reissued his challenge for a duel, claiming that I am no gentleman if I do not meet with him."

"You are certainly no gentleman." Mentor smiled at his own wit. "Who else?"

"Defender of the State says I am a traitor for exposing the profiteering of MPs in wharf legislation. He claims he will find me and hang me from the nearest tree. And Deus Grammatica describes in quite bloody terms what end I deserve for abusing the King's English."

"None of those sound like threats you can't handle. Or would you prefer a guard?"

Olivia hesitated.

"What? I know that look—even under all that . . . is it dirt?"

"It's dirt, but it's clean dirt." She rubbed the dirt from the ends of her fingers.

"Spare me your distinctions. Tell me what you are thinking."

"There are three others." She breathed in deeply, then pushed another packet across the table. "They don't use a pseudonym—in fact there's no signature at all. But they are all in the same hand. There's something about them that feels different, angrier."

Mentor took them, a frown growing as he read. "Is there anything else?"

"After our last meeting, I thought I was being followed. Then after I met with Cerberus, I was accosted in my dressing room. I think someone might have discovered who I am."

"Who *you* are or who An Honest Gentleman is?"

"I don't know. Somehow those three letters seem more personal, but they were sent to An Honest Gentleman at the *World*. So they can't be about me—whoever I am."

"Why not?"

"Only a handful of people know who writes as An Honest Gentleman. As the editor of the *World*, Wells wouldn't betray that secret, not without risking her increased profits. I think these letters are meant to make me reveal myself as HG."

"There's another possibility. You agreed to Sir Roderick's proposal that you marry his son because you needed the protection of a new name. If someone from your past thinks they have found you . . ." Mentor's voice trailed off, then with efficient motions he tied the letters back into a packet with the twine. "Go home, Olivia. Go back to your estate. Today."

"Is that an order or a suggestion?"

"You don't respond well to orders. Never have." Mentor smiled.

"I'll go tomorrow. It's already too late today—I don't like to travel those roads in the dark if I can avoid it. But as for my father, do you have any information?"

"No progress. If Sir Roderick couldn't find your father all those years ago, I hold little hope we will. But I have given the case to one of our best men, and he continues to look. If your father is alive after all these years, we want to find him as much as you do."

She wanted to press him for more information, but she knew the settled tone in his voice. "Thank you."

"You will go home first thing in the morning. Promise me."

"I promise."

"We'll remain in touch. The usual methods."

Chapter Ten

Harrison signaled the coachman to stop. The last inn before his father's house was only a half hour's travel from his familial lands. But he wasn't ready to see either his ancestral estate or the woman who might not be his wife.

As a young man, anxious to arrive home, he'd never stopped here, and it had been more than six years since his last visit. No one was likely to recognize him.

"Have we arrived?" His valet, Walker, stirred from his reading of the *Sporting Magazine*. Looking out the window at the tavern, he yawned. "Have we not dawdled long enough? Not an hour ago we stopped to find her ladyship a gift, though that would have been better done in London. And what you bought her . . ." Walker rolled his eyes and straightened his cravat.

"I am in need of refreshment. Will you come?"

Beside them a hired hackney belched forth its occupants.

Walker sniffed dramatically. "I have had enough of the sights, sounds, and smells of the rural tavern."

Harrison, long used to his valet's idiosyncrasies, jumped down from the carriage, then waited, allowing the hackney's passengers to bustle into the tavern. He took in their details by habit, a skill he kept up even when he had no need for it. A boy of about five with too-large shoes hid behind an old woman with a heavy mustache. A portly man held the hand of a comely girl twenty years his junior. A beak-nosed parson—his wife and daughter wearing the sober clothing of one of the evangelical sects—clutched a prayer book, while a severe-looking woman with drab clothing held herself apart. Any other time, he'd have teased out their stories, but he had his own to consider.

Married or free?

He should answer that question before he saw Olivia. On the drive, he'd broken the problem down into smaller and smaller pieces, hoping that eventually his answer would appear in a sort of syllogistic glory. But every time he tried to create a logical proposition, he ended in nonsense.

Stymied by the mess of his emotions, he'd tried another tack, completing the sentence "I want." That too was a failure. Everything he wanted was impossible, spoken in the voice of his grief, not yet assuaged, though decades old. *I want my father to call me son and ruffle my hair with his hand. I want to pretend to be irate that my family is drinking port instead of claret. I want to arrive at the house and find my family waiting for me. I want the dead not to be dead. I want not to be alone.*

At the word *alone*, he remembered Olivia as he had last seen her, face drawn, hands twisting, as he left for the wars. In that long-ago moment, his heart had called out to hers. He'd considered throwing himself from his horse and taking her in his arms for one last passionate kiss. But his father, ever jovial, had ruined the moment. Patting Olivia on the shoulder, Roderick had declared, *She'll be here, boy, when you return.* His anger at the marriage had returned in an instant, with Olivia a living reminder of his subjugation.

He felt a tap at his elbow. A small boy, one of the tavern's grooms, pointed toward the tavern door.

Since he'd opened the box of his memories, Harrison found himself beset by them.

He handed the boy a ha'pence and walked to the tavern door.

To avoid being alone, he could reconcile with his wife, but he needed to know his limits. Would he have to live in the country? Would he have to bring her to London? And, for both questions, he needed to know how often and how long. The clench in his stomach tightened. But was it caused by imagining the possible restraints on his life or seeing Olivia again? He was uncertain. Damned uncertain.

Olivia. At the thought of her, a suffocating tangle of emotions ground into the center of his chest.

He'd wanted a wife who was brave, daring, funny, sweet, and clever enough to beat him at chess. But his father chose otherwise, giving him a dutiful wife, competent, smart in her own way, capable of being satisfied with a quiet life in the country. Had she been mousy, bland, or dim-witted, he could have justified his behavior.

But instead he had acted like a cad. After the wars, he should have returned to the estate. It was not Olivia's fault that she became a pawn in the larger struggle between his sense of self and his father's expectations. But with his father dead, he had delayed the visit, postponing for one day, then another, until somehow a year had passed. Unable to justify the delay, he decided not to go at all.

He had buried his unresolved feelings about his wife in a deep well already filled with other emotions: anger at his father's manipulations, unresolved grief for his family—all dead—guilt for his own negligence, and his desire for the woman his father had chosen. Then, with practice, he sequestered the mess of emotion behind a strong wall of practicality.

"Sir?" The innkeeper's voice cut through his memories. "Would you like a bit of food or drink?" The slight man with mismatched eyes gestured toward the room reserved for men of rank or money.

"Claret. No: Whiskey. A deep glass."

At a table against the back wall, he sat facing out, watching the travelers, the innkeeper, and the barmaids, noting their heights, sizes, clothing, quirks of expression.

"Abbey-bound?" The oldest barmaid, thick pale hair twisted under a cap, filled his glass from the bottle.

"What makes you say that?" He hid his surprise behind the whiskey.

She nodded at the hackney passengers. "The coach passengers stop here on their way to somewhere else. Locals stop at the village, not here. You are neither on the coach nor local. That leaves the abbey."

"Many people go to the abbey then?"

"Fair amount. Most that go there, stay there." She watched the room, just as he did, noticing which tables might need attention. "Should be near a dozen there now."

"A house party?" He downed the whiskey to keep her at his table.

"Not parties exactly. Just them Oxbridge men."

"Oxbridge?"

"For the library—or so they say. I say it's for the food, drink, and easy lodgings. But perhaps her ladyship finds consolation in the good-looking ones."

The maid canted her head, hearing the arrival of another company.

"Consolation?"

"If you are going there, be wary." She'd moved far enough away that he barely caught her sentence. "It can be a dangerous place."

He downed the second whiskey in frustration. What Oxbridge men? How dangerous? What sort of consolation?

He could call the maid back and pay for the information, but it was not worth calling attention to his presence.

He put some coin on the table, and picking up his hat, strode from the room.

He'd see for himself.

In the yard, Walker broke away from a conversation with the severe-looking woman from the previous coach. The valet's step bounced with gossip, but he waited patiently as Harrison gave the coachman directions.

"Interested in hearing what the stable-yard thinks of the management of your estate?" Walker settled himself back into his seat.

"Let me predict. Unsavory characters are sating their bellies at the table of the estate's generosity." He held back the tidbit that the men were handsome.

"And no one sees her ladyship for days on end. She supposedly sequesters in her rooms, but no one is certain." Walker looked out the window. "Wait! Isn't this the way we came?"

"I have decided to call on an old friend for his advice." Harrison's tone was clipped, and Walker fell silent.

Twenty minutes later, the carriage stopped at the bottom of a low hill dotted with sheep. Sitting outside a large stone cottage, a tall, gaunt man with silver hair regarded the carriage with suspicion. Mr. Herder, his father's old estate manager, looked as forbidding as ever.

Harrison approached the cottage in long, powerful strides.

"Is the abbey this way?" Harrison tested if the old man would remember him without prompting.

"The path by the river is narrow but serviceable." The

old man pointed into the distance. His gaze rested for a moment on Harrison's oldest carriage and on Walker standing beside it, then he examined Harrison slowly. Tears welled in his eyes. "Oh, my boy, you look the image of your mother."

The older man reached for his shepherd's crook, then struggled to his feet. Harrison stepped forward instinctively, supporting Herder's elbow. Herder turned the support into a hearty embrace, but when the gray-bearded man released Harrison, his face was grim with suspicion. "Why would you pretend not to know the road home? And why do you travel in a carriage without your family crest?"

Harrison helped the old man back to his seat. "I had hoped, after my long absence, to investigate the estate from the position of a stranger. I was hoping you would give me an introduction—as your relative—for a position belowstairs. I would have little risk of encountering her ladyship that way."

Herder grimaced. "I understand your plan, but I don't like it. An earl in service at his own estate can only cause ruptures later when you are no longer a servant. Pretend instead to be one of them scholars. Pert, quarrelsome men with more intelligence than sense, they are."

A woman in her midfifties called out of the door of the cottage. "Da, I'm going to check on the lambs."

Harrison stepped out of sight. But Herder waved away his concern. "No need to worry about my Molly recognizing you. She and my Harriet were in service in Tunbridge Wells when you were a boy. The girls only came home when Molly's husband became estate manager, and now my Harriet is Miss Olivia's parlor maid."

Harrison winced at the reference to his wife, the countess, by her first name, as if she were an unmarried younger daughter. "Are you happy here?"

The old man held his hand out toward the chalk hills.

"I was born in this valley. My wife bore our children in this cottage. I know these trees, these streams, like my own hand. If I can't find happiness here, then I haven't the resources to be happy anywhere. But this is your land, and now that you are home, you can set some things to right."

"Is the estate not managed well?"

The old man looked torn. "Miss Olivia does the best she can. She's a proud woman, and she might not tell you, but she faces obstacles that you will not."

Harrison looked into the distance for some time, watching the sun begin its evening transit. A proud woman—a secretive woman—a house filled with suitors. He tamped down his rising jealousy. It wasn't rational to be jealous of a woman he hadn't wanted. But whatever the state of their marriage, the world knew her as his countess, and her behavior reflected on him, for good or ill.

"I'll need your help, Herder, and your son-in-law's. I'll play a scholar, but first I need a key to the abbey. I'd like to look around the estate, without anyone knowing."

"How long are we to stay here?" In Herder's cottage, Walker looked around the small room with the single cot bed with an assessing eye. Clean, neat, serviceable, it could accommodate two trunks of clothing and the other goods they had brought with them, but nothing more. He removed his upper clothes, cravat first, then his waistcoat.

"You chose to remain instead of going home with the coach." Harrison pulled his cravat loose, leaving the ends hanging as he unbuttoned his outer clothes.

"No, no, I would hate to miss the intrigue. Husband stealing home in disguise to test his wife's fidelity. Whatever you need, I will be here."

"A lovely declaration, Walker, but I saw you eyeing that pie in the window." Harrison picked up Walker's waistcoat and tried it on. Walker's love of sweets made the waist a bit loose on Harrison, but that would add to the illusion.

"The fact that Herder's daughter is a better cook than any you've hired in London is irrelevant." Walker rummaged through the trunks. "It's good that I ignored how long you said we would be staying. I've brought enough clothes for the both of us. Ah, here." The valet pulled out a pair of trousers and one of Harrison's oldest waistcoats and jackets. "I also brought some of your older clothes for mucking about the estate. Those should nicely convey the sense of a scholar in secondhand clothes."

"I look like a poor exhibitioner stealing into the college common room." Harrison stepped to the window. The sun had not yet set. He would have more than enough time to arrive before dark. "Where is my traveling desk? I need a letter of introduction."

"In the corner here." Walker lifted the desk and handed it to Harrison. "Who will you be?"

Harrison chose a piece of paper boasting his ducal seal as the watermark. "This intrigue puts me in mind of the *Odyssey*. I'll be T. L. MacHus, a scholar who has gained his lordship's patronage."

"T. L. MacHus." Walker repeated the name slowly, then a grin spread across his face. "Ah, Telemachus, the son of Odysseus, who searches for his father! Too bad you can't simply be Odysseus: You've come home to find your wife surrounded by suitors."

"They are scholars, Walker, not suitors." But Harrison tasted the words like alum.

Having borrowed Herder's nag, Harrison traveled the main road that led to the family manor, an old abbey deeded to an ancestor by Henry VIII.

His mind turned to other times he had ridden this road.

Winter carriage rides for religious services in the village, his country-bred family, all energy and little formality, six children vying for the forward-facing seat. His mother, wearing a wan smile, would sit in the middle, one child on each side, his youngest brother in her arms. In his memories, she was never older than twenty-nine. His brothers, dressed for war, each riding a sure-footed, even-tempered horse who wouldn't start at the sound of rifles, the smoke of the guns, or the cries of the wounded.

All dead.

He turned his mind away from memories too tender to bear for long.

Home. He could imagine every twist and turn of the road.

At the next bend, he would turn downward, where a slow river split the valley into pasture and woodland. The road would bend away from the river, leading him up a long hill into a dense ancient forest.

At the crest of the hill, he would look into a soft valley where seven hundred years before, monks built their abbey in native stone. Harrison's ancestors had acquired the abbey through good service to Henry VIII. His great-grandfather had saved the great sanctuary, building alongside it a new manor house holding the public rooms, the dining hall, ballroom, drawing rooms, library, and the family and guest rooms.

But from the hill, he would see only the very tips of the abbey towers peeking between tall oaks and alders. A fairy city, built by magic, he'd always thought it. In that moment, with the abbey barely visible, he would know he was home.

From that high point, he would descend through deep forest, then emerge in a broad clearing, his home still nestled in trees. The outer buildings in ruins served as each generation of Walgrave children's playground.

The road made him yearn for home. The scent of the trees, the sound of the river, the play of light on the road, the sweet memories of his family, all pulled him on, through the forest, up the hill. Before he reached the summit where he could see glimpses of his fairy castle, Harrison closed his eyes. He wanted to take in his first view of home all at once. It was uncharacteristically sentimental, but he indulged himself.

But when he opened his eyes, he felt as if he'd been struck in the gut. The trees were gone. His trees. His playground with his brothers. He felt flayed, chest split open, heart wrenched from his body. Nothing could have prepared him for the sense of loss and betrayal. All cut down, and for what?

For someone else, the view of a wide green plain, punctuated occasionally by ancient trees, might have been beautiful, even picturesque. But not to him.

He flung himself from his horse. He stood, looking at the rows of coppiced orchard, the large garden extending from the stone abbey, and the river in full view along the distant edge of the scene. Was he still in his bed at Herder's cottage? And was this scene of desolation only a nightmare?

Overcome with sorrow, he placed one arm on the side of his horse and buried his face in the bend of his elbow. Tears welled from deep inside him, in big wrenching sobs. He wept for all his losses: brothers, sister, mother, father, all gone. He wept even for himself, left all alone.

Eventually the wrenching of his shoulders slowed. He was left breathing heavily in short bursts, until his tears were spent.

He did not know why she'd cut down the ancient forest. Perhaps she had not known how much the trees had meant to him. Rationally, he knew there was no way she could have known. But he didn't care. After the tears, he felt only an implacable anger. She had destroyed his home, his lands, and having destroyed everything he loved, she wanted to escape.

His anger was cold, cunning, perhaps even cruel. He tied his horse to a tree in the shadow of the woods and circled toward the ruins behind the abbey. He knew a dozen places to steal into the abbey, and he had hours until dark to decide exactly what to do.

Chapter Eleven

Olivia cursed as she tried to pick the lock. Her skills were rusty from lack of use.

Six perfectly respectable years as a perfectly respectable wife. Yet, she was crouched in the dark, using a hat pin to steal quietly into her own home. Mrs. Pier never forgot to leave the conservatory unlocked. But it wouldn't do to call for the butler to open the main door. No, that would make clear to the household that she had been gone, and only Mrs. Pier knew her secret. Seeing Harrison on the street in London had made her suspicious and wary. Though she trusted the servants to protect her, she needed no more rumors about her behavior.

The lock wasn't giving. She bent down in the soft earth and tried again. At least she traveled in breeches. The lock finally surrendered, but with a snap and groan that made her wince. She could only hope that none of the scholars were wandering the grounds. She entered, taking off her slippers to make her way in stocking feet. She had slipped in more than once since becoming An Honest Gentleman. Even so, she had to remember every squeaking floorboard, every step on the staircase that might send out an alarm. By the time she reached her bedroom, she was past exhaustion. She stripped off her clothes and fell into bed.

She dreamed that night that her husband had come home. She entered their bridal suite to find him standing in partial undress at the window, looking out into the garden. She recognized the curve of blond hair at his neck, the way his shoulders narrowed into slender hips, the muscled curve of his calves. She walked to him, stood behind him, smelling the hint of green lemon and pine-wood in his cologne, until he'd turned. But his face, when he turned, was not his own. Instead, it was all white, with the eyes blackened out, like the beaked masks worn by doctors in the plague or at carnival to terrify children. She recoiled and stepped back, wanting to turn and run. He caught her hand before she could escape and pulled her toward him. But before he pulled her into the abyss that was his mask, her dream filled with music and the monster disappeared.

The dream faded, but the music remained, haunting, beckoning. She sat upright, listening; the dreamlike chords seemed to sound from everywhere. For a moment she let it lull her, then it struck her: the music room. Someone was playing the instruments. The elegant instruments Lord Roderick had acquired with such care hadn't been played since his death. She'd offered Mr. Nathan, the music scholar, his own key to the room, but he had tugged on his beard dismissively. *No, Miss Livvy, I study the music of the people. I don't want the elite instruments of the wealthy. I want the humble reed pipe of the shepherd, the gut-stringed harp of the bard. I want the songs of the common man.* The music room had remained unused and locked.

For her, the room was filled with memories of Roderick, who had been her second father. Roderick had taught her all the skills Mrs. Flint left out of her curriculum. Her own father's tutelage had been of a different sort—how to reach her hand into a stranger's pocket for a wallet or watch, or how to stand pitifully on the corner before a fine house, hand out, begging for a ha'pence to ease her churning stomach. Perhaps she had been lucky her father abandoned her. Even so, she had never been able to forget that he'd promised to return.

She wrapped a dressing gown tight over her nightshift and raised the flame of the oil lamp by her bedside. Splaying her household keys out across her palm, she identified the music room key by the decorative outline of a harp at its head.

The music room was beyond the corner where the family wing met the body of the main house, on the same level with the family bedrooms. After Sir Roderick's death, only she slept in the family wing. Usually, after managing whatever commotion the scholars created, she found it peacefully quiet.

Tonight, however, knowing an intruder was in the music room, she wished briefly she had someone to lean on. But she had been on her own for so long that she likely wouldn't know how to confide or even how to trust. She'd tried with Harrison. She shook off the momentary sadness—if Harrison had wanted this life, he would be here, taking care of a lute-playing intruder.

Her flame made dark shapes dance on the walls, but the melody drew her on.

The broad corridor was lined with marble-topped commodes, displaying pieces from Roderick's collection of curiosities.

She bumped her knee with a soft thud against one of the commodes.

The music stopped. At the far end of the corridor, past the music room, a dim light rose up the stairwell from the entry hall. Anyone leaving the room would be outlined by the light.

She watched for the intruder.

But seconds turned to minutes.

She sighed. Of course, the culprit would wait, hoping not to be discovered.

Turning the knob on the music room door, she found it locked. A circumspect intruder locks the door behind him. Lovely. With a big sigh, she unlocked and opened the door.

From the doorway, she lifted her lamp, slowly illuminating each part of the room. The window curtains were pulled back, allowing the moonlight to diffuse softly through the room. The instruments were in their places. But no one was there.

Impossible.

She walked the edges of the room, then looked out the window to examine the open lawn. Nothing, and nothing to indicate how her phantom musician had escaped.

Reluctantly, she gave up, unlocking and locking the door to test the bolt, then she returned to her room for a restless night's sleep.

"You are not expected, and we have no more places for scholars. Write to Lady Walgrave. Perhaps you can be admitted next month." The housekeeper, a shrew named Mrs. Pier, placed her body between the door and its jamb.

Arriving as a scholar had its disadvantages. As lord of the manor, he would have handed his hat and gloves to the butler, strode into the drawing room or bedroom, and demanded an explanation from his wife. He hadn't expected to be kept standing on the threshold, or he would have simply made himself comfortable in the family wing last night.

"I have permission from Lord Walgrave to use the library." He held his letter of introduction.

The housekeeper snorted and rolled her eyes.

So much for the respect due Walgrave's rank and status as lord of the manor.

"We wouldn't know Lord Walgrave if he rode up on a white horse."

As if given a cue, Harrison's horse—white—whinnied.

Mrs. Pier, with instructions he couldn't hear, handed his letter to a footman behind her. She stepped onto the porch and pointedly locked the main door.

"I suppose we have to make room for you. You can wait in the scholars' parlor for her ladyship's determination on where you will lodge."

She led him briskly around the side of the house. There a covered walkway connected the main house to a two-story building built onto the ruins of the old rectory.

"The scholars lodge here." Mrs. Pier unlocked the main door and led him down a long corridor. "Names on the doors." She gestured at the framed pieces of slate scribbled on in chalk as they passed. But when he paused to read the names, she hurried him along. At the end of the hall, she gestured for him to precede her into an open drawing room.

Arms akimbo, she recited a much rehearsed speech. "The scholars share this parlor, so be neat. If you leave piles of paper lying about, the maids or other scholars might use your research to kindle a fire. Her ladyship provides a morning and an evening meal, with tea in the afternoon. Scholars eat on the terrace in summer, in this room in winter. No one is welcome in the kitchen without Cook's permission. If you need help with your washing, the scholars' maid is available on Saturday mornings."

"Scholars' maid?"

"Lady's maid, scullery maid, scholar's maid—isn't that clear?" Mrs. Pier shook her head as if he were dim, then returned to her script. "Her ladyship welcomes new scholars on Wednesday afternoons when she hears the weekly reports."

"Weekly reports?"

"All scholars explain their research on Wednesdays before tea."

"I see."

"Undertake what experiments you wish, but do no damage to limb or library. Do you have any questions?" Mrs. Pier's annoyance was barely contained.

He opened his mouth to ask but reconsidered.

"Her ladyship won't turn you away unless you can't give a good reason to use the collection. If you are wise, you will come up with a good reason by Wednesday." Mrs. Pier walked to the door.

"Can I see her ladyship before then?"

Mrs. Pier didn't bother to turn. "Her ladyship welcomes new scholars on Wednesday afternoons when she hears the weekly reports. Once we've settled where you will be laying your head, Mr. Pier will show you to your room." He heard her mutter as she left, "Muddle-headed manners, these scholars, every one."

The parlor was large, with a fireplace in the middle of one wall. Several chairs clustered around two low couches, the pillows askew. He pressed down on the padded seats of the chairs—well cushioned, with brocaded upholstery both expensive and relatively new. He wondered how much he had paid for such well-appointed rooms.

Walking back down the corridor, he read nameplates, quietly turning the knob on each door until he found one room unlocked. He tapped and called the scholar's name. No answer. He opened the door and peered in: a cot, a desk, a chair, a set of bookshelves overflowing with books. Little else. Utilitarian but comfortable.

Hearing voices approach, he ran back to the drawing room. He took a seat in front of the fireplace and, closing his eyes, pretended to be asleep. He heard the shuffling of feet, then a pregnant hush. He opened his eyes to find a half circle of seven men, mostly in late middle-age or older, of varying heights, watching him.

"Ah, a new man. Welcome, welcome." A tall, thin, grandfatherly man standing at the center of the circle extended his hand. "I am Otley, law and political economy. We are the Seven, the original scholars brought to the estate by the late Lord Walgrave, Sir Roderick. We'll begin the introductions on your left."

"Lark here. Natural history, ornithology, and herpetology." A narrow-faced man squinted at him, then held up a magnifying glass which made one eye appear enormous.

"Martinbrook." A coarse-haired man with a ruddy complexion held out grubby fingers. "Geology, antiquities, agriculture."

"Nathan." A dapper white-haired man nodded his head rhythmically, his voice a reedy tenor. "Music. I used to play the bassoon for the Royal Opera—but it's not much of a solo instrument. Now I am reconstructing the transmission of our native folk songs."

"You'll have to excuse me if it takes a bit to learn your names." Harrison wondered if this was the way Snow White had felt.

"Simply remember your alphabet," Otley offered in a well-modulated voice. "Sir Roderick used to joke that he would eventually fill the alphabet up, but for the first seven he used the letters L through S. You've already met L, M, N, and me—O. You only have P, Q, and S left."

"What about R?" Harrison questioned.

The seven men grew silent and bowed their heads slightly. After a moment, Otley spoke, "Our R was Sir Roderick himself. He was our patron, our colleague, and our friend."

"Yes, the best of antiquarians, so knowledgeable about

the best places to excavate." Martinbrook rubbed dirt from one of his fingers.

"Yes, a true scientist." Lark tucked his peering glass in a special pocket sewed to the front of his waistcoat. "He could identify any bird by its call or shadow."

"Yes, a fine musician. I miss his hearty baritone in the parish choir." Nathan waved his index finger, as if leading a chorus.

"Yes." "Yes." "Yes." "Yes." The remaining men's heads bobbed with agreement.

Harrison was struck into silence, the men's memories spurring his own. In his grief and anger, Harrison had locked away the sweetest memories, instead holding tightly to his father's authoritarian orders and to their contentious final conversation. But at his ancestral home, the tender memories crowded out the rough. Suddenly he remembered the last time he and all his siblings were together. Every summer, his father had led his children on rambles through the woods, hunting for ruins or birds or some other interest. That summer they had spent weeks tracking a family of wildcats, his sister riding on their father's shoulders. Harrison had imagined wildcats to be the size of large dogs, so in the end, he was disappointed to find them barely bigger than a barn cat.

A man with rumpled clothes twisted his monocle nervously as he broke their mutual silence. "Partlet here. Classics, logic and rhetoric."

"Quinn. Astronomy." A stocky man with a tonsure—Harrison immediately thought of Friar Tuck—fluffed his cravat to a more precise arrangement.

The last man in the row, a neat, broad-bellied man with a thick mustache, pulled a pipe out of his mouth. "Smithson. Engineer. I built fortifications in wars against the American colonies. Now I write biographies of famous men of science."

"Let me see if I can remember your names." Harrison made his way around the circle. "Lark, Martinbrook, Nathan, Otley, Partlet, Quinn, and Smithson."

The men bobbed their heads, smiling and repeating "yes" as he called each name.

"Three other men hold fellowships this month." Nathan's rhythmic finger counted them off. "Fields is a mathematician. I understand not a bit of it, but he is a handsome boy. Jerome, our philosopher, a wary but quite charming man. His only flaw is that he loses his spectacles every day."

"You've forgotten Lord Montmorency, who has a year-long seat." Martinbrook rubbed a dirty hand across his chest. "He divides his time between his research and his estate, but he's here now. Last time he was unable to articulate how to distinguish Celtic and Pictish ruins from the Roman, and I hope he's developed a better answer."

"And what do you do?" Quinn leaned in, the hollows of his cheeks making him look severe.

"Do?" Harrison was caught off guard.

"Research, my boy. Why are you here?" Lark held his magnifying glass up to Harrison's face.

Disconcerted, Harrison struggled for an answer. "My interests, I regret, are fairly pedestrian. Having served in His Majesty's Navy, I wish to write a history of famous sea voyages, from Odysseus to Admiral Nelson."

"Admirable aim, young man, admirable." Smithson, the engineer, slapped him on the back. "We haven't had a Nautical with us for some time. Hakluyt and the other maritime books are to the right as you enter the library above the main doors. You'll find an empty desk there too, but most don't like it. It's a dark corner, though Miss Olivia provides a nice lamp and sufficient fuel. We'll show you the way. Come along."

Chapter Twelve

Olivia had made a list of what she must accomplish before she left the abbey. The list was like an hourglass, each completed task a grain of sand falling to the bottom, measuring out her remaining time. She had to end one part of her life, before she could begin the next. But she couldn't yet see the next phase of her life—it was as if she were in mid-leap, and she couldn't yet see the ground. The sense of uncertainty and the sorrow of ending made all the tasks harder than necessary.

Today, she was to gather all her belongings into her bedroom to decide what to take and what to leave. The unpleasant task of packing she'd listed for another day.

She'd come to the marriage with few possessions: some clothes, a valise of books and papers, some mementos of the children she'd taught. But from Sir Roderick, she'd acquired a cabinet full of treasures. When Roderick had discovered her love of antiquities, he had begun to give her little things. Once a month, she would arrive in the morning room to find a box sitting before her place at the table. She'd objected at first. But he'd shaken it off: *You've given me back a daughter, Livvy. Indulge an old man.* Eventually she'd relented, allowing herself the sensation of being valued and loved.

She smiled at the memory of slowly unwrapping the gifts, Sir Roderick urging her on. *Come on, Livvy girl, untie it now. Here, give me that twine. Now the box lid. My girl, you'd think you'd never gotten presents, you move so slow.*

She wondered if he hadn't intended to give her so many, except she'd burst into tears at the first one. Her marriage gift—but not from Harrison. A set of volumes by different authors, all bound to match in a rich burgundy morocco, each one examining the history and antiquities of a different area or city in Britain. She'd caressed each volume, then over the next two years, she'd read them to her father-in-law. As they read, they made a list—a tour of England that would have taken the better part of a year—but he'd laughed off the time and distance. *If one is going to see the finest antiquities, then one shouldn't say before one begins "but I must be back in time to milk the cows."*

The gifts had continued for two years after his death, each one meticulously described in a codicil to the old man's will, which the solicitor had included with the last present. She read the note once more, wiping away a tear.

> *These little gifts have I hope eased your grieving, Livvy—but they cannot repay the solace you have given an old man before his death. They are yours to enjoy and dispose of as you wish—my will makes that clear, even to a man as timber-headed as my son.*

She had wept for Sir Roderick until there was no more weeping. But today, as she wrapped each one of his gifts, she felt the enormity of her action in leaving Harrison. The weight of her decision threatened to bow her to the ground.

To avoid her grief, she took out the codicil and began to inventory her things. But she couldn't forget the phantom music that had woken her for two nights—it was as if someone had read *The Deserted Wife* and decided to torment her.

A tap at the door drew her attention.

Mrs. Pier entered. "The September scholars arrived last week and have settled in. Such handsome blokes. They'd make excellent footmen, so tall and well built."

"Are you thinking of setting Mr. Pier over for a younger man?"

Mrs. Pier shook her head. "If I did, I'd have to listen to them talk, and there's nothing more comforting than Mr. Pier's silences."

Olivia laughed. She would miss Mildred's practical good humor, but until she knew if Harrison would agree to her terms, she couldn't risk inviting any of the servants to leave with her.

"I indicated you would welcome them at tea this Wednesday."

"Of course, Mildred, that's perfect. Do you happen to remember their interests?"

"Yes, miss." Mrs. Pier straightened to recite. "Lord Montmorency continues his investigations into the Roman ruins at Bignor. I gave him a place far from Mr. Martinbrook to avoid too easy disputation."

"Good decision. Martinbrook nearly caused him a fit of apoplexy last time he was in residency."

"Mr. Jerome is consulting the Boethius, Mr. Fields the Euclid."

"I remember their applications now: philosophy and math."

"We also have an unexpected guest with a letter of introduction from his lordship himself." Mildred held out a heavy piece of monogrammed paper.

"Strange. Walgrave never sends us scholars." The seal was a version of her own. "But as he grows more engaged with the estate, we must expect things to change."

"The house will not be the same without you, my lady," the housekeeper offered with a solemn shake of her head.

Olivia placed a hand on the housekeeper's arm. "Thank you, Mildred. But it's for the best." She opened the introduction. "Let's see here: a Mr. T. L. MacHus. Scottish?"

"Uncertain."

She read aloud only the most important details. "'MacHus . . . Oxford . . . Historian . . . Welcome him as you would me.'" She grimaced. Should she embrace or throttle him?

"An unfortunate choice of words." The edges of Mildred's mouth ticked upward. "With Mr. MacHus we have eleven scholars, and the lodge only houses ten."

"If we were to follow Walgrave's recommendation, we could house him in the pigsty. But that would probably violate some rule of hospitality." She closed her eyes, imagining the available rooms. "How are the repairs to the guest wing windows?"

"Most of the rooms have one window missing, if not more."

"Not the guest wing, then." Olivia shook her head. "Is he an able man?"

"Appears to be."

"If Mr. MacHus is to be welcomed as we would his lordship, he will take his lordship's old room."

"In the nursery?" Mildred brushed her hands on her skirt.

"No, after his mother died, Walgrave moved out of the family wing. His father converted the front corner tower into a suite." She rejected keys on her ring before holding out an ornate old key. "This should be the one. Tell

MacHus his room offers the most spectacular views in the county."

"The tower will have to be aired."

Olivia rubbed the key, suddenly unwilling to let anyone else reopen her husband's room. "I should ensure that Walgrave left behind nothing of any consequence. Have whichever of the maids you can spare meet me there."

"Of course." Mrs. Pier turned to leave.

"Mildred, did you hear music last night?"

"No, Miss Livvy, I sleep as sound as a hedgehog in winter." The housekeeper's gaze grew sharp. "Was one of them scholars in the music room without permission?"

Olivia shook her head. "No, it was a dream, nothing more." She tucked Sir Roderick's letter in the front of the trunk and rose. "I'll follow you down."

In the days after their wedding, when Harrison had seemed smitten with her charms, Olivia had been grateful his rooms weren't in the family wing. Having lived with his father for so many months, she'd found herself unexpectedly private when it came to the pleasures of married life.

She wondered what she would find in Harrison's old rooms after all this time: spiders and cobwebs and the musty smell of stale air, or a return of the desperate longing she'd felt when she'd closed them up so many years before?

When he'd left, he had pressed the key into her hand. "Remember me, Olivia, until I come home again." In the weeks after Harrison had left her, she had made his room into a private retreat—as it had been during the week after their wedding. She had lain on his bed and imagined his body beside hers. She would close her eyes, and pretend her hand was his, letting it trail down her neck, across her breasts and the flat plane of her belly, as he had done, allowed her fingers to touch again all those places he had touched, even the places she had believed led him to glimpse her very soul.

But one morning, she'd awoken, shivering, to a room long grown cold, and she'd realized that her dreams had no more power to bring him back than they had to keep her warm. That day, she'd moved everything she'd wanted to remember him by, locked the door, and never returned. Sometime later, Sir Roderick had moved Harrison's furniture to a room in the family suite, on the expectation that Harrison would eventually move home.

Perhaps it was time to face those memories, then let them go. If she were lucky, she would open the door and find only dust, cobwebs and the musty smell of stale air.

She was still reminiscing outside the door, key in hand, when the two maids arrived, their arms laden with fresh linen. Two footmen followed behind, carrying buckets of warm, soapy water.

"Ah, Miss Livvy, I've often wondered what was behind this door." Susan—one of the older maids—carried a broom.

Joan, the newest upstairs maid, looked cautiously over her shoulder. Olivia had found Joan, molested and abandoned in a dangerous alley in Manchester, and had been unable to leave her to her fate. Believing that Miss Olivia had been sent to her by the angels, Joan had proved as loyal as she was superstitious.

Olivia turned the key, then the knob, and pushed, but the door didn't budge.

"Should we call for Mr. Pier?" Joan whispered, as if her words might disturb any ghosts behind the door. The maid looked anxiously at the door, then down the corridor behind them.

"No need, Joan. I can open it." Olivia turned the key, making sure to hear the bolt pull back. She pushed again, but nothing. Olivia felt frustration tighten along her jawline. Once she had determined to open the room, she would not leave it to the butler. Turning the knob, she leaned into the door with her shoulder; then, when that failed, she gave it a swift and angry kick.

The door released from the jamb. Creaking eerily, it swung inward, revealing only a pitch-black darkness.

"By all the saints at the back door of purgatory!" Joan, eclectic in her religious beliefs, crossed herself and stepped back.

Olivia, used to Joan's superstitions, pushed the door open to the wall. Breathing in courage, she walked forward into the darkness, counting her steps. "His lordship's great-grandfather added the turrets to make the abbey look more like a fortress, but he wanted windows for the light."

"Ah, miss, be wary. No telling what power might be hiding in that dark."

At fifteen paces, Olivia felt heavy curtains at the tips of her fingers. She pulled aside the heavy cloth to reveal small square windows. Behind her the maids set to work.

Joan stepped cautiously around the century-old heavy furniture standing against the walls. She yelped when she pulled open a set of curtains and found a door.

"That's the staircase up to the drawing room, and beyond that the bedroom. Let's start at the top and work our way down. You will find the bedroom views spectacular."

At the uppermost floor, the maids gaped at the window, giving Olivia a moment to think.

The rooms felt different from the day she'd locked them. Then, they had simply felt empty, reduced to a bed, a desk, a chiffonier, a table with two chairs; but she'd been able to imagine them once more being filled. Now that emptiness mocked her. How had she ever been so young as to believe he would return to her?

She remembered their last kiss. He'd pulled himself out of bed, out of her embrace, and she'd watched as, with every piece of clothing, he transformed from her passionate lover into an officer in His Majesty's Navy. She'd watched greedily, memorizing each inch of him, as he covered his bare flesh one piece of clothing at a time. He'd realized she was watching and turned so she could see him more fully. She'd watched as his strong arms slipped from view, one, then the other, covered by the crisp linen of his shirt. He'd stood there for a moment, letting her drink in the sight of him, as he buttoned each of his cuffs. He'd buttoned his shirt from the top down, teasing her as each inch of flesh disappeared, and she drank in the flex of his chest, the sinews of his belly, the jut of his sex telling her that he wanted her again, even as he left her.

He'd tortured her a little then, leaving his hips and legs unclad, while he pulled on his waistcoat and began to tie his cravat. She'd been emboldened by his game, and she'd leaned back against the headboard, pulling the sheet away slowly to reveal her still naked body, until he could see her fully.

She'd delighted in his growl and in the leap of his sex. And when he'd caught her by one foot and pulled her to the foot of the bed, she had squealed in anticipation. She hadn't resisted when he'd turned her to face the sheets and pulled her hips back against his member. When he'd entered her, she'd felt only pleasure and passion.

She turned her mind from the memory. Only later had she realized none of his touches signaled more than desire, and that in their last coupling, so spontaneous, so heady, he'd likely thought her no better than a whore.

She looked around the room one last time. Only furniture. She opened the drawers in the closet chiffioner. All empty. Out of long habit, she ran her hand across the back of the drawer, then pulling each one out, she looked at its underside.

"Miss Livvy? Are you looking for something in particular?"

"No," she responded quickly. "Just making certain all is clean for our new guest."

Joan shrugged acceptance and returned to washing the window.

There was nothing that couldn't be left for the use of Mr. MacHus.

Nothing here of any value at all.

Chapter Thirteen

Harrison had been surprised when the butler, a dour man who examined him as he would an insect, led him to his old turret rooms. The choice had to be merely a coincidence, or perhaps Olivia housed all the extra hangers-on in his old rooms.

The rooms were not as he had left them. He would have been surprised to find they were, but at the same time he felt disappointed, even saddened. What had he hoped for? A locked room, never opened, and all his belongings lovingly kept exactly as he'd left them?

The maid placed his clothes in a giant wardrobe, looking at him anxiously as if she were afraid to turn her back to him. Had one of the other scholars abused her? He would never have allowed such behavior in his house. But he had been absent. If he had wished to protect his tenants, he should not have entrusted the responsibility to another.

"I don't bite." He removed himself to the far edge of the room, nearest the windows and farthest from the door.

"Ah, no, sir, I'm sure you don't." But he noticed that the maid looked relieved that he had left the way to the door open for her to escape.

"Tell me about your mistress."

The maid looked at him suspiciously. "I owe her ladyship too much to gossip, sir."

"Then tell me about the other scholars. What are their characters? How long do they stay?"

"Right now we have the seven, the three visiting scholars, and you, of course. We never go over ten, but you weren't expected."

"Expected?" he asked, absently, running his fingers over the grain of the wood in the newel post of the bed.

"Those who want to study here send her ladyship letters, telling her their goals, and she and the parson choose who can visit. Usually those stay a fortnight or a month, sometimes longer, but the seven are always here."

"The parson? Is that the Reverend Woodbridge?"

"Oh, no, sir!" The maid laughed, then looked nervous and shy. "Rev. Woodbridge retired to live with his brother in Devon. The new parson, Mr. Southbridge, is a young man, not thirty, if I were guessing."

"He advises her ladyship?" This would be the man who supported her request to separate. What motivation could he have for such a bold act? A tendre for Olivia, perhaps?

"Oh, yes, he comes to the house every Wednesday for tea and stays through dinner. Her ladyship relies on his help with the scholars."

"I look forward to meeting him. How will I know him?"

"Ah, let's see. Blue eyes, the color of cornflowers, and tall. A nice voice—good for the pulpit." The maid's voice grew a little softer as she described the parson. Finished with Harrison's things, she began to edge her way toward the door.

"A handsome man?" He moved farther away from the door, and she scooted past.

"Oh, yes, sir. All the ladies think so."

Did his wife think so as well? Would she leave him for

a parson? The frustration that tightened the back of his neck surprised him. Why should he care?

The maid curtsied at the door. "If you need anything, sir, Mr. Pier's office is at the bottom of the servants' stairs. He manages the extra scholars."

"Not the housekeeper?"

"No, sir, only Mr. Pier. The housekeeper—Mrs. Pier—says she has enough to do keeping the seven in line." The maid escaped.

He turned to look at the room, freshly cleaned, the windows still damp from being washed. The bed was freshly made, the pillows fluffed.

The only furniture that remained from his residence was the bed. The stately old oak bed had been built during his great-grandfather's time, and his father had once thought to move it to one of the grander bedrooms. But the original builder had embedded some of the supports into the wall itself. Nothing—not even his youthful passion for his wife—moved it even an inch.

He smiled at the memory. She had been a pleasure to hold. His body flushed with desire at the thought of her, so willing, so generous, so trusting. If Olivia were present, they could muss the sheets quite pleasantly.

He pushed the memory away. All that mattered was that she wished to leave him.

In his head he heard Capersby's words: *You left her first.*

For the past two nights, Olivia had woken to the sound of music. But by the time she'd opened the music room door, the musician had fled. She'd considered setting one of the footmen to guard the room, but decided against it. Somehow the music felt personal, a message she was intended to interpret. She'd investigated the room by daylight, but could find no way—other than the two-story drop to the ground—for the musician to come or go.

Tonight, however, she was ready. During the day, she'd made a space for herself to hide in the large wardrobe at the end of the room. Then she'd lit a lamp near the window in her bedroom and filled it with enough oil that the lamp would go out around the time she usually retired to bed. Once in the music room, she'd pressed herself against the edge of the door, able to hear the quietest sound. A piece of heavy paper kept the lock from engaging, allowing her to observe without risking the sound of the latch.

She curled up and waited. At some point she fell asleep, waking to the first bars of a tantalizing musical piece. Once more, the room was dark. The casement windows were open, letting in the pale light of the moon, but the player was too far away to be illuminated. All she could see was his back, broad and strong. The music he played was delectable, tender and passionate, all at once. The tune was one of Roderick's favorites, from an old handwritten ledger book filled with musical settings, written out in a spindly hand. She'd learned to play it on the pianoforte just to please him. The piece had tripped her fingers for months, but the old man had never minded. *Soon, Livvy, you'll play it with the best of them, then I'll accompany you on the lute.* He'd never played with her, his fingers too gnarled with age and pain to manage the lute's delicately paired strings.

So lost was the intruder in his music that Olivia slipped from her hiding place unnoticed. She drew herself up to her full height.

"If you wish to use the music room, you need her ladyship's permission."

The man's back stiffened, but he did not turn. "And if I don't wish to ask her permission?"

"Then, her ladyship will call for the magistrate and have you removed from the premises."

"Sir Roderick allowed me to use this room whenever I wished. His old servants will remember me."

"His old servants are either dead or happily retired on the pensions Sir Roderick left them."

He made no move to face her, only continued playing softly, adding to the undercurrent of tension that flowed between them.

The tune was complicated, but he played it without a stop or a misstep. She would have preferred simply to listen to that music all night, but her preferences mattered less than her obligation to the estate. Soon that obligation would be over, but for now, she was still bound by it.

"Will you call for your mistress then or leave me to play in peace?"

"I have no need to do so."

"Ah, so you are going to let me play as I wish."

"No, I am her ladyship." She held herself up to her full height, short as that was.

The man's shoulders stilled, and his fingers hesitated only briefly.

"I remember when Sir Roderick bought this harp. He was in Ireland with his children. A gypsy in a brightly painted carriage was playing just exactly this tune, cheerful and pensive by turns. Sir Roderick bought it, and then insisted that the gypsy meet him and his family at his estate in four months' time to teach the whole group. Sir Roderick's daughter had a gift for making this sing."

"You were here as a boy?" She tried to keep disbelief out of her voice.

"Roderick's son found me a boon companion, and I accompanied him to Cambridge."

"Then you must know a great deal about Lord Walgrave." She wanted to believe him a fraud.

"More than anyone alive, I suppose, except of course his wife."

"Oh, I know very little about Lord Walgrave; we have rarely met, and I am soon to leave on a long-anticipated journey."

"You speak very freely to a stranger." The tune changed to something equally seductive, mesmerizing.

"You have disturbed my sleep for three nights now. I am petulant and overtired." The song's seduction combined with lack of sleep and the darkness of the room made her direct.

"My apologies, my lady. I was drawn to my old friends here. Tell me, how far will you travel?"

"As far as the end of the world. Perhaps to a land so far from the sea that they don't know the use of an oar."

"You will be Odysseus then."

"Better than being Penelope. Better to travel the seas, taste the adventure, than be the one stoking the hearth, waiting for the sailor to return."

"The sea is a cruel mistress, though. She kills as many as she leads to shore."

"Perhaps. But boredom or worry kill those left behind. And one must die, one way or the other."

"I suppose you are right." He lifted the globe of the lamp and lowered the wick slightly, all without missing a note in the evocative melody.

"What tune is that?"

"Something I learned on the road," he answered.

"How did you get in?"

"The door has a faulty lock. It always has, from my youth. I grew up on the estate, and Sir Roderick educated me as a son, even letting me play this instrument any time I wished." His voice was gentle, soothing, the voice of a magician or a mesmerist. "Did you not consider that it might be dangerous? Coming here alone to confront a ghost or a burglar?"

"Burglars rarely come night after night merely to play the instruments. Ghosts, well, that's another matter—but were you a ghost, I would have little to fear."

"Ah, but my lady, some ghosts can be vengeful."

"I have my prayer book, and if need be, I can call the parson to bless the house."

"Not superstitious, then."

"I simply know this house's ghosts."

"Does the house have ghosts?" He drew the music to a close, drawing out the final sounds of the last notes, then stopping them altogether.

"Every house has ghosts. Most people choose to ignore them."

"But you are not most people."

"I prefer to know what secrets sleep inside a house's walls."

"An interesting perspective. These walls have many secrets. Have you discovered them all? Would you like me to play another? Perhaps on the viol this time. I see my old favorite still stands in the corner." He rose, but did not step forward.

"Only if you promise that you will let me sleep tomorrow night."

He stepped into the greater darkness of the corner. She heard the creak of the floor where his foot trod.

"For a ghost you are quite talented—you can even make the floor creak." She listened, hearing nothing but her own breath.

Watching the corner he had disappeared into, she raised the wick of the oil lamp. The light shone brightly. She was alone.

Chapter Fourteen

"I don't like his lordship's scholar. He's one of those who misses his dinner, then wants to scavenge in the kitchen for victuals." Mrs. Pier poured Olivia a cup of tea. "He roams the house, looking in rooms not open to the scholars, as if he's searching for something particular and hasn't found it yet. He claims he gets lost, so I set the hall boy to keep him in the library."

Olivia grew silent. Could it be that her troubles had followed her from London? "What does he look like? Short, a bit fleshy, broken front tooth?"

"No." Mildred looked at her with concern. "This one's tall, strong I'd wager, dressed as you'd expect, but carries himself as if he could afford better."

Olivia released her breath. "Other than wandering, what about him makes you uneasy?"

"It's merely a feeling," Pier admitted reluctantly. "Sure, when you look at him, he's scribbling away like the rest. But something makes you wonder what he's doing when you aren't looking."

"We expected that his lordship would send an agent to examine the estate." Olivia sipped her tea.

"His lordship's obligation is to come back to the estate himself."

"Perhaps he will after I am gone." Olivia gave a half shrug in agreement. "But until MacHus declares himself, we are under no obligation to make his investigations any easier. I will pay no attention to him at our meeting today, and I will neither meet nor engage with him. However I will ask Mr. Southbridge to take his measure."

"That's best." Mrs. Pier looked out the front window. "The parson's horse is on his way to the stables. I'll bring more tea and whatever biscuits Mr. Stanley has created for the day." Mrs. Pier slipped from Olivia's study. A few moments later, Pier's butler-husband led in the parson.

"Olivia, you look well." The parson crossed the room to kiss her hand.

"As do you, Noah." She gestured him to a seat before the desk.

"What business do we have today?" He rubbed his palms together in mock glee.

"Three petitions for supplies." She pointed to a stack of papers to his left.

As Noah read silently, Olivia returned to her list of unpleasant tasks. The next one: determining which books she would add to Sir Roderick's library.

"The three petitions are reasonable, though I have qualms about Professor Lark's proposal to reproduce one of the experiments in Joseph Priestley's *Experiments and Observations on Different Kinds of Air.*" Noah scratched his temple. "Are you certain that's wise?"

"To use one of Sir Roderick's favorite words, I feel cantankerous. Lord Walgrave should understand to the fullest extent what managing the estate requires. Lark's experiment should provide that opportunity."

The parson shook his head slowly, trying not to laugh. His eyes, when they met hers, were a brilliant blue. "Instead of offering you sound advice, I find myself cantankerous as well."

"Then the estate will order the appropriate supplies." Olivia made a notation in her ledger, smiling.

"In fact, take whatever amount Lark asks for and double it." Noah leaned forward conspiratorially. His blond hair was thick, like Walgrave's, but already lined with gray. "I'll even post the order myself at the village."

"I've made you devious, Noah. You will have to say an extra prayer tonight to set yourself back on the right way." She dipped her pen in the ink and wrote out the order.

"If we have concluded our only business, we have time for a walk in the garden. It's a cool day, but clear."

She sanded her paper, then set the ledger to the side to dry, giving herself time to consider his offer. Noah was an easy companion, good-natured and kind. He'd lost his wife in childbed poisoning and the child with her. He hadn't re-married, but occasionally she wondered if she were the reason why.

"I would like a walk. But I would value your advice on one other problem." She paused as the tea service arrived. A footman set it on the desk beside them, then disappeared.

"Of course. Explain while I pour." He prepared her tea perfectly, just the right combination of milk, sugar, and tea, added in the appropriate order.

"As you know, Sir Roderick left detailed notes on which books to acquire for the library, and he established a small annual endowment to cover the expense. When he died, his list included more than six hundred titles, along with instructions to keep current on new books in specific areas."

Noah bit into one of the biscuits and groaned in pleasure. "I must say, Olivia, your company is delightful, but I would visit merely to eat Stanley's biscuits. As for the books, no one could have overseen that account better than you have."

"Yet one hundred books remain to be purchased. I recently contacted Constance Equiano, the bookseller at the African's Daughter, to see if she would take on the task of locating those that remain." She blinked away unexpected tears. "But I don't see any way to fulfill my promise to Sir Roderick, and it makes me inexpressibly sad."

"You have more than repaid Sir Roderick's kindnesses, and, if Walgrave fails to honor his father's wishes, that is not your fault." Noah looked into her face and read it well. "Why can't you finish?"

"I'd need at least another hundred pounds beyond what's left in this year's endowment."

"Answer three questions then. Can this bookseller even find all the books? Is there sufficient money in next year's funds to pay for the purchases? And, do you have sufficient reserves in the estate accounts to cover the difference until the beginning of the year?"

"I don't know. Yes. And yes."

"Then engage Equiano to find the books, and if she does, buy them. Do what you must to avoid regrets." His voice, as usual, was kind, and it gave her strength.

"Then I shall do it. Roderick's list will take some time to copy out, if you wish to walk without me."

A look of disappointment flashed across his face, then disappeared. "Give me paper and pen, and I'll take half the list. But I must be repaid, my lady."

"What payment will you require? You must choose something cheap as I've just committed to spend estate funds on books," she teased, her heart already lighter. One fewer item on her list of unpleasant tasks.

"It will cost the estate little: a walk on another day . . . and more biscuits." His smile was easy, allowing all that was unspoken between them to remain so.

* * *

Harrison stood at the head of the long library table, calculating which chair would offer him the most obscurity. Under his father's supervision, the library had expanded up and out, adding another room along its length and opening up the center to double-height. Around the open second story, a wrought iron walkway provided access to books on the upper level. Along the innermost wall stood the long table where the scholars met. Harrison settled on a chair partially veiled in shadow and next to the seat designated for Mr. Quinn, the astronomer. A broad man, Quinn would help block Harrison from Olivia's view. From that seat, he could also observe Olivia in the long pier glass near the table's head. He felt his heart quicken in anticipation, the way it did before an important debate in Parliament.

He took his place at the table and began to work. The presentations, he anticipated, would be gruelingly dull, so he'd brought several sets of newspaper correspondence to review, including those signed by An Honest Gentleman. In the background, the scholars rehearsed their speeches, each one stopping periodically to tighten his sentences. He found their revisions obsessive, but chalked it up to competitiveness. As for his own report, he spent no time preparing. Why should he? He'd given dozens of reports before heads of state and parliamentary committees. How hard could it be to justify a pretend project?

He tried to focus on the articles, but his thoughts kept turning to the moment he would see his wife once more. Sparring with her in the dark music room had proved unexpectedly satisfying. But she had not known who he was. How would she respond when she saw him today? Would she blush red, embarrassed to be caught off guard, or would she respond coldly, even angrily, to the knowledge he'd been stealing into the house? Her letter on their marriage had startled him; it was only fair to startle her as well. It would give him the upper hand in their negotiations.

Soon the table filled around him, the seven scholars in their established seats nearest the head, the four visitors below them. He sat between Lord Montmorency, an addled man obsessed with antiquities, and Quinn.

He knew the moment Olivia entered the room. The scholars rose as she approached the head of the table, and Harrison stepped slightly behind Quinn. He had no wish for her to recognize him just yet. A thin man in a blue waistcoat stood by her side, between her and the mirror, interfering with Harrison's line of sight.

"Be seated, sirs, be seated. We will begin momentarily."

The group sat as the thin man pulled out Olivia's chair.

His first look at his wife for more than six years hit him like a blow to the gut. She looked nothing like he remembered. He had the details right: thick brown hair, wide dark eyes, full lips, high cheekbones and firm chin. But remembering her constituent parts had not prepared him to see the whole woman. The whole, breathtaking woman.

Over the years, his frustration and anger had transformed her into a dowd, demure and compliant. He'd painted her as the sort of woman who would accept the insanity of an arranged marriage to a man she'd never met, in exchange for a comfortable life in the country and a title. But he should have listened more closely to Palmersfield's and Capersby's descriptions. This woman needed no title to make her fascinating. She was temptation personified.

The man in blue leaned close to whisper in her ear, and her eyes responded with delight. Though he had no right to be, Harrison felt suddenly possessive. For the first time, he realized how much he had lost in letting Olivia go.

"Quinn," he whispered. "Who's that man in blue?"

The portly astronomer chewed on an empty pipe.

"The parson. Noah Southbridge. He helps her ladyship decide who to admit and for how long."

The parson laughed at something Olivia said. Their heads were bowed together over a set of papers, and when they looked up from their work, the parson patted her hand. Harrison wanted to yell at the man to stop touching his wife, but he held himself back. His response, he knew, was irrational.

Harrison watched Olivia's face grow serious. She hit a bell with a small mallet. "Gentlemen." She waited until the room fell silent. "Please observe our time limits: Our sand glass gives you three minutes to outline your purpose, your most recent findings, and your plan for next week, then we have three minutes for questions."

"Is it true, my lady, that if one goes over time, he is expelled from the library?" Jerome, a new scholar with a voice like a frog, wiped sweat from his brow.

Olivia smiled comfortingly. "We expel no one on their first Wednesday."

"No, she waits until the second for that." Quinn chortled, and the other originals laughed heartily.

"Gentlemen." Olivia's voice, mellow and smooth, offered a firm caution, and the laughter stopped. "We begin as usual with the Seven, and with Mr. Otley moderating." Olivia turned her attention to a document she was copying.

The reports of the Seven sped by, all sharp, concise, and entertaining. Each man spoke convincingly until the last grain of sand fell. The questions were pointed, and sometimes difficult, but each man defended his research admirably. Harrison shifted in his seat, regretting having been so flippant about preparation. It would take all his skill not to embarrass himself before Olivia.

"And last, our unexpected scholar, sent to us by Lord Walgrave himself." Mr. Otley smiled at him. "Mr. MacHus, share with us your research."

He stood, expecting her eyes to widen with surprise and shock when she recognized him, but she was paying no attention at all. She did not even look up when he stood. Instead, she was whispering some confidence in the parson's ear, and the parson was nodding. His anger flashed hot, but he tamped it down, an experienced orator faced with unexpected opposition. But watching the pair in the mirror, he waited for her reaction to his voice. She had heard it in the music room already, but now she would realize he was her husband.

"In my excitement to begin my research into a history of famous sea voyages, from Odysseus to Admiral Nelson, I spent my morning in the library, marveling at its wonders. As a result, I have little to report, though I now have the fine model of my fellow scholars to follow in preparing my report next week."

The scholars puffed up with his praise.

"However, I was wondering if you all could advise me in how to approach a second project." He watched Olivia from the corner of his eye. The housekeeper had drawn her attention away to some other business. It was almost as if she were deliberately ignoring him.

"Well, it depends on the area. We all claim authority in our fields, but outside of that, we sometimes know little or nothing at all." Martinbrook examined the tips of his fingers.

"Yes, it depends on whether your question intersects with our interests." Nathan nodded rhythmically.

"I wish to examine articles published in several different newspapers under a variety of pseudonyms to determine who the authors might be. It's an intellectual game a dear friend who is an invalid proposed to me." It wasn't a complete lie, Walgrave thought. In fact, given Mr. James's health, it was perilously close to the truth.

"What are the pseudonyms?" Otley deftly managed the conversation.

"An Honest Gentleman, A Pursuer of Peace, Hannibal, and Prosperity Once More."

Olivia's hands stilled and her face blanched, but she did not look up. The parson placed his hand on hers. She sat, unmoving, head bowed, as if she were afraid to meet Harrison's eyes. Her reaction made it clear that she'd finally linked the voice of MacHus to that of her long-lost husband. But her posture told Harrison far more: The parson was her reason for leaving him.

"Are you wondering if one person writes all the letters, regardless of pseudonym?" Partlet, the rhetorician, asked. "The challenge will be to identify the origins of the person from only the words he uses."

"Why, yes, I suppose I mean that as well." What Harrison actually wanted was to beat the parson into the ground, but he forced himself to sound calm.

"Or she," Lark added.

"She?" Walgrave raised an eyebrow. Olivia leaned into the parson's ear once more, the parson nodded, then she rose and slipped out of the room, never once looking in Harrison's direction. He wanted to follow, to force the conversation she was so obviously avoiding. But his duty stopped him. He could confront Olivia at any time. When would he again find a group of scholars so willing to help?

"Yes, many educated women write in the newspapers using their own or assumed names. Mrs. Barbauld wrote a lovely series on natural history some years ago, or was it Mrs. Wakefield?" Lark's voice trailed off as he caught sight of something out the window.

"Ah, yes, I remember a long debate in the *Gentleman's Magazine* between Anna Seward and a bombastic man . . ." Smithson rubbed his mustache between his fingers.

"Joseph Weston," Nathan supplied confidently. "I used

to set people's names to music to remember them. His had two long initial syllables. JO-seph WES-ton. But that was over twenty years ago."

Harrison felt his head start to spin. The conversation of the scholars was filled with so many rabbit holes, and one could never tell which would lead to important information or to nonsense. The scholars made an afternoon arguing in Parliament seem like child's play.

"Ah, yes. Weston harangued Seward for almost two years—but in the end, I must say, Seward won. She told me she regularly used pen names: A. S., A Constant Reader, Benvolio. Brilliant woman and quite lovely." Partlet blushed slightly around his ears. "We once had tea, in my younger years."

"Is there evidence that any of these writers are women?" Otley attempted to lead his colleagues back to Harrison's question, but no one followed.

"One can tell a great deal about a writer from the words on the page. For example, have you ever noticed the tool laborers use to beat down a hedge?" Partlet shifted his monocle by squeezing his cheek.

"The one that looks like a cross between a mattock and axe?" Smithson drew a quick sketch and held it up.

"Yes, exactly! If you were in Cornwall or Devon, you would call it a *visgy*, but in Somerset it's a bisgay. Small difference to be sure—but if a man uses one term and not the other, you have some hint to his background." Partlet removed his monocle, puffed a breath of air on it, then rubbed the glass clean with the edge of his shirt.

"Yet by itself one word isn't sufficient to place a writer from a particular region," Nathan said. "I face this problem in tracing the roots of a ballad."

The scholars began speaking over one another in their excitement to be useful.

"It might mean the writer grew up in a place, or lived there for a time, but no longer," Martinbrook opined.

"Or that he was close to someone from the region and picked up the word that way," Lark interjected.

"Or he has adopted the words used by his neighbors," Smithson countered.

Harrison raised his hands to quiet them. "If I were to look at each set of articles separately by magazine and pseudonym, could I tell if the writer was the same in every article?" He divided his papers into piles by author and passed them to the scholars on either side of him. The stacks slowly made their way down the table. The scholars quietly passed each other the sheets, careful, Harrison noted, to keep each set together and in the original order.

Finally Otley spoke. "You must add two other factors: The writer may have intentionally tried to hide his identity, or the editor may have revised essays to make individual authors sound alike."

"That seems like a lot of effort." Another rabbit hole. Harrison began to wonder if the scholars would be any help at all.

"When I was at the court of Catherine the Great, such efforts were routine." Otley rubbed his chin. "Since Peterloo, publishers must be wary of printing anything that draws accusations of sedition or treason."

"Let me ask this: If we assumed that all the articles were published before Peterloo and that each one appeared in essentially the same form as the original writer wrote them, could we make any generalizations about the authors?" Harrison sighed inwardly, berating himself for having framed his initial questions so broadly.

"Well, if you want *only* generalizations, then, certainly." Quinn straightened the pile of papers before him.

"Yes." "Yes." "Yes." Each scholar pronounced his agreement and buried his attention in the papers.

"Look here." Lark pointed at three sentences. "A Pursuer of Peace uses a periodic sentence each time he disagrees with his opponent's position."

"He also frames his own positions as questions," Otley observed.

"I see that," Fields agreed, tentatively, then grew more comfortable when no one objected to a newcomer talking.

"None of the other authors do either of those," Jerome chimed in, given confidence by Fields's experience.

"Can we hypothesize that these four articles share one author?" Harrison asked, hopefully.

"Yes." "Yes." "Yes." The agreements circled the table.

Harrison rolled the pile into a tube, then tied a string around it.

"Prosperity Once More likes the word *eleemosynary*." Nathan spread out three essays and pointed to the word in each one. "See here: 'Are not our parish lists eleemosynary in nature?' It's in every article."

"Not only that"—Quinn straightened his pile until it had neat clean edges—"his arguments are always rooted in the effects of inflation or government regulation on the common laborer."

"What of the others?" Harrison prompted, knowing how long it would have taken him to discover the similarities. The scholars were a windfall, a confusing, unpredictable windfall.

"Hannibal comes from the North." Lark squinted at his page. "My friend John Brockett lent me his glossary of North Country words. Fascinating reading. Hannibal frequently reverts to North Country usage."

"Such as?" Harrison prompted.

"Well, here." Lark, nearsighted, held the essay close to his face. "He uses *abstract* as a verb with the meaning 'to take away unlawfully.'"

"Then, that leaves our Honest Gentleman. What do we

know of him?" Harrison waited, anxious to hear what the scholars would notice.

The room grew silent again, the scholars reading over a page, then passing it on.

"They all appear to be by the same person," Partlet said, but his voice was unconvincing.

"Why?" Harrison waited. The men seemed far less confident than before.

"Because they are unremarkable," Partlet explained. "We would have to spend several hours to find any identifying features at all."

"We can say he's a university man." Quinn fluffed his cravat into a new arrangement.

"Yes, and Cambridge rather than Oxford." Jerome watched to see if any of the other scholars objected.

"Why?" Harrison questioned.

"His examples are scientific rather than religious or philosophical," Jerome explained. "He is very practical in his application of logic, no sophistry and little theoretical speculation."

"Thank you, gentlemen. You have saved me hours of time. I know now how to proceed." Harrison looked up to discover that the parson had escaped as well as Olivia.

"Then, we are done." Otley hit the bell with his mallet. "We will adjourn to the lodge for tea. I should tell our new colleagues that Mr. Stanley's biscuits are not to be missed. Today we have a new shortbread with persimmons, taken from a handwritten manuscript he examined during his travels in Pennsylvania."

Chapter Fifteen

"Your ladyship, your presence is required in the library." Mrs. Pier's lips pursed into a thin line.

"Already? We left them only an hour ago." Olivia set down her pen.

"I'll wait for you in the corridor, your ladyship." Pier walked crisply, shutting the door behind her.

"Oh, dear. Pier only reverts to rank when she's reached her limits." Olivia rose from behind her desk, and Noah, from his regular chair, rose as well. "Thank you for finding me. I was somewhat distressed."

"But understandably. You could not have imagined Walgrave would send a scholar with an interest in An Honest Gentleman. As for now, I'll post these in the village." He held up two letters, one for Lark's supplies, the other for Roderick's books.

"I can't imagine what mess the scholars have made in so little time."

Southbridge took his leave at the door. "If I may be of assistance, you know where to find me."

Nodding goodbye, Olivia turned her attention to Mrs. Pier.

"According to Mr. Calder, all the bridles are missing

from the barn." The housekeeper's face was a cloud of dismay.

Olivia hurried down the stairs, grateful for the distraction. She was still reeling from the moment she'd realized that her new scholar MacHus was in fact her husband—well, not quite husband. And for him to return here with the purpose of unmasking An Honest Gentleman! If not for Noah's steadying hand, Olivia feared she may have swooned for the first time in her life. It was still too overwhelming to think about. For now, she'd turn her mind to whatever disaster the scholars had managed to inflict on the library.

She had learned early that the scholars would unthinkingly appropriate items from the household for their experiments. A pot Cook had liked for stews—when filled with rocks and suspended from a makeshift crane they'd built in the meadow—became a fine wrecking ball for testing a theory that Smithson, the engineer, had read in a recent article. But it wasn't until she'd discovered the lot of them on the roof, preparing to launch Quinn, the astronomer, off the edge in a flying machine, that she had established some rules. After Quinn had dismounted and the machine had plummeted straight down to break into pieces on the roof of the porte cochere, the scholars had agreed to her edicts with only a minimum of grumbling.

The primary rule: no harm to limb or library.

Opening the library doors wide, she surveyed the room. The large central library table had been cleared of its books and papers. Unaware of her entrance, the scholars were huddled around a diagram laid out flat. Seven white heads were muttering, pointing, and disagreeing with varying degrees of civility, while two younger men were watching with a complicated mix of dismay and fascination.

Occasionally she could make out bits of disconnected

argument. But even so, she was not quite able to determine what they had planned.

"No, I'm certain that position is right. See here. Below the main diagram, it says that 'the center of gravity of a body suspended on one cord always lies beneath the center line of that cord.'" Quinn motioned toward the ceiling where the height of the room rose to two stories.

Looking up, Olivia inwardly gasped. Somehow the scholars had tied ropes to the ancient chandelier above the central library table, then tied the other ends of the ropes to the wrought iron grating of the balcony. Between the ropes hung a system of weights, pulleys, and cylinders—all attached, she realized with bridles.

She refused to let herself wonder how they had managed it. If she did, she'd never have a peaceful night's sleep again. Suddenly, she imagined the ropes pulling the bolts of the walkway free and the scholars toppling to their deaths.

What would happen to the lot of them when she was gone? Would Lark again forget to cover his magnifying glass and set the papers on his desk on fire with the afternoon sun? Would Martinbrook dismantle another fencerow in search of rocks moved by the ancient Britons? If the local magistrate arrested them again, who would bring them home? Would Harrison even wish to?

She wiped unexpected tears from her eyes. She would miss each gray hair on their troublesome heads.

Eavesdropping carefully on the scholars' debate, Olivia examined the ropes and their cylinders, tracing their path across the ceiling.

"Smithson might be the expert at building fortifications, but as an agriculturist, I can tell you: One must account for the difference in the material." Martinbrook rubbed his hands through his coarse hair. "The sketch assumed a linen cloth, and we have only wool."

Olivia looked quickly to the window curtains. They were still in place.

"The problem isn't the materials; it's these angles here. I believe the translation from the Italian isn't accurate." Nathan rubbed the top of his nose where his spectacles rested.

"If you compare this version to Smithson's original notes, you will see important variations in the design here and here." Lark objected as loudly as his narrow voice would allow, but the louder, more assertive voices overshadowed him.

"If Smithson's copy isn't exact, then we have to interpret the data based on our own experiences." Quinn fluffed the lace of his cravat. "We don't know this design is da Vinci's at all. Only Smithson believes it to be authentic."

Olivia approached the desk and silently looked between the shoulders of the scholars. The diagram was sketched, she realized with a bit of dismay, on her largest and most expensive drawing paper. It was held down flat at the corners by a variety of objects: a brick, a doorstop, a globe, and a shoe. She immediately looked at the scholars' feet, but all were clad. She'd have to collect the shoe after the experiment; otherwise, later one of the scholars would be distressed to be missing a shoe, forgetting entirely that he'd sacrificed it to science.

Olivia stepped in close to the group of scholars. Lark moved over to let her see the drawing better, then realizing who she was, looked up with rabbit eyes. She lifted her finger to silence him, but not before he'd elbowed Nathan in the ribs. She watched as each of the scholars realized she had joined them, surprise giving way to guilt, and guilt to apologetic resignation.

Soon, only Smithson—his head bent over the drawing— remained unaware of her presence. "In Italy, I reviewed Leonardo da Vinci's works extensively. Though the papers I copied from the Duke of Arundel's library at Gresham College are unattributed, I'm certain they belong to da Vinci." Smithson chewed on the end of his cheroot, kept empty because the taste of tobacco made him unwell.

"But can the original drawing be trusted?" Olivia asked, as if she had been part of the scheme all along.

"Oh, yes!" Smithson offered without raising his head. "As you see here, we are testing Leonardo's theories related to balances and weights."

Lark, unable to manage his discomfort any longer, poked Smithson in the ribs. "Miss Olivia is here."

"Of course Miss Olivia is here, Quinn. We've just been discussing our little experiment. And besides . . ." Smithson's voice trailed off as the consequences of Olivia's presence registered. The stocky man grew silent, rolling his cheroot between his thumb and forefinger. Then realizing something, he grinned widely. "And besides, Miss Olivia only minds if we break something. This experiment will break nothing! See!"

Smithson reached to his left and loosened the rope from the back of the chair, letting it swing free.

Olivia watched with a fascinated dismay as the ropes loosened each in turn and the cylinders moved up and down their lengths, depending on the direction of the force. For a moment she almost felt as if she were watching an acrobat at the traveling fair. The heaviest weight finally let loose, and it began careening toward the large stained glass window that had been in the family for generations. She felt her stomach twist and her breath stop as the cylinder shifted to the bottom of the rope. Coupled with the knot on the end, it swung closer and closer to the window, gaining force and momentum as each weight set free. She couldn't turn away. Like the others, she was trapped in the moment, watching the disaster unfold.

Closer, closer, the weighted cylinder swung, then

stopped. With near misses, and complicated movements, Smithson's ropes and cylinders finally came to a rest less than an inch before the large stained glass window.

"All right, then, gentlemen, I think that concludes today's experiments." Olivia tried to keep her voice level and calm, though her heart was still pounding against her ribs. "Professor Smithson, I assume we will hear your report on your findings at our Wednesday meeting."

"Ah, yes, Miss Olivia. Of course. I'll begin it now." The engineer grinned all the way to his chair, then turned back to the group. "Next week I would like to test da Vinci's studies on curved mirrors."

"Oh, yes," Partlet agreed, "I'd like to see what he says about monocles."

"Yes, we should gather all the mirrors from the abbey," Martinbrook suggested, innocently. "Perhaps we can also examine how shallow curves create a faster fire."

"Yes." "Yes." "Yes." The scholars bobbed their heads as if in a roll call.

At the word *fire*, Olivia turned quickly. "Professor Martinbrook, please remember that we do not kindle fires in the library. And with the lack of rain, I would prefer no kindling of fires in the fields as well."

"Ah, yes, certainly, my dear. Excellent point." Martinbrook nodded his agreement. "A fine display, Smithson. Let us know when we can be of use again."

The scholars drifted back to their desks, promising to dismantle the experiment before they retired for the evening.

Olivia watched them, waiting as her heart returned to something of a normal rhythm. They were never easy, her scholars. But she who had never had a reliable father felt she had gained one, first in Sir Roderick and then in the Seven when they arrived. Even with their quirks and peccadillos, all had kind hearts, even at their most competitive.

They had become an odd family, and she would mourn their loss. *But not now: For now, we are still together.*

"I believe that's mine."

She heard his voice as if from a long distance, its tones echoing in her bones. Harrison had found her, and she still hadn't decided how to handle him. She wasn't ready, not for this.

"What is yours?" She waited for the obvious answer—*everything*—but he did not give it. But she would not give him the satisfaction of recognizing him—not when he had propositioned her only a week before.

"The shoe." He held up his foot, revealing a single white stocking with an obvious repair to the heel. The sewing was badly done, and for a moment she regretted that his housekeeper couldn't darn a smooth sock.

"Ah, yes." She set the shoe on the table and began her escape.

He rounded the table to speak low to her ear. "Might I speak with you in private? My three-minute allotment proved unsatisfactory."

She stepped back, dread settling in the pit of her stomach. "The regulations of the library allow only one presentation per week. If you wish for an exception, you should petition his lordship." He caught her wrist as she turned to go.

"You know who I am. I saw your eyes widen with recognition."

"How could I not recognize you, Mr. MacHus? We met not two hours ago. But our acquaintance is not long enough for the liberties you take. Please release my hand."

He let her hand drop. Confusion and disbelief crossed his face, and Olivia felt a moment of triumph. How dare he assume she would know him? He had not recognized her at the theater.

"Excuse me, your ladyship." He struggled for words.

"I must speak to you on a matter of great importance, but this"—he gestured to the library and the other scholars all bent over their work—"is not the place."

She would not let him off so easily. "Matters of great concern should be directed to your patron, his lordship."

"I . . ." He looked over his shoulder at the other scholars. He rallied; she could see it in the way he drew back his shoulders. "I have news from his lordship that can only be shared with you—in private."

"Have you any proof of that? You cannot think me so gullible that I believe you—a stranger—simply on your word."

He stood for a moment, thinking. She watched his thoughts in the quick movements of his eyes.

"His lordship wishes to convey his regrets for the current situation."

"If his lordship has regrets, he should convey them himself." She raised her chin and turned to go. She could not keep up the pretense for long, but she enjoyed baiting him.

"Damn it, Olivia," he whispered through clenched teeth. "I'm trying to do just that."

She turned to face him, making sure to keep her face impassive. She focused on his face, tracing the planes of his cheeks, the line of his jaw, then she let her eyes move downward, across the breadth of his shoulders, the narrowness of his hips, the length of his legs. Her eyes raked his body with calculated disinterest. When her eyes met his again, she was pleased to see a spark of desire. "I do not know you, sir. And your position as a scholar does not include the privilege of my name." Then, as if she had never lain awake at night wondering if he were dead or alive, she stared at him, impassive, waiting—the way a parent, a priest, or a judge would wait for a confession.

The expression on his face hovered somewhere between surprise and regret. Out of a slit pocket in his waistcoat he pulled a smooth, flat stone and held it out in his palm. Brown, with luminous stripes of gold and black, the tiger's-eye had belonged to her father. Longing wrenched the inside of her belly, and she reached out to take the stone, but pulled back, refusing the emotion.

Steeling her face to reveal nothing, she looked up into his eyes, a bottomless blue. "Follow me." She left him, to follow or not, as he chose.

As he followed her silently to the front of the house, she quickly considered what she would need to do to manage Harrison's investigation and his presence at the estate. She had imagined a dozen ways they might meet again. In none of them did he sneak into the house pretending to be a scholar, then announce that he intended to unmask her as a traitor.

Strangely, the situation offered its consolations. She now knew Harrison had found Cerberus's list. It was clear he hadn't recognized her as the actress or he wouldn't have asked the scholars for help so openly. If he had brought the document with him to the estate, she might find a way to retrieve it. And having him on the estate while he was making his investigation meant that she could intervene if he got too close to the truth. It was an odd situation, a series of unlucky coincidences that had led him home, but not to *her*.

But she'd never expected her secret investigations for Mentor to lead her husband back to her door. Since the wild success of her novel, she'd expected him to arrive sooner or later. No earl with a rising career in Parliament wants the scandal of having a novelist for a wife. She imagined the scene a dozen times: He would arrive in his best carriage, storm into the library, throw a volume of her book on the desk, and demand an explanation. *She* might be of no value to him, but he would not allow a blot on the family name. And eventually, she knew, someone would let slip that that Lady Walgrave was the author of *The Deserted Wife*. She might do it herself if Harrison got too close to An Honest Gentleman.

Sadly, all of it signaled that she could not be herself. Olivia-the-deserted-wife felt only frustration, anger, and regrets for the former lover who still haunted her dreams. She would have to play another role. But what? She had no script to follow. She only knew that she had to keep him from discovering An Honest Gentleman's identity, and Mentor would expect her to use every wile in her considerable arsenal, be it anger, or sympathy, or even—though she hoped it would not come to it—seduction.

She looked over her shoulder. Harrison followed, as silently as Eurydice had followed Orpheus out of Hades. But unlike Orpheus, when Olivia looked over her shoulder, Harrison did not disappear. He only glared at her.

Sighing, she unlocked the drawing room door. "I have used this room as a study."

"You keep it locked?" He examined the room.

"It allows a little privacy. The scholars wish to celebrate when they make a discovery. If this room doesn't suit, you might prefer the estate office, once it's refurbished." Though she would have preferred to sit at the desk, she chose instead the chaise longue, leaving him a nearby chair.

"Refurbished?" He pulled the chair closer to the chaise, positioning himself closer than an acquaintance, but not so close as a friend. A perfect distance, she thought.

"You will find answers to any question about the estate in those green morocco volumes on your right. Every six months, I've had the weekly reports bound. 'Bind final reports' is an item on my list, if you wish me to take care of it."

"List?" Harrison raised one eyebrow.

"Loose ends to tie up before you take over."

"What loose ends?" Harrison sounded flippant, like a rake just woken after a night of carousing.

"The footmen have grown too tall for their livery; a lightning strike damaged the roof of the lodge; dry rot destroyed many window frames in the guest wing. Do you even read my reports?" She stared at him, both confused and annoyed.

He said nothing, only turned the tiger's-eye between his fingers.

"I suppose you will learn soon enough." She breathed out slowly. "Might I see it?"

"What?"

"The stone." She held out her hand, and he placed it in her palm. She ignored the warm brush of his fingers against hers. "I thought I'd lost it."

"I shouldn't have taken it. I wanted . . ." He paused. "I'm not sure what I wanted."

She pulled a tiger's-eye drop necklace from beneath her chemise. "When I discovered mine was gone, your father found me this one. Professor Martinbrook told me that tiger's-eye is a pseudomorph—a class of minerals which appear to be something other than they are or which change their composition without changing their appearance." She turned the stone in her hand toward the light. "My father gave me this stone before he left. I always thought it might be a clue." She realized the moment the words had left her mouth that she had revealed too much. But what did it matter? Whatever relationship they might have had was already ended.

"Forgive me. Had I known, I wouldn't have taken it." His apology sounded sincere. When she met his eyes, blue as the sea, she felt them pull her into a whirlpool of conflicting emotions. "A clue to what?"

She dropped her gaze and focused on the stone. "A child

who loses parents early always has questions about family and place."

"I thought your father and mine were old friends."

"Of a sort. My father disappeared when I was young, but he left me in Sir Roderick's care. Your father sent me to school, made sure I had the means to support myself, helped me find employment as a governess. It was more than many men would have done."

"I had no idea you were one of his foundlings. Did you marry me out of a sense of obligation to him?" His voice was soft, almost sincere, but something in it made her wary. Or perhaps *he* made her wary.

"I have done many things out of a sense of obligation, but marrying you was not one of them." She breathed out slowly, waiting for his response. Her story about her father's relationship with Sir Roderick was true as far as it went, but it would not bear too much scrutiny. Nor could she explain why she had married him. If she'd told him honestly *I needed the safety that marriage to an earl provided*, he would have demanded to know what she had done. And that past was better left buried.

Chapter Sixteen

Harrison watched her turn the stone in the light, and he felt pleased. He had taken the tiger's-eye all those years ago on a whim—a memento, but of what he hadn't been sure. Yet it had turned out to the good. By returning the stone to her, he had created a sense of trust. Already she had confided in him about her father. After their wedding, he had been too busy discovering the delights of her body to engage deeply with her mind or her heart. But knowing she was an orphan—that gave him an opening, some ground on which to respond to her stance on their marriage.

His goal was simple: to gain some time. He didn't need for Olivia to remain his wife for long; only until the end of Parliament's special session. After Peterloo, the tide in Parliament was turning toward reducing the freedoms enjoyed by free Englishmen. Though it was unlikely that the Whigs could stem that tide, Harrison had to try, and any hint of a personal scandal would justify the opposition in ignoring his appeals. Olivia had already waited half a dozen years. What could a few months more matter? Surely he could keep his longing for her under control for that short a time.

He had already mapped out an argument to convince

her to wait. Though his wife was clearly intelligent, she'd been educated at whatever middling boarding school his father had chosen. Her weekly estate reports showed that her mind leaned toward numbers in columns, toward ensuring the estate held adequate fuel for the winter or sufficient feed for the stock. But she was not philosophically or theoretically inclined, leaving him an avenue to use his debating skills to his advantage.

First he would build a greater rapport. Clearly Olivia found the scholars a burden—she'd been inattentive during their presentations, she locked them out of her study, and she had recoiled at Smithson's experiment. He would play to that, offer to lighten her load by removing the scholars. Having shown that he had both her best interests and those of the estate at heart, he would turn the discussion gently to their marriage, to why she needed his support to make a claim of invalidity. He would assure her he was amenable to a separation and even a settlement. He might even, if she remained agreeable, pay her price. But his sticking point would be the timing. No action could proceed until after the special session. She would have her separation; he would have his parliamentary special session, and it would all be reasonable and pleasant.

As long as he could keep his mind off the parson.

"I must admit that I've been enjoying my masquerade. Mr. MacHus has already learned much that Lord Walgrave would never have been told. But one thing baffles me: How did my father's house come to be an asylum for mad scholars?"

"I assure you they are all quite sane." Olivia did not look up from the stone.

"That doesn't answer my question."

"All of this was well explained in your father's letters—

or did you not read them as well?" Olivia set the stone down.

"Why do you think I haven't read your letters or my father's? Have I not provided you with answers in a timely fashion to your questions?"

"Through your agent." Olivia sat still, with her hands folded in her lap, distant, even aloof. He was surprised by her posture. A tiny voice in his head started to wonder if he'd made a mistake.

"No, I believe I am aware of everything."

"Then why ask me to repeat what I've already written?" She furrowed her brow.

"I learned in war and Parliament that one gains different information from letters than from conversations, and vice versa." Harrison extended his hands in a gesture of openness.

She shook her head slightly in disbelief. "In the arenas of war or politics, a single sentence can doom a campaign or a vote. But when one is discussing the parish church's need for a new roof, there is little need for concealment."

"Indulge me: How did the scholars come to the estate?"

"You were gone. Your father needed something to distract himself." Her sentences were clipped and direct. "He found amusement in collecting. Books, papers, manuscripts, even instruments, as I'm sure your midnight revels in the music room have revealed to you." She paused, watching him for a confession.

"Guilty as charged. But proceed."

He could see the objection in her face, but she shrugged it off. "News of his collection spread, leading him to open the library."

"He must have hated all those people underfoot."

"At first, perhaps, but he soon found a way to manage it. He built the scholars' lodge to give everyone privacy; he established a schedule for using the library; and he gave even the most engaged scholar an incentive to retire for the evening by having dinner served promptly and just as promptly taken away."

"I still can't imagine why he opened the library at all."

"He missed having a family, and he found one with the scholars. With Otley, he debated the nature of man and governments. He and Quinn spent months trying to develop a better method of predicting comets. He and Nathan sang ballads every day." She smiled, a soft, gentle smile. "His favorite was about a ram with enormous horns."

"I remember that one. My father would sing it in a booming baritone." Harrison had never imagined that a silly song could evoke his grief so poignantly. He looked at the floor so she could not see him blinking away tears. "What he lacked in ability, he made up in exuberance."

"He was a man of enthusiasms, and he reveled in the scholars' interests. When he was too ill to leave his bed, they kept his spirits from lagging. Nothing short of your presence could have made him happier. As a result, each year when the Seven apply for readmission, I approve them all."

"And when they succeed in destroying the property?" Harrison asked, hoping to encourage her to confess her annoyance with the scholars.

"The estate is almost uniformly better for their help. Martinbrook's experiments in the kitchen garden have increased our yields enough to share with the cottagers. With Smithson's help, we've built more cottages for the tenants, and he has stabilized many of the more precarious abbey ruins. The expense of their room and board is negligible against their contributions."

"Even so, I will have to consider my father's expectations for the scholars and whether the current system meets his goals."

Her voice grew cold. "If you were concerned about the scholars destroying your family home, you could have intervened when they were setting up their experiment. Or, perhaps better, you could have revealed yourself as lord of the manor when you arrived, and taken up your responsibilities. I must wonder, then, what your game is, and to what I owe the . . . pleasure . . . of your company."

"If I said I wished to see my family home . . ."

"I would think you were lying. Since I'm sure that you did not come here to impersonate a scholar, you must have received the paperwork from my solicitor."

He walked to the window and looked out. That had not gone as well as he'd predicted. He decided to try a different tack. "Do you hate me?"

She looked puzzled. "Why would I hate you? You made it clear that you had no wish to be married, and you have refused to be married in every way that matters. Hating you would be foolish, for it would mean that I refused to acknowledge what you have made perfectly and repeatedly clear."

"Then if you do not hate me, what are your feelings?" Perhaps he could gain some insight into her motivations, since he had miscalculated her thoughts at every turn so far. Not in all his years in Parliament had he felt so out of his depths.

"My feelings are my own. If we were married, I might feel obligated to share them, but we are not married nor have we ever been."

"What if I wish to share my feelings?"

"You may do as you wish, but it does not require me to reciprocate."

"You have grown into a hard woman, Olivia." He realized this with some sadness.

"I was always a hard woman. You simply didn't realize it."

"Ah, how can that be? The Olivia I remember was sweet, open, dutiful."

She shook her head, rejecting his words. "I have long credited you with greater skills of observation than you apparently possess. I was even then a woman of many secrets. You simply were uninterested in knowing them."

"What if I would like to know them now?" Harrison was surprised at how true that question was. He'd known he would have to fight his physical attraction when he saw Olivia again, but hadn't been prepared to be so interested in the woman herself.

"You had six years to discover all you wished. You only want to know them now because I have refused to be convenient. That has captured your attention. Believe me, sir, like indigestion, this interest will pass." She looked at him with clear disdain. "Accept that we are not married. It frees us. You may follow your interests, I mine. It's all very civilized."

"I may well come to that acceptance, but for now, I have many questions. Most concern the estate and its management, but others concern how you imagine this separation would proceed." He shook his head. "To be blunt, you can't pursue the court case without my help. I can hold any judgment up for years, simply by refusing to pay any solicitor's fees. I have all the power in this situation, so why not be reasonable?"

"I am being *reasonable*, as you put it. Let me explain the situation as *I* understand it. But since I have not studied for the bar, as you have, you may correct me where I go astray."

"That seems fair." Harrison fought a smile. Now he was back on solid ground. He almost felt sorry for her, but he would be gracious and correct her missteps gently. "Please, begin."

"We face two problems here: one of my legal status and

the other of money. If we are *married*, I—as your wife—do not have any legal standing as a person before the law. Any money I might make from some venture—say, if, like Charlotte Smith, I chose to become a writer—that money would be yours, not mine. Any money or property I brought to the marriage became yours the moment we were wed. The only exception would be the monies provided to me through our marriage settlement, my pin money. Am I correct thus far?" She paused, waiting for his comment.

Harrison nodded, growing increasingly aware that he had underestimated his "meek, compliant" wife. "That's correct. As Blackstone's *Commentaries* say, 'A man and a woman are one person under the law, and that person is the man.'"

She inclined her head with exactly the right amount of noblesse oblige. "If we are married, I may use my pin money as I wish. But I cannot use my pin money to hire an attorney to represent me, because I—separate from you—do not exist. If we are not married, however, I cannot use my pin money because pin money exists in the context of a marriage settlement."

"Correct. If no marriage has occurred, then you have no pin money."

"But if I am not married to you, then I have the right . . . to exist. I can have my own money, and, as a legal entity, I can use that money to hire a solicitor to petition the courts on my behalf. I can do this even if I am petitioning to have my invalid marriage declared invalid."

"Yes, all that is true. But practically all you have proved is that for you to have any money at all to pay a solicitor, it must come from me." Harrison felt a hum of energy from their debate.

"I paid my solicitor with the remainder of the funds your father gave me to consider marrying you. I have a deed of gift from your father, making that agreement explicit. I also have the marriage settlement, where you agreed to exclude that gift from your possessions. And so, I have it both ways: If I am married, you agreed the funds are mine; and if I am not married, the funds are mine. So my using them in any way I wish poses no problem. And I wish to petition the courts to declare our invalid marriage invalid."

"Damn it, Olivia. We stood before a parson and took vows. We are married."

"A marriage is more than vows—there are forms, conventions, that must be observed. We did not observe them." She raised her hands palms up, then dropped them to her sides. "But putting that aside, I am merely setting forth a proposition and its logical conclusion. If . . . then. That is the way that you prefer to think, is it not? Rational, detached, logical."

"What does *how* I think matter?" He felt the skin at the back of his neck tighten as it did only when he was facing his most accomplished opponents in Parliament. And even they could not twist him in knots quite like this. He wanted to chalk it up to distraction caused by his desire for the woman in front of him, but in truth, he had simply been outmaneuvered.

"For years, I've read your parliamentary debates in the London *Times* and other periodicals. As a sort of game, I began to predict what you would argue before I read the summaries."

"How often were you successful?"

"Almost always."

"Then you are unusual. My fellow MPs rarely anticipate my arguments. If they did, I would lose far more often."

"I originally wanted to understand how you think." She

shrugged. "But given our present dilemma, I thought it would be best to use the terms you prefer."

If she weren't so calm, he could imagine her words carried an undercurrent of anger. But how could she be angry, if she believed their marriage had always been a sham? If she was angry, then he would have to consider why.

Oh, God, he thought, *I* do *think in terms of* if *and* then.

"Is there some other way that I should set out the problem?" Her voice sounded indulgent, as if he were a recalcitrant child who refused to eat his dinner.

"No. *If* you have spent so much time studying my responses, *then* you should at least gain the benefit of that effort." He put the slightest pressure on the words, enough to show that he had acknowledged her observation.

For the first time, she smiled—a wan, thin, almost sad smile. "*Then*, I will proceed." She folded her hands before her. "At stake here are not my funds or your power. It is your reputation, your family's reputation. If you refuse to set me free, I will destroy it. Because I have the power here, not you."

He began to object, but she cut him off.

"For years, you have claimed I am your wife and allowed me to act on your authority. I have run your estate, most would say admirably, and for that service, you have paid my bills. Nothing more. If you continue to insist that I am your wife, then legally you must pay your wife's expenses—and I am certain, I can spend enough that you will regret keeping me. Conversely, if you wish to be free of me, but you wish to avoid paying a settlement, you could show me to the door, with no settlement, no clothing, and no means of support other than what I have left from your father and what I can create from my own ingenuity. That would be your right, but again, it will come at a cost. Neither of us wishes for a scandal. No, the best course is the one I have proposed: United, we petition the courts for a ruling. They will find the marriage invalid—because it is. You will give me the modest settlement I've requested, and I will retire to my own life. It might take some months, but your rank will redeem you. Soon you will find that you are invited to every dinner and ball by every eligible debutante's family. My proposal is a reasonable response to an unusual situation. To show you are also reasonable, accept the proposal."

Harrison felt stunned. It was a different argument than he expected, but one that showed a fire in his wife that he had not seen before. He'd seen glimpses of her wit in the music room. But this was different; here he saw a fully formed, deliciously seductive brain. And he admired it. Had he seen this woman at his marriage, he might have come home to spar with her before. But he hadn't allowed himself to see anything but his own righteous anger.

"If you want me to agree to present a unified front to the courts, then make it worth my while."

"I never knew you to be a blackguard." She looked surprised, then resigned.

"You misunderstand me. Certainly I find the thought of once more enjoying the pleasures of your . . . company . . . quite appealing. But my proposition has nothing to do with mere physical entertainments."

"What do you want?"

"I want time. I need to conclude some business too sensitive to endanger by a scandal surrounding my marriage. I wish for you to do nothing, to make no changes, to remain here on the pretense of being my wife."

"How long?"

"Till the end of the special session."

"That's three, perhaps four months."

"But in the end you get your reasonable solution: the settlement you've requested and my agreement before the courts. But I want one more thing. Until we separate, it must appear to anyone who observes us that we are a devoted couple." Harrison found himself surprised at his own words, but he let them stand.

"Why would I agree to that? It will only make the scandal greater when our marriage is declared invalid."

"I am not saying that I wish to remain married. I only wish to be certain that we have not taken one hasty decision and replaced it with another."

"Six years, Harrison. There is nothing hasty about this decision."

"I don't wish to argue, Olivia. I simply need time. If you are to leave, I need to be tutored in the status of the estate and its tenants. It will make that tutoring easier if the tenants merely believe I have finally come home, not that I am about to set you aside on a legality." It was true and wasn't, but what mattered was that she believed it.

"But you are doing nothing. The marriage is invalid."

"And yet my father is the one who arranged the marriage, so any criticism of its forms will fall to his—and by extension, my—door. If I am to agree to your settlement, I must have this time to learn the estate and its functioning without the specter of scandal hanging over my every decision."

"Of course." Her voice was slightly less cold. "I'm relieved to hear you consider the needs of the estate. It deserves an engaged lord of the manor."

"Then, tomorrow, I would like to review the estate accounts. Will you show them to me?"

"I will put the steward at your disposal. He's a fine man—the son-in-law of your father's manager, Herder."

"No, Olivia. I would like *you* to give me the benefit of your experience." He watched her stiffen at the familiar name, and he resented again that she allowed everyone else the use of it, but not him. "It's the least you can do for leaving me."

She crossed her arms over her chest. "Meet me in the morning room tomorrow."

"One more thing. I'd also like to remain as one of the scholars for a little while at least, to see from the inside, as it were, how the program works."

"I will inform them that you will be working among them."

"No, I mean that I would like to remain Mr. MacHus."

"You wish for me to lie to them."

"No, I wish simply for you to not inform them."

"Is there a difference?"

"Yes. In one case you are asked to play an active role in a deception; in the second, you simply omit to answer a question that no one is asking. Besides, as you have just told me so explicitly, this is my house, and you have no standing here."

"And to think I once believed I might love you, given time and mutual interests."

He ignored her words, and what they stirred within him. "Do we have an agreement?"

She shook her head in disbelief and frustration. "I agree to teach you about the estate, but I will have to consider the rest. I'm not certain I can pretend a devotion I do not feel and have never been given cause to develop."

As it always did, the dream came to torment her shortly before dawn. When she awoke, she would remind herself that the dream only came when she felt unsettled or insecure—that her conflict with Harrison had reminded her of all the ways her security depended on someone else and not her own actions. But until she awoke, she was a child again, not more than five or six, and her father was gone.

She tugged her knees into her chest and pulled the thin blanket up over her shoulders. She wouldn't cry. She wouldn't. But the tears streamed down her cheeks whether she wanted them to or not. She brushed them away with an angry swipe of the back of her hand.

Nothing of his was left. Not his best suit, or his second best one, or the boots she kept polished and shining for him in the corner by the cot.

Before the empty hearth, on a three-legged stool, she could see the small beaded reticule he'd given her for her sixth birthday. His little lady, all grown up he'd called her, and she'd stood extra tall. Beneath it was the letter he'd pressed into her hands three days before. "Now, keep this safe for me, just until I return." She could read the name on the front: Lord Walgrave.

She'd flung the letter to the floor and wrapped her arms around his knees. "I want to go with you! You!"

He'd put his hand on her head, brushing back the hair from her face. "Ah, sweeting, it won't be more than a day or two. I've left you tinder and some bread. Wait for me like you always do."

She'd felt the rising panic in her stomach as she always did when he left. The bile tasted strong on her tongue.

"You know what to do?" He waited for her answer.

"Stay in the cottage. Hide if someone comes by. If they find me, run for the forest and hide until they leave."

"Good girl, sweeting."

But a day or two had lengthened into three, then five, then seven. He'd never been gone so long, not without telling her at the start and making sure she had enough provisions.

She pressed her hand into her stomach. Hunger had

burrowed its way into her belly and spent each day trying to gnaw its way out. The bread—rationed out so carefully—had lasted only four days. When she'd run out of the tinder he'd left, she'd collected sticks in the woods. But yesterday the snow had come down thick, and she'd run out of kindling. The room was cold, so cold. She wore both her dresses and both pairs of socks.

She slid her body down into the center of the cot and curled into herself, trying to find some warmth. He'd come back. He always came back.

The dream always ended then—on the sickening realization that her father would not return. That as much as she loved him, he had abandoned her.

Chapter Seventeen

Olivia sat in the morning room, waiting for Harrison to come for his morning coffee. The night before, in her study, she had laid out the ledgers in which she recorded expenses and profits for each aspect of the estate. She even provided her receipts, wanting him to know how hard she'd worked to keep his estate running smoothly and well. But it had made her melancholy. When she'd placed the estate ledgers and the folders of receipts on the desk, she had torn out the pages on which she'd calculated the size of her settlement. She'd done it a dozen different ways: a small cottage, a larger house, a house abroad, servants, no servants, etc. She'd anticipated every possible budget, from Harrison giving her nothing to Harrison giving her the full amount she'd requested. The full amount was more than she needed in any of her calculations, but it was the amount that she imagined his friends and solicitors would find appropriate for a woman of her former rank.

She had no interest in remaining on the estate, but she didn't wish to leave her home either. It was a difficult position, for no matter which choice she made, she would be left unsatisfied in one way or the other.

Outside the window, the resident scholars were taking

their morning constitutional in the garden. The scholars exercised for twenty-one minutes exactly (a number Partlet and Lark had established through some logical syllogism based on the longevity of pigeons). Their routine was unvarying, a circuit from the lodge through the kitchen garden and back again, while performing an exercise with their arms and legs that Quinn said was based on the movement of the stars. As she watched them wave their arms and lift their knees high, Olivia realized that she didn't want to say goodbye to them just yet. Harrison's proposal appealed to her because it meant she could delay saying goodbye to her scholars so soon, but she still would have to do it sometime. Was it better to act precipitously or delay?

As it was, nothing had yet gone as she had planned. She'd imagined a clean break. Send Harrison the letter, file the claim, wait for the determination of the court, and leave. But even so, she'd held the papers her solicitors had drawn up for a month before steeling her heart to send them to Harrison, and she'd almost called the mail carrier back a dozen times before he walked out of sight. If she hadn't grown to care for Harrison in that wedding fortnight long ago, she might have been able to remain his countess. But somehow it felt like a betrayal of herself, of Harrison, and even of Sir Roderick to remain when he could never love her.

And what damage could that do to her heart? She'd waited for him for six years on the basis of a fortnight's acquaintance. What other foolishness would seem reasonable after three months of pretended devotion? She couldn't do it, as much as she might wish to find herself in his arms again.

No, since her marriage, she'd been in stasis, always waiting for Harrison. Even Odysseus's patient wife had had suitors during her twenty-year vigil. Olivia often wondered what Penelope had thought during those years, but the writer of the *Odyssey* had been uninterested in a woman's perspective. What happens, men, when you leave a wife behind for twenty years? Will you come home to discover her faithful to your memory, like Penelope? Or plotting your murder, like Clytemnestra? Olivia had drawn a mental line with Penelope at one end and Clytemnestra at the other, and at the end of each day for a year she'd plotted her position. When the dots fell consistently at Clytemnestra's end of the line, she knew she needed to make a change. She'd begun to write, some time later she'd become HG, and a little later she'd renewed her contact with Mentor. Before, as a governess, Olivia had given the Home Office eyes and ears in the homes of foreign aristocrats like Baron Ecsed. This time, Olivia used her essays to promote the public good, even when that meant helping Mentor identify traitors among her English correspondents.

The scholars began their strange ostrich walk back to the lodge, and Olivia looked at the clock. One minute. Where might Harrison be?

Harrison settled himself at the desk in Olivia's study, having borrowed a set of keys from Herder's son-in-law. He'd risen early and, still smarting at Olivia's friendship with the parson, he'd written a letter to Aldine, asking his solicitor to investigate both the parson and the scholars. In particular, Harrison asked Aldine to recommend measures to limit their influence on the estate and its reputation, even if that extended to closing the library and dismissing the scholars. He'd written *estate*, but he meant Olivia. He'd sealed his letter with a smug satisfaction and carried it to Herder's for Walker to post. He still had an hour to review the materials before his meeting.

But he found himself pondering instead his conversation

with Olivia on the previous day. He'd come to realize that he had made a tactical error early in their marriage. His father had assured him he'd chosen a practical woman for him, and as a result, in every communication, practicality was all he saw. But what place does a record of crop rotations leave for demonstrating an agile wit? Now, having lost her, he was intent on discovering all those things about her he'd never seen.

Perhaps that was the reason he'd asked Olivia not just to remain his wife until the end of the special session but also to pretend marital devotion. Perhaps he'd hoped that by acting as if she loved him, she might discover some affection for him after all, might feel a fraction of what he'd felt for her so quickly six long years ago. But that was the question, wasn't it: Could pretend devotion become real love?

He'd spent years protecting himself from Olivia and from the memory of her face. But now he could imagine nothing else. Olivia was not a traditional English rose, but he found her beauty enchanting. He always had. It had been part of the problem in the marriage. He'd feared that if he opened his heart to her, even a little, he would find himself bound to her not just in the law, but body and soul. And then he would run the risk of turning into his father, who, having lost his loves and his dreams, surrounded himself with useless objects, entertaining himself by manipulating the lives of others.

The clock chimed on the mantel, and he shook off his reverie. If he were to review her records before their meeting, he had to begin.

Before him lay several ledgers, the figures all entered into carefully ruled columns. Beneath each ledger was a folio containing receipts and invoices to match the ledger entries.

The completeness gave him pause. Eventually, of course,

he would have asked for supporting documents in order to audit the ledgers. But for Olivia to have provided them from the first suggested much about her idea of him. Too much. He would have liked to think she thought him thorough and careful, but more likely she imagined him petty. The thought disturbed him. But when did he concern himself overmuch with the feelings of those he was investigating?

At the word *investigating*, he caught himself. He hadn't intended—at least not consciously—to investigate her. But he couldn't set aside his conviction that he'd seen her in London and that she'd run from him. The housekeeper had insisted Olivia was at the estate on that day, but the housekeeper was loyal to Olivia. All the servants were. It was another reason that he needed for her to remain at the estate as his countess a little longer. It would make taking over the management of the estate difficult if they all felt she had been wrongly displaced.

He forced the thoughts away. He would address the attitudes of the servants when the time came. At this moment, he needed to discover all that he could about the management of his estate. *His estate*—the words still gave him no pleasure. Once again he felt the tightening of a noose around his neck. This was his estate, these were his people, and he would have to be part of their lives. Laugh at their jokes, send gifts when they married or bore children, grieve with them when they lost a child, a spouse, or a parent.

It was the engagement with the people, not the estate itself, that felt suffocating. He had inherited so few of his father's and his mother's skills. His father could talk to a stone, and the stone would talk back. His mother's compassion and foresight had made her universally beloved. Guilt pressed heavy on his conscience, consuming him as it always did. As a coddled and cosseted boy blindsided by grief, he had taught himself to be impervious to doubt, to remorse, to pain. To love. But he hadn't been impervious to Olivia, or her letter saying she was leaving him. If he had been, he would have stayed in London, where it would be easier to pursue his suspicions about An Honest Gentleman.

He shook the thought away. He was torn as usual between obligations—between his duty to the estate and his duty to the nation. Olivia managing this estate had allowed him to devote himself to his career with the Home Office. Perhaps if he could make her happier—promise to visit and to take her to London, even give her children—she might consider staying on as his countess and continue managing the estate. But he wondered if that was even a reasonable thought. The Olivia who explained the legalities of their marriage was unlikely to be easily swayed.

Once more he forced his attention back to the estate records—a task he could manage. The stack in the center related to the kitchen. The week's menu sat on top, with a brief note carefully lettered at the bottom: "One additional scholar this week." Harrison harrumphed. Had she written it before or after she had discovered he was MacHus? If Olivia expected him to take over the management of the estate, then he would begin with the menu.

He focused on the orders for foods not grown on the farm, and their cost.

He read over the meals. Crimped Cod, Curried Rabbit, Roast Suckling Pig, Jugged Hare, Vol-au-Vent of Pears, Cabinet Pudding, Fenberries, Pineapple.

Pineapple? He followed the entry to the right. At *two guineas*? That was more costly than a scullery maid for six months! He crossed it out and moved to the next item.

The menu was odd. But with a tweak or two, here and there, he could make it more to his taste. He began adding, deleting, and altering as he moved through the week's meals. Five minutes later, he was pleased with his work.

Having placed his imprint on the kitchen, he moved on

to the stack of papers related to the estate produce, then to the tenantry. In each case, he made small but deliberate changes. He kept two lists—specific questions for which he wanted specific answers, and larger issues he wished to investigate himself. Already he was making the estate his own.

A footman—perhaps eleven or twelve years old—came to the doorway. Seeing Harrison behind the estate desk, he blanched and began to back away. Harrison called him back.

"May I be of help?" Harrison tried to make his voice warm and gentle.

"Cook needs this week's menu." The boy remained, but his body was poised for flight.

"Let me see." Harrison dug out the menu. "I believe this is it." The footman took the menu and ran.

Harrison had only just returned to his other piles, when Olivia entered the room. Her morning dress was simple, a white muslin that hugged her body, caressing each curve. Uncovered, her hair was pulled back into a loose bun. Tendrils fell in soft ringlets around her face. What would it feel like to loosen her hair and bury his fingers in those curls? To kiss those full lips? His heart beat faster at the thought. Somehow his body couldn't accept that she wasn't his. But he tamped it down. He needed to gain her agreement to his proposition, and he would do that by making their time together agreeable.

Her eyes looked at the clock on the mantel. Five minutes after their meeting time.

"I waited for you in the morning room." Her voice seemed almost tender.

"I thought we could meet more usefully if I had reviewed the information in advance." He felt almost sheepish. He'd avoided the morning room deliberately.

"Of course." She inclined her head slightly in acceptance,

then pulled a chair to the side of the desk. "I thought we would begin with the estate's crops, particularly those we send to market. It was the stack on the far left."

He lifted the pile and placed it between them. "I have listed several questions already."

"Then we should start with those. May I see your list?" She read his questions carefully. "I'm pleased you are taking the estate's management so seriously."

"You have always managed the estate with great skill. I would be a fool not to learn from your experience."

A tap at the door drew their attention. The housekeeper looked from Olivia to him, and back to Olivia.

"My lady, you are needed belowstairs." The housekeeper looked uncomfortable, even sheepish. Harrison was immediately suspicious. "It's Mr. Stanley. He's telling stories of his experiences in Queen Catherine's court."

"Oh, dear. I'll be there in a moment."

The housekeeper melted from the room.

"What did you do?" Olivia's eyes were narrowed in suspicion.

"Me? Do?" Harrison held his palms out. "I don't even know Mr. Stanley."

"Gilbert Douglas Stanley III?" Olivia repeated the name as if doing so would jog Harrison's memory.

"Is he one of the scholars?"

"Yes and no. He arrived years ago as a scholar." Olivia began searching the desk. "But over time, he's become our cook. Where in these piles did you move the menu?"

"The menu?" Harrison shifted uncomfortably in his seat.

"Yes. It was here last night." She worked slowly through each stack of papers.

"I gave it to the footman perhaps twenty minutes ago."

She sat back in her chair and studied his face. "Please tell me you made no changes."

"Why would he give you a copy of the menu if he didn't expect changes?"

"You made changes." She stared at him unblinking. "How many?"

"Not so many. I retained the dishes themselves, but I re-arranged the meals in which some occurred. I reduced the amount of port and increased the claret. With the wars over, choosing Portuguese wines over French is no longer a matter of patriotism."

As he outlined his changes, Olivia covered her face with her hands and shook her head slowly.

"Finally, I eliminated something called a Crown Jewel Tart."

"Oh. Lord. No." She rose, but pointed him back to his seat. "Stay here. I'll return shortly."

"I would like to accompany you. Meet the chef, hear his complaints. Surely I can explain my preferences." Surely this wasn't so difficult.

"That would be unwise. Mr. Stanley has very particular ideas about food, developed after years of travel around the globe. He has supplemented that travel with investigations into the recipe books of every manor house from here to Rome."

"But I insist."

"Come along, then." She was already walking away from him. "But don't speak—not unless you wish to be preparing all of our meals for the next month, while inter-viewing cooks."

"Have I told you, dear ones, about the day I first wore a hat?" The chef—Gilbert Douglas Stanley III—waved his arms, a spatula in one hand. "It was unfortunately cold that day in Queen Catherine's court when I was called upon to make my famous Crown Jewel Tart. I could only find a straw hat—because of course one must keep one's head covered to avoid the cold that causes consumption. We knew it was the cold that killed the poor footman—God rest his soul—so untimely a death, it was."

Harrison watched the chef with a sort of morbid awe. Stanley had wrapped a wool throw around his head, making him look like a mad peasant escaped from bedlam.

Harrison felt the heat of the kitchen, but the chef seemed unfazed, warming his hands in front of the oven door. When he saw Olivia, the man twisted, jumped, then pounced as if he were a giant predator waiting for a mouse.

"Mr. Stanley, I must apologize." Olivia approached Stanley slowly, as one would a rabid dog or a lion in the wild. "I had no intention of altering your menu in the slightest. You are, as always, our impresario of taste."

"Then how did it come to be changed?" One edge of the wool flopped in front of his left eye, but he didn't move it, merely tilted his head to regard her with his right. He looked like a giant, ill-dressed, one-eyed owl.

"My friend, Mr. MacHus here, wrote on the menu, because he was imagining how his own cook might prepare a menu close to yours. He made alterations because his cook is less skilled and his audience is less adventurous. But he didn't realize the menu as he adapted it would be returned to you."

"Is that true, MacHus?" Stanley pointed at Harrison with one crooked finger.

"Lady Walgrave is far too generous." Harrison ignored Olivia as she glared at him over her shoulder. "I might have hoped my cook could approximate your dishes, but the truth is no one who is not a master of the culinary arts could even hope to approach the originality of your design."

For a moment Harrison feared he might have misstepped. The tall man, scowling, turned away from Harrison and Olivia in a slow circle, his arms outstretched above his head. But then when his back was fully toward them, he leapt to face them again, smiling madly. "Apology accepted! Now to make my famous Crown Jewel Tart!"

Running across the kitchen, the chef grabbed a bowl of flour from the arms of one of the kitchen maids and held it out of her reach. "No, no, no. My dear, you cannot simply throw the butter and the flour together. The marriage of the ingredients must be harmonious, or my famous Crown Jewel Tart cannot be delightful. No, my dears, we must compose it happily of happy ingredients!" He wagged a long finger at a maid who stifled her laughter behind her apron.

"Do we know that the chickens were happy when they laid these eggs, dear ones? And were Eliza and Beth happy when they churned the butter?"

"Yes." The maids spoke in a giggly chorus.

"But what do we know of the mill? Was the grain crushed with the appropriate weight? Was the grinding of the grain evenly fine? No?" Stanley's voice was melodic. "My dears, listen: For my famous Crown Jewel Tart, you must use only the flour that has been milled in the morning by a fresh horse, and one who has been fed an apple before he begins so that he starts his work with a sweet taste in his mouth."

Harrison leaned into Olivia's ear. "Is he mad?"

"Quite," she whispered back. "But he is kind to the staff, and his food is divine. Whatever you do, never comment on his hat."

"What is his name again?"

"Gilbert Douglas Stanley III."

"Is there really another Gilbert Douglas Stanley?"

"We are afraid to ask, but the thought that there might be others—in a long line—boggles the mind."

"Are we happy?" the cook declaimed to his disciples.

"Yes."

"Then we must cook!"

The girls began to complete their tasks, as Stanley threw himself into a cooking frenzy only an artist of equal talent could understand.

Olivia motioned to Harrison to follow her, and they slipped out while Stanley was declaiming, "Walnuts on the bottom, then the fenberries, then the pineapple rings—but prettily, prettily!"

"We can count that as a disaster averted." Olivia led Harrison toward the servants' stairs. "You've tasted Stanley's meals; I'm sure you understand why we accept his eccentricities. But of course you might have different preferences for the kitchen."

Harrison kept his thoughts on that to himself, the constant jabs about his palate from friends like Palmersfield echoing in his head. "I can't imagine he would be able to find another place, as mad as he is."

Olivia looked surprised, then suspicious. "Do you have any idea how hard it is to retain a good cook? Or is your cook no better skilled than the person who darns your socks? Oh, never mind. You will learn soon enough the hazards of offending talented servants."

At the foot of the stairs, Mrs. Pier waited, a small, dirty boy by her side. "You are needed, Miss Livvy. This is Bertie, the Davis boy come for help."

Without hesitation, Olivia knelt before the child, no more than five or six, and began to ask questions in a low, gentle voice. Harrison could not hear what she said. But the boy's eyes never left her face, and when he began to cry, she wrapped him in her arms, petting his head, and cooing gentle words. When she stood, she never let go of the boy's hand, and the child buried his face in her skirt. He'd never wished to have a child, but seeing Olivia comfort the boy made him wonder briefly if he had been wrong.

Then, Harrison watched admiringly as Olivia marshaled her troops. She sent one footman to the pantry with Mrs. Pier, another to the stables to harness a wagon, and the third to the butler, telling him to find the boy—Bertie—a warm cot near the horses. She acted as efficiently as any general in Wellington's army. Only when Mrs. Pier returned with the maid who had unpacked his clothes did Olivia release the boy's hand, giving him into the care of the two women. He was most surprised when Pier—who he had believed a bitter shrew—held out three biscuits from the larder. The boy had taken them slowly, an action that tugged at Harrison's heart.

"We will have to continue our . . . discussion later." Olivia returned to his side. "His parents are sick."

"Might I accompany you?" He wanted to see more of this Olivia. "I might be of use."

She looked suspicious briefly, then recovered to respond graciously. "It is your estate. These are your people. If you wish to help, then you should."

Chapter Eighteen

When they reached the stable yard, a wagon was already loaded with three large baskets and a pile of woolen blankets. Olivia inspected the baskets, while a ruddy-faced man adjusted the saddles. Missing something she wanted, Olivia sent a groom back to the house.

"Mr. Davis rarely asks for help. I don't know what to expect, but I know it will be serious."

"You are going yourself? Why take such a risk?"

"I am not high-born, my lord. My own health is of little consequence to me if I preserve it by refusing to help those in need. However, we do not know what illness plagues them, and I would understand if you wished to remain here."

"I lived through the wars, Olivia. What have I not seen?"

"But *you* must consider the good of the estate, whereas I am the last of my line. Once I leave the abbey, if I die, no one will notice, and no one will be inconvenienced."

The sadness and truth of her sentiment struck him profoundly. He too was the last of his line, and he'd felt a similar recklessness.

"Even if I have inherited this"—he extended his hand

to the abbey—"we are alike in that. No one will much regret my passing."

Something indecipherable flickered in her eyes, and he started to say more. But the stable master joined them.

"All's ready, Miss Livvy." Calder looked Harrison over suspiciously. "Would you like one of the grooms to escort him back to the house?"

"No, Mr. MacHus will be going along."

"Of course, Miss Livvy." The ruddy-faced man helped Olivia onto the wagon.

When she lifted the reins, Harrison was startled. He had not expected Olivia to drive herself.

He pulled himself up beside her. When she saw he was seated, she pulled from the yard with a speed that surprised him.

"So fast?" His words were lost in the rumbling of the wagon on the road.

She guided the rig skillfully, if terrifyingly fast. None of the young rakes who raced their curricles around Hyde Park could approach her in either daring or expertise. Even at the curves where he had to hold on to his seat to remain in place, she never lost control of the wagon or the horses.

Almost an hour later, she pulled the wagon to a stop.

The cottage was barely habitable. A large tree limb had fallen on the roof, caving it in at the corner. Two windows were filled with dirt and stone to block the winter air. Before he could stop her, Olivia jumped to the ground.

"This isn't my land." Harrison looked around with relief.

"No, your neighbor, Lord Heron, has been running this estate into the ground for almost a decade."

"But if it isn't my land, then these are not my people." He jumped down beside her.

She looked at him with one eyebrow raised and walked to the back of the wagon.

He followed. "Of course we will help. I only meant that Heron is responsible for his cottagers' well-being. This level of disrepair is criminal."

"It's a responsibility he has grown accustomed to shirking. And little that a lord does is criminal—short of murder, and sometimes not even then." She pulled one of the baskets out and settled it on her hip. She reminded him of an Amazon, defiant and strong. "Would you prefer to wait in the wagon?"

"Of course not." He lifted one of the other baskets. "What do you wish for me to do?"

"Watch for the dog." She started for the house. "We had to circle round by the bridge, but Bertie was able to cross the river—it's shallow enough here, even for a boy his age. But even at that, he left home hours ago."

The door stood ajar. "Davis? Polly?" Hearing no answer, she pushed the door inward with her foot. "It's Lady Walgrave. Bertie came to the abbey for help."

Only silence met them. She set her basket on the ground. Her face when she lifted it toward him was grim. She called the cottagers' names once more, then stepped toward the door.

"Let me. I think we know what we are going to find." He set his basket on the ground next to hers, then stepped ahead of her into the one-room cottage. A rank smell, fetid and rotting, made him cover his nose.

In front of him, a man slumped over the table, his eyes staring. Beyond him on the cot, a woman lay motionless, a rat sitting on her chest. Her arm hanging off the cot's edge was covered with open sores. Harrison backed out of the room, just as Olivia began to enter.

He caught her in his arms, stopping her. "There's nothing to do. They probably sent Bertie to the abbey because they knew they were dying."

"No!" She pushed past him, then seeing Bertie's dead parents, she turned her face away. She pressed her hand against her mouth to hold back a sob. Harrison, wanting to comfort her, wrapped her in his arms and led her out into the sunshine. Once outside, she leaned her head against his chest as she wept quietly. He wanted her never to move.

"He's just a little boy," she said, as if to herself. She brushed tears away with the back of her hand, then straightened her shoulders and walked out of his arms toward the house.

Harrison, stunned, caught her hand. "What are you thinking? The mother has the pox. We have to burn the cottage, not go inside for a tour."

"He needs something to remember them by." She looked so determined, he wondered how old she was when she lost her parents. Suddenly, he felt guilty to have taken her tiger's-eye. If it was her only memento of her father, taking it had been cruel. Somehow he would make it up to her.

"Then I'll go. Stay here."

He wrapped a cloth around his nose and mouth to reduce his chance of infection, then entered. The rat glared at him, before scurrying away. Harrison's stomach turned. The Davises had kept their cottage neat and clean, but even so, he saw nothing a child might cherish.

He returned to the yard, empty-handed, knowing Olivia would object. He'd seen the determination in her eyes. But she was gone.

He turned in each direction looking for a sign of her. Nothing. As long as she stayed out of the cottage, she was in little danger. But where could she have gone? Just when he was about to call her name, she appeared around the side of the cottage.

"Harrison, I need your help." She grabbed one of the baskets and disappeared again.

At the back of the cottage, he found her lying on her stomach facing into a small shed. The basket was open at her side. What was she doing?

"Shhh. Don't scare him." She looked intently into the dark.

He saw no other option; he lay on the ground beside her. "Him?"

"When Bertie's parents fell ill, they made him stay here. It's filled with blankets—he's been quite warm—and some toys from his father. I've put them in the basket. Do you hear that?"

"What?" Harrison was rarely taken off guard, but this version of Olivia—sympathetic and daring—was baffling and fascinating all at once.

"That! Listen."

Harrison waited, unmoving, then he heard it, a soft whimper or perhaps a grunt.

"I think it's a puppy or perhaps a piglet. I've been throwing bits of food in to tease it out."

"Have you considered that it might be something less pleasant? A skunk, vole, weasel?"

"Shhh. You'll scare him."

He fell silent as she threw a handful of crumbs to the edge of the shed.

A very long time later, after the damp of the earth had thoroughly soaked through Harrison's waistcoat, a small red fox pup crawled to the edge of the shed. Olivia reached out slowly and scratched behind its ears, then patiently waited until it allowed her to scoop it up.

When she rose, the pup cradled against her chest, Harrison could see she'd been lying on a blue blanket from the wagon.

"You had a blanket!"

"And?" She looked at him as if he were mad.

"So, you're not wet."

"Wet?"

"You weren't lying in the dirt, so you aren't wet."

She looked puzzled, then amused. "I suppose you are cold as well."

"Yes, I'm wet, and I'm cold . . . and all for a fox who might well be shot in Heron's next hunt." He shook his head in disbelief.

"Oh, no. We're taking the pup back to the estate. Without his parents, Bertie is going to feel lost and alone. I won't deny him his pet." Her face was delightfully animated.

"Wait. Is Bertie staying at the estate?"

Her face fell, and he wished he had said nothing. "I forget that I haven't the right to make those decisions. It is, of course, up to you. But Heron will put the boy in a work-house. That's why his parents sent him to the abbey."

Harrison wondered if hers was the zeal of one orphan for another, and found he could not deny her.

"Then I suppose we should find a way to get that pup home safely."

The smile on her face was worth the damp and the cold.

Chapter Nineteen

"Where are we?" A wiry man looked out the window of the carriage. "We should be smelling peat by now."

"I changed the plan. I've secured us lodgings at an inn not far from here." Archer leaned back into the shadow, the embers in his pipe providing the only light in the coach. "Our gypsy has continued her investigations, ignoring your warning. It seemed wise to follow her home."

The wiry man rubbed his shoulder, remembering the hard shove from the actress's rescuer. "I told her what you said—that she wouldn't be the only one to suffer if she kept looking into other people's business and that sometimes secrets are best left as secrets. But we were interrupted before I could tell her the rest."

"That's unfortunate. We will have to try again."

"I don't understand the game you are playing. We join forces with that madwoman. We hire Charters and his thugs. All to find out which journalist is asking all the wrong questions. But when we find out who she is and where she lives, you try to warn her off. If she keeps digging, Calista or one of the others will likely kill her. Why not let them?"

"I believe we can resolve this peaceably, Brinker." Archer began to say more, then stopped.

"She didn't seem peaceable." Brinker chewed on a bit of a stick he used to pick his teeth. "Did I tell you she threatened me with her penknife? As if she thought she could best me."

Archer laughed slightly. "She likely could. She takes after her mother. A hellion, that one was, with a pretty ebony-handled penknife she carried in her boot."

"I thought you said she lost her mother in infancy."

"She did. But the resemblance is uncanny—even under all that paint, no one could mistake it. When I saw her on the street last year, I thought I'd seen a ghost." The man's tone grew thoughtful, perhaps even wistful. "The cheekbones, the lips, the hue of her skin, that's all her mother. In the right circles, she'd be recognized in an instant. Luckily those circles are far from here."

"Do you want me to try again? Make it clear that if we found her, others can too?"

"For now, we'll wait, perhaps on reflection she'll take our advice. Ah, we are here. They should have rooms under your name."

Brinker hopped from the carriage and pushed the door shut. Inside, Archer sat silently. He opened the window and rapped his pipe against the coach door to empty the spent tobacco. Then reaching into his boot, he pulled out a penknife and caressed its ebony handle.

Chapter Twenty

Olivia approached Sir Roderick's room with Harrison close on her heels. She unlocked the door with one of the keys hanging from a watch-chain at her waist. An old-fashioned device, he noticed, like his grandmother's chatelaine.

"You will find your father's room much as he left it. His private papers and his favorite books remain here. If a scholar wishes to use one of Sir Roderick's books, I remove it for the day, then return it before I retire." She directed him to enter before her.

The room was recently aired, the windows open wide. Even so, for a moment, Walgrave imagined he smelled a hint of his father's favorite tobacco, sweet-scented and mild. The furniture was heavily carved, a vestige of times past. Unlike his room in the tower, everything remained as it had been the last time he'd visited.

He walked in, measuring his steps with memories. "You have been very scrupulous. I should thank you."

"I preserved this room for myself, not you. Sometimes when I need advice on how to manage some aspect of the estate, I come in here to think it through." She placed her hand on the table, rubbing the wood absently with her thumb. "I sit here, and I imagine what he might have done if he were making the decision."

Her obvious affection for his father grated. "And does his ghost speak to you?" His words sounded caustic and dismissive, even to his own ears.

Her reaction was telling: a quick roll of her eyes, a slight disapproving nod of her head. "As I said in the music room, every house has ghosts. But while I would welcome your father's, he does not visit me. You are the one he haunts."

"What do you mean?" Harrison bristled.

"Your anger. You carry it everywhere. But I think I have the means to help you exorcise his ghost." She opened the tall wardrobe in the near corner. "In the last months of his life, he dictated to me a journal of sorts." She held out a volume in a limp vellum binding. "These were his last thoughts for you. I recorded the words as exactly as I could, hoping you might hear his voice once more."

He took the book from her hands, not certain he wanted to untie the cover.

"I'll be in my dressing room if you have need of me." She walked to the door adjoining his father's rooms, and he raised one brow quizzically. "In your father's last illness, I removed to your mother's room to be close to him." She regarded him closely. "He loved you, you know. You might not have felt it was love, but he loved you all the same."

Harrison sat at the table at the foot of his father's bed and opened the diary. But at the first entry he stopped cold.

I did what I thought was best, son, in marrying you to Olivia. I hope you have come to see the wisdom of that choice.

He flung the book across the room. Wisdom? He had never hated his father as much as he did when he'd discovered his father's marriage plot.

"How did you do it?" His voice had been cold, and he'd felt a bone-deep anger that he could still taste, even after all these years.

His father hadn't answered, only twisted his cane back and forth.

"I would bet on senna and valerian—two of your favorite remedies." Harrison worked out the details as he spoke. "That would explain my sudden illness and my resulting stupor. Your men had only to wait, then help me into a carriage."

"I've begged you to come home for months. I even offered to come to your club in London." His father's voice was quiet, his face worn and tired. "You left me no choice."

"Forcing me to marry isn't going to bring them back. Mother, Celia, my brothers—they will all still be dead. Marriage only gives me more to mourn—a wife, children."

"It's not about mourning, boy. It's about living. You've been adrift, your eye always on the horizon. Marriage will settle you, tie you to this land. You are my heir, and I want to die knowing you will honor your responsibilities. A wife, children, that is your future."

"The world is at war, and you want me to marry, have children, live a small life on a country estate. I want to live a big life, whether that's abroad or in Parliament."

His father had rammed his cane into the floor. "Big? What sort of criterion is that? What is a life of responsibility to others, to your family, to your tenants, if not a big life?" His father spat the word. "Here's my offer—it's the only one you will get—I'll let you go abroad, test your wings, have the Grand Tour, whatever you wish, but only if you honor my wishes in this. You must marry before you go." *The old man fell back in his chair, coughing, blood on his handkerchief.*

"My ship leaves in a fortnight, Father. I haven't time to court some miss and marry her in only fourteen days' time." As an afterthought, he offered a gesture of conciliation. *"If there were time, if some perfect miss wanted to marry me, then I would marry before I go. But there's no time, and there's no perfect girl."*

His father smiled, a smile that he'd seen too often, a smile that meant his father thought he had the game tied up. "I'm glad to hear that, boy, because I've managed it already. I've got a nice young miss for you to marry, even a pretty one. Knew her father years ago. All the agreements have been signed, got a special license from the bishop. All we need is the ceremony, and the parson comes tomorrow."

Harrison had felt his heart grow hard. "Father, that's not fair to the chit or to me. Let me come back in three years' time. I'll court her, and if we suit, I'll marry her."

"I'm dying, son." His father's voice had softened, and Harrison had turned away so his father wouldn't see his tears. "I won't be alive in three years' time, and before I die, I need to know you are settled. I haven't asked you for much. I've let you learn what you wanted, go to the schools you wanted, even to Cambridge—though, for the life of me, I don't know why you had to have that school instead of Oxford with your brothers. Now I'm letting you sail around the Continent, while there's a bloody war in France. I want you to have a reason to live through whatever it is you have planned."

Harrison looked up, trying to read the old man's face.

"Don't think you've fooled me pretending to be all foppish and silly this last year. I'm not sure exactly what you are planning, but I've still enough friends in the government to confirm something's afoot. I've even heard

your berth is on a navy ship, but you know I would never allow that."

Harrison sat down, surprised . . . and not. "Then you should understand why I don't wish to marry." He leaned forward, meeting the old man's eyes, blue like his own. "The wars rage on apace. Why saddle a young woman with a husband who might not return?"

"You can marry—and you will—or you won't go." His father's voice grew hard, harder than Harrison had ever heard. "The old king might be ill, but he remembers an old friend."

"You can't expect an heir—not in only a fortnight."

"It's not an heir. It's you. You need ballast, something to give you weight. A wife, the possibility of children—that's the cure for your wandering. And Olivia, my boy, she doesn't know it yet, but she's the kind of woman who makes civilizations tumble. I've never met a woman who could match you but her. Meet her. If you would only give her a chance, you might find you want to marry her."

Harrison looked at the door to his mother's, now Olivia's rooms, and he picked up his father's journal from where he'd flung it. The cover was bent back, and the first pages torn, but he smoothed them out. Perhaps it was true; perhaps there had been wisdom in his father's choice for him. Olivia was right as well: He needed an exorcism, but reading his father's journal wasn't the only way to do it.

Olivia stood facing an open trunk, her back to the door. Beside her a tall glass-fronted bookcase held a collection of . . . Harrison squinted . . . rocks? It couldn't be, not when she was wrapping each one with the care one would give one of the crown jewels.

She was half turned away from him, giving him ample

time to admire her form, her bearing. His eyes caressed the gentle line that led from her neck to the curve of her shoulder, then down the length of her torso until it flared smoothly at her hips. When she bent down to tuck the object in a safe position in the trunk and her skirt clung to her rounded bottom, he felt the ancient pull to take her in his arms. To convince her to remain his countess, he would need the careful words of a seasoned orator, not the heedless lust of a hot-blooded boy.

He turned to look at the room. Once again, nothing was the same. His mother's wedding gift from his father had been furniture, and she'd chosen frivolous rococo pieces with dragon-headed finials, pagoda shapes, and painted monkeys. *That damn chinoiserie*, his father had called it, but he'd never refused her.

Olivia's taste ran to simpler lines. A Pembroke table with reeded legs sat near an elegant, almost Egyptian-inspired settee. Incongruously, she'd kept his mother's heavy tester bed, but replaced the curtains with lighter colors and more symmetrical patterns.

"You have refurbished the room."

"Ah, there you are." Olivia shut the doors to the cabinet holding her collection. "When I moved into her room, your father insisted on replacing the furniture. He claimed it was part of my wedding gift, allowing me to feel the estate was my home. But, in truth, he wasn't ready for someone else to use your mother's things. He loved her very much."

"We all did." He turned away from the sudden and unexpected well of grief. "She painted this room a cold slate-blue. This green is better, lighter, even sunny."

"Your father picked it. He hired a firm of colourmen from London to make recommendations, then he threw them all out. He mixed the paints himself from pigments he ordered from Ackermann's." She looked at the walls. "If we ever need to make a repair, we will simply have to begin again." She hesitated, then corrected herself. "I mean you, of course. It is hard to stop saying *we*."

"Then don't. Stop, I mean. We can work something out. Perhaps I could come to the estate more often, or you could come to London. We could have children."

She hesitated, then looked away.

He didn't press; he would convince her slowly. He walked to the window. The old dark brocaded curtains that had covered the window when he was a boy had been replaced with light-colored figural tapestries. "Let me guess: ancient mythology."

"That's not even a guess. The figures are all wearing classical robes. No, if you are to guess, you must pick the specific stories."

He held the tapestry out, intending to look at the images. But before he could answer, a towheaded child—not more than seven—ran through the courtyard. The little girl turned and waved at his window. He tried to breathe, but the wind had been struck from his lungs. It was a ghost, his childhood companion Trist, waving at him to come play.

"Harrison, are you well? Your face has gone quite white." Olivia followed his gaze out the window, then waved at the child. "That's Cora, Mrs. Pier's granddaughter. She attends the village school in the mornings."

"I thought she. . . ." He stood staring at the child by the servants' entrance, then shook himself. "She reminded me unexpectedly of a friend who died too young."

"You were close." It wasn't a question. Olivia stood at the window with him. The nearness of her, the sweet scent of her perfume, in a moment so fraught with grief, encouraged his confidences.

"More than that. Trist saved my life."

"She did?" Her voice carried all the surprise he'd expected. He'd never told anyone, not even Trist, how much he owed her. But now that he was home, it was inevitable that he would remember all of it. But just because the memories were inevitable didn't mean he had to bear them alone. Perhaps if he told Olivia, she might be less determined to leave. And he wouldn't have to spend the rest of his days missing her.

"My mother died from the whooping cough. For days, the coughs racked her body, turning her blue from lack of air. Between bouts, she would gasp for breath, until the next set of coughs began. Eventually exhaustion turned to pneumonia. I blamed—still blame—myself. I knew I was sick when I came home for the holiday, but I wanted to come home so desperately. I never fit in well at school, not even with the friendship of the Somervilles, and I thought it was merely a cold."

"From what your father told me about your mother, she would never have left you at school if you were sick. She would have demanded to retrieve you."

"She didn't like me being gone any more than I liked being away. After she died, I would stay here for hours on end, lying in her bed, praying that my coughs would take me as well. But they never did.

"My father had brought Trist home while I was still recovering from whooping cough. Bringing home strays, my mother would say, but she was dead by then. We'd met, but I was grieving, with little interest in a friend, though I believe that's what my father intended her to be. On that particular day, I was standing here wondering whether that tower there was tall enough to kill me quickly if I leapt from its top."

Olivia put her hand on his shoulder but said nothing, simply offered silent comfort.

"My father had been called to the fields, so I knew I would have time to steal up to the balustrade. Then I saw her, in the courtyard there." He pointed at a spot across the courtyard from the window. "She was so thin, with clothes bare and worn. She looked more alone than any person I'd ever seen. She was playing quoits and saw me in the window. She held out a disc, inviting me to play. I refused. I was still often racked by coughing fits when I exerted myself. But she didn't know I had been sick, and she simply shrugged, as if she never expected to be anything but alone. She turned back to the game, throwing one disc over the spike, then another, until she had no quoits left, then retrieving them all, she'd begin again."

"You must have been very lonely, if an invitation to quoits diverted you from suicide."

"That wasn't it. It was what happened next." He folded his arms over his chest, reliving the scene. "A large man rode into the carriage yard, and seeing her, flung himself down from his mount, yelling. She recoiled and ran to that door there, but it was locked. Then, she ran to that one. But the household had been given the day to watch the hunt, and all those doors were bolted shut. She looked up at me and mouthed just one word—*help*—before the man grabbed her and lifted her from the ground by one arm."

He waited for Olivia's next question, but she gave him only comforting silence. Eventually, he picked up the thread of his story. "I didn't know what I could do. But I had to intervene."

"You were a child. What could you do?" Her voice was quiet, thoughtful. He didn't look at her, not wanting to read pity for the melancholy boy he had been before he knew Trist.

"I was six. I could shoot. I took my father's dueling pistols from the box beside his bed, and I loaded one—two would have been too heavy. My hands shook as I poured the powder. I hurried down the stairs as fast as I could without triggering an attack, cradling the gun to my chest. I went out there." She followed the line of his finger.

"That was brave. You could have been hurt yourself."

"I was afraid, but not for myself—I'd already imagined my death fifty times that week. I was afraid of failing her." He turned back toward the window as if he were watching the play in his mind. "Apparently, her father had won a great deal of money by cheating at cards. The brute kept hitting her, first with the front, then with the back of his hand. He spaced out his words to accompany each blow. *You. Will. Tell. Me. Where. My. Money. Is.* I kept my breaths shallow—sometimes that helped—but I couldn't risk speaking. I found a handful of pebbles and threw them at his back, then I cocked and lifted the gun."

"The girl, Trist. What was she doing? Surely, she was fighting or screaming for help?"

"She said not a word. She simply clenched her eyes shut and bore each blow."

"Poor child. How did the man respond? Did he let her go?"

"Well, faced with a six-year-old holding a pistol at his chest, what could he do but surrender?"

"Is that what happened?"

"I saw his face. I think he was afraid that I would make a mistake and shoot him. He threw Trist against the wall, and she crumpled in a heap. Later, he told my father that he had no intention of harming us. But he wanted more than his money; he wanted to punish someone—anyone— for having been duped. I believe he would have beaten her to death the moment he gained the information."

"Did she know that? That by refusing to speak, she forced him to keep her alive?"

"I never asked. She remained on the ground for so long, I was afraid he'd hurt her badly. I kept backing away, making him follow me, to give her room to run, if she could. I kept willing her to look up. I wanted her to know that I was there to save her. And then she did. She opened her eyes, and our gazes met. She started toward me, crawling at first, then pulling her legs under her, she stumbled the rest of the way. I could feel the breath wheezing in my chest. I had only moments before I would be as useless to her as I had been for my mother. I held out the pistol to her, and she took it. Then I fell to the ground, coughs racking my body." He stopped, trapped in the dual losses of his mother and Trist. He crossed to the settee, not sure if his legs would hold him up through the remainder of the telling.

"And then?"

"She shot him. She raised her pretty chin with the bruises purpling her jaw, and pulled the trigger. The man howled in shock and pain, leaning over his leg, where a line of blood seeped through his fingers. Then she pulled me to my feet and dragged me, still coughing, back through the door I'd come through, and she braced a nearby chair below the handle."

"Was the shot enough to stop him?" Olivia sat on the edge of the bed across from him, listening intently.

"We didn't know. But I knew where to hide." He leaned back on the settee. Telling the story alleviated some of his guilt. "This house is filled with hidden rooms and secret passages. The shot would draw my father, so we only needed to hide. We came here."

"Here?" She looked startled. "There's a secret passage here?"

"And in the music room." He waited until she rolled her eyes, realization dawning. "These walls were painted with faux paneling and monkeys. One of the monkeys' tails, when pressed, opened a passageway to the nursery. My mother could sneak up to see us—or we could sneak down to be with her. Many a nursemaid was terrified to find us missing. Children of the Devil, one called us." Harrison walked to the corner the room shared with his father's old quarters. "It should be about here." With a click, the door opened.

"No. There is *not* a secret passage into my bedroom." She looked into the darkness with its spiderwebs hanging down, then drew back. "I hate cobwebs." She pressed the panel, sealing the door again.

"That was Trist's reaction. Apparently she could fire a gun at a man three times her size, but a dark passageway was terrifying."

"I know how she felt. It's the cobwebs. Dark is fine. Cobwebs mean spiders."

"I told her she wouldn't be safe if I started coughing. But she refused to leave me; instead, she gave me hard candy she'd gotten from the cook."

"And what did you learn from it?"

"Learn from it?"

"Yes. Did that day change you in some way? It must, for you to still remember it so vividly after all this time?" There was a hint of some emotion in her voice, but Harrison was too caught up in the past to be able to identify it.

"I suppose it taught me to be brave, even against incredible odds. It taught me to have the strength of my convictions. And it made me realize that in addition to adventure, I wanted my life to make a difference. To use whatever skills I had to help, as she helped me that day."

"That's a lovely legacy."

"I suppose it is." He had always known that Trist's bravery that day had been the standard by which he measured himself. How could he rest, comfortable on an estate, when a six-year-old girl had been willing to risk her life to save his? The fact that being around Olivia these past few days had left him questioning that standard was just one more blow to his carefully crafted world.

"Do you think you've honored that legacy? Have you been brave, Harrison—in all things?"

He stared at her, unable to speak for the tumult of emotions clouding his mind. With a resigned look on her face, Olivia turned away.

Harrison caught her hand, drawing her back to him. She wanted to resist, but she could not refuse. He'd been in her dreams, her thoughts, for years, and if she were to leave him, at least she might enjoy a kiss. He wrapped his arms around her as if trying to decide what to do next, and she nuzzled her face against his chest.

He raised her chin, looking into her rich brown eyes, waiting. She said nothing, only caught the bottom edge of her lip between her teeth. She saw desire flame in his eyes, then he lowered his lips slowly to hers. He kissed her gently at first, then more firmly. She matched the delicious pressure, opening her mouth to him, feeling the warmth of his tongue on the back of her teeth.

She felt his hands drift downward, until he cupped her bottom in his hands, warm and strong. Soon, all she could think of was the warmth of his mouth and the power of his arms. His kisses grew more insistent, and she matched him at every stroke of his tongue.

It wasn't wise. It was weakness. She had never been able to resist him, even from their first meeting. She was close to abandon.

"Miss Livvy." The knock on the door was soft, then louder. Livvy felt Harrison groan in her mouth. But the moment was gone. "Miss Livvy, you are needed."

She stepped out of his arms, and he turned toward the window. She felt a fool.

"Yes, Joan. One moment." She turned back to Harrison. "I think it would be best if you returned to your father's room."

Without speaking he left her, and the room grew suddenly cold.

Chapter Twenty-One

In the morning mail, Harrison had received a packet of papers from Mr. James, giving him the task of breaking the code that Lord Wilmot had sent home shortly before his death a year before. He had set himself to work immediately, taking a well-lit place at the long table in the middle of the library. But instead of focusing on the code, he found himself wondering—as he had for two days now—where Olivia had been hiding.

He wanted to apologize. Though he could never regret the kiss—except that it had ended too soon—he did not wish for Olivia to believe he'd sought consolation in her arms because she had been convenient. No, he had wanted her with every sinew of his being. But how to apologize for something he could not regret, except that it might have made Olivia uneasy.

But every time he looked for her, she was nowhere to be found, not in her study, or in the morning room, or in the library, or any of another dozen places. He had even stolen into the music room each night, hoping his music would call her to him. But she had not responded.

At the far end of the library, a workman was replacing some of the panes in the large window. And suddenly

Harrison knew where she was: the guest wing, unused because of repairs to the windows.

He returned his work to the brown paper wrapper and left it on the long table. It would be fine, he reassured himself. None of the scholars would look at another man's work, and if they did, they would find nothing but pages and pages of an undecipherable code.

Once in the guest wing, he found her quickly. The sound of laughter led him to the end of the corridor, where a salon for large dinner parties could be entered from any of four doors. He intentionally chose the door farthest from the laughter so that he could slip into the room unobserved.

Olivia, the parlor maid, and the housekeeper were giggling. In one of the pier glasses he could see Olivia's smile: mischievous but sweet. He had never seen her look so at ease. Of course, he'd denied himself any opportunity to experience such a moment.

Olivia sat behind a short table where she cut a heavy brocaded fabric. From the pile of cloth on the floor next to her seat, the maid was sewing what appeared to be new slipcovers for some chairs, and the housekeeper was applying what smelled suspiciously of horse glue to one of the seat bottoms.

"He was so embarrassed. But *later*, he asked if he could escort me home through the orchard." Herder's daughter, Harriet colored at the recollection.

"He's a handsome lad to be sure, and with fine prospects." Mrs. Pier nodded approvingly.

"Just a bit clumsy when it comes to talking to pretty young women, it seems," Olivia teased.

Strange behavior for a countess, making her own upholstery. The women were clearly friends, not a noblewoman and her servants.

He entered the room, and the women stopped talking.

The maid grabbed her sewing and the housekeeper her pot and brush, and within moments they both were gone. Olivia, however, kept moving the material on her table and cutting to the pattern he could see stenciled upon it.

He stood, not knowing what to say. If they were married, he might have offered a disquisition on the appropriate distance a countess would keep from her servants, but she claimed she was not a countess. And he couldn't truly bring himself to care about such social niceties. Besides, something in the set of her shoulders made him choose another tack.

"Have I not provided you with an adequate allowance? I would imagine there are plenty of craftsmen who would appreciate the trade."

"There are. But it seemed foolish to pay for a service that Harriet, Mildred, and I could do. Usually we would wait until after Christmas to do such work, but as I will be gone . . ." She let the words trail off.

"It's another one of the items on your list of things to do."

"Yes. One of the last. I should have the house in fine shape in another week or two."

"They seem to be more your friends than your servants."

The corner of her mouth lifted in a partial smile. "I have long considered them so."

He suddenly realized that he had never seen her visit or be visited. Certainly, she had gone to care for his tenants, but no one from the village had sent her an invitation, and as his presence was not yet known, there had been no invitations on his behalf. "But the estate is not so isolated that you would not have ample companions in the gentry. What of Squire Landry's wife and her daughters? Or the gaggle of widows in that manor house past the village? Do you not visit?"

She stopped cutting, and, looking into the distance, she

considered her answer. "The circle of village life is a small one, and its inhabitants often narrow and unforgiving."

"Did you offend them in some way?" He couldn't help the note of suspicion that colored his words, the closeness between her and the parson springing to mind.

"I haven't done anything to draw their disapproval. They have merely mirrored your distance."

That brought Harrison up short. "What do you mean?"

She sighed and looked into his eyes with a sort of plea, as if she wished to protect him. "It doesn't matter, you must know. I've had the scholars and the staff. I haven't been lonely."

"*What* do you mean?" He pushed the emphasis on the first word. He would not let her defer. "It's not necessary to protect me from the truth."

"It was widely known that your father forced the marriage, just as it was widely known that I had been employed as a governess. I was unknown, my family unknown, and I had stolen the possibility of one of their daughters marrying the earl. We still had invitations when your father was alive, but after . . ."

"After . . ."

"You remained away." She rose and walked away from him to the window. "And your absence raised questions. Eventually, someone spread the tale that some fault of mine kept you away. Your absence was interpreted as a punishment. The presence of the scholars only complicated matters, but even so, by the time your father died, the stories were already well rehearsed."

"You've been shunned."

"By all but the parson. He thought that his presence at dinners or our Wednesday meetings would signal that I had not committed some great sin that kept you away."

"But it hasn't worked."

She shook her head. "Sadly, no. It has only caused him to

have a string of complaints that he should not countenance my sin, nor lighten my punishment by entertaining me."

"I had no idea." He felt ashamed that he had been so disengaged, that he had simply done what suited his own purpose without considering what his actions signaled to others. What man leaves his wife to manage the vagaries of community life on her own, unless she had committed some transgression? No wonder they had thought his absence a punishment.

"It stung at first, but they were right. I wasn't of the gentry, and I certainly am no aristocrat. Besides, my interests never intersected well with theirs. With the scholars here, I've spent too many years in the company of intelligent, well-educated men, men who allowed me to speak my own mind, to pursue my own interests as they did theirs. It made me ill-suited to an afternoon discussing the latest French fashions, what color best complemented some young miss's complexion, or what soup would best go after fish."

"I never meant to punish you, Olivia. It wasn't your fault."

"No, you wished to punish Roderick, and I was simply an unfortunate bystander."

"All this time I thought you had a rich circle to keep you company. I never realized you would be alone."

"I have only been alone if you consider the company of your class to be the only one that matters. I've been well entertained and well loved. I will miss my little circle."

"Still, I wish I had known. It would have been an easy situation to redress."

"But an impossible letter for me to write without sounding petulant or demanding."

"You could have made a demand, Livvy." He let himself use the shortened form of her name, the syllables gentle on his tongue. "You were my countess."

The fact that she hadn't called upon him when she had every right to do so made him feel chastened. But, of course, she had no reason to trust him.

Coming home had been as difficult as he'd always imagined, but for far different reasons. Instead of feeling trapped by unwanted duties, Harrison found himself facing failure at every turn.

Mrs. Pier knocked on the door, and Harrison returned to the library with much to consider. All these years he had believed Olivia happy on the estate, only now to realize he'd had no reason but his own peace of mind to believe her so. Then to discover he'd sentenced her to a kind of prison! She'd made the best of it, but it would make persuading her to remain almost impossible.

When he entered the library, his stomach fell. The brown paper lay open in the middle of the large central table, and the papers spread out in short stacks across its length. Each scholar huddled happily over their own portion.

Harrison rubbed his forehead with his fingers, trying to determine how to react. Anger would only raise their interest.

Martinbrook welcomed him. "Oh, MacHus, you're here. This is very exciting."

"We didn't mean to open your packet. We thought it was the proofs Otley has been expecting, and we had all promised to help read them," Nathan explained with a bob of the head.

"Yes." "Yes." "Yes." Smithson's, Partlet's, and Quinn's heads bobbed in agreement.

"But when we saw the note, we realized this must be your friend who wanted your help with the newspapers," Otley explained. "And we thought it wouldn't hurt to try our hand at your latest puzzle."

"Note?" How could he have been so careless as to miss a letter?

"Yes, MacHus, you have a great correspondent." Partlet adjusted his monocle. "What a lovely game."

"Game?" Harrison tried to keep his tone level, but he was already baffled.

"Yes," offered Quinn absently, "here's the note that set up the rules." The portly man pushed a sheet toward him, never looking up from some calculations with his pencil.

"We're sure we can win . . . and wouldn't it please Miss Livvy for us to contribute something to our holiday feast?"

"Yes, she's always so generous."

"Yes." "Yes." "Yes." The heads bobbed one after another. He was so used to them now, he didn't even stiffen at the reference to his wife as *miss*.

He hadn't paid much attention to the letter in Mr. James's broad, distinctive hand, but he read it once more. It began without salutation.

Here's the puzzle I promised. I've sent it to the others—same rules apply. Whoever solves it first will get a Christmas ham, 50 pounds, and a box at Kean's next performance of Lear. *I've sent along all the materials that might help you solve it, but I make no promises that I've provided everything. But what sort of a puzzle would it be if I gave you all the parts?*

Harrison knew Benjamin well enough to hear the frustration and sarcasm, but on the surface the note could read just as the scholars had understood it. A game with a prize.

"The prizes are very generous. Your friend should have been more careful." Lark lowered his magnifying glass.

"Why?" Harrison scratched his head, always feeling with the scholars that he had come into a conversation already half over.

"Well, we've only been at it for an hour or so, and we've made good headway." Martinbrook waved his grubby fingers over the pages.

"Have you?" Harrison's interest rose. Perhaps they could discover the clue that helped break the code. "Tell me."

"Yes. It posed some complications," Smithson explained.

Harrison was not surprised. He'd known fewer minds finer than that of Tom Gardiner, the late Lord Wilmot. "What were the complications?"

"First, we couldn't decrypt it using normal rules of substitution." Quinn held out a sheaf of pages with attempted decryptions.

Otley jumped in to explain. "By that he means, we looked for the most used characters in the code then we assumed that those characters stood for the most used letters in the language. In English that's e, t, a, o, i."

"He must understand, Otley. Or his friend wouldn't have sent him so complicated a puzzle."

"Please, proceed." Harrison knew he had to keep the scholars focused on their task, or he would hear a hundred stories about famous codes, codebreakers, the consequences of using bad codes. *Oh, no*, he realized with some despair, *I can now predict the way one of their stories leads to the next*.

"The problem is that this code frequently includes words from other languages, Latin, Greek, German, French." Partlet wiped his monocle on his cravat.

"And those languages don't use the same letters as frequently. In German, for example, the most used letters are e, n, i, s, r, but in Italian they are e, a, i, o, n." Smithson twisted his thick mustache.

"Without knowing the language, we couldn't successfully use letter frequencies." Nathan nodded his head rhythmically. "Your friend who created this code must be very clever."

"Yes, quite clever." Walgrave carefully avoided any verb tense, for Wilmot had been dead for more than a year, murdered—the Home Office believed—for the information he'd hidden in his code. In a flash he remembered the day he'd met Tom Wilmot. Harrison's first year at Harrow had been lonely, and he'd counted the days until he could go home for the holidays. When the day arrived, he'd waited all afternoon on the porch steps with his bag. But no one came. The headmaster had just informed Harrison that an outbreak of chicken pox had quarantined his estate, when the last carriage pulled up. Before Harrison could refuse, Tom threw Harrison's valise up to the carriage driver, announcing, "My friend is coming home with us." He'd gained fast friends in Tom and his boisterous, welcoming cousins, the Somervilles, but his youngest brother had died during the quarantine.

"So, in summary, Mr. MacHus"—Quinn fluffed his cravat—"the problem is that the code key changes with every pair of lines."

Harrison shook off the memory, realizing he'd missed too much of the explanation. "Could we start at the beginning, gentlemen? I'm having a little trouble catching up." He picked up a page from Mr. James's packet. "You are telling me that this page of gibberish is a list of 101 items."

"Use this one." Otley held out a neatly penned sheet. "I've laid out each item on its own line." The length of the lines alternated, one short row followed by a longer— sometimes much longer—row.

"How did you determine where the lines began and ended?" Harrison compared the two sheets to each other.

Fields, the mathematics scholar, said generously, "Montmorency figured that one out."

Montmorency, always silent, looked up, nodded, then went back to work.

"Montmorency realized that the Greek letters α and Ω were sometimes symbols instead of letters," Smithson explained. "Since in the Greek alphabet, α is the first letter and Ω is the last, we speculated that those letters marked the beginnings and ends of the individual items."

"But how did you sort out when the Greek α and Ω were acting as symbols instead of letters?"

"Every time we found an Ω preceding an α, we assumed that marked the end of one line and the beginning of the next." Otley showed him an example.

"We must hope that our game-builder remembered not to include any words beginning with oa." Smithson observed.

"Yes." Harrison shook himself as soon as the word left his mouth. Now they had him using their odd verbal tic. "I mean, I agree."

Montmorency looked up, smiling. Perhaps he didn't speak to avoid the constant yeses.

"So, yes, the 101 lines of text make 50 pairs. But to decrypt the first line (which isn't part of a pair), we needed a code key," Lark said, almost shaking with excitement. "Your friend complicated the puzzle by sending us two possible sources for that. This page." He held up a botanical drawing, a rose in bloom being fed upon by a hummingbird. "And this one." A second page showed an agave alongside two botanical descriptions. An agave and a rose.

"Very different plants. I saw the South American specimens of the agave at the Physick Garden in Chelsea. Impressive."

Lark smiled indulgently, but kept talking. "To prove the theory, we began to test all the words on these pages. It took less time with all of us working together."

"Eventually, we realized that the key was *hummingbird*. Probably the unlikeliness of the image was supposed to point you to the key word," Smithson chimed in.

"Unlikely?" Harrison felt as if he were standing in front of a distorted mirror. If he moved even the slightest bit, his image came back warped beyond recognition.

Lark harrumphed. "No hummingbird would feed on a rose. No nectar there. It might drink water from its leaves after a rainstorm, but not feed. And hummingbirds aren't even British—one finds them exclusively in the Americas."

"I see." Harrison realized that the Home Office had been approaching Wilmot's code as spies would, but Wilmot had been a scholar. An American bird feeding on an English rose would have struck him as an obvious clue. "Now that we have the code key, we can decode the whole document."

"No, hummingbird decodes alternate lines but only until line forty." Lark wagged a correcting finger.

"Don't confuse the matters yet," Quinn objected. "Just explain how the code works."

"Line forty?" Harrison felt himself falling behind again.

Quinn took over. "Only look at the first pair. Using *hummingbird*, we translated the first line to read

*Charlotte Smith Celestina three fifty-four
eleven five*

Nathan figured out, using Sir Roderick's copy of Smith's book, that the other numbers indicated the volume, page, line, and position of our code key. The fifth word on the eleventh line of the fifty-fourth page of volume three is *dialogue*, and using that word as our new code key, we deciphered the next line. A name: Sir Walter W. Greg."

"Does dialogue decipher the rest?" Harrison felt hopeful for the first time in months. Perhaps they were about to discover the information Wilmot had died to send them.

"No." Quinn shook his head.

Harrison much preferred the yeses.

"For the location of the next code key, we had to go back to hummingbird. That's how we discovered the pattern: the first line directs you to the location of the code key, and the code key decrypts the second line."

"But only up to line forty-one." Lark corrected, pushing his spectacles up his nose.

"Still not yet, Lark." Otley patted the musician on the shoulder.

"I understand that something horrible happens at line forty-one." Harrison offered a sympathetic smile to Lark. "But *hummingbird* gives us half the books we need. Does the library hold any of those?"

"Yes, at least five." Partlet called out from the card cabinet that indicated which books the library owned.

"Let's spread them out among us."

Lark, Martinbrook, Nathan, Otley, Quinn, and Smithson each took a book. Finding the code key in each one, the men began to decrypt.

"I have translated a name." Smithson worked faster than the others. "Sir Ronald MacKerrow."

"He was a historian at Oxford, but he's been dead two, three years now. Died abroad, as I remember. Some story about highwaymen," Partlet explained.

"I have another: Sir Philip Gaskell," Nathan called out.

"And I have Sir Fredson Bowers," Martinbrook added. "But didn't he die in a duel last summer?"

"Gaskell's dead too. Carriage accident last month." Lark began to look concerned.

Harrison felt the hairs on the back of his neck stand on end: four names, four dead men, five if one counted Wilmot.

"Why would someone go to the trouble to encrypt a list with the names of three dead men?" Otley asked.

"We don't know yet what the list contains, so we can't yet speculate. It might be that the list was made before their deaths, and they have something else in common," Harrison replied.

The scholars grew quiet.

"Most likely, my friend knew the men were already dead, and that's why he used them in his game. It might offend people to have their name used thus."

The scholars looked relieved. "Yes, that makes sense."

"Then I'm sure that's it, gentlemen." Harrison kept his voice light. "It's just a game, after all. But I'd like to see if we can win the prize."

The scholars became animated again.

"Ah, yes, that would be lovely."

Lark grimaced. "I hate to bear the bad news, but we really must explain what happens after line forty-one."

Otley nodded. "Go ahead, Lark."

"Well, it's simple really. By translating all the titles with a single code key, it makes it too easy to finish the game. You don't have to go in any particular order. So, your friend abandoned the hummingbird code key entirely, making one pair dependent on the one before it."

Harrison nodded. "Let me make sure I understand. With the first twenty pairs, using the word *hummingbird*, I can translate the book titles all at one go. As a result, if I don't have one of the books at hand, I can simply skip that name and move on to one of the books I do have. It made the code too easy to break. All I needed was *hummingbird* and the help of a good library, and my friend would be paying out his prize."

"Correct."

"But after line forty-one, I have to translate in order. Each pair gives me the key for the next."

"Yes!"

"Yes."

"Yes."

"How did you figure out that the system changed at line forty-one?" Harrison was struck by their ingenuity. "Trial and error?"

"Your friend told us. He included this line—all alphas and omegas. It signaled a change in the pattern."

"How do we proceed?" Harrison asked. "How many more books can we find here?"

"Sadly, we've exhausted our resources here: Your father's tastes led elsewhere." Lark waved at the stacks of books in front of them. "Whoever made this game has a robust, and rather eclectic, library."

"Or he lives near one—perhaps in London or Cambridge or Oxford."

"If you remain here, it will take several weeks to locate all of these volumes and have them sent to you. But you might save time by making a trip to London to visit the British Museum and whatever booksellers who might sell the books you need. Doing so would increase your chances of winning," Otley suggested.

"Forty-two books," Smithson corrected. "We've completed eight of the pairs. You only need forty-two books to reveal the remaining names and win your game!"

"I suppose that's why your friend offered a Christmas ham. He knew how long it would take."

"Do you suppose, MacHus, you would share your box with us?" Partlet asked almost timidly. "Nathan has always wished to see Kean."

"If this works, I'll make sure that Miss Livvy receives the Christmas ham, and my friend finds box seats for all of you."

The delight in the scholars' eyes was unmistakable.

As they drifted back to their desks, Harrison shook his head. The Home Office had been working on the code for weeks, and ten scholars in a remote library had deciphered it before breakfast.

As he was drafting his letter to Mr. James, Harrison noticed the library had grown exceptionally quiet. Only Otley and two of the October scholars—Fields and Jerome—remained. Montmorency, the silent antiquarian, had slipped out shortly after the scholars had deciphered the code.

The door at the far end of the library crashed open, and Lark and Nathan, giggling, stumbled to their desks. Laughing behind their hands, each man collected a stack of paper before racing each other loudly back to the door and slamming it behind them. Drunk, both of them, Harrison thought with annoyance—and with alcohol likely purchased by the estate. Mr. MacHus might not be able to put a stop to such foolishness, but he could at least investigate.

Harrison sealed his letter and hurried onto the terrace at the back of the house. The men, arm in arm, were already far down the lawn, skipping toward the dower house. *Skipping?*

Harrison followed them at a discreet distance, but there was no need for any subterfuge. The men were completely focused on their own pursuits.

The dower-house door was unlocked, and Harrison followed the sound of excited voices to the kitchen at the back.

He stood somewhat out of sight, watching six of the Seven perform some experiment. In the middle of the room on a low table sat two large tin cylinders connected with tubing and filled with liquid, and between them a glass bell. A still of some sort. He craned his ear to hear their conversation.

"Ah, yes, just as Sir Humphry Davy predicted, the experiment produces 100 cubic inches of gas, when the temperature is 55 degrees and the atmospheric pressure 30 pounds, while the gas itself weighs 75.17 grams." Smithson recited the numbers with pleasure.

Martinbrook licked the end of his pencil and recorded the numbers in a small notebook. "Should we record the color as well? I would call that a pale green."

"Davy calls it pale green too."

"How much gas did we recover last time?"

"We recovered 160 cubic inches of nitrous gas—just as Sir Humphry Davy predicted."

From his position Harrison could only hear their conversation, but not distinguish who was saying what.

"I think we have quite enough for another trial."

"Oh, yes, that's quite a lot."

"Now we should test the properties of the gas itself on human subjects. Should we begin? Volunteers?"

"We need to know the dose and the temperature for each of the effects."

"I've written that down here: 'giddiness, fullness of the head . . . feelings resembling those of intoxication, feelings of a most ecstatic nature.'"

"We'll try another round, giving Partlet, Lark, and Quinn a portion in quick succession."

"Are you ready? Then breathe in, men."

All seven breathed in deeply from the tubing.

"Ah, the sensation is quite thrilling. A delightful sensation in my toes and in my fingers."

"Oh, no, for me it's more exquisite, a pleasure akin to flying, as if I am ascending in a balloon."

"Yes, exactly that. The air seems to have grown thinner and more potent all at once. My body feels more vigorous— as if I could run up and down the stairs for hours."

Lark began to giggle, while Partlet and Quinn began to laugh involuntarily.

"Come now, be serious. This is an experiment, not a game." Smithson took measurements from a series of tubes.

"But this all feels so . . . as if the world were the most amusing spot in the whole of the galaxy, and we are merely . . . I can't think of the word, but something very, very small." Quinn gestured wildly toward the sky.

"Ants! We are ants." Lark lifted his magnifying glass, and Partlet pointed, laughing at Lark's one enormous eye.

The men fell into laughter once more.

"I believe that is a reaction you must record in your data," Harrison suggested from the doorway. "That some persons are afflicted with humor—even laughter."

"Oh, MacHus, come in, come in! You must participate in our experiment. We need another subject!"

"Why are you in the dower house? Has Lady Walgrave thrown you all out?"

"Sometimes we wish to replicate an experiment we find in the books. But Miss Livvy won't let us conduct experiments in the lodge."

"So you've taken over the dower house?" Harrison queried.

"Oh, no, Miss Livvy said that we might use it occupationally as our needs demand."

The scholars began to disperse, but Harrison remained behind. "Where does the money for these experiments come from, Smithson?"

"The materials are quite expensive, but my monthly stipend from the residency covered most of it," Smithson carefully explained. "For supplies that go beyond our allowance, we apply to the parson and to Miss Livvy."

"Do those expenses often receive approval?"

"Oh, yes. I don't know anyone who has ever been turned away." Smithson stopped to consider. "Except perhaps that man who wanted to purchase a drift of pigs."

"Pigs?" Harrison was baffled, a feeling he seemed to be experiencing with greater and greater frequency. "What does a research library have to do with pigs?"

"It wasn't exactly clear, so Miss Livvy didn't support it."

"Does the money for supplies come from Sir Roderick's endowment?"

"I believe it comes from her ladyship's allowance," Smithson speculated.

"Why do you believe that?"

"She said something once about not needing her allowance as long as she was living on the estate, and she also mentioned being concerned about the support of the scholars if she were to leave."

"Has she discussed leaving with the scholars?"

"Oh, no, but every year around this time, she grows sad and restless."

Around this time. Harrison tried to imagine what happened in the winter to make her melancholy. But he couldn't identify a cause. Of course he didn't know her well. Indeed, he'd never attempted to know her. Increasingly he saw the mistake in that.

"Don't you feel uncomfortable taking a woman's pin money?"

Smithson looked at his feet. "I never saw it that way. Miss Livvy manages the estate better than any ten men. I always assumed that if she needed the money for something, she would use it for that. It would be the practical thing to do, and she's a very practical woman."

* * *

Harrison walked back to the abbey alone, considering everything he'd learned about his estate and his not-wife thus far. Though he was increasingly comfortable with the details of managing the estate, he was not equally satisfied with his knowledge of Olivia. The glimpses he'd seen revealed a woman far more interesting than he'd imagined, and he wanted to know her better. But she had still not told him if she would remain his devoted not-wife until after the special session. Perhaps what the situation needed was the same sort of concentrated attention that made his work with the Home Office so successful.

Yes, he thought with satisfaction, getting to know Olivia better was exactly what was in order.

Chapter Twenty-Two

Olivia heard Harrison's step in the corridor outside her study. It was strange how quickly she'd learned the determined sound of his walk. She'd been drafting her next essay for the *World*, a continuation of an earlier essay on corruption in shipping. She slipped the draft under a piece of drawing paper on which she'd begun a sketch of Bertie with his fox pup—a decoy in case she was interrupted.

Harrison of course entered without announcing himself. "What do you think of An Honest Gentleman?" He dropped a copy of the *World,* turned open to her most recent article, onto the desk.

"Good afternoon, your lordship. I trust you had a pleasant morning." She stared at him, hoping to divert his attention to the social niceties and away from the *World*.

"Forgive me. In our years apart, I've grown used to my own company, and you must civilize me." But he looked unabashed. "Let me try again. Good afternoon, Olivia. What do you think of An Honest Gentleman?"

"Would you believe me if I said I don't read him?" She picked up her pencil as if returning to her sketch.

"Everyone reads him—you simply don't wish to acknowledge reading the *World*."

"Perhaps. But you clearly dislike his work, and I'm not in the mood to be lectured. So, away, Harrison." She waved her hand. "Go learn your estate, and leave me to my drawing."

He paused. "Actually, I think he's smart. His articles are knowledgeable without being pedantic or dull. But some of the information he provides is incendiary—like throwing a lit match on dry hay. He must have informants on half a dozen parliamentary committees."

"But his efforts make no difference. Parliament continues to resist reform."

"I would say instead that his efforts do influence Parliament, simply not in the way he wants. The more convincing An Honest Gentleman is, the more the Tories fear reform, and the more they retrench."

She raised an eyebrow. "Are you suggesting that good arguments in favor of reform lead to bad laws suppressing it?" She hoped that had not been the Home Office's purpose all along. She preferred to believe she was helping unmask a spy in the government. But she typically only knew the outcome of her missions when, as at the Baron Ecsed's, they ended in tragedy.

"Exactly." Harrison pulled a chair out to sit facing her.

"That's a somewhat blinkered view."

"But one justified by years of arguing before the very men An Honest Gentleman wishes to convince."

"An Honest Gentleman, if he is arguing from his convictions, might be disturbed to find you right." Olivia focused on giving the fox pup Kit a delicate snout.

"Let me see." He whisked the drawing out of her hand, picking up her essay as well.

She felt her stomach drop and prayed he would not notice the second sheet of paper.

"You have a nice precise hand. Bertie's smile hints at

melancholy." He lowered the drawing to his lap. "You have an attentive and perceptive eye."

"Why, thank you." She willed Harrison to put the sheet down.

"Working with the scholars, I've learned that collaboration can sometimes have unexpected results. As a result, I'd like you to help me uncover An Honest Gentleman's origins. What he's like. Where he's from. Perhaps even where he lives."

"But doesn't it go against the whole purpose of a free press to hold a writer's words against him in such a fundamental way?" She watched as he flexed the paper and her draft separated from the bottom of her drawing. She swallowed her dismay.

"Not if we intend no harm to him. I simply wish to meet a man who has such original ideas and such a clear way of expressing them."

She held out her hand for the portrait, and miraculously he handed it to her without noticing the letter below. If she agreed to be his partner in researching An Honest Gentleman, then perhaps she could keep him from looking her way. She could make sure the evidence never pointed to her or Mentor.

"What do you think?" Harrison watched her face with interest.

She raised her hand. "I will help you, *not* because I believe this could or should be done, but because it should be done respectfully and carefully."

"Agreed!" Harrison's eyes lit a more brilliant blue, and she felt like she could stand there staring into them forever. "I have the periodicals in my room. Would you like me to retrieve them to work here? Or would you prefer to work in my drawing room?"

"Let's work here. We might find having a lock on the door convenient."

"I always find a lock on a door convenient." Harrison made the words sound like an invitation.

Olivia looked away unable to meet his eyes. "I was supposed to meet with Mrs. Pier this morning, but the parson came to discuss the new scholar applications. I put her off until now. Might we meet later this afternoon?"

"Certainly. I will be waiting."

Olivia walked with Harrison to the servants' staircase, then taking leave of him walked toward Mrs. Pier's office. But once she was certain she was not followed, she changed course for the village churchyard. She made sure to keep away from the library windows until she was out of sight. At the churchyard she waited by a large monument. Mentor, who rarely left London, had sent a letter requesting a meeting. She'd escaped the abbey from the servants' quarters, walking briskly through the kitchen garden, and from there across the estate to the village.

Mentor stepped from the shadow of a nearby tree.

"We must talk quickly. I cannot be sure that I wasn't followed."

"I came about the threatening letters the *World* has received."

Her stomach turned, but she tried to act unconcerned. "It must be serious for you to come all this way in that disguise. You make an untidy beggar."

Mentor held out his cap. "Yet I've made a pretty penny. You should put something in—in case we are watched."

She opened her reticule. "How much have you made this way?"

"Almost a shilling." Mentor shook the hat to make the coins bounce. "About the threats, you were right to be concerned."

She felt apprehension crawl like a spider up her spine. "How bad?"

"One is a rumor. Our investigations into your father may have stirred up old hostilities. But it's unclear how easily those will lead to you. The other is more substantive: Your old employer may have discovered that you are alive."

She stiffened. "Calista? How?"

"She's been free to roam the country for the last year. A local magistrate overturned her house arrest, finding it too strict for such a gentle lady."

The information turned Olivia's insides cold. "He didn't see what she did."

"No. Only the Home Office had that pleasure. Given that she swore to kill you, we would prefer if you remained near your husband for the future."

"Not husband." She raised one eyebrow archly. "How could any girl graduate from Mrs. Flint's school without learning how to protect herself?"

"You know the danger—he does not. He might need *your* protection."

"And the Home Office would prefer if he remained unaware of that danger, correct?"

"Not necessarily. He already knows you were a governess, so you could let him know that a former employer wants you dead. He could know that when you discovered the crimes Calista and her husband were committing, you went to the magistrates. Any of that would be believeable enough that it wouldn't lead him to your other secrets. At this point, however, you should continue to conceal your spying with the Home Office, as An Honest Gentleman, and before that your training with Mrs. Flint."

"You make it sound so clear-cut, but those are very slippery lines. It's like a skein of yarn: You pull one string and the whole unravels." Olivia watched Mentor's face carefully. "But if you wish me to keep my role as AHG secret, why did you tell him to *investigate* An Honest Gentleman?"

"What?" Mentor's eyebrows shot up. "He was told to let that go."

"Getting you to admit that Harrison works for the Home Office should have been harder. If I need to trust more, perhaps you should trust a little less, old friend."

"Ahh, clever girl. You have always been one of our best. What does he know?"

"I'm not certain. Could Harrison be so intent on finding An Honest Gentleman because he is the spy we seek?" Olivia couldn't help feeling slightly sick at the mere suggestion that Harrison was a traitor.

"No, he's already been excluded. Mr. James warned him off investigating An Honest Gentleman for just the reason you mention—his interest can easily put him under suspicion." Mentor paused, thinking. "Find out what he knows, Livvy, and if he's making headway, distract him. Seduce him—whatever it takes to divert his attention. That shouldn't be too hard. He *is* your husband, after all."

"But he isn't. That's the point." She raised her hands in frustration. "It's a void marriage, never valid."

"Would he seduce you, given the situation, if doing so would help ensure the safety of England and all Englishmen?"

"It's dishonest, and I don't want to lie to him."

"Olivia, you have been lying to him since the day you first entertained Sir Roderick's proposal. And you know the stakes. We need to find who in the government is using the newspapers to undermine the state. We've already investigated three of the men who brought you information, and none of them is our man."

"But over the last year, I've received letters from dozens

of correspondents. Investigating all of them will take months."

"Yes, and if Harrison interferes, he could make identifying the real criminal impossible. If you don't want to seduce him, find some way to keep him occupied. I'll try to think of something as well. As for Calista, if she knows you are alive and where to find you, it might take both of you to thwart her."

Mentor gave her an overly elaborate bow and then disappeared back into the trees.

Olivia walked home slowly, thinking. If Calista was free, she might not attack Olivia directly, at least not at first. The abbey, its servants, the scholars, even Harrison—none were safe. And if Harrison revealed her as An Honest Gentleman, it could overturn all her work for the last year.

But it was the seduction that gave her pause. Mentor was right. It would provide the perfect distraction. And, more to the point, she *wanted* to seduce him. She wanted to let her hand run down the side of his face, to kiss his lips, to press her body into his until there was no distance between them. Since she'd decided to end their non-marriage, she'd felt a chill in her bones that no amount of fire or blankets could take away. And once he'd returned to the abbey, she'd felt his warmth like a beacon. *More like a moth to a flame, ready to consume me.* But he'd already abandoned her once, and he would do it again. She could hear her father's voice, "But did wanting him justify the lie of seducing him? Keep your heart close, my girl. Never tell a lie when a half-truth will do."

She was torn between desire and love. Could she love him *and* seduce him *and* still walk away somewhat whole? Because to tell him she loved him would require her to tell him everything. But no one could know her secrets and still want her to stay. No, "'if it were done, then 'twere well it were done quickly.'" Olivia quoted *Macbeth* to herself, and hoped the end of their story would be less bloody.

Olivia had searched for him in the obvious places: in his turret rooms, the music room, the library. Up- and downstairs. Then she searched the less obvious places: his father's room, her study (which was unlikely since she kept it locked), the conservatory.

Finally she found Harrison in the billiards room, his back to the door, playing a solitary game. His waistcoat was discarded across the back of a chair and he had rolled up his shirt sleeves. She watched for a moment. His back was strong, his shoulders broad, his waist narrow. His arms, strongly muscled, pushed the cue with precision and skill, as he hit ball after ball into the corners he wanted. As he rounded the table, he saw her, giving her a slow smile and an equally slow assessing gaze.

She was ruddy from her search. Her bosom rose and fell with exertion . . . and anticipation.

"As I remember, you owe me a game."

"I do?"

"Yes. When I was here last, we had each won one game out of three, but we never finished the set."

She flushed, recalling how he'd circled the table and caught her, kissing her, until they had both discarded their cues. Pushing the remaining balls to the side, he'd taken her passionately on the green of the table.

"Ah, I see you remember, as well as I, the last game we played here." Harrison grinned. "Would you like a rematch?"

Olivia swallowed before she answered. "Of which game?"

"Perhaps we should play to decide? But we will need a wager."

"What do you have in mind?" She chose her cue, then

held it in front of her for examination, caressing the end slowly.

It was Harrison's turn to swallow before speaking. "If I win, I . . ." His voice tapered off as he watched her hand stroke the cue up, then down.

She leaned forward. "Lacking imagination, my lord?" It was her job to make him want her, to make him think only of her, because when men lost themselves in their lovers, they also lost control of their secrets. She was to distract him, even if it broke her heart.

Harrison coughed and looked away. "I think you are trying to ensure you win."

"I certainly intend to." She met his eyes and paused provocatively. "Because the stakes are my body, if I lose."

He regarded her suspiciously, but with undeniable interest. "And if you win?"

She set the cue against the wall and stepped close to him, the space between their bodies a mere inch, close enough that she could see the pulse in his neck increase. She lifted her eyes to see his filled with desire. "I'm sure you can forfeit something equally pleasurable." She ran a slow finger down his cheek and rested it on his lips. "But of course if we play, you will have to promise to keep all my secrets—or at least those I tell you." She let her hand trail down the middle of his chest, down his belly, until she let it rest boldly on his sex, waiting until she felt it stir.

"What secrets, Olivia?" He put his hand on her breast. "Two can play this game."

"Play me and find out." She dared him with her word and her eyes, all the time hoping she would never have to tell him her darkest secret. She could not bear to see him turn away from her in disgust.

"Then my body will be my forfeit as well. So, it's your body, if I win, and my body, if I lose. I claim the match now."

"That's not the way the game works." She backed toward the closed billiard room door.

He followed, stepping between her and the door. "It is, if we want it to be." She backed away again, but he was ready, and he pressed her against the wall, his hands on each side of her face, his body boxing her in. As he breathed on her neck, he reached out to the billiard room's door. She heard the lock turn.

She could feel his heat warm the whole of her body, and rebelliously her own answered it. He pulled her body into his and kissed her with all the ardor of a man long denied. She felt her own heat rise in answer.

"And after the end of the special session, what if I refuse to end this non-marriage?" Harrison brushed his hand from her jaw down her neck, then kissed the base of her throat.

"It's done, Harrison. Or not done. Never done."

"I remember." He trailed one finger down the side of her cheek, down the soft sensitive skin of her neck, across her chest to the spot where her breasts swelled full and lush. She felt the finger as a trail of fire, warming her with each inch of movement. "I remember this."

He moved his face near hers, so close to her lips she thought he was going to kiss her, and her lips reached out toward his, but at the last moment before their skin touched he bent his lips to her cheek then her neck, breathing without touching the line his finger had traced. Then he touched her with just his tongue. No kisses, just the teasing flicker of his warm flesh on hers.

Then suddenly his mouth was on her neck. She closed her eyes, and lifted her chin away from him, increasing his access to her tender flesh at the join of her neck and chest. Then he moved lower, his mouth on the crown of her breast. As he moved down her body, he pulled her buttocks against him with one free hand, and pressed their bodies together.

There with her back pressed against the wall, he began

to plunder, taking what he wanted, and once more she offered no resistance. She'd wanted him again, told herself that if he offered, she would take it, let him give her another week of pleasure before disappearing from her life again as he had before, this time for good.

But when his other hand moved from the wall to her lower body, pressing against her mound with his hand, letting his fingers squeeze and tease, she stiffened. Was she sure? Could she survive another heartbreak?

She closed her eyes, lost in the sensation, in the memories of his body on hers, in hers.

His hand moved more insistently, and his mouth took possession of hers. She kissed him as fervently as he did her. It was heady, his body pressing her into the wall, his hands teasing her to greater and greater heights.

His mouth moved lower again, stopping for greater pleasure, then a hand replaced his mouth, pulling and kneading her breast to hard points, and his mouth replaced his lower hand. He groaned as he took her sex in between his lips, again pulling and caressing, until she thought she could bear no more, and then he plunged one finger into her depths, and she cried out in an agony of sensation. All her senses were tied to the movement of his lips and hand, in the strokes of rough flesh against unbearably soft. Then his mouth was gone, and she felt herself widening as another finger joined the first. "Do you remember this, Livvy?"

And all movement stilled. "Tell me you remember. That you want this again."

"Yes. Please. Yes."

And his mouth moved against her again, inside her, teasing, tormenting, until she shattered in his arms.

He held her a long time, both of them leaning against the wall. He listened to her breath come back to an even rhythm, enjoying the moments before she came back to herself, where the only emotion between them was satisfaction. It wouldn't last; she would still leave him. But this, at least they could have this timeless moment. Until time intruded again.

"I didn't know an invalid marriage could come with such benefits." Harrison leaned his shoulder against the wall, gazing at Olivia.

"As I cannot be your wife, think of me instead as your eager mistress." She stood upright, straightening her clothes. "For six long years, you left me without satisfaction, and now, I find I require it." She stepped from the wall and picked up her cue.

"Able, my lady, and oh so willing."

"This means nothing, Harrison. It's only pleasure," she cautioned, pulling back to look him in the eyes. "I'm making no promises."

He answered by plundering her mouth once more. If she thought his kisses signaled agreement, so be it. He could not refuse the offer of her body, when he'd been faithful to their marriage for so long. But he wasn't releasing her from their marriage merely because she had found a way to escape. No, not when he hadn't tried being her husband in all the ways that truly mattered.

As they kissed, he backed her against the table, then lifted her until she rested against the finely grained wood. The material in her skirt was sufficient to allow him to spread her knees and step into the space between her thighs.

For some moments there was nothing in the world but their kisses and the warmth of their bodies touching through their clothes. But soon they grew more urgent.

Slowly, as a dancer at one of the less respectable establishments, she pulled her skirts tantalizingly up her legs.

Her legs spread wide, her skirts barely covering the entrance to her sex. He pushed the skirt up the rest of the way and tucked it behind her legs, revealing all of her. The slit in her pantaloons was wide, offering a study in dark and light, the white cotton framing the flushed darkness of her sex.

Lifting one leg over his shoulder, he knelt down to worship her. He kissed a line from her ankle to the top of her inner thigh, touching his finger to her most sensitive skin. He pressed his finger into her darkness, until she groaned his name, and when he pressed farther she rocked against his hand.

He pushed her morning dress down her shoulder, ripping some of the old material as he revealed the skin of her chest and her breasts, smooth and firm. He squeezed, and she moaned in response. So responsive. He tried other more subtle techniques. He kissed from her nipples down to her belly button, where he began to suck against her belly, leaving small blue marks as he moved, marking her as his.

She clutched his hair in her fingers as he worked his way down, and when he reached her soft flesh, she guided him even lower, to that spot so sensitive and so private. When his lips reached their goal, she barely could contain her desire.

He raked his fingernails against the softness of her thighs and teased until her moans grew more and more fevered.

When Harrison pressed into her, he felt as if they were connected in every cell, with every nerve, every muscle. As her body welcomed him, he felt her ache intensify, tensing and releasing then tensing again. They fell out of control, out of their bodies, except for the welling passion that kept them tied to this one spot and this one time.

* * *

He held out his hand to help her up, then in quiet helped her repair her clothes once more. He brushed her hair with his hand, smoothing it, luxuriating in its silken smoothness.

She looked at him with an earnestness that touched his heart.

"Harrison, this, between us—" She struggled for words. "It changes nothing. I'm still not married to you, and I have no intention of changing that."

And just like that, the past rose up between them.

"You knew the marriage was invalid from the first, didn't you?" He tried to keep the hurt out of his voice, but knew he did not succeed.

"I suspected, but your father was so ebullient, I wanted to believe him when he said all the formalities were being observed. Had you come home, I might never have investigated it, but once I did, once I discovered we weren't married, I couldn't continue the lie."

"But it was my father's lie, not mine. I've believed all these years that we were married. My friends will tell you, in matters of my own affairs and my own choice, I'm hopelessly honest. It's the only way to remain sane in a political world which shifts by the minute under your feet."

"And yet you lied to the cook."

"I had a choice: to give the lie to your story—which would have only magnified a problem I unwittingly created—or lie to support you. But you are not playing fair. I was speaking of the important things in life: whether I have been faithful to you, whether I will care for you and the estate, whether you can trust me to do as I promise. Part of being honest requires that we treat those who live in community with us with kindness and respect. Sometimes it requires omitting a truth or letting a half-truth pass without remark. But in things that matter I try never to lie, even when it might benefit me."

"You are a Member of Parliament; you lie as a vocation."

"But not about things that matter. You have read my speeches. Have you not noticed how scrupulously I hold to the truth?"

"I have considered it was merely an artifice, to gain a reputation for honesty so that when you lie, no one will notice."

"Then you do not know me."

"You have not given me much occasion to learn your character."

"That is why I'm telling you this now: I will not lie to you, Livvy. You can trust me on that. If nothing else, that is something solid between us. If I promise something, you can trust my word. If I lie to you, then you have every right to leave me, and I will not follow."

Her face changed. Had he known her better, he might have thought that he saw regret as well as guilt and suspicion. But, he told himself, he didn't know her.

"I still believe it would be best for us to separate, for you—and me—to pursue different lives."

"Will you tell me why?"

"You have promised to be honest, Harrison. I'm not sure yet if I have that luxury. I have made decisions that require me to keep my own confidences."

"I accept that. But if you allow me, you will find me as stalwart as my friends complain I am."

"Yet you have carried such anger with you, even though your father has been dead for three years. When you couldn't punish him, you punished me."

"I felt you were complicit, but I see now that by refusing to come home, I made you a victim of his lie as well. What would it hurt, though, to see if we might suit?"

"There is *no* marriage." She shook her head emphatically.

He held up his hand, asking for a pause. "I know. I understand the legality of it. But in the eyes of society—this community, the ton—we have been married for six years."

She turned her face from him.

"I came home to address the question of our marriage. True, I might not have come home otherwise, but I'm here now. We could start over, but you don't seem to wish to."

"You say that you will not lie to me. But I can't promise you the same. I don't know who I am, Harrison. I don't even know my own name, not really, and the only person who can answer my questions is my father. So, until I find my answers, I can't be your wife . . . or anyone's." And with that, Olivia quit the room, leaving Harrison to wonder if he truly wanted to know the secrets she kept.

Chapter Twenty-Three

"A gentleman is sleeping in the drawing room, your ladyship." Mr. Pier held out a dog-eared calling card. "I told him Lord Walgrave is not present, but he insisted on speaking with you. He assured me he is not a scholar."

"That's good. We are overrun with scholars. If he is one of Walgrave's friends, we must accommodate him, but he might be traveling on." She signaled for the footman to follow her, as she read the calling card: Adam Montclair, Esq.

Montclair was slumped on the edge of the chaise longue, his clothes dusty from travel. To arrive so early, almost at sunrise, he must have traveled all night.

"Mr. Montclair." Olivia shook the man's shoulder gently. He did not respond. Shaking his shoulder a little more forcefully, she tried his first name. "Adam."

"Em? Em? Sweet Em. Forgive me." He nuzzled her hand with his face, clearly asleep.

Annoyed, she shook his shoulder harder, less gently. "Wake up, sir. You must wake up."

He opened his eyes slightly. They focused for a moment on Olivia's face. "You're not Em." He slurred.

"No, I am not Em." Olivia found herself suddenly

annoyed. One of the first lessons Mrs. Flint's School for Exceptional Girls taught its pupils was how to appear unremarkable, even invisible. Perhaps she had learned that lesson too well; even Harrison hadn't recognized her at the theater. She placed her hands on Mr. Monclair's shoulders and shook more insistently.

The man finally awoke, shaking his head against the last vestiges of sleep.

"Excuse me, your ladyship." Montclair pushed himself upright. "I left London last night in search of Lord Walgrave."

"Even during the day, that's a difficult journey, with a dozen places to go astray if you don't know the route." She stepped back, looking him over. Even dust-covered and weary, he was a handsome man: Dark hair, green eyes, his voice cultured.

"I believe I found each one of them." He brushed his forehead with his hand and yawned. "Can you tell me where your husband is? Your butler seems to believe him in London, but I had it on good authority Harrison is here. I carry a letter for him."

Olivia gave Montclair a closer look. He had called her husband by his first name. Montclair was a friend then as well as a messenger. That explained why, when waiting until light to leave London would have been the better choice, Montclair had chosen to leave while it was still dark. But she did not know if Walgrave wanted his presence known—he had gone to such lengths to hide it. How could she handle Montclair's request without revealing that Walgrave was present? "Might I see the letter?"

Montclair pulled out a pack he wore against his chest. He withdrew the letter and held it out, letting her see the address and the seal. The handwriting was Mentor's. Mentor had promised to find a distraction for Harrison. Perhaps Adam was it.

She turned away to give herself time to think. Knowing that Harrison worked for the Home Office should have made her feel more at ease: A man who trafficked in secrets, no matter how much he personally tried to tell the truth, might understand the choices she'd made. But knowing that Harrison continued his investigations over the Home Office's objection made her wary. What could be his reason? Mentor had assured her that Harrison was not complicit in the passing of secrets abroad, but his insistence on continuing to investigate suggested otherwise.

"Lady Walgrave? Are you well?"

"Yes, of course." She shook off her reflections. "I take it you are a friend of Walgrave's."

"I am—though sometimes that role is challenging." He tried but could not keep himself from yawning. "Excuse me, my lady. My body refuses to accept I am awake."

The footman stood at the door. "Mr. Montclair will be staying the night. Please tell Mr. Pier to prepare a room in the family wing, then join me here." She waited until the boy pulled the door shut behind him.

"Whose authority tells you Walgrave is here?"

"I cannot say." He looked away, not meeting her eyes. "Parliamentary privacy, and all that."

She thought for a moment before answering. "Walgrave will meet you in your room. Since he has been so long absent from the estate, he wished to learn about it as a stranger might. He plays one of the scholars and goes by the name T. L. MacHus."

Montclair burst into laughter, shaking his head. "Well, that's Harrison for you. He has returned home in secret to observe the inhabitants of his estate, and he chooses Telemachus as a name. Why not just call himself Odysseus and be done with it? Has no one noticed?"

"I must admit, Mr. Montclair, until this moment I had not realized it either. Telemachus, Odysseus's son who searches for his father. I suppose choosing Odysseus would have been too obvious. But the parallels are amusing: Odysseus returns from sea and he finds his home invaded by suitors. Here the Walgrave home is invaded by scholars."

"Having been at Cambridge, I won't speculate which are the more dangerous: suitors or scholars."

"I have no need to speculate. Scholars. Every time." At a tap at the door, she nodded the butler into the room. "Mr. Pier, we have been speculating on Homer's *Odyssey*, and whether suitors or scholars are the more dangerous. Given your experience on the battlefield, have you an opinion?"

"Scholars, my lady. They are unpredictable . . . like fighting a battle with only Punch and Judy for your allies."

"We must make sure our hospitality equals that of the ancient world, Pier. A bath, a meal, and a bed. Does that suit you, Mr. Montclair?"

"Very much, my lady."

She found Harrison in the corner of the library he had claimed as his own.

"I have had the most interesting discussion with a friend of yours."

"A friend?"

"A Mr. Montclair, come from London to meet with Lord Walgrave."

Harrison stood abruptly. "When?"

"Just now."

"Where is he?"

"Perhaps it would be wise to first tell me who he is."

"An associate."

"An associate who knows you are here and who traveled all night to reach you. That sounds like more than an associate, more even than a friend."

"Parliamentary matters are sometimes urgent."

"You and I both know it isn't Parliament." She pushed his books aside to lean against the table in front of him. "I think it is time to be more honest with me, Harrison."

He stared at her, confirming all her suspicions. "Is Montclair still here?"

She waved him silent with a hand. "During the wars you were supposed to be at sea."

"I was at sea."

"In the years before his death, your father found it increasingly difficult to read handwriting. Printed books—as long as they had adequate space and clean margins—troubled him less, but eventually I became his sight, reading everything to him. Every week, we waited for the newspapers, anxious to know that you were still alive. The mail packet would arrive, and he would immediately pull out the newspapers, ignoring all the other mail. He would hand them to me, hands shaking with fear, and ask me to read for him. We would begin with the general listings, then the wounded, then the dead. One day, we saw a notice for your ship— 'the frigate *Peaseblossom*, sunk, all hands lost.' Eyes wet with tears, he refused to believe it. He demanded I write a letter for him to some person he knew in the Home Office, and when the answer came, it fell to me to read it. I know you weren't at sea. What I don't know is whether you are *still* a spy."

"If Montclair is here, one of my projects is in trouble."

"You haven't answered my question."

"I think I have."

"Is that why you didn't come home to me?"

She could see Harrison consider lying before his face became resigned. Perhaps he truly was an honest man. "I had decided not to come back before I returned to my other work."

Olivia felt the words like a blow, but she straightened, determined to show him only strength.

"Thank you for your honesty. That explains a great deal. You should go to Mr. Montclair. He is in the green bedroom."

"What brings you here? And so early?"

"A foolish desire to see the world?" Adam could barely keep his eyes open.

Harrison brushed aside the sarcastic response. "Tell me quickly, and then you can sleep."

"Mr. James believes he's found a pattern in the news we've received from some of our northern informants. But he doesn't know enough of the background to be sure. And he believes you are the only man who does. So, my purpose here is twofold: To bring you that giant pile of documents there on the desk, and to remain until I learn how you manage the remote agents. And I get to stay until I've learned it all, or caught up on my sleep." Adam yawned wide.

"Since you already have the files laid out on the table, do you mind if I review the documents here?"

"If I can sleep while you do it." Adam's eyes looked bleary. "In fact, I'd prefer keeping them here with me. Some are quite sensitive, and until I understand fully what is in these reports, I should hide out up here. You *will* have my meals delivered, won't you?" Adam yawned again.

"Of course." Harrison pulled a chair up to the table and began to separate the papers into precise stacks. "It will be best to keep these documents locked in here with you. The scholars have a habit of reading my mail."

Adam stripped to his underclothes and pulled back the covers on the tester bed. "There's also a letter from Aldine. Something about whether he should proceed as you instructed with the situation you asked him to look into. I assume that means something to you."

Harrison picked up the envelope. He knew already what it would contain: the results of Aldine's investigation into the validity of Harrison's marriage. The packet was fat. Harrison knew he needed to open it, but especially after their delicious game in the billiards room, he couldn't face learning that Olivia had never been his wife and that he couldn't object when she left him. He wrote Aldine a short letter: "If the situation is clear, proceed as you think best. Harrison." But something niggled at the back of his memory, so he set the letter on the edge of the table to consider it further.

Several hours later, Harrison realized, ruefully, that the only way to keep all the various reports straight was to pencil a makeshift map on the large table in Adam's room. He would have to swear Adam to secrecy, if the man weren't snoring so loudly.

With nothing more to do until Adam woke, Harrison returned to his turret room. He wanted to surprise Olivia with a gift: a set of drawing pencils he'd bought on the way down. He'd never expected Olivia to come to him. It seemed a sign that he was right to try to get to know her better. And for her to have given herself to him with such sweet abandon . . . he smiled at the memory.

Olivia's drawing of Bertie remained on the table. He picked it up, again admiring this time her depiction of Kit. Her delicate lines caught the emerging fox in the pup's face.

He began to set the drawing back on the edge of the desk, but it slipped from his hand. In trying to catch the drawing before it reached the floor, he knocked the blotter askew and revealed a piece of paper hidden under it. Looking over his shoulder to see if he was alone, he pulled the paper out of its hiding place. It was a long letter in Olivia's hand. To whom did his wife write such long missives? Was it a lover? Jealousy flashed in a second before he tamped it down. He looked for an address but found nothing.

He began to read the letter itself and within only five sentences, he felt as if his world had shifted.

It was a draft of a letter from An Honest Gentleman to the *World*. This one took up again the question of corruption in the local magistrate offices. He sat down, stunned. The letter was in his wife's hand. Was this one of her secrets? Was Olivia An Honest Gentleman?

It couldn't be.

He'd come to admire An Honest Gentleman's agile wit. Was that the same wit he'd seen in Olivia? And if not, why? What were the differences? He read through the other papers on her desk, taking care to leave each positioned exactly as it had been.

It had to be her. She kept her study locked.

Who else might have occasion to visit Olivia's office? Any of the scholars? Pier and his wife? The parson?

At the thought of the parson, Harrison remembered that Olivia herself had told him Southbridge had paid her a visit only that morning. Was Olivia serving as Southbridge's amanuensis, making a fair copy of his letters to send to the *World*? Southbridge hadn't seemed like the type to engage in letter wars—but Harrison had been surprised before.

He would have to be more attentive now.

He replaced the essay and the drawing and removed his gift of the drawing pencils. He didn't wish to give any clue that he had been in the study alone. Or that he had found out one of her secrets.

Harrison worked late in the library, hours after it was closed to the scholars. Since no one knew yet that he was

Walgrave, if he were discovered he would have to return to his room, and he wasn't yet ready. Learning that the parson was likely An Honest Gentleman had renewed his enthusiasm for analyzing the letters. But Olivia's involvement with Southbridge posed a problem. Now he understood her reluctance to help him discover An Honest Gentleman's identity as well as her cautious agreement. Perhaps she thought she could protect the parson. But if Southbridge were An Honest Gentleman and if he were selling secrets, Harrison would have to distance Olivia from his plots before telling Mr. James.

At a soft sound in the corridor, he snuffed his lamp, waiting. The door to the garden creaked. Then, a few moments later he saw Olivia, dressed in a dark robe, pass through a pool of moonlight outside the library windows.

His hand was on the latch of the long glass doors before he realized he had risen from his desk.

Of course he would follow her. Whether she wanted him or not, he still considered her his wife. And after holding her in his arms once more, he found himself possessive. But he couldn't force her to marry him again. Perhaps finding her in a tryst with a lover—with Southbridge—would be just the medicine he needed to let her go. But he didn't have to like it.

Harrison could already predict where she was going: the summerhouse by the lake. Moonlight lit her way, making it easy to see her at a distance.

At a sound to her right, she stepped into the shadow of a thick-trunked oak. A fairy tree. He could easily imagine Olivia as a member of the fairy folk, deceiving and bewitching in equal measure.

A buck burst past, followed by two does. Harrison wondered if Olivia's lover caused their flight. Though Harrison had tried to convince Olivia to trust him, she had refused, instead telling him that *she* could not be trusted. Had a lover been the reason? But if she had a lover, why had she taken Harrison to her bed? Was she punishing him for leaving her alone so long?

He almost turned back. He suddenly didn't want to follow her. He didn't want proof that Olivia loved another. In part he didn't want to lose Olivia because she was his last connection to his lost family. Olivia had known his father, remembered him fondly, and even though Harrison had bristled at his father's interference, he'd loved—and mourned—the old man. In part he didn't want to lose her because he'd never stopped thinking of her, and after their tryst in the billiard room, he realized he never could.

As he followed, his jaw set with determination or anger, he couldn't tell. He should have let her go and not traveled to his estate until she was gone. What had been his motivations, and why was he following her now? Why not consign her to another man's arms and be done with her? An invalid marriage would allow him to marry again, to have heirs if he wanted them. But the thought of enduring a matchmaking season turned his stomach. If he needed a wife, he would simply follow his father's lead and ask Mr. James to find him one.

In the past when he'd followed a suspicious person, he'd felt a heady mix of exhilaration and caution, ready at any moment for the situation to change. His senses heightened, he often imagined he could anticipate the other person's emotions, excitement, or reticence or fear or anger. All he'd imagined left an almost visible imprint on the path, guiding him in how to behave, whether to stay in the shadows and observe or step into the light and demand a reckoning. This uncanny perception had made him Mr. James's most trusted agent, one who could accomplish missions that no one else could.

But tonight his perceptions were clouded by his own visceral emotions. Anger, frustration, disappointment, determination—all formed a bitter stew in the pit of his stomach. And though he wished to deny it, desire and jealousy also colored his plan.

At the edge of the thicket, the path split, the left going farther into the forest and from there to the village, and the right to the summerhouse and the lake. He began to angle toward the summerhouse, so that if she looked behind her, there would be no chance of her seeing him.

But as he turned, he saw her disappear into the greater darkness of the woods. The village, not the summerhouse. So. It *was* the parson.

But what a coward the parson was! Why should he expect Olivia to come to him through the darkness? The man deserved to be beaten silly, not simply because he was Olivia's lover, but because he hadn't the gentlemanly good sense to come to her.

Harrison began plotting revenge, more on the parson than Olivia. She was a fine woman, seductive and completely unaware of her power over him. She couldn't know how, for years, his body had ached for hers. But, he'd left her few choices, and he should let her go. But of course it was only now that he'd lost her, that he wished he had tried to know her better. Harrison knew, if he were being as honest as he claimed to be, that this was entirely his doing. But there was no room for self-recrimination when vengeance was so much more appealing.

He circled back to the path, relying on the hard-beaten ground to allow him to move quietly behind her. But she seemed unconcerned, walking swiftly but not fearfully. No backward glances or quickening pace, just a steady progress.

The edge of the forest ran down the bottom of the parsonage garden, and past the churchyard. His stomach tightened, knowing he was about to be proved a cuckold.

No, not that. She was not his wife, she had never been his wife. But he'd thought of her as his for so long, it was as if he'd learned that his parents weren't his at all, but just a couple who'd taken him in when he was too young to know the difference.

She was not betraying anyone, except perhaps herself. The parson would never marry her. Even though she and Harrison had no legal marriage, it would still be too much to overcome for a clergyman intent on rising in the ranks of the church.

His stomach clenched in dread and disappointment. Just a few more feet and she would be at the parsonage, and he would return to the house, sign the separation agreement, and then return to London.

From his position in the shadow of a poplar, he could see the garden gate and door of the parsonage. But the house was dark. Surely she was not meeting a man with so little income as to be unable to afford even a fire? Was she so lonely that a country parson was her best company? The blame for this, too, could be laid at his door.

He was so caught up in his storm of regret that he almost missed seeing her turn, not to the house but into the churchyard. Suddenly, he was suspicious, but for entirely different reasons. Something felt wrong here. Off. Mr. James would call it his "confounded intuition."

If he hadn't been so obsessed with his failed not-marriage, what would he have noticed that he needed to know now? Whatever it was, he was sure, without being able to pinpoint why, that Olivia was in danger. This wasn't a tryst, but something else, something nefarious.

When every muscle in his body wanted to run, he held himself back. At the bottom of the churchyard she'd left the gate wide open—no bar to a quick escape, but no impediment to being surprised from behind. He had to find her. But where had she gone?

"Ah, Lady Walgrave. I see you've followed my instructions. Now take one step back into the moonlight so that I can see you." The voice was cultured, educated, with the hint of a foreign accent. French, perhaps? Or a refugee of one of the other European countries during the wars? Or was the accent merely a ruse to obscure his true voice?

She stepped back.

"One more step. No, not too far. I want you close—if you prove uncooperative. Ah, yes, that's good."

The man was fully in shadow, though still within arm's reach.

Livvy kept her hand on the pistol in the pocket she'd sewn into the folds of her skirt. It was powdered and loaded; all she had to do was pull the primer and aim. She kept her fear in check, focusing instead on gathering what little information the man might give her.

"Following your instructions wasn't terribly difficult. I've walked to this churchyard at least twice a week every week for the last six years."

"But it's the perfect venue, don't you think? A place where the dead keep their secrets and you give up yours."

"I doubt that." She stood with her back straight, refusing to appear cowed.

"It's such a shame that Sir Roderick couldn't see what you've become. I wonder what he thought he was making of you, transforming a governess into a countess."

"What do you want?"

"Money, of course, and a great deal of it. But you must understand: I want much more than money. I want you to stop looking. It's a scandal you are courting, unless you pay me."

The man remained in the shadows. She needed to see his face. She needed to be able to recognize him later. Perhaps if she baited him, he would step out of the shadows . . . but it was a risk.

"Not a cent," she said confidently.

"What false bravery, your ladyship. What would your husband do if he knew where Sir Roderick found you or what you've done since becoming his lady? Would he welcome losing a bright future in Parliament?"

"My husband knows everything he needs to know about me." She kept her tone level and firm; in normal circumstances—oh, to be able to remember normal circumstances—she would refuse to engage. But with Harrison at the house, and with her orders from the Home Office, she had to play this man's game. "I have nothing to give you, so tell my husband whatever you think he would wish to know."

"Do you wish for me to tell him what you've been doing in London? All those men meeting you in dark places. All those essays. Many would pay for that information."

She took a shallow breath. "I don't know what you mean."

Harrison couldn't hear any of the words, but he could see the stiffness in Olivia's back, the tension in her voice, and as he drew closer, he could hear a tone of triumph in the voice of the one who taunted her.

She was too close to the man. Her back was straight, tense. At that distance, she wouldn't have time to escape if the well-dressed man chose to restrain her.

Suddenly she recoiled as if struck, backing away from

the man. But it was too late. From the shadows behind her, a familiar-looking wiry man grabbed her arms and pulled her, struggling, against him. The taller man seemed surprised, even dismayed.

Harrison saw the flash of a knife in the moonlight and heard Olivia's stifled scream. Fear brought bile to his mouth. He ran forward, trying to reach her before the man could do her more harm. But before he could reach her, he heard the firing of a gun, and the man flung Olivia to the ground. The wiry man, clutching his arm, ran away, leaving a trail of blood through the gravestones. The elegant man disappeared into the shadows.

Olivia lying on the ground was like a nightmarish painting. Beautiful and macabre. The moonlight fell fully on her body, blood pooling from a cut, likely on the back of her head, where her head had struck the edge of one of the gravestones. He prayed she was not dead, and that her injury wasn't grave.

He brushed her hair back from her face and pulled her into his lap. "Livvy, wake up. He's gone."

He pulled his flask out of his boot and poured whiskey across her lips, patting her cheeks gently with his fingers. It seemed like an eternity before she began to moan and then to open her eyes.

"Harrison? Why are you here?"

"I thought I'd visit my father's grave."

"At night? Now?" Her brows furrowed in confusion.

"No, I followed you . . . I thought you were meeting a lover."

"Lover?" She tried to focus on his face. "I don't have a lover. I mean, except for you."

"Well, certainly those men don't care for you very much."

She tried to push herself out of his arms, but fell back, the corners of her eyes tight with pain.

"My head." She reached up and pulled away fingers wet with blood. "Oh, my." Her face blanched.

"No, no, Livvy, don't faint, I need you to stay awake. Do you think you can make it to the parsonage?"

"The parson is spending the night in the next village over. No one is home to help."

"Perfect. We'll make ourselves at home while we treat the wound on that pretty head of yours."

"But Southbridge . . ."

". . . Will be pleased we were able to take refuge in his home. Now, up."

He arranged her body so that he could more easily lift her to her feet.

"Hold on to me."

She did, clinging to his side and arms as if she were in love with him.

"There's a key."

"Key?"

"To Noah's kitchen. At the back of his house." Her words were breathy, forced, as if she was putting all her energy into speaking.

His relief that she wasn't meeting a lover soured. How did she know where Southbridge kept a key, if she hadn't used it?

As if reading his thoughts, she said, "He's absentminded—locks himself out. I suggested he hide a key so that he can always get back in."

The feel of her body curved into his side, the support of his arm curved around her waist, the smell of her hair, scented with lilac water, all made him wish she weren't wounded, so that he could kiss her until she remembered how good they were together—until she forgot the parson even existed.

He sat her in the chair by the back door of the parsonage,

leaning her upper body against the wall of the house, then retrieved the key from under a rock.

Unlocking it, he lifted her and pulled her into his side. The kitchen was at the back of the house, and with the door open, Harrison had enough light to maneuver Olivia into the kitchen and into a chair beside the long harvest table. He lit a lantern, then bolted the door shut, and pulled the curtains over the windows. Her attackers might imagine Olivia had taken refuge in the parsonage, but Harrison saw no reason to make it easy to find her.

He poured fresh water from the pitcher on the counter and blotted her head clean. She flinched at the bite of the cold water against her scalp.

After a few minutes of letting him care for her, she pointed to a canister low on the counter. "Willow bark. He buys dried strips from the gypsies."

"Good. Can you sit on your own?"

"Yes."

He retrieved the willow bark and handed her a narrow strip.

"Thank you." She chewed on it.

"What were you doing there? And who was that man?"

"I don't know who he was. He's been sending threatening letters, and I wanted to know what he was capable of."

"Threatening letters? About what? And why did you meet him? You might have been killed."

"But I wasn't—*might have beens* are for children and fools. If you will return to the abbey and awaken Pier, she can doctor my wound. Tomorrow I'll be good as before."

She tried to stand, then swayed. He caught her in his arms before she could fall.

"Perhaps you will stay right here. If the parson is gone he cannot be angry that we have borrowed one of his rooms."

"Not just one."

"Yes, one. I'm not leaving you, not with that wound splitting open the flesh on your head."

"No one can know."

"Can know what?" He immediately assumed she wanted to keep him a secret, and his anger flared.

"The meeting. The man. You can't tell anyone . . . too dangerous."

He felt relieved that she wanted to keep something else a secret, not him. "You are bleeding all over my best boots. Of course we will call for the magistrate."

"I'll agree to your bargain—remain your wife at least in public—if you keep this quiet."

He stilled. Her secrets must be serious if she would remain his wife to keep them. And if it were that bad, then he needed to know just what it was.

"Then, wife, let me tend to your wound. We'll discuss our bargain tomorrow."

Chapter Twenty-Four

When Livvy woke the next day, she didn't recognize the room or the bed. But she knew all too well the man next to her. Still asleep, with his hair tousled over one eye, he looked as he always had to her: as a golden-haired Adonis. She reached out gingerly, careful not to move anything connected to her aching head, and ran one of his curls through her fingers.

He opened one eye, then a smile grew across his face. "I see you."

"That's a child's game."

"But a good one. How do you see me? Are your eyes telling you I'm one man, or two, or four?"

"Just one. I couldn't manage four of you."

"Well, that's fine then. Did the willow bark ease the pain? Or do you wish for more?"

She started to sit up, then blanched. "Perhaps a small willow tree would be in order."

He reached over the side of the bed and lifted a tin canister from the floor. He held out another thin strip of bark. "I'll cut the tree down when you've finished the can. Perhaps while you chew, we can determine how I'm going to become Lord Walgrave to my devoted servants."

She took the small sliver of bark and chewed it.

"Do you look so sullen because your head hurts or because you have decided to remain my wife for a while longer?"

"Does it have to be one or the other?" She squinted with pain.

"I can always call the magistrate to report the attack on you. Who is the magistrate, by the way? Sir Gerald?"

"Lord Hocksley." Impossibly, she looked even more sullen.

"You don't like him?"

"He reminds me of a toad."

"Do you mean the way his neck flares out in layers of fat, or the way he has a tendency to say every sentence in a throaty staccato?" Harrison placed his hands at his neck, spreading his fingers, then mimicking Hocksley's speech: "What! My word! An attack! Lady Walgrave! Oh no! Bad business! An attacker!"

"I once told your father that when Hocksley visited I amused myself by counting how few verbs he used. After that, it became a game, each of us predicting the number whenever he arrived."

"Why were you in the churchyard last night?"

She held up her hand, stopping his question. "I agreed to your terms. I will pretend to be your wife until the end of the special session. But I have no interest in being under your thumb or answering your questions."

She threw her legs over the edge of the bed and tried to rise, but before she stood up, she swooned. He barely kept her from falling out of the bed.

Olivia awoke to find Noah sitting by her bed, his face a mixture of fear, concern, and disappointment.

"Why didn't you tell me?" Noah searched her eyes.

"Tell you what?" Olivia felt confusion beating against her forehead in rhythmic pulses.

"That I am your beloved husband come home to reconcile." Harrison stepped forward on the other side of her bed.

Noah on the right, Harrison on the left. *Oh, no, not this. Not them together, vying for my affection.*

She looked at Southbridge, grimacing. Already her duties were bearing consequences, and one of them was the hurt she saw in Southbridge's eyes. "He has come home." She tried to push herself to a seated position, and immediately both men reached out to help her.

"I've told the parson that this would be a good time to announce my return." Harrison grinned. "Otherwise, it might look awkward for you to have been found in his bed."

"His *house,* not his bed. And I'm wounded."

"Ah, details." Harrison seemed to be enjoying himself. "But you are caught between a rock and a hard place, as they say. It's the parson's house, and you weren't alone. Either you have spent the night with Mr. MacHus, taking advantage of the parson's absence. Or you and his lordship—that would be me—encountered a footpad and took refuge in a nearby, unoccupied cottage. Which rumor will do the least harm?"

"Fine. You may announce your return. And while you are at it, can you borrow a carriage? I don't believe I can walk back."

"Already done. While Southbridge here stayed by your side, I sent for Herder to bring a carriage from the estate."

She leaned back, watching her options disappear as Harrison built a new narrative of their evening. "The staff will be hurt that I kept you a secret from them, as well as anxious that you have been observing among them under a false identity."

"We'll tell them the truth. I didn't even let you know I was coming, and after you discovered it, I demanded your cooperation. Besides, I have no complaints about the staff, though I still think that Cook belongs in an asylum."

"But he makes lovely biscuits." She felt sleep come, and, feeling strangely content, she let it.

Olivia woke to the wet nose of a fox pup nuzzling her neck. She opened one eye, slowly, turning her head from side to side to see whether the pain would return. Bertie stood at the side of her bed, holding the pup next to Olivia's face.

"I didn't wake you." Bertie tucked the fox under his arm, gently.

"But I'm awake." Olivia leaned up on her side, waiting to discover what the child wanted.

"Mrs. Pier said I could wait outside your door until you woke up, but I wasn't to wake you." He looked at her with earnest eyes.

"Who woke me, then?" She reached for the dressing gown lying next to her on the bed.

"Kit." Bertie scratched the pup behind her ears.

"I see. Did Kit want something in particular?" Olivia examined the boy's face. His eyes were red and swollen.

"Kit wants to sleep in the nursery tonight. The stable frightens her."

"It does? But wouldn't that leave Mr. Calder all alone? Won't he be frightened if Kit isn't there?"

He looked thoughtful. "I don't know."

"Have you asked Kit why she's afraid of the stable?"

"She misses her parents. I found her last month after Lord Heron's fox hunt. Her eyes were still closed. I fed her berries and snails. My da said I had to let her go in the spring."

"Foxes like the woods because that's where the other foxes live."

"I know." The boy looked crestfallen. "But then I won't have anyone."

Olivia brushed his hair back from his face. She wanted to tell him he would have her, but until she knew whether Harrison would give her the settlement she requested she couldn't make that promise. "I know it's hard, Bertie. I lost my parents when I was your age. But Lord Walgrave's father took good care of me. I promise that you won't be abandoned. Lord Walgrave will take care of you too."

The boy's eyes filled with tears. "They burned my house down."

"I know." She knelt beside the bed and hugged the boy to her chest, both of them weeping. The fox wriggled between them. And suddenly she needed to make him some promise. "How about this? In spring, when Kit goes to her fox family, if you wish, we will find you a dog, a puppy who can sleep in the nursery when she's scared."

The boy wiped his eyes on his sleeve. "I would like that."

"Bertie Davis!" Mrs. Pier exclaimed from the door. "Didn't I tell you to leave that fox in the stable? Now come along. Mr. Stanley has made you some special cakes."

Bertie brightened slightly, then turned to Olivia. "At least I didn't wake you up."

Olivia watched the five-year-old leave with Mrs. Pier, holding the housekeeper's skirt in one hand, and his fox in the other. His losses broke her heart. She knew all too well what it felt like to grow up alone. She tested sitting up slowly, and finding no ill effects from her injury, she rose and began to dress, Bertie's plight weighing heavily on her.

She had never forgotten how frightened she'd been when Sir Roderick and his friends arrived at the cottage where her father had left her.

"Fallon, you swindler. Where's my money?"
"Break the door down. That will teach him."

"We know you are there."

"You can't escape us."

Fear hardened like an anchor in her throat. There was no time to run. She had flung herself onto the floor and crawled under the cot, pressing her back into the corner as far as she could. She had tucked her feet under her skirt, making sure that no part of her body or clothing stuck out. The damp of the wall had leeched through the top of her shift, making her shiver, but she'd willed herself to ignore it. She brushed a spiderweb away from her face, trying not to think about where the spider might be.

The door shook under the weight of the angry men's fists. "Fallon!" Giving under the pressure, the cottage door swung back hard against the wall, dislodging pieces of failing plaster. She could see boots, five pair. Her only hope was that the angry men might overlook her in the deep darkness surrounding the cot. Her heart beat hard and fast, and the sound of blood coursed in her ears.

The men moved to search the room, each taking a different corner. The man by the window held the lamp up, illuminating the hearth and the front corners of the room. One of the men bent down in front of the fireplace, getting ashes on his shoes. "Hearth's cold. No embers even. No one's been here for at least a day, probably more."

"No food either." The man by the cabinets in polished boots shut the doors. "But he left this. Lady's reticule. Wait, something's in it."

She held her hand over her mouth to keep from crying out Mine! It had been her mother's.

"Tell me it's that fat pile of banknotes he's been showing off." The man by the window sneered.

The scuffed boots closest to the door met the recently polished boots at the center of the room. "No luck, Hardcastle. Just a letter addressed to Walgrave."

"Lucky devil," Hardcastle tore it open. "Listen to this:

'I leave you my greatest treasure to care for until I return.'
Fallon's pinned Walgrave for the sentimentalist."

"I take exception to that." The ash-covered boots
walked closer, the man's voice cultured and low. "I'm the
smart one."

"What does that make the rest of us?"

Walgrave laughed. "Archer is our dandy, Manning our
diplomat, and you Hardcastle are the brawn."

"I think that letter is Fallon's last joke. He wouldn't have
left anything of value. Not in his nature, the swindler."

Her father might be a thief, but he was her father. The
only family she had. She felt an anger so deep that she
wanted nothing more than to kick the man in the shins. But
she knew she had to keep still, keep quiet. Her only hope
was to be overlooked. She watched the frost curl with her
breath, and she covered her nose and mouth with her hand.

"Worthless bastard left you a beaded reticule and calls
it his greatest treasure. I always said he had a sense of
humor."

"Yes, Walgrave, I want to see you carry that to the next
ball at Almack's."

"Anything we've missed?"

One of the men—the one with the lantern—walked
around the room. She could see the light move in a circle,
from the door to the far wall to the hearth to the near wall.

"Knew we should have brought more light."

"What's there to see? He's long gone—and left only a
freezing cottage and a reticule."

"I'll look under the cot all the same—perhaps he's left
me a strongbox full of jewels. Then you'll wish he'd liked
you better."

The ashy boots approached and set a lantern on the
floor next to the head of the cot. A man bent on his hands
and knees. His face, illuminated by the lamp, looked like
the crags on the side of a mountain. She shrunk into the

wall, *trying to be as small as possible, curling into herself as if trying to ward off a blow. Then she kept very still, like a deer, hoping if she didn't move he wouldn't see her.*

"Nothing here." His voice was cultured, deep. The man stood. She watched his boots walk away and stop beside her mother's reticule. "Looks like we'll have to try another route."

The other boots walked to the door, the men grumbling, but the man who hadn't seen her held back. Before he left, he kicked the reticule under the bed, then pulled the door shut behind him.

She pulled the reticule to her and clutched it to her heart, as if it could protect her, as if it could bring back her father. She knew to wait in her hiding place. It might be a trap to get her to bolt. She counted her heartbeats like her father had taught her. At four thousand she knew it had been at least an hour. She started to crawl out from beneath the cot, but she heard more horses, and she pushed herself back against the corner.

The door opened again. The man who hadn't seen her had come back. This time he lay down on the cold floor and looked under the cot at her.

"There's no need to be afraid. I know your father." He held out a letter. "See? This is my name here. Walgrave. Your father asked me to take care of you, and that's what I'm going to do. I have a friend. Her name is Mrs. Flint, and she runs a School for Exceptional Girls, as she calls it. Would you like to go to school? You'll have a warm bed and plenty of food and friends."

"I have to wait until my father comes back. If I leave, he won't be able to find me."

Sir Roderick's eyes were kind. "I understand that. Why don't we do this? You'll go to school, while I look for your father. And I'll find him for you, even if it takes until the day I die. Is that acceptable?"

Cold and hungry, she nodded her agreement.

"Then come along." He held out his big, warm hand, and, scrambling out from under the cot, she took it.

She'd never been that afraid again, except occasionally at night when she dreamed her father had returned to the abandoned cottage for her, and she wasn't there. At least Bertie had—or would have—the cold comfort of knowing his parents were dead.

She picked up the tiger's-eye stone that Harrison had returned to her, and began to rub it in slow circles between her fingers.

Mrs. Pier entered Olivia's room, her face a lecture. "Well, Miss Olivia, I am hurt. His lordship arrives, and you did not trust me to know about it." Sir Roderick had hired the older woman shortly after Olivia's wedding, and over the years Mildred had been her truest friend. The scholars had taken the news of Walgrave's return in stride; very little ruffled their feathers—or registered at all, if it was not related to their research. Olivia knew that Mildred Pier would require an explanation. And yet, she could not give her the truth—not all of it.

Sitting at her dressing table, Olivia raised her hands in helplessness. "He insisted no one was to know, and I was afraid if I objected he might discover my trips to London."

"He'll find out soon enough, what with your novel at every bookseller's stall in the country." Mildred helped Olivia step into her walking dress.

"Yes, but I've wanted to find the best time to tell him." Olivia tightened the drawstrings around her bodice.

"The best time to tell him is before he finds it out on his own." Mildred adjusted Olivia's fichu. "I'd confess, and soon."

"To what should she confess?" Harrison stood in the doorway between Olivia's room and his father's.

Mildred, turning red, looked at Olivia with apology in her eyes, and quickly excused herself.

"One of those secrets you cannot trust me to keep?" Harrison lounged against her wardrobe. "Have you been selling off the family jewels, the silver? I saw what you did with the trees."

"I wrote to you about the trees, and I refuse to explain it again." She searched his face for evidence of anger, but found none. "If you wish to know, ask Herder."

"Then what secret does Mildred fear I will discover?" His face was placid but curious.

"I suppose it will reconcile you somewhat to our parting ways." She breathed deeply, calming the fast beat of her heart. But whether her heart beat fast from the anxiety of telling him or from remembered passion, she couldn't tell.

"I wait on bated breath."

She looked up to see Harrison holding his breath, cheeks puffed out, face contorted like a five-year-old. She began to laugh. Letting his breath go in a giant swoosh, Harrison laughed with her.

"Now, what secret am I to keep for you today?" Harrison's voice was gentle, even kind.

"When you didn't come home, I grew . . ." She searched for the word.

"Argumentative? Angry? Anxious? Apoplectic? Apprehensive? Should I move on to the Bs?"

She knew he was trying to make it easier, and of all her secrets, this one wasn't all that significant, at least to him.

"I grew restive. I had just read Matthew Lewis's *The Monk*, and I wanted to see if I could write a novel that outdid him, as he had outdone Ann Radcliffe."

"Ah, my bloodthirsty girl, should I fear you will murder

me in my bed? Or perhaps will you run mad with a woolen hat and torture the servants? We have that tower, perhaps you might throw me off next time I frustrate you."

Olivia knew he was only teasing, so she continued. "The scholars ensured every detail was apt, and Mr. Bentley published it several months ago. Already it's gone into a second edition. Apparently, there is money to be made in gothic novels with a bit of gore."

"What is the title? Perhaps I've heard of it. Palmersfield and Capersby—you remember them—are great fans of a new one called *The Deserted Wife*."

She waited, watching his expression shift with recognition.

"It's you. The lady author of *The Deserted Wife*." He laughed until he turned red. It wasn't the response she'd expected. "Lord, you must have hated me."

"You've read it?"

"In a single night."

"You aren't angry?"

"How could I be angry? I couldn't put it down. My valet, Walker, had to bring our meals to my rooms."

"Your valet read it as well?"

"One volume behind me all the way. My dear, it was brilliant! I especially liked the section where the offending husband was torn apart by vultures . . ." His face grew introspective. "Oh. I suppose you meant that particular punishment for me."

"It's a novel, not real life. However the book began, in the end, the characters behaved according to their own logic." She stared at him for some minutes. "You honestly aren't worried my novel will damage your career, if my identity becomes known?"

"Perhaps it might if it hadn't been such a good book. But everyone in the ton has been desperate to know who the author might be. You'll see: I'm going to introduce you to everyone as the famous author of the most talked-about novel of the year."

"Miss Livvy, you are needed." Mrs. Pier stood at the door. It was unclear to Harrison whether Olivia was truly needed or Pier had decided the time for their conversation was over.

"It seems our conversation will need to wait once more." Olivia rose.

"Perhaps I can assist you," Harrison offered.

"As you wish."

In the corridor outside the library, Quinn pointed an angry finger at Martinbrook. "I've told you time and again not to use my telescope."

"Gentlemen, what is your dispute?" Olivia spoke softly, but the men immediately included her in their debate.

"Martinbrook has tampered with my telescope again."

Martinbrook sighed audibly. "Quinn told me I might use it in the mornings when he is still asleep after his nighttime vigils. I need it to observe whether the land reveals any barrows from our ancient Pict ancestors." He rubbed the back of his hand across his nose, leaving a black smudge behind.

Harrison looked at the antiquarian's hands, both showing the dirty remains of his excavations, as did his shirt and trousers, while Quinn, the astronomer, was perfectly clean, his cravat a crisp white, his clothes recently laundered and pressed.

"I did agree to let you use it, but a telescope is a delicate instrument. You can't expect it to work properly if the gears are jammed with jam! Elderberry, if I'm correct."

"It's a very fine jam, one of Cook's best batches."

"Miss Olivia, Martinbrook would be perfectly happy as one of those medieval hermits who lived their lives at the top of a pole, never bathing and sitting in their own excrement."

"Well, from a pole I'd have an excellent vantage point to observe the lay of the land."

The men fell into their argument once more.

"Gentlemen, gentlemen." Olivia waited for the men to heed her. "As I remember, the telescope was purchased for Dr. Quinn with monies from the fellowship fund." Quinn beamed in victory. "As a result, we must maintain that equipment for the benefit of all." Quinn's face fell.

The men's voices rose once more.

"I believe the solution"—she looked to Harrison and grinned mischievously—"would be to let his lordship make the determination. Lord Walgrave?"

The men turned to Walgrave, each expanding on his own position in louder and louder terms. When Walgrave looked for Olivia, she was gone.

Walgrave caught up with Olivia in the library, where she was sitting at his desk in the dark corner. "You abandoned me."

"It's hardly abandonment when it's your estate. Adjudicating the disagreements of the scholars is your obligation." Olivia finished a letter and set it aside.

"Are they always that difficult?" Harrison picked it up, an order for supplies.

"Only when one of them impinges on the other's research." Olivia took the sheet from his hand and placed it on the far end of the desk. "More often, they are quite happy with their books and papers, and with something sweet at afternoon tea."

"I see you are hard at work . . . at my desk."

Olivia held out a fat packet from Constance Equiano at the African's Daughter bookshop. Written in a crisp hand, Equiano listed the books she had located—every one on Sir Roderick's list. Over the next five pages, Equiano outlined the condition of the various copies, their current owners, and the costs of acquiring them. In other months, Olivia would have written queries requesting more information about some of the books. But these copies would do. Another of her tasks completed. "Your father left a plan for how he wished his library to grow, as well as a list of books he especially wanted to buy." She held out the list. "These are the last he specifically indicated he wished to acquire. Of course you will have your own ideas about how to build the library's collection."

"Some of these are quite expensive." Harrison scratched the skin in front of his ear.

"Your father made some lucrative investments before his death." She paused, intending to elide the fact that estate funds would cover some part of the purchase. He could discover that from his review of the accounts. "The money supports the library and its maintenance, though the scholars' meals do come from the estate accounts."

"I suppose it wouldn't do to let them starve." He returned the list. "Will you finalize the purchases before you go?"

"If you wish."

"I do. You've been a better manager than I would have been, Livvy. My father would have been proud."

She was surprised at how much his praise mattered. "If I go, you will keep them then—the Seven? They will always have a place here?"

"Of course, Livvy. I have promised never to lie to you. If you leave me at the end of this, I will keep them on, even if I grieve your loss each time I hear one of them say yes."

Smiling, she pushed the rest of his papers to the far side of the desk and sat on the edge, her knees open wide. "I desire an afternoon sweet, my lord, and I wondered if perhaps you could give it to me here."

There she was, perched on his desk like his wildest fantasy. Anyone might knock on the door at any moment. It made him want her even more.

"The scholars could return at any minute. Are you sure you wish to begin this here?" But he moved to her and began to kiss her neck all the same.

"The scholars will arrive thick in the middle of some debate or other. We will hear them in time to repair our clothing." She drew him close. "And you *did* choose the darkest corner for your desk."

He bit her neck as he pulled her close. Kneeling, he lifted her buttocks in his hands and kissed her thighs, gently at first, then with greater appetite. Her climax when it came was shattering, but he would not rest, his fingers and mouth still caressing her, pushing her to another more dazzling height.

Readjusting her clothes, he then took her by the arm and led her to his turret rooms.

Each time they had awakened, their passion had renewed, and he'd spent himself in her body several times before they had both fallen into a fast sleep.

Now in the half-light before dawn, he lay beside her, having no intention of letting her leave his bed.

He rolled over onto her, pinning her arms under his hands and kissing her neck. She nuzzled his face with hers as he entered her once more. Pushing them once more to climax.

"Is it like this every time you take a lover? Hire a whore? This hunger? This . . ." Her voice trailed off.

He watched her face and pressed his hips into her body; though spent, he still needed the connection.

"Nothing is like this. No one is like you."

"I have listened for years now to the servants. Those

who are wives, of course. And none of them has ever mentioned . . ."

"Then they have very boring lives."

"Is this not how one treats a whore?"

"This is how one treats his wife, if he is very lucky."

"Then I hope you find this again."

No matter what he did, no matter how many times he held her in his arms and brought her pleasure, no matter how solicitous he was of her opinions, her desires, no matter what . . . she was still leaving him. It made no sense. She might not love him, but he knew she loved the estate, its people, her scholars. Her life, even with the allowance she'd requested, would be far less comfortable. No woman would give up such security for the risks of spinsterhood.

And now, with the passion between them so strong, it could not be simply distaste for him that drove her away. That meant she was under constraint to leave. And that was a mystery he meant to solve.

Chapter Twenty-Five

A week had passed since the attack on Olivia. Every morning Harrison would tutor Adam in how to oversee the Home Office agents. And every afternoon, he would change from master to student, and under Olivia's gentle guidance he learned how to run the estate. If in the middle of their studies, they grew amorous, they would simply retreat to Harrison's turret rooms for a different sort of lesson. The fact that the servants believed them married meant they didn't even have to hide their pleasure.

But the last packet from London had called Adam back and suggested strongly that Harrison needed to complete his decryption of Wilmot's code.

Adam had ridden out at sunrise, with the assurance that Harrison would follow close behind. An hour later, Walker had their bags packed, and two horses stood ready in the courtyard.

He had only to give his regrets to Livvy. He found her in her study, standing by the window.

"Business calls me back to London." He had hoped for perhaps a kiss goodbye or an embrace, but she looked at him blandly.

"I see."

"You see?" Her response made little sense. "I will return in a few weeks, after this is settled."

"Then this is goodbye. It was . . . good . . . to see you again, my lord." Her voice was reserved and distant, and his stomach twisted.

"Goodbye?" he repeated, feeling that there was something more to it.

"Yes. Only a week or so ago, you manipulated me into agreeing to maintain the pretense of our marriage for the sake of your career." He could hear the edge of frustration now. He was beginning to be able to read her voice.

"And to see if we might suit," he offered, his sense of helplessness growing.

"As you said. But today, you must leave."

"But I will be back. A friend sent a code to me to decipher. He made it a contest of sorts." Even to his own ears, the excuse sounded thin. "He wrote to say that he needs the results by the end of the week. But I can only finish in London."

"I have been here before, standing in front of you, saying goodbye, the feel of your lips on mine still fresh. It took you six years and a . . . legal proceeding . . . to return home. I will not devote another six years to your next return."

"What do you mean, Livvy?" His suspicions were fully awake now.

"I have called for my trunks to be brought down, and I've called for a carriage. I will not be here when you return."

"Livvy." He put out his hands in supplication.

But the stern set of her jaw, the hint of disappointment in her eyes, told him she was not lying. If he left now, there would be no returning. His chance would be gone. His heart sank into his shoes. There was only one solution, if she would agree. "Then I suppose we will take the carriage. How long will you need?"

"As I said, my trunk is already packed."

"Then come with me." His heart lightened immediately. "And any provisions you need in London we can simply purchase. But bring a dinner dress. We'll be spending the night at the home of a local magistrate. Squire Baldwin knew my father from before the wars. His name is one of the few on my friend's list who isn't dead, and I want to see if he might know what this list means. If he doesn't, I want to warn him to be careful."

The countryside rolled past, cold and barren, the winter having arrived early. Harrison and his valet took turns riding on the outside. Harrison was concerned about high-waymen, given the recent attack on Olivia. Walker, when he was in the carriage, slept or nattered on about the latest fashions in London. He was sleeping now.

Olivia was thinking on her not-marriage, trying to piece together what she might need to know if she were to stay with Harrison. She hadn't told him she was considering it; it was too new an idea to share. But being near him had brought her a sense of peace and home that she'd never felt before.

But she wouldn't fool herself either. She still feared she was merely convenient and that if she agreed to remain married (or rather, to marry), he would leave her again, just as quickly, and never return. Wasn't this morning an indication of how little he considered her when making plans?

She let her mind return to the day she'd first met him. Even as angry as he had been, she could still see the characteristics his father had described so lovingly.

He'd walked into the library—much smaller then—

where she had been reading a book, and took her breath away.

"I'm sure you are aware that I haven't been consulted in the arrangement of this marriage."

Uncertain of her voice, she'd nodded her assent.

"And knowing my father, I'm sure that your wishes weren't considered either. I hope that he didn't bully you into agreeing to his scheme."

"You misjudge your father." She looked at her hands. She needed to appear demure, the sort of woman a man would choose for his countess. "Though he was quite persuasive on the benefits of a marriage to his son, he was actually quite solicitous of my wishes."

"So, you agreed to this marriage?" He raised one eyebrow in disbelief.

"It's surprising what one will agree to when one has few prospects." Her voice sounded sad, even to her ears.

He looked at her closely, as if for the first time. "Meaning?"

"My family are all dead. When your father contacted me, I had been working for several months as a governess to four disagreeable children. Marriage to a man I had never met seemed a pleasant alternative." She hadn't mentioned that she needed a place to hide, a place to resurrect herself as someone new, and a new name to protect her.

"But you know nothing about me. I could be cruel, profligate, violent, or perverse . . ." His voice had been filled with frustration and even confusion.

"I am neither a child nor a fool." She folded her hands primly, hoping he would not see them shaking. "I entered into this agreement after careful consideration. I made certain . . . inquiries concerning your character."

"What kind of inquiries?"

"If you must know, I hired a Bow Street runner to

investigate your friends, your pastimes, your accounts."
She lied. She'd investigated him herself with a little help
from Mentor.

"Your income is insufficient to live on, but you had
enough to hire a runner?"

"Your father gave me a small fortune merely to consider his offer, and I used a portion of that money. Had I
discovered you were cruel, or profligate, or violent . . ."

"You left out perverse."

"I would not be here now." She ignored his baiting, and
kept her voice low and soft.

"What did you discover?"

"You excelled at both Harrow and Cambridge, especially in philosophy and natural sciences; your closest
friends tend to be men of intellect, but your circle also includes more frivolous companions. In the last year, you
have spent a great deal of time at your club and at the
races, though your worst expenditures tend to be in keeping up with the latest fashions. No more the serious schoolboy, you have gained a reputation as a wit and . . . if you
will excuse me, my lord . . . a bit of a fop."

"That tells you little of my character. Does it not concern you that in the last year I have spent considerable
time drinking and gambling?"

"That part of the report did give me pause, but it was
balanced by the reports of servants who find you responsible and fair, and of the reports of your closest friends."

"Which friends?"

"Lords Capersby and Palmersfield."

"You spoke to Capersby and Palmersfield?"

"Yes, and at some length. They were most obliging.
They made it clear I could do far worse in a husband."

"Really?"

"They in fact assured me that you would be unlikely to

beat me if I displeased or angered you," she tried to tease a little, but he was too angry to notice.

"I may beat them, however."

"Well, if I had friends who met secretly for such a purpose, I would likely wish to beat them too."

Later that night, she had retreated to one of the parapets to look out over the peaceful countryside. She heard him on the stairs, and she pulled her cloak around her body, waiting. When he stepped onto the parapet, he looked like Lucifer in moonlight, all rugged beauty. He'd faced her, the light illuminating his face, the line of his chin, and she'd been struck with desire. In his anger, he strode to her. He pressed her body roughly against the parapet wall, forcing a kiss, expecting—she thought—to shock her. She'd stiffened for only a moment, but she'd made no effort to refuse him.

He'd continued kissing her, his hands feeling the curves of her body, coming to rest on her breast. She'd lifted her arms to encircle his neck, then she'd returned his kiss with passion. The softness of his lips, the smell of his skin and hair, struck her viscerally. He had wanted her, and she had not refused.

The memory left her flushed, wanting his arms around her even now, but Harrison was outside and she was left to miss him, accompanied by the snoring of his valet. She turned her mind away from her longing, to consider the other threats that faced her. The news that Calista knew she was alive was not welcome.

Calista's husband had been a foreign count, wealthy beyond measure. It was Olivia's third mission after leaving Mrs. Flint's school—and, due to the outcome, it had been her last until she'd begun writing as An Honest Gentleman. The Home Office had sent her to investigate a series of disappearances—all young women who had worked for a foreign baron, Calista's husband. Olivia had been hired as a lady's companion, and though she'd found the baroness odd and temperamental, she'd felt some affection for her.

Olivia had rebuffed the advances of the count, and he'd turned his unwelcome attentions on the upstairs maid. One night soon after, Olivia had found the maid's body, broken and beaten in the castle garden. But by the time she'd roused the magistrate, the body had disappeared. She'd searched then, using all the skills she'd learned at Mrs. Flint's. And she'd found what she was seeking—and more: the bodies of all the missing girls buried together in an ancient sarcophagus in the churchyard. When the baron had tried to silence her as well, she'd felt few qualms about protecting herself.

Reviewers had praised the gothic gore of *The Deserted Wife*, finding it a remarkable achievement of the imagination, but she hadn't imagined any of it, not even Calista arranging the bodies to make room for one more.

She shook off the memory, but couldn't forget Calista's insistence that Olivia too would die. The Home Office had protected her, announcing her death in the papers, and Sir Roderick had secreted her away on his estate. She'd chosen a new name and hoped to begin a new life. But she'd chosen the wrong role to play: believing Harrison wanted a reliable, domestic wife, she'd turned her energies to that, and she'd run the estate admirably, until she'd realized her success would never win his heart.

Olivia knew she could not go back to being domestic-Olivia; no, her old adventure-loving self was too happy playing the spy again. And that might cost her Harrison.

It might cost her everything.

They spent the afternoon at Squire Baldwin's estate, on the excuse of accepting a standing invitation to hunt on his manor lands. The man had immediately picked up his fowling-gun and led them into the fields.

Olivia stood watching the flight of the grouse. Their host, a garrulous old man, had bragged about his skill in shooting, and she had no wish to reveal herself as more skilled than he. Instead, she made sure to hold the gun awkwardly and allow him to give her lessons on its use.

"In my day women could shoot or they went hungry when their man was away. None of this accomplishment stuff. Who cares if a woman can draw or paint or sing an aria? What matters is whether she can feed herself and her family when times grow hard."

Olivia was listening to Baldwin with half an ear when she heard the grasses rustle to her left, and instinctively stepped into the shade of a tree.

"No need to be afraid, dearie, I'll not shoot you." The squire leaned over to check his weapon, when Olivia heard the snap of a gun's hammer falling into place behind them. She threw herself at her host, knocking them both to the ground, as the shot fired. It missed her, but grazed Baldwin as it passed.

Baldwin, the breath knocked out of him by the fall, looking questioningly at Olivia, stunned by the turn of events. She moved a finger to her lips, signaling him to remain silent. They both lay on the ground in the shadow of the trees, unmoving, in case the assailant came to see if his bullet met its target. Olivia pulled Baldwin's gun, already primed, to her side, prepared to shoot if necessary. They remained there waiting.

Eventually, Harrison, drawn to the sound of the gunshot, found them, helped the old man to his feet, then lifted Olivia from the grass and held her closely in his arms.

That evening, Baldwin was still visibly shaken, and he grew more so after Harrison asked if the old man had any connection to the dead men listed in Wilmot's code.

"I only know four, all school friends. Some I haven't seen for years. The only one I've had any contact with at all recently was Bowers. He'd become obsessed with old plays, and we had a delightful chat about *The Merry Wives of Windsor* at a coffee shop." The older man shook his head. "Tragic. All of them dead, and in senseless accidents, every one."

Olivia could barely concentrate on Baldwin's reminiscences. Yes, Baldwin was on Wilmot's list, but had the bullet been meant for him, or her? Was this all tied to An Honest Gentleman? Olivia desperately wished she could confide in Harrison, give him all her secrets and see what he thought. But the trust between them was a fragile thing and she could not risk her safety—and that of countless others—until she was sure how he would react.

The sooner they reached London, the better. Once she and Harrison deciphered the rest of the items on the list, she hoped all would become clear.

Chapter Twenty-Six

Aidan Somerville, Lord Forster, lounged on the chaise in front of the fire in his fiancée's library. He watched Sophia, Lady Wilmot, at her easel, painting. She sat in profile, looking out the window. Today she was sketching the trees in their stark late-autumn appearance; the lines appeared ghostly, dark on the prepared white of her canvas. He loved looking at her, the thickness of her nut-brown hair, the trimness of her dress, the elegance of the line of her arm as she raised it over the paper pinned to the easel.

"Are you certain I can't convince you to retire to your bedroom? We have at least another hour before Ian and Lily return from the park." He followed her gaze to the clock over the mantel. "But your children are always a bit late."

She shook her head. "Why, Lord Forster," she teased, "have you no concern for the proprieties?"

"Never with you." She was tempted, he could tell. But before he could make a move toward her, a knock sounded at the door, followed by the butler's entrance.

"Lord Walgrave has arrived, my lady, on pressing business. He requires the attention of both yourself and

His Grace. I placed him in the front drawing room, though he did ask to meet you here, in the library."

"Walgrave is always welcome, and if he prefers the library to the drawing room, that suits me as well."

"He has brought with him his wife. Should I prepare tea?"

"His wife?" Sophia looked to Aidan, who nodded affirmation. "Well, then tea, certainly. Before you escort them back, ask Cook to prepare some refreshments. I need a moment to consult with Forster."

Dodsley nodded and withdrew.

Sophia turned to Aidan. "I didn't know he was married."

"I knew. But I didn't know the two of them spoke."

"Why not?"

"It was an unwelcome marriage—arranged—and he's resented it and her. As far as I'm aware, she has lived entirely on their estate."

"Then perhaps he wishes our help in introducing her to society? Dozens are better suited than I am to that task, but I feel the obligation to help him quite strongly. Without Walgrave's help this fall, I fear we would have had a difficult time with the magistrates."

"I can't imagine it's a social call: Walgrave isn't the sort who would stoop to a purely social visit."

"Perhaps that's why he asked for the library rather than the drawing room, to make it seem less social. This should be an interesting visit."

When Harrison had announced that they needed to travel to a library in London, Olivia had imagined they would go to the British Museum. But standing in the entry of Lady Wilmot's house, she found herself wondering how Harrison knew the lady, and how well. If the library had been so robust that they traveled to London to visit it, wouldn't she have heard about it through antiquarian circles?

Perhaps Lady Wilmot would be plain, hunchbacked, old, toothless . . . Olivia thought of any number of scenarios with some pleasure.

But she would be gracious, whatever Harrison's relationship with her ladyship proved to be, or had been. Besides, Olivia was claiming that their marriage was invalid, so what right did she have to be jealous at all? If she didn't want him, what would it matter if some other woman did?

The problem was that she did want him. She had from the moment that he'd thrown open the drawing room door to confront her for agreeing to an arranged marriage.

But when they entered the drawing room, she realized that Lady Wilmot was the woman who had helped her at the bookshop. In comparison to Lady Wilmot's elegance and beauty, Olivia knew it was she who looked plain and old.

Harrison escorted her to meet their hostess. He even seemed as if he wished to remain by her side, though his embrace of her ladyship made clear that the two were old and good friends.

"Sophia Gardiner, Lady Wilmot, may I introduce my wife, Olivia Levesford, Lady Walgrave."

Lady Wilmot's eyes widened only briefly at seeing Olivia again, then her smile broadened. "I am grateful for the honor of your visit."

She took Olivia's hand and led her to the couch. Livvy was surprised at the woman's warmth. Perhaps not a mistress. "Walgrave has been a dear friend for years, visiting me and my late husband during our years in Italy, and more recently helping protect us from a mysterious enemy who threatened myself and my children."

"You are too gracious," Harrison objected. "I believe Forster protected you most."

"Hear, hear, man! Sophia, do you hear that? Harrison has declared that 'Forster protected you most.'"

"Lady Walgrave, you have not yet met my fiancé, Aidan Somerville, Duke of Forster."

Olivia had not noticed the man in the room, standing in the corner to the right of the door. But once she did, she wondered how she had missed him. One arm holding a book, his leg resting on the bookcase ladder, he seemed larger than life, filling the corner of the room behind her. She wondered why he had chosen such an obscure corner, and she found it suspicious. Had he wanted to see without being seen, at least at first?

"Your Grace." She offered the requisite half curtsey, rising to discover that Forster held his hand out for hers.

"Lady Walgrave, I have wished for some time to meet the woman who stole Walgrave's freedom. I hope your trip to London was uneventful."

Harrison intervened before she could answer. "Somewhat more eventful than expected. But we came today because we were hoping for your help, Lady Wilmot. We believe we have found the solution to your late husband's code, but we need your library to finish deciphering it."

"If you need the library, then you need the library. And, of course, I will help. I've wondered what Tom's code contained, but I'd almost reconciled myself to never finding out." Sophia held out her hand for the list. "May I see what you have thus far?"

Harrison held out the copy he had made from the scholars' notes. "The clues lead from one book to the next. In each pair of lines, the first line indicates the book to use to decode the next."

"Was Tom playing some sort of merry joke?" Sophia examined the list carefully.

"I think it was a matter of necessity," Walgrave said. "Tom was weak, collecting the information over years and as his body allowed. He knew someone might notice if he kept the same book by his side for weeks or months on end. He chose a code word—*hummingbird*—to begin the code, then encoded the remaining items with whatever book was at hand. His contact here could easily use the British Museum's collection to decipher the code."

"Walgrave is right. What we see here is Tom carefully using the resources he had at hand," Forster chimed in.

Sophia looked up from the list of items already decoded. "These three titles at the top came in a packet together from a friend in Paris. These next four are my books, purchased from a bookseller in Naples who catered to the English-speaking population. The next two were a gift from one of the English tourists returning home." She shook her head slightly. "I always wondered why our books seemed to migrate all over the villa."

"Did Tom read them?" Olivia asked gently.

"Always. We had lovely conversations over most of them. That's how I remember." Sophia read over the rest of the decoded titles. "It's almost a record of the last year of our life together." She grew silent, and Forster stepped to her side, but she waved him away with a wan smile. "But this makes it more difficult. These aren't just Tom's books—which we would find in those shelves there—but they are the family's books. These could be here, in the nursery, at Tom's country estate, or still in Italy. It's a bit daunting."

Olivia put her hand on Sophia's elbow. "Perhaps we would find it more manageable if we worked through until we reach one that is difficult to access." She looked around the library. Bookshelves alternated with the long windows on the garden side, but even so, the books filled the cases from floor to ceiling, leaving only a space at the top of each case for a marble bust of some famous philosopher, scientist, or author. "Is there an easy way to identify where each book might be?"

"Yes, of course. I have a set of ledgers in which I record every book and where it should be shelved, though Ian and Lily challenge that system daily." She removed two large ledger books from the shelf nearest her partner desk. "Lady Walgrave, if you would sit here, we can begin identifying where the books might be found."

Forster nodded. "That sounds reasonable. Then Walgrave and I can locate and decipher the code to provide the name of the next title we'll need."

Olivia held out her hands for the ledger and sat in the chair across from Sophia at the desk.

"The system is a bit complicated. This ledger is our acquisition list. It proceeds in chronological order, so I'll use it since I can somewhat predict when a particular book came into the library. The ledger you have is the shelf list. It is divided by bookcase and within that contains the actual location for each book. Shall we begin?"

Olivia nodded yes.

"Our first book to locate is Mary Robinson's book of poems, *Sight, the Cavern of Woe, and Solitude.* That was a gift from Frederick Buchanan when he painted Tom's portrait in fall of 1817." She turned the pages swiftly. "Olivia, it will be in the section for Sappho. It should be somewhere in the middle of the list."

Olivia turned to her ledger.

"Oh, and the entries are organized, not by the title or author, but by their location on the shelves. Sappho I.1 is shelf one, place one. You'll see."

Olivia found Robinson's book some five pages into the section for Sappho. "This says 'Sappho V.3.'"

Harrison walked to the Sappho shelves. "Let's make sure I have this right." He pointed up. "Sappho?"

"Correct."

"V would be the fifth shelf down from Sappho's bust, and three is the third book in . . . from which side?"

"Left."

Harrison removed a small slender volume and opened it. "Forster, what does the code say?"

"Thirteen, thirteen, six."

Walgrave turned the pages. "Find page thirteen, count thirteen lines down, then six words in. I have it: *scorpions*."

Harrison and Forster bent their heads over the substitution code. "I have the next book: Horace Walpole's *Essay on Modern Gardening*."

"Would that be under the busts of Ray, Theophrastus, or Linnaeus?" Olivia paged to the appropriate sections of the ledger.

"Theophrastus. I have it here." Sophia removed the volume from the shelves. "Where should I look?"

"Page twenty-five, line fourteen, word three," Forster read out.

"The word is *transpicuous*."

"Is that a word?" Walgrave asked.

"Yes, it means something one can see through—a transpicuous forest," Olivia answered, without thinking. "If an argument is easily understood, it can be transpicuous."

"That leaves out any of Forster's arguments," Walgrave joked.

"And yours," Forster retorted.

"I think we ladies are wholly transpicuous," Sophia countered.

"Not Olivia. As she tells me on a regular basis, she is a woman of secrets," Harrison said.

Olivia looked up to find Sophia, clearly intrigued, watching her.

Harrison bent back over the solution grid. "Oh, dear.

Perhaps Forster and I should manage this next one. It could be a bit salacious."

"Not fair. If it's entertaining, you cannot keep it to yourself," Olivia chided.

"Certainly, Walgrave, tell us."

"The next clue is Cleland, *Memoirs of a Woman of Pleasure*. The numbers are eighty-eight, nineteen, three. I withdraw my assertion that Tom wasn't making a merry joke, and I'm certain I don't wish to learn what word he chose."

"Look at Harvey, third shelf down, perhaps five or six in. It's a small book covered in a crisp blue linen." Sophia gestured to the bookcases.

"Lady Wilmot, should we ask how you know your Cleland so well?" Harrison teased.

"That's for her to know and for me to find out," Forster warned laughingly.

"I found it. Let's see. *Intemperately*. At least it wasn't pleasure, or kisses, or . . ."

Olivia rose and took the book from his hand. "Let's see what else Lord Wilmot could have chosen. 'Charles waked, and turning towards me, kindly enquired how I had rested? And, scarce giving me time to answer, imprinted on my lips one of his burning rapture kisses, which darted a flame to my heart, and that from thence radiated to every part of me; and presently, as if he had proudly meant revenge for the survey I had smuggled of all his naked beauties, he sprung off the bed cloaths, and tossing up my shift as high as it would go, took his turn to feast his eyes on all the gifts nature had bestowed on my person; his busy hands, too, ranged' . . . ah, here it is . . . 'intemperately over every part of me.' Lady Wilmot, I find I have never read Cleland. Might I borrow it?" Olivia looked not-so-coyly at Harrison.

Walgrave and Forster both began to cough, then quickly

placed *intemperately* into the substitution code to arrive at the next book.

"Pliny. Thank God. Something temperate."

After some minutes, Olivia looked up, confused. "I see Pliny listed here, but there's no shelf marked."

"I'm afraid I left some of these in our villa in Italy. The Pliny, for example, was in Italian. I had no idea how much room I would have here, so I left all the foreign language books behind."

"I believe I have a copy of that in my library here," Aidan volunteered.

"Can we send a footman? Or is your library organized by some equally arcane system as my father's and your fiancée's?" Walgrave scribbled *Forster* beside the title of the book.

"It's equally arcane, but luckily my bookish brother Clive is reluctantly staying at my house—something about renovating the rooms at his club. He will be able find anything we request."

Lady Wilmot and her fiancé acted in concert. Sophia called for a footman, while Forster took a piece of paper from the desk and scribbled a note. The footman was come and gone within minutes.

"I suppose we are stuck until the next book arrives."

"Then that seems a perfect time for tea."

"Once our library grew too large for a ledger, Sir Roderick determined to follow the French system, with each book recorded on a single card."

"Did he use the backs of playing cards as they did in France?"

Olivia laughed. "I can't tell you the row it caused the first time he realized that the scholars were taking the records out of the catalogue in order to play whist with them. But the problem eventually disappeared."

"How?" Harrison looked up from his work.

"Sir Roderick insisted that if they were to play with his card catalogue he had to be included in each game."

"How did that solve the problem?" Harrison raised an eyebrow. "My father never had much aptitude with card games."

"But he had two things in his favor. He had made it a sort of game when we made the catalogue, to match the content of the book to the suit of the card, and he had an excellent memory."

"He simply memorized which books were on the backs of which cards?" Forster interrupted.

"Exactly."

"How long did it take the scholars to discover what he had done?" Sophia asked.

"Almost a month. It might have taken longer except he found the ace of hearts so funny he could never see it without laughing." Olivia smiled at the memory.

"Knowing my father, I'm almost afraid to ask what title was on the back of the ace of hearts."

"But we must know," Sophia insisted. "I say we make a game of it and guess."

Forster shook his head. "We can't guess until we first know the relationship between the suit and the book title on its back."

"Yes, with my father, the match could be quite idiosyncratic," Harrison agreed.

"I can tell you that books about agriculture tended to be recorded on the backs of spades; and books on mining on the backs of diamonds," Olivia teased.

"What about the clubs? What content matched them?" Harrison queried.

"Why pugilism, of course!" Forster announced.

Lady Wilmot shook her head and ignored the men. "If the suit is hearts, then can we assume that the book has to do with love?"

"If that's the case, my father owned a fine medieval manuscript of *Song of Songs*."

"But it could as easily be books on physiology," Forster said.

Olivia shook her head, holding back a laugh, her hand on the thin blue volume.

"You must give us a hint, Lady Wilmot," Sophia implored. "Otherwise we could be choosing everything from ancient erotic poetry with Sappho to mystical religious passion with John of the Cross to treatises on midwifery."

Olivia smiled and asked, "Should I give a hint?"

"No," Forster joked, teasing Harrison happily.

"Yes. At least give us a century," Sophia said.

"It was from the last century, and it was a book often regarded as somewhat . . . indelicate."

Harrison turned a slight shade of purple. "Not again! Cleland?"

Sophia burst into laughter and Olivia covered her mouth, trying not to laugh at Harrison's response. For a man so knowledgeable in how to please a woman . . . he could be a bit of a prude. "I must admit that from then on, I found it simply easier to give each scholar a pack of playing cards when he arrived at the library."

"Walgrave, come with me. The ladies will call us for tea. I've purchased a new pony for Lily, and she's in the mews. Fine piece of horseflesh." The two men talked horses and Newcastle as they left the room.

Chapter Twenty-Seven

As soon as the door shut behind them, Sophia waved Olivia to her chaise longue.

"In the last several weeks, I have often worried about a desperate woman who came to a bookstore I patronize and asked for help." She looked up, searching Olivia's face for a response. Olivia remained silent, waiting to see how much Sophia might intend to reveal to Walgrave.

"I'm sure you were able to offer her the help she needed."

"I have consoled myself with that thought, but today, I find that my concerns have been renewed."

"I am sure there is no need for concern. Circumstances often change."

"I would hope that if that woman needed help again, she would somehow know that I would be available to offer assistance . . . whether it would be as simple as a shared confidence or a request for help."

"I am certain, your ladyship, that any woman you have helped in the past would know she would not be turned away."

"Then, please, ease my mind further and tell me your story."

"Why?" Olivia demurred.

Sophia shrugged. "Because it's clear you love him, and equally clear that he's hurt you badly. Perhaps I can help."

The appeal of a woman friend was too great to reject, and given that Sophia had helped her once, without question, Olivia found herself uncharacteristically confiding in the other woman.

"After our wedding, I lived with Harrison's father. Each week, we waited for the wars to end and for Harrison to come home. After Sir Roderick died, I'd waited so long that I forgot exactly what I was waiting for. Then one morning I realized that he was never going to return."

Lady Wilmot extended her hand, placing it on Olivia's knee, in sympathy.

"I can remember the exact moment. I walked into the morning room, sun shining in the long windows, my breakfast on a tray on his desk, and a copy of the latest London newspaper tucked under the table linen. I skimmed through the advertisements for servants, read the theater and society news, shook my head over the police reports, then settled in to read the parliamentary debates for the previous week. And there I saw it, the evidence that made it clear just how foolish I had been to believe that I—of all people—could have drawn him back to me."

"What did it say?"

"I'll never forget it. 'The opposition's position was well argued by Lord Walgrave, returned last month from the Continent.' Returned, and no word."

"Oh, dear. You must have been crushed."

"I knew he had been opposed to the marriage, but somehow I thought with his next visit we could start anew. First I cried; then when my tears were spent, I forced myself to face honestly each of the illusions I'd allowed myself to cherish. One by one, I set each aside, until there was nothing left, not even the dreams I brought with me to Sir Roderick's home."

"But you still love him," Sophia said gently.

"Yes, unfortunately, I do."

"Thank you for your confidence." Sophia poured the tea. "I would like for you to consider joining some friends of mine this evening for dinner. We are thinking of forming a salon, of sorts, but one whose purpose is somewhat unusual. You may bring Walgrave, of course."

"Unusual?"

"So often salons are managed by a woman, but for an audience of men, whereas this would take as its model the muses of Parnassus. Each woman brings a particular skill, and we share that knowledge or expertise with the others when it is needed."

"Might I speak frankly, Lady Wilmot?"

"I would prefer it."

"When we first met, I was running from Walgrave. It was essential then that he not catch me, and it is essential now that he not know who he was following."

"I saw the desperation on your face. It is the primary reason I am willing to keep your secret."

"But we meet today, in the company of a man I was clearly trying to escape, and then you invite me to dinner tonight, to discuss a salon that takes on . . . causes."

"That's not quite what I intended."

"Why me, then?"

"Because you are resourceful. You have trusted me twice, when you had no reason to. And I believe that when we know one another better, we will find ourselves not so different, you and I. Certainly you are not so different from the other women."

"Then we will come."

A rap at the door ended their conversation. Harrison carried a tea service, and Forster an armload of ledger books. Behind them two footmen each carried a box filled with books.

"My tastes in books and Tom's often ran parallel, so it seemed easiest to bring my ledgers in which I record my purchases," Forster explained. "Unfortunately, unlike Tom and Sir Roderick, I have no system for my library. I simply write in one of these ledgers what books I have purchased then put the book on the shelf. It makes for some uneasy shelf-mates, but at least I always make sure to put a book or two between Wordsworth and Byron."

"We've brought all the books Forster purchased in the period Tom was making his list." Harrison set the tea service down as Lady Wilmot directed. "This way, if the book isn't in Tom's library here, we can perhaps find it in Forster's."

"Then, let's have our tea, then resume our work. Perhaps we can even be finished before dinner."

Lady Walgrave's salon was held in a large unused banqueting hall at Lord Forster's London house. Most of the wing beyond the hall had been converted into estate offices, leaving the banquet hall isolated except for a lucky connection to the library.

Surprisingly, to Olivia, however, the table in the middle of the hall was set for only fourteen. Membership in the salon did not extend far past Lady Wilmot's or Lord Forster's relations. The Muses—as Lady Wilmot called them—included a cousin by marriage, Audrey Hucknall; Sophia's sisters-in-law, Ophelia Mason and Kate and Ariel Gardiner; and Forster's sister Judith. Only Olivia and the bookseller, Constance Equiano, were not relations. As soon as dinner was concluded, the men—Forster, Walgrave, Malcolm Hucknall and Sidney Mason—all retreated into Forster's billiards room, leaving the ladies to plan their salon.

"As you all know, Aidan has encouraged me to open a salon. I hosted one in Italy until my husband fell ill, a lovely community that would help each other whenever a need arose. I'd like to create that combination of intellect and skill again. We would contribute our talents in whatever way we feel will best benefit the group, and eventually, we would use our knowledge and skills to help others. But to use our skills, in some cases, we must keep them secret. We promise, then, not to reveal each other's gifts outside of our circle."

Each woman agreed with nods and, in some cases, relieved sighs.

Sophia pointed at the ceiling. Ornate painted beams were spaced evenly down the hall, and between each rib, carved medallions waited for paintings to fill them. "Since all the paint on the ceiling has chipped off, I decided to reimagine its decorations. Each of the medallions will house a portrait of one of us—the Muses in the Muses' Salon—with the emblems of our talents." She waved to the side, and a woman in a painter's cap and smock stepped forward, holding a drawing board. "My friend Angelica has agreed to join us as the official painter for the Muses' Salon, and she has agreed to be bound by the same promise of secrecy. Tonight as we talk, she will be making your sketches. As for me, I design gardens. I know plants and their seasons and I have been developing a community among the plantsmen and nurserymen in London. Angelica has decided to present me as Flora, goddess of flowers."

Sophia extended her hand to her future sister-in-law, Judith, inviting her to make her own introduction.

Judith wrinkled her nose. "Though Sophia finds it a talent, I find it more of a curse. I have an unusually sensitive palate. I can distinguish ingredients in a dish or drink either by taste or smell. I can recall and recreate dishes and perfumes with a fairly high degree of accuracy. But don't ask me to do anything useful with it. I can't, for example, tell if a meal or a potion is poisoned, unless that poison has some distinctive aroma or taste."

"I'm sure that skill will prove very useful at some point." Ophelia leaned forward encouragingly.

Sophia turned next to her sisters-in-law. "Kate can remember anything she's read, even if she has only read it once, or only read it swiftly."

"It's even odder than that." Kate shrugged her shoulders. "Sometimes, I can even recall a page later, even if I didn't actually read it before. I can 'see' the shapes of the letters in my mind and I can 'read' it later."

"Ariel, describe your talent."

"I have a surprisingly accurate sense of direction. Once I have visited a place, I can return there with ease, even if by a different route."

"Now you, Ophelia," Sophia prodded.

"But I haven't a skill." The auburn-haired woman looked uncomfortable.

"You can make anyone feel welcome, and you create communities wherever you go," her sister Ariel suggested.

"And no matter whether you are telling the truth or the most extravagant lie, people always believe you. Well, people not related to you, that is." Kate grimaced. "It isn't fair."

"Malcolm will tell you I am a dancer, and that's true, to a point"—Audrey looked bashful—"but horses and ropes are far more difficult to dance on than any stage! My family was famous on the Continent as acrobats, performing for kings and queens before the Terror."

Olivia and Constance turned to each other with similar looks of chagrin.

"Constance?"

"I suppose I am like Ophelia, in that people underestimate me. I have connections to tradesmen across the country as well as to some religious groups through my sister."

"Olivia?"

"I can pick a lock; read a letter upside down, even if it's written in a bad hand; and disguise myself so that I'm not recognized, even by those closest to me."

The other women oohed.

"I think Olivia has the best skills." Kate laughed. "And she should teach us all."

"Oh, yes! yes!" the women exclaimed all around, and for a moment Olivia felt that she was at home with her scholars.

"Now that we know each others' skills, we can begin our good work. If a woman comes up to us on the street and asks for our help, I want us to offer that aid, in whatever way would be most helpful to her. And I'd also like for each of us to bring causes to the group for our help."

All the women nodded their heads in agreement and quickly began to outline even more ways in which the Muses' Salon could work.

Chapter Twenty-Eight

"Leaving us already, Lord Montmorency?" Mrs. Pier cooed. Montmorency knew he was one of her favorites.

"I'll be back at the end of the month, dear Pier. But until then, I must see to ditching my moors, troublesome things." Montmorency took her hand and with an elaborate bow, brushed his lips across the back of her hand. Mrs. Pier blushed—as usual. "But I have six months left in my residency, so you will be seeing me before the end of next month. The Roman artifacts to be found in this region are exceptional."

"Well, and of course you have other interests that keep you from us."

"Ah yes, my dear, other interests." He smiled, rubbing the thick raised scar on the back of his hand. *If only they knew.* "But I must be off, I'm expected at my estate tomorrow night." With a self-satisfied air, he picked up his valise, letting his finger play along the edge of a pocket sewn into his waistcoat. He'd put the list there. All safe and hidden.

As Montmorency climbed in the waiting unmarked hackney, Flute held out a large rag and wet it from a drinking flask. "Ready to remove those paints and become yourself again?"

Montmorency began to wipe off layers of his face, becoming Charters with each pass of the linen.

"Learn anything useful from playing the scholar?"

"Ah, Flute, I have gained us a world of information, so much that I find myself losing interest in our newest client. I don't like being lied to, and we have not heard the full story of why the names of these newspaper correspondents are so valuable. The authors we have traced so far have been zealots or fools, goading the state because it suits them. But there is no real stratagem in their essays—excepting of course those of An Honest Gentleman. If there's something to be discovered here, it will be with him."

Flute looked up, intrigued. "And the new information?"

"After a year of searching for Tom Wilmot's papers, I have them and the code key to boot. A couple hours of work, and I'll have it all decoded."

"Then you don't yet know if your name was mentioned."

"It was, but it is no longer. I removed it and substituted another man's in their list," Charters remarked with barely contained glee.

"But how, if it was in code? And without being seen?"

"Flute, my father was silly and a fool. Since, as his third son, I was not to be the lord of the estate, he found no harm in naming me after a foolish whim. I believe it was even a bet, but I have never been able to prove that."

"What's your name?" Flute seemed only moderately interested.

"Let's make it a quiz. I will tell you how I was able to remove my name and replace it with another's. If you can guess my name, you may choose our next client."

Flute looked interested. "Then tell me."

"My first name is nine letters long, but uses only six unique letters. The first and the third letter of each triplet is the same, and there is no repetition of letters across triplets. As much as I hate the name, I spent my childhood fascinated by it—making it into anagrams and other tricks."

"So the pattern is one and three, four and six, seven and nine?"

"Exactly. Assuming that the first three letters of most items would spell out Sir, I ignored those. Then I looked for a series of letters repeated as you describe. When the scholars divided the list, I chose the portion with my name in it, and I simply worked it backward. I knew what letters appeared in my name, and I used those to code in a new name—that of a dead man. Simple. It is the only time in my life I have been grateful my father was a boor."

"What did you learn from the list? Other than that your name was on it."

"I learned that having your name on that list is tantamount to a death sentence, and I want to know who the executioner is. I want to know that, almost as much as I want to know the true identity of our friend An Honest Gentleman."

Chapter Twenty-Nine

The next morning, Olivia dressed while Harrison was still sleeping. She'd received a note from Mentor asking her to meet at the usual place and time, and she needed to escape before Harrison woke.

She was torn. A disguise would help keep her safe, if Calista was in London. But with Harrison so close by, she couldn't risk donning one without him discovering her secrets. She would have to rely on her wits instead.

She slipped from the room as he snored lightly.

She gave herself the luxury of a hackney, hailing one from a corner two blocks from Harrison's London house and leaving it two blocks before her meeting place.

Inside the coffeehouse, Mentor waited at a table in the back room.

"Ah, I'd expected some guttersnipe with the pox," Mentor teased. "But instead I have coffee with a beautiful woman. It is good that you could meet me. After your last letter, we felt it necessary to see that you were well."

"Ah, you were worried."

"Yes. But don't tell the others; they already feel that we play favorites with you."

"Don't you?"

"Few of the others can boast a marriage, even an invalid one, to an earl. But you are the best agent Mrs. Flint ever trained—she says it herself."

"How is old Flint?" Olivia watched the doorway for any sign of being followed, but she saw nothing.

"The same. I keep thinking that some day when we meet, I'll suddenly realize that she's aged, but it never happens. She is still as quick with a lock as anyone, and you are still the only one who ever matched her." Mentor crossed his leg over his knee, pulling a piece of paper from his upper boot.

"Do you have anything for me?"

Mentor watched over her shoulder. "The list that you and Harrison deciphered. We've traced all the names. We don't know what Wilmot believed they had in common when he made the list, but that was more than a year ago. Now it is little more than a roll call of the dead."

"We'd hoped Baldwin would know the connection, but now . . ." She hesitated, remembering the sound of the gunshot and knocking Baldwin to the ground. It had been so close. Her mouth went dry. "How many on the list are still alive?"

"Only five. We've set agents to protect them, and perhaps in that way we will discover who killed the others, and why. But we'd also like someone to look into the others—the dead men. We've thought to give the task to Montclair." Mentor rarely made small talk, so this was significant . . . somehow. "But we would like to give the job to you. Sometimes a woman's skills unlock secrets more successfully than a man's. Of course, you can sort out the question of your marriage before you decide."

"I'll consider it. But what of An Honest Gentleman? Do you wish for me to continue?"

"For the time being." He pressed a slip of paper across the desk. "Here's a little information you might use to good effect in your next column. If this doesn't make the lout bite, then we will have to find another way to flush him out."

She concealed it in her bodice.

"But more importantly, do you believe you *can* continue? Walgrave is observant, almost preternaturally so. Has he noticed your avocation? Or more to the point, does he suspect?"

"He suspects everything now that I have been attacked."

Mentor put a handful of coin on the table. "Be watchful, Livvy. None of the information we have is concrete, and that means an attack could come from any quarter." He set his hand on hers briefly, then walked away.

Joe Pasten.

A traitor.

Harrison still couldn't believe it.

When Olivia had risen before the dawn, he'd pretended to be asleep so that he could follow her. Since her meeting in the graveyard, he'd been prepared to discover Olivia was An Honest Gentleman. But he hadn't expected to find Pasten passing her information.

Harrison brushed his hand through his hair in frustration. Why did he have to be the one to discover Joe's treachery? He couldn't imagine how he was going to inform Mr. James. Joe was Benjamin's dearest friend—the man who had saved his life at Waterloo and had spent years as his valet-cum-physician. Harrison had often watched Joe and Mr. James with a kind of admiration. Each time he had seen their heads bent over a shared document, or he had watched the way their minds interrogated a problem from all directions and came to a mutually satisfying end, he had been jealous. He had seen that sort of marriage of minds with Forster and Lady Wilmot, and it was the sort of closeness that he'd grown to want with Olivia. If Harrison were a different man, he could ignore the devastation turning Joe in would cause. But he wasn't. He only wished he had stopped looking when Mr. James told him to do so. Because now he had to consider not only his duty to the Home Office, but his obligations to Olivia as well. Did she know what she was doing? And if so, did he want to tell the Home Office that the woman he loved was the one distributing secrets through the press?

As Harrison struggled with his duty to the Home Office, and his love for Olivia and Mr. James, another man approached Olivia's table. She stiffened. He couldn't hear the man's words, but he knew what aggression looked like. Beneath the table, Olivia slipped her hand in her reticule and pulled out a pocket pistol, keeping it hidden in her lap.

Harrison rose to help her. She didn't think she could shoot someone, did she? And not in a coffee shop! He had to intervene, even if it meant revealing that he had followed her.

He kept his gaze firmly on Olivia's reactions. She seemed calm, even complacent.

The man held out his dirty fingers, passing her a tightly folded letter. Folded several times, it was small enough to fit into the palm of his hand. He rose, saying something that Harrison couldn't hear. Olivia's face grew anxious and strained.

As Harrison hurried his way forward, the man brushed past him. He was dirty and wiry. Immediately Harrison remembered where he had seen the fellow: He'd thrown him out of the actress's dressing room not a month ago.

Suddenly, it all began to line up: the letter from an informant addressed to An Honest Gentleman in the dressing room, the attack on Olivia in the churchyard; the shot that may or may not have been meant for her; her meeting with Joe. He didn't know if the feeling in his gut was anger, betrayal, regret, or shame. Of all Olivia's secrets, he'd never imagined that one of them would be that he'd propositioned her like a common whore.

By the time Harrison reached her table, Olivia was seated alone.

"Tell me who's threatening you." Harrison slipped into the empty seat before her, reading the anxiety on her face. "I've got the pieces. I just need to know which game board we are playing on, and I need to know who the players are."

She said nothing and her silence frustrated him.

"I followed you to your first meeting. I saw who you met with, so I'm also sure that you don't wish to reveal anything I don't already know. So let me lay it out for you." He paused, but she only looked at him. "In the last few months, I've followed you on the street and propositioned you at the theater. I've discovered you are a novelist, a newspaper columnist, and after this morning, perhaps even an agent of the Home Office."

"I had hoped you wouldn't put the puzzle together."

"Why wouldn't I? You are my wife."

She held up her hand to object, but he ignored it.

"Don't say it. What matters is that you have been threatened. At least three times by my count. If I'm right, you've been assuming that the threats have been coming from the same quarter . . . or are at least rooted in the same cause. But what if they aren't the same? Yours is the elegant solution, but is it the correct one?"

Olivia thought for a minute, realizing he was right. But by her count the threats came from at least three quarters: the threats to *An Honest Gentleman*, those springing from her investigations into her father, and those from Calista.

"You are suggesting that I could have different sets of people threatening me for different reasons?"

"Exactly."

"I'm simply not that interesting."

He barked a laugh. "Think about it. It's too easy to see this all as tied together. But if you haven't found a connection, perhaps it's there isn't one. Tell me what the man in the churchyard said."

"My memory of that meeting is fuzzy." She thought for a moment. "I know that he knew things about me and my father that he said that I didn't want you—or the ton—to find them out. But I can't remember much else."

"What did the man say today?"

"That's easier to remember. He said, 'My master knows you won't stop until you have answers, so he'll meet you once. Tonight. At that address.'"

"What answers do you seek, Olivia?"

She turned her face away. "You never believed me when I told you I was a woman of many secrets."

"I was wrong. Perhaps if I had listened, you wouldn't be leaving me." The idea of her leaving him made him feel both inexpressibly sad and a bit frantic. Without meaning to, he'd come to depend on her, on the regular receipt of the letters he read in secret, wishing, and not wishing, they had held more of her heart. At first he had pretended not to read them on principle, angry at being married, then later, he had pretended not to read them because it had become a pattern, a dance between them. If she believed he didn't open the letters, then perhaps she might reveal some part of herself unintentionally. Even as he pushed her away, he always wanted to draw her close.

"The problem is that I have so many secrets, I've even forgotten some. If I knew why I was attacked, then I could predict the what and the where." She lifted her hands, then let them fall.

"What might they be angry about?" Harrison waited. "You owe me this much, Olivia. I have a right to know at least as much about you as you discovered about me in those blasted interviews you held before our marriage. Start at the beginning."

She gave a rueful smile. "The beginning is not as clear as you might imagine. I have only the vaguest memories of my childhood. My mother died when I was an infant; my father, though I loved him, was a thief and a swindler. My father entrusted me to your father when I was only five. Sir Roderick used to joke he won me by losing a bet." She smiled, a sad smile that pulled at his heart. "I loved your father. He sent me to a somewhat unusual boarding school, where the headmistress taught us how to make our way in the world. I became a governess. That failed. Then, your father decided I was the perfect wife for you, and I let him convince me to marry you. The rest you know."

"Then why are they threatening you?"

"My father had enemies, and because I knew that, I've made sure to investigate him under an assumed name. So I don't understand how this man had made the connection. He appears to wish to punish me for my father's sins." She looked away. He took the note from her hand, and she did not resist.

"What is this?"

"It's the time and place for a meeting."

"With that man?!" He read the message. "I'll never let you go. It's too dangerous."

"Harrison, I'm not your wife." She plucked the note from his hands, and rising, put her hands on her hips. "I can come and go as I please."

And rising, she left.

* * *

Several hours later, Olivia arrived at the abandoned building described in her directions. She arrived two hours early, as Mrs. Flint had trained her, to find and occupy a position of strength.

As she mounted the stairs of the porch, she found Harrison sitting behind a large column, hidden mostly from view.

"I suppose you thought that by intercepting me here, I will let you stay."

"If you can come and go as you please, I can stay or go as I please. I thought you might like some help."

She rolled her eyes and harrumphed but did not demand he leave her. Mentor had told her Harrison was a good agent, and Mrs. Flint always cautioned her girls never to work alone if they could help it.

Harrison escorted her to the door. "It's locked, but we can break in around the side if you are amenable."

"Here. Let me." She nudged him out of the way and knelt in front of the lock.

"What?"

"Shh." She pulled a pin from her hair and put her ear to the lock. He watched, stunned.

"There." She smiled broadly. "Not so hard with the right tools." She stuck the pin back behind her ear. "After you?"

"We will discuss your ability with locks later." Stepping in front of her, he led them both into the darkness. "Keep your hand on my back. I want to know where you are." Together they explored the house, ensuring that no one had arrived before them. The upper rooms had been used for storage, the lower most recently for a milliner's shop.

"We should wait here."

"For how long?"

He opened his pocket watch. "Another hour." He sat on the floor, his back to the short end of the closet.

She settled in across from him, knowing that the last thing either of them wished to do was talk.

She watched him, listening to the rise and fall of his breath. She noticed the muscles in his chest, the strength of his arms. If this would be their last night together, then she would make the most of it.

She crept to his side.

"I thought you preferred distance."

She shrugged.

"What is it that you want, Livvy?" His voice was tired, almost bored.

She reached out her hand and placed it on his thigh, then slid it up slowly. "I haven't decided yet, but I thought you might deserve a bit of turnabout."

"What do you mean?"

"Shush." She placed her finger across his lips. "My turn."

After they had sated themselves in each other's bodies, Olivia drew herself up and crossed the room to the window, looking out from behind a shabby curtain.

"Why would you come here alone, Olivia? You have been assaulted and threatened. What if they intend to kill you, or worse?"

"Why do you care? You ignore me for years, then when it becomes clear that I am leaving you, you return home and think you can tell me what I can and cannot do."

"But you don't understand. I have experience in these things."

Olivia felt her years of fruitless longing well up into words, and she could not contain them. "*You* don't understand, Harrison. I do too." She paused, remembering that she should keep her secrets, but she had grown tired of hiding from him. "You don't think that your father just happened across me at the secluded estate of some rakish lord, discovered I was desperate to escape his petty children, and decided I'd be the perfect bride for his son? No, I went to Mrs. Flint's school."

His face fell with the realization.

"I work for the same men that you do. Joe, Mr. James. I once even worked for you. You knew me as Peggy. You might remember her: She discovered a series of murders in the North."

"Peggy died."

"And like the Phoenix rose again. New name, new mission, but still not the kind of woman you'd want for your countess."

"But my father described you as the perfect wife."

"No, your father described me as perfect for you. We both assumed that meant I would be docile and compliant, and I tried—for two weeks, and then for six years of letters. But I've started to wonder if we misunderstood him. Of course now, it's too late."

"Why did you accept his offer? Why resign yourself to a country life when you'd been living a life of adventure?"

"I'd been abandoned as a child, left cold and hungry in a cottage with no money and no friends. I wanted a father, a family, a place to feel loved and cared for. Something to balance all those years of standing on street corners hoping to beg or steal enough to ease the hunger in my belly. I had the first part at least. Your father was that for me, and I mourn him still. I remained on the estate for him. But he's dead, and it became perfectly clear you didn't want me."

"How do you know I don't want you? All these years, and I've remained faithful to you."

"Faithful?" Incredulous, then angry, Olivia let her whole body change. Her stance became more open, and she leaned forward provocatively, shoulders back, breasts forward, one hip canted out. "Perhaps, my lord, I misunderstood your offer. I thought that dinner at your club was merely a euphemism for other delights."

He colored, the light flush of embarrassment quickly turning dark with anger. But his voice when he spoke was cold and controlled. "As *you* have told me repeatedly, we are not married. I had received your papers that very day."

"And that very night, you propositioned the first actress whose performance spoke to your blood."

"*You* spoke to my blood, Livvy, even in disguise. My body knew it was you."

"If I believed that, I would be a fool. I've been a fool to believe you before."

"Why? Did I ever promise you I'd come home? Did I ever tell you I wanted to be lord of the manor? Or from our first moments together did I not tell you I was meant for a different sort of life, for the sea, for adventure?"

"Yet you left the sea for Parliament."

"I thought you were happy. I thought you wanted a quiet sort of life, that you enjoyed the fields and crops and adjudicating the woes of your tenants. I didn't know you were one of Flint's girls."

"And had you known, what difference would that have made? On our best days, you would only have distrusted me. You would have wondered what my game was and why I was marrying you instead of seeking some adventure. On our worst, you would have wondered if I had been sent to spy on you. A marriage without trust is no marriage at all."

"I've already told you that you can trust me. Would it mean anything to say that I wish we could go back, back to that moment when there was a possibility?"

"As a sentiment, perhaps. But would you have made a different decision?"

"If I knew then what I know now?" He shrugged. "Perhaps."

"That's the seduction of it, isn't it?" Olivia shook her head. "The idea that, if you could, you would make a different choice. But at that moment, you made the best decision you could, given the set of choices you faced. It might not be the choice I or your father would have preferred, but it was the choice you believed was right for you."

"You give me too much credit."

"Perhaps, but we were wrong—your father and I. We wanted to help you, to give you a home to come back to, but we would have done better to let you alone, whether you came back home or not."

"He was a very determined man."

"As are you. But I'm tired, Harrison. Every room in the abbey reminds me of all I've lost, or never really had. My father, yours, my hopes and dreams."

"Give me a little more time, Livvy—"

At the sound of approaching footsteps, both of them grew immediately silent. Olivia reached into her reticule and tested the powder in her pistol. Before Harrison could stop her, she stepped into the light.

"Ah." The well-dressed man stepped into the half-light, a pistol in each hand. "I see you have your father's daring and foolhardiness in equal measure."

"My father taught me resilience and ingenuity as well."

"Perhaps." The man tilted his head as if listening to an unheard melody. "Your father left a great many men angry. Even after all these years, some of those men would like to find him, if, of course, he is to be found."

"Is he?" She hated the note of hope in her voice.

"I have never known—and I suspect neither did Sir Roderick. But your father's enemies would be equally happy to take their vengeance on you. When you were young, Sir Roderick claimed you had died in a shipwreck, then he changed your name and hid you away at a boarding school that would give you the skills to survive. His actions kept you safe, but by looking for your father you are removing yourself from the protection of the Walgrave name."

"Why are you telling me this?"

"Because I owe your father my life, and warning you is my repayment. Stop looking. If you stop now, you should be safe."

"Why? What harm would it do to find him, if he is still alive? To know where I come from and who my people are?" Olivia heard her voice break with tears.

"Did you trust Sir Roderick, Lady Walgrave?"

"Yes."

"Did you ever know him to act in any way that wasn't in your best interest?"

"No."

"Then you have your answer." The well-dressed man began to back into the darkness. "But I offer one more piece of advice. Given that you are dead twice over, your marriage is as valid as Sir Roderick could make it. Go home to your husband, Lady Walgrave. Don't court this scandal."

Olivia watched the shadows for some time, wondering what her father might have done to create such an enemy or such a friend. But at length her thoughts turned to Sir Roderick, who had, in all the ways that mattered, been her father. Perhaps the well-dressed man was right. If Sir Roderick had gone to such lengths to protect her, maybe she should trust his decision.

She looked over at Harrison, still hidden in the shadows. If Sir Roderick had believed so strongly that she and

Harrison were a match, perhaps she should trust him in that as well.

"Have you learned what you needed?" Harrison's voice was gentle.

"I suppose, but it's hard to let go of wondering."

"You can always trust me, Livvy. I do what I say." He put his arm around her shoulders. "What would you like to do now?"

She touched his face. "I think I'd like to spend some time in London . . . getting to know my husband."

His smile was brilliant, lighting his eyes. He picked her up, her small frame against his, and swung her around in a circle. "Then, wife, let me show you London."

Chapter Thirty

"Miss Livvy?"

Olivia started in surprise. After five glorious days in London, seeing every sight, and spending every moment in Harrison's arms, the couple had returned to the estate late in the night. If love was what she had felt for him before, then she had no word for what she felt now, except that it was also love, just quieter and more confident and less troubled by questions of who he or she was.

But the voice—Lark's—was anxious, almost frantic.

Lark almost stumbled over his own feet as he hurried toward her, one hand extended holding a piece of paper. When he got closer, she noticed the sheen of tears on his cheeks.

"Miss Livvy, please tell me it isn't true. I have nowhere to go, no family. I gave up my rooms at the university years ago."

"What has upset you?"

"This." He held out the paper. His hand shook as he extended it. "Don't you know?"

The letter was from the firm of Leverill and Cort, and signed H. W. Aldine, solicitor. She read it once, then shaking her head, read it again. By the time she lowered the sheet to look in Lark's face, she felt both sick and angry. She could not believe that Harrison would be so petty, so callous, but the evidence was here. He had told her she could trust his word, that the scholars would be safe, that the library would continue as his father had intended. How had she believed him? Harrison pretended he told the truth, but everyone lies. Quickly, she began to reconsider how much money she would have when she left.

"Then it is true." The old man searched her face, and his shoulders began to shake. "But you, the others, are my family, my home."

She placed a hand on his shoulder, felt the bones frail beneath her fingers. "I can't speak to how Lord Walgrave will admit scholars in the future, but I can assure you, you will not be abandoned. If his lordship does not relent on this plan, then you may come to me. I won't be able to offer you the ability to continue your research, but you will not be alone."

The old man folded himself into her arms and wept. As she held him, she felt trapped, torn between love for Harrison, duty to country, and concern for the men who had become like benevolent uncles. There was little she could do to change what was going to happen, but at least she could try to ensure that as few people were hurt as possible. But, she thought with her stomach turning cold and hard, at least he had made it easy to leave him.

She entered the library a short time later, having reassured Lark that he would have a place with her. The old man had drawn himself together admirably. Wiping the tears from his eyes, he had announced, "Then I will begin to copy all the materials I need before I leave," before shuffling away.

The library was quiet, without even the quiet sounds of

research. No pages turned, no pens scratched across paper, no inkwells clinked with the dip of each pen. The scholars looked forlorn, even broken. She could not take them all, not on the settlement she'd requested, but she couldn't abandon them either.

All eyes turned to her on her entrance, and not a few hands hastily wiped their faces, but she could see from their red eyes and noses that more than Lark had been crying.

"All of you received dismissals?"

Slowly each head nodded as she surveyed the room.

"I never imagined he would dismantle the library entirely. Had I known . . ."

"We don't blame you, Miss Livvy. It is Lord Walgrave's decision."

Seven heads nodded in unison.

"Not all of us will be destitute," Otley began to explain. "Quinn can go to his sister."

"Since her husband died, she's been lonely, and her house is not so far from the British Library," Quinn explained. "I can continue my work there."

"Smithson can request to return to Lord Marlby's employ."

"He's written me for years to come write his family history. I'd resisted only because this was my home, and his family is so uninteresting. No rebellion, no heroics, they changed sides every time there was a new side to change to, no character in them at all."

Olivia tried not to cry as Otley told her each man's plans. Their family—strange as it was—would be broken up. It was even now in the process of separation. And there was nothing she could do to change their fates.

"As for me, my letter asks that I remain to oversee the sale of the books." Otley sighed. "He doesn't care how much he gets for each book, only that they be sold. I was hoping, however, in honor of Sir Roderick, you could help me value the items."

Suddenly Olivia knew what she would do—could do—for them. She walked deliberately to the catalogue and opened it. "Of course. We can begin now. Would each of you bring me the ten items you need most for your research?"

The men looked confused, then hastily collected their books. After a few minutes, the men came to her with piles of books of varying heights. Partlet's books, all heavy folios, were tucked up under his chin.

"Do you have ten pence, Partlet?"

"Why, yes"—he balanced the books, then patted his coat until he found a pocket—"I do." Then he looked puzzled. "But these books would cost twenty pounds together."

"Not today, Partlet, not today."

"Then, Miss Livvy, might I change the books I'm choosing?"

"Of course."

The men scattered again to the ends of the room, coming back with very different books than the ones they had chosen before.

For the next hour, she and Otley "valued" the books, pricing the books at whatever she knew the scholar could afford.

Nathan got the nine-volume set of Boydell's *Illustrations of the Dramatic Works of Shakespeare* that he had often petted over the years; Martinbrook a set of rarely used maps of the world, including a volume on the various counties of England.

None of the men chose the most valuable or the rarest books. Instead, knowing somehow that she was giving them a precious gift, each one took only what he most loved and what he would most miss.

"We won't sell them, you know. None of us could part with these."

"I know." She smiled sadly. "It will be a remembrance of our family here."

Each man brushed back tears, until no one could brush them back anymore. Then they all wept together.

Later that afternoon, having wrapped each man's books carefully in oil cloth, she sent Pier to the village to post them to her solicitor in London, with instructions on how to distribute them once the scholars had moved to their next lodgings.

Later that night, she took the ledger and wrote in more reasonable prices. She would not cheat him, not even of books he didn't want. When she added up the row of figures, she sighed. She would still have enough, but barely. Leaning back in bed, she turned her face to the wall and wept for all her losses.

The next morning, Olivia instructed Calder to rig a carriage and instructed two footmen to come to her room in twenty minutes. The trunks had been packed for weeks; all she had to do was put in the final pieces and pack her valise. She could be in London by nightfall.

The footmen's eyes widened at the sight of her luggage, but they said nothing. The news would travel quickly through the staff, and she would have to rely on Mrs. Pier to pass on her regrets for not saying goodbye. But who would expect her to remain after he had dismissed the scholars? No, she could not stay, not when her heart was broken into too many pieces ever to heal.

Finished, she adjusted her hat, and gathering her courage, knocked on the door of her study, which Harrison had slowly made his own. She did not wait to be invited in.

He was seated behind the desk, reading one of the household account books. When he looked up, he smiled, broadly. Then taking in her coat, gloves, and hat, his face changed. Wary, perhaps. Guilty, more likely.

"I thought you didn't visit in the afternoon. I could have gone with you."

"I've decided to leave, my lord." She didn't care if her voice sounded cold or angry. "We do not suit. Our values are too different for us to find any lasting peace in each other's company."

Even now, his surprise looked genuine. If she had not seen the letters to the scholars for herself, she might have thought his face revealed hurt and dismay. As it was now, she didn't know what emotion it was, but she didn't care. He had lied to her, and that was enough.

"You've hidden for years behind that logical façade. I thought for a while it was just a pretense, a wall you put up to protect yourself from further harm, but perhaps that is the real you. Aloof, disengaged, interested only in facts. The Harrison I knew . . ."

"You never knew me. All you knew was what a lonely girl thought she wanted."

"Yes, you are right. I had only a dream of you, and now I've woken up. I had always hoped that, when I woke up, the dream and the real man would be the same, but I was a fool." She looked away, blinking back tears.

"I'm sorry not to have been that man, Olivia."

She felt the corners of her mouth turn up in a sad half-smile. "As am I, Harrison." She turned away from him, picking up her shawl. "But I take my leave of you. It's past time. I will wait, of course, to petition for a determination of invalidity until after the end of Parliament's session."

"Why do you want to leave me?" Harrison rose and started towards her, but stopped.

Olivia stared him in the eyes, wondering how he could even ask such a question. "I'm putting to rights your father's injustice. The laws say marriages like ours should never happen. Perhaps, had we met in a marketplace or at the theater, or any of those places where young men find their brides, you might not have hated me. You might have eventually decided I was the sort of woman you wished to marry. But Sir Roderick went about it wrong, and we have suffered for it."

Harrison grabbed Olivia's arm as she turned from him. She stopped but didn't turn back. Instead, she pulled her arm out of his grasp, until he was left holding only her hand. It felt so intimate, palms together, and Harrison held Olivia's hand, feeling as if the whole world were slipping through his grasp. "I know what that man said about you and your father, but I think you know more than that. Part of your claim of invalidity rests on the question of your name, and before you go, I want to know the truth."

She shrugged. "I don't know the truth. I don't even know my own name with any certainty, except I know it wasn't Olivia. That was the name Roderick and I chose for me when I went to Mrs. Flint's and that I took up again after I came to the estate. My earliest memories are of a boat and water, endless water. But how reliable are an infant's memories? I remember the boat because I felt the swaying of the sea as a lullaby. But was it the sea? Or simply a trip from Liverpool to London? Without finding my father, I will never know."

"Where will you go? Your settlement, where will I send it?" He knew the answer to the last question. He'd read each of the pages a dozen times, trying to find a way to tie her to him, or at least find her again. But he asked the question because he needed some way to prolong the moment, to keep at bay the hole that would tear at his belly with her loss. When she left, he would become again thorough, stolid Walgrave and not the passionate man he was with her. Even so, he could not ask her to stay. She had made her choice.

She looked back at him, the tears now fully visible. "Even now, you pay no attention to my letters. The payments go to my solicitor, who will forward me the funds. As for my destination, I will be comfortable, perhaps even happy."

"I am sorry, truly sorry, we could not reconcile our differences. But the man you want doesn't exist."

"But he did, Harrison. He did." She pulled her hand from his grasp. He turned toward the window, not wanting to see her leave. When he turned back, she was gone.

He didn't understand what had just happened. He had thought they were getting along well, discovering all the things they shared in common. They had spent a week laughing and loving. He had even begun to see how with Olivia he might have that marriage of minds he had envied so much in his friends. He poured himself a glass of port. He could go after her, but she didn't want his help. And she'd made it clear that she certainly didn't want him. He refused to feel her loss. He refused to mourn her.

He listened to the carriage pull away from the abbey and disappear into the distance, then sought comfort in the library, but the room was empty. The tables were cleared of all their papers, the books returned to the shelves. It was as if no one was in residence at all. But more likely, the scholars were off in the dower house, trying to blow up his estate with their experiments. Shaking his head, he returned to his tower room with a bottle of port and drank, until he could drink no more.

The next morning, Harrison returned to the library to find it still empty and the tables still cleared. Wanting company, he went to the lodge. Partlet and Nathan, heads bowed together outside the building, retreated quickly down the garden path, and Lark—who looked as if he had been crying all night—ran into the corridor and slammed the door to his room shut. Down the corridor, all the other scholars scuttled away as soon as they saw him.

But what had he expected? If he had been one of the scholars, he would have taken Livvy's side too, though he wasn't exactly sure what side she was on. He'd thought she finally trusted him.

At the drawing room, only Otley remained. The old man looked up at him with disappointment, then rose slowly. "I understand that it's your right to close the library, Lord Walgrave, but such an announcement to the scholars should have come from you directly, rather than from your attorney. I will stay on as you request, but I do it for Sir Roderick's sake, not yours."

Harrison felt as if the world had shifted on its axis and he had not moved with it. "I regret that I have done something to offend you, Otley. But I have sent no letters to the scholars, and I haven't corresponded with my attorney in some time. In fact, the last time that I wrote to him . . ." The realization dawned suddenly. His angry insistence that Aldine investigate the scholars and close the library if he uncovered even the hint of impropriety, the letter from Aldine he'd never read, his vague response left on the edge of the table in Adam's room—it all tore out the bottom of Harrison's heart. "Do you have one of the letters here?"

Otley held it out, and Harrison's hands shook as he took it. And suddenly he understood why Olivia had left him— she'd thought he'd broken his promise to keep the scholars. He could explain—he could even get Aldine to write a letter on his behalf. But it would be useless, because she was gone, and he had no idea where or how to find her.

He sank into the chair next to Otley's and buried his face in his hands so that the old man would not see him weep.

Chapter Thirty-One

"Flute. Remember that actress I met with some weeks ago?"

"The one I followed?"

"Yes."

"I thought we decided she wasn't of interest."

"We were wrong. We thought that Mrs. Wells was using her as a blind to conceal the true author of the articles. However, she is not an actress at all, but Lord Walgrave's wife in disguise."

"Is she An Honest Gentleman?"

"A woman who used to be a governess? I don't think so. No, before I arrived at the abbey, Lord Walgrave had some long discussion with the scholars about word choice in the newspaper essays. I believe *he* is An Honest Gentleman, and his wife is his agent. And that makes him ripe for a discussion of our fee."

"Fee?"

"For keeping his secret. A peer exposing the secrets of other peers will not sit well with the ton. His career will be over."

"What if he refuses? Idealists are unpredictable."

"Then he might have to die."

There was a commotion from outside Charters's study, and Calista pushed her way into the room.

"I have come for my jewels."

"They are my jewels now. A retainer for our services, and we have discovered the information you desired."

"I figured out who An Honest Gentleman is by myself." Her eyes darted around the room, as if more people were going to appear from the corners. "You did nothing for me, and I'll pay you nothing in return."

"Your being unhappy doesn't mean we did nothing."

"I don't have anything more to pay you. The jewels weren't even mine, not anymore, at least. My relatives weren't supposed to discover them missing, but they have. I must return them."

"That is no concern of ours." Charters lifted his finger, and Flute opened the door to three large men. They flanked the woman.

She looked at the men. "You told me nothing. And I must have my jewels."

"Irrelevant. You knew the terms when you hired us."

"Don't discount me! I found out their names, you fool, and I will discover yours. I will tell everyone that you are a swindler, a cheat, and a murderer."

"If you have the time before you are tried and hanged for theft . . . Goodbye, Baroness Ecsed. See: I already know *your* name." The men lifted her by her shoulders. "I would recommend a swift retreat to the Continent; perhaps you can convince your husband's family to take you in. Try France. Montpellier." He flicked his finger again. "See her out, gentlemen."

Chapter Thirty-Two

Though Harrison did not know where exactly, Olivia received reports that he had followed her to London, methodically searching each place where she might be. He'd visited her solicitor. He'd accosted Mrs. Wells at both Drury Lane and the *World*, demanding she deliver a letter to his gypsy, Calypso. He'd even demanded that Joe and Mr. James reveal her whereabouts, but they had refused. Instead, they had written to reassure her that Harrison now knew that the Honest Gentleman affair—and their involvement in it—had been approved by the Prince Regent himself. Harrison had also, Joe wrote, gone into the archives and spent two days reviewing the Ecsed affair, declaring himself horrified anew at the Baron's depravities. But, Joe had assured her, all references to her own actions after reporting the Baron to the magistrates had been carefully expunged. It was cold comfort, but she appreciated Joe's words.

Her cottage would not be ready for another week, so Olivia had taken temporary lodgings with Mrs. Wells. Or rather, in the nicely appointed apartment adjacent to Mrs. Wells's offices at the *World*. Olivia hid there, surrounded by friends.

In the evening she'd attended in secret a meeting of the

Muses' Salon. But the ladies did not know where she lodged, and, true to their promise, they told no one of her attendance. The salon was her only comfort.

When she returned to the *World*, however, a note was stuck to the door with a sharp penknife. Dread clenched at the bottom of her belly. She pulled out the knife, noticing the emblem of Baron Ecsed on its edge—Calista's husband. Looking over her shoulder, she let herself into her rooms, then raising the lamp, she read Calista's uncontrolled scrawl.

You killed my husband. Tonight I kill yours. I'm waiting by the presses.

Olivia dropped the note on the floor, stunned. Calista had found her. But worse, Calista had found Harrison. Hands shaking, Olivia loaded her pistol, then shoved it in her reticule. Whatever she had to do, Harrison would not die.

She met Penn, one of the pressmen, on the street downstairs outside the offices of the *World*. He had heard something loud from inside the shop and was going to investigate. She sent him away, afraid the big man's presence would force Calista's hand.

The office was dark, and she maneuvered slowly through the piles of printed materials. By the time she reached the pressroom, she could see a dim glow next to the central press.

Olivia stepped into the light and walked forward slowly, not taking her eyes off the woman across the room, unable to believe that it had come to this.

Calista held the pistol awkwardly, her hand shaking. Two feet in front of her spread a pool of liquid. Olivia traced the line of liquid: It extended around the presses and to the walls on either side.

"Ah, Lady Walgrave. That smell is linseed oil, and these rags are soaked in turpentine. With all this wood and paper, this place will burn brilliantly. But will you live to see it?" She gestured with the pistol. "Or will he?"

Olivia looked at Harrison, leaning against the wall, his face pale, his shirt red with blood. From the way his shoulder hung forward, she could tell it was dislocated. Sweat beaded on his brow and his lip.

"What have you done to him?"

The woman laughed with glee. "After I stabbed him? I merely pulled back the arm of the press and let it go. Shame it only hit his shoulder—I was hoping to stop his heart."

A thick line of oil ran across the floor in front of Harrison and connected with the line encircling the presses. When the solvent caught fire, he would be trapped. "I'm not Lady Walgrave. We are not married."

The woman spat on the floor at Olivia's feet. "Liar. You have been his wife for almost a decade. His *countess*. You have enjoyed the pleasures of life, of rank, while I have enjoyed nothing but suffering. I used to have pretty dresses and an estate and money, so much money I thought I could buy the world if I wanted it. But then you came, and now it's gone. All of it. I have a room and an allowance from my husband's cousin that lets me buy one new dress a year. I sit in my room, with my chair, and my bed, and my dress, and I think of how much I hate you. Even when you were dead, I thought about how much I hated you."

Olivia watched the woman carefully. It was clear she had gone mad. "What are you waiting for, Calista?"

"Don't you call me that. After what you did, you can call me *vengeance* or *fury*." Calista stopped. "I'm nobody now—the ton no longer invite me to their parties. But before tonight is done, you will be nobody too. The only question is whether I kill you or him . . . or both."

"Punish me. Harrison had no part in what's between us."

"But you care for him, and killing him would hurt you."

"She's mad. She keeps saying you killed her husband." Harrison spoke with obvious pain.

"Be quiet, Harrison," Olivia ordered softly.

"Oh, he won't be quiet, Lady Walgrave. He's been trying to convince me that you are not capable of that treachery." She turned with glee to Harrison. "Do you know what your pretty wife has done to you, my lord? Do you know that she's been writing to the newspapers? But whether I kill you or not, you will die." She turned back to Olivia. "The men I hired to find you think he's An Honest Gentleman, and I let them believe it. He'll pay their price to keep silent or he'll die. But it's you who is writing those essays— just as it was you who killed my husband."

Olivia saw Harrison's face beg her to defend herself, but perhaps it was better this way. He would finally know who she was and what she was capable of. But he would live— that's all that mattered.

"Walgrave doesn't care for me at all—so my part in your husband's death won't matter to him." She watched his face change as he realized the madwoman was right. "I mean nothing to him, and he means nothing to me."

"He must care for you. Why else did he come when I wrote him? Why else would a lord marry a servant with no more money than a common whore?"

"Your husband was a monster who enjoyed his cruelties." She looked at Harrison. Then at the printing press near him. His eyes followed hers, and he nodded almost imperceptibly. If she could draw away Calista's aim, he could put the press between his body and Calista's bullet. "Do you think you would have fared so well over time, Calista?"

"He never would have hurt me. I brought him the girls. I knew once he saw you he would fancy you, so I hired you. It was his right to expect more of you than just teaching his children. But you rebuffed him, and he accepted the advances of that little whore. If it's anyone's fault, it's yours. If you had accepted him, he wouldn't have killed her. No, I will destroy you as you destroyed him."

"He threw her body from the tower, Calista, and you laughed at her broken bones. And she was not the first. He delighted in killing, Calista, and you delighted in helping him."

"Why do you value the lives of servant girls more than the life I had? A scullery maid is a scullery maid is a scullery maid. But I was a baroness. I danced with kings. How did her life even compare to mine? And no one cared what my husband did with the servants. It wasn't anything that every other lord hadn't done. The magistrates even said that the girl didn't know her place."

Olivia clenched her fist until the knuckles were white.

"Besides, who are you to worry about killing? You were quick enough to take his life. Tell him, Lady Walgrave, about the man you killed, about the children you left fatherless, about the wife you reduced to penury. He doesn't know how bloodthirsty you are, but I know. They told me you were dead, but then I saw you on the street a year ago, going to a play. I thought I'd seen a ghost. But you weren't a ghost, were you? No, you were alive, with a new name, married to an earl."

"I'm not married to him. I gave a false name. The marriage is invalid. You can let him go."

"Of course you gave a false name. Do you even know your real name? After I discovered you weren't dead, I found out everything I could about Olivia, Lady Walgrave. But she doesn't exist. But I had an advantage, because before you were Olivia, you were Peggy—Peggy who murdered my husband. And with that name, I found out others. I even know that your father called you Elise."

"What do you know of my father?"

"I have friends, even now. Do you know that fire near

St. Bride's? I set it, and all to stop a little journalist from finding her father. I know where he is. But I'll never tell you. And your mother—do you even remember your mother? Her name for you was . . ."

"Enough, Calista." The well-dressed man stepped into the room, holding his own pistol. Harrison, it seemed, had been correct—the threats she'd been receiving weren't linked. Or at least, not in the way she had thought.

"Lady Walgrave, take your husband and leave."

"No! She's mine! I've waited years for my revenge." She swung the pistol around to face this new intruder, supporting it with both hands.

"Put the pistol down." The well-dressed man moved slowly forward.

"Why are you protecting her? She's nothing compared to me—I was a baroness." Calista's face contorted with madness and rage.

The printing press in the shadows behind Calista creaked, and she turned, firing. The bullet lodged in the body of one of the presses.

From behind her, Penn appeared. The big man tried to knock Calista to the floor, but she heard him at the last moment. Calista threw the lamp into the linseed oil. The liquid burst into flame, spreading almost instantly down its path. And Calista disappeared in the smoke.

"Penn, the presses!" Olivia cried out. She ran to retrieve one of the large buckets filled with water near the piles of paper.

Though the line of oil extended across most of the back of the room, it was not evenly thick in all places. At each press, she and Penn and the well-dressed man emptied the water buckets, then they emptied the ones filled with urine that the pressmen used to clean the type. The scorched smells burned her nose.

Harrison, using only one arm, poured water on the

rags. "If it gets too hot, linseed oil will combust without a flame."

The smoke, however, still billowed.

"There's no more water, but I think the fire is out," Harrison yelled.

"Whether it's out or not, we must leave before we can't find the door," Olivia directed. "Penn, help Harrison. We'll follow you."

The large man nodded and helped Harrison stumble to the door. But seeing another flame, Olivia turned back to smother it. The no-longer-well-dressed man took her by the shoulders and pushed her in front of him toward the door. "You, too, Elise. No daughter of Fallon's dies when she still has a chance for love. But you must stop searching—no one else can know you are still alive."

The four of them struggled against the doors. Just when Olivia feared that Calista had locked them, the doors gave way. Running from the building, Harrison, with Penn beside him, fell coughing on the ground. Olivia bent over her knees, feeling as if her lungs were tearing apart with every cough.

The man who called her Elise began to rouse the workers who lived behind the press. Within minutes the yard was full, people carried buckets of water into the pressroom to make sure the fire—if any remained—did not spread.

Some women, seeing Harrison was bleeding, took him across the street and began to minister to his wound. Seeing he was cared for, Olivia began to search for the man who called her Elise. But he was nowhere to be found. By the time she returned to where Harrison had been, he too was gone.

"His valet took him away." Penn came and stood by her side. "He was stabbed. But not too badly, Miss Livvy. It will heal. He'll be just as he was in no time."

Just as he was. No, now that he knew exactly what sort of woman she was, he would be something else. The slender hope she'd clung to that they might someday reconcile faded and disappeared.

Broken, she called a hackney and took it to Lady Wilmot's. When she arrived, dirty and weeping, Lady Wilmot opened her arms and led her into the house.

Chapter Thirty-Three

At first, Harrison remained in London, waiting for his wound to heal and for Olivia to inquire after his health. A letter, a visit, either would have told him she might still care. But he could still hear her voice, so confident, declare *I mean nothing to him, and he means nothing to me.* At the time, he'd thought it was simply a ploy to divide the madwoman's attention, but as the days passed with no communication, he began to see it as the truth it was.

He returned to the estate, and each day he sat at her desk and waited for the dozen crises he would have to manage. He did nothing else—truth be told, he had no energy to devote to anything else, not even Parliament. Managing the estate was his penance for not knowing how to keep her.

"You asked me to come, my lord."

He rose and embraced the old man, leading him to a comfortable chair. "Yes, Herder, thank you. I wanted to know about the trees."

"The trees?"

"What happened to them?" Harrison wanted some bitter thought to balance his longing. "I thought the estate did well enough without selling them."

"Oh, no, sir! I would have thought Miss Livvy would have told you." Herder lowered himself carefully. "Bad storm, five, six years ago. We woke up to find most of the trees broken, and those that weren't yet broken were bowed to the earth. We worked through the night, lighting pots to save those we could, trimming the most damaged ones. She never slept, not for three days. Far more would have been lost if she hadn't acted. Then she planted new ones, giving each one enough distance from the other to grow and thrive as well as give the best views. Even had that man Repton out here to survey the estate and make recommendations, but in the end, she and I set out with a map and decided how best to create the impression of the former landscape given that we lost so much."

Herder's words brought an old memory to the surface. Olivia had indeed written of the storm and of the estate's losses, but Harrison simply hadn't connected it to his beloved trees. And of course, he hadn't remained at the estate long enough after his marriage to indicate how much the trees meant to him.

Each time he questioned Olivia's motives, she always seemed to have acted conscientiously, though never predictably. Harrison knew his affair with Olivia was over, but still he waited every day, hoping that she would write or that Aldine would discover where she had gone, but neither ever happened.

"Molly, the new housekeeper, has asked that you come to the kitchen, sir." Otley nodded at Herder from the door. Overwhelmed with the details of the estate—or perhaps simply too sad to bear anything for long—Harrison had asked Otley to help with the new staff. Between the estate-manager and Molly and Otley the estate was almost as well run as when Olivia had done it on her own.

"Can you manage it, Otley?"

"I'm afraid not, sir. Molly asks that you come to the kitchen or reconsider your alterations to Dr. Martinbrook's bathing schedule."

For the fiftieth time that week, Harrison asked himself how Olivia had managed the household and its humours. "I only wish to be fair, Otley. All the scholars choose a night to bathe for the week. Martinbrook, however, bathes any time he wishes simply by application to the house-keeper. And while all the other scholars bathe in the servants' quarters, Martinbrook bathes in the dower house. It's deferential treatment, and I see no reason to continue it. Last week, he bathed every day, and twice on Thursday."

"I understand, sir. Will you be coming belowstairs?"

"I'm going to regret this, aren't I?"

"I wouldn't presume to speculate, sir."

That meant yes. He knew it, and so did Otley, but they played their roles. Harrison pulled himself reluctantly from his chair. "Thank you for the information, Herder. I appreciate your perspective."

The old man nodded his agreement, and Harrison left with Otley.

"Might I ask, your lordship, if any of the household have complained of deferential treatment?"

"No."

"Have any of the staff complained that drawing Martinbrook's bath every day was too onerous?"

"No." Harrison was starting to feel ill at ease. He had only looked at the household register and noticed that a scholar appeared to be taking advantage of the estate. It was only a bath, or rather only eight baths, but curbing Martinbrook's access had allowed him to make a point: He was watching.

* * *

At the top of the servants' stairs, he started to notice hints of an unusual earthy smell, more like the stables than the kitchens, but certainly some foods took on a peculiar scent as they were cooked.

"Do you smell that, Otley?"

"What do you mean by *that*, sir?"

"That smell. It's somewhat like manure, but more . . ."

"Rotten, sir."

"That would be one way to describe it."

They opened the door at the base of the stairs, and the smell overwhelmed them.

Harrison covered his nose. "My God! What is that?"

Molly came from the nearest doorway, a handful of posies under her nose.

"Martinbrook, your lordship. It seems on his most recent expedition, he found an entrance to a burial mound."

"From the ninth century," a voice piped from the back doorway. "A very nice one, still largely intact."

"The entrance, however, required him to crawl on his belly through the home of a large badger," Molly continued.

"A collection of badger tunnels called a sett," Martinbrook called out. "A badger sett. Some are used for hundreds of years. Notoriously clean animals, discard their refuse in latrines."

"By latrine, he means . . ." Harrison found himself almost overcome by the stench.

"Yes, sir," Molly continued. "At the end of the entrance, he discovered that the mound was in fact a cave, home to dozens of small bats."

"*Plecotus austriacus*, Lark says. Unusual creatures, but lovely," Martinbrook interjected.

"On the way out of the mound, he came across the lair of a red fox."

"Poor thing," Martinbrook said. "Woke it right up."

"Let me see. You are telling me that in a single afternoon, he crawled through badger refuse, bat guano, and fox urine. Is this typical?"

"Yes, your lordship." Molly waved her posies for emphasis.

"I keep telling them that I lost my sense of smell in the war," Martinbrook interjected. "Great gift, allows me to investigate places no other naturalist would."

"He has no sense of smell," Harrison repeated, feeling baffled.

"No, your lordship."

Harrison retreated in defeat. "Molly, please allow Martinbrook to bathe as frequently as necessary."

Molly followed him out. "You must remember, Miss Livvy didn't run the household on a whim. Every decision was related to a particular circumstance she wanted to avoid. Have you never wondered why we have all the rules about not kindling fires in the library?"

Molly turned on her heel, calling for all the maids to help bathe Martinbrook.

Harrison returned to his office, once more chastened. He picked up his father's journal, rubbing the soft vellum with a tender hand. Now that Olivia was gone, perhaps it was time to discover what Sir Roderick had thought it essential he should know. Perhaps he could even discover why his father had thought Olivia was his perfect wife. He had a feeling he already knew, now that it was too late to make any difference.

Chapter Thirty-Four

The cottage was large enough for her and her maid Joan, along with Mr. and Mrs. Pier. The three came days after Olivia had left the abbey, claiming that maintaining the house for another mistress would be unpalatable. She didn't believe them, but she was grateful.

The novel she'd finished before Harrison had come home—*The Revenging Maiden*—was more of a success than her first. Now, she had enough income to pay the three servants the same wage they had received at the manor. The rest came from the village each day and returned to their families each evening. She missed—as she'd expected—the regular interruptions of the scholars. Harrison had relented on dismissing them, so Lark had remained at the abbey, among his books and colleagues.

Bentley had been pressing her for a third novel, but she couldn't imagine what she might write. She seemed to have left her fight at the abbey. Each day, though she stared at the page, she found she had less to say, not more.

Her hand brushed across the newest letter from Joe. Before she'd left London, he and Mr. James had thanked her for her patriotism, and confirmed for what seemed like the fiftieth time that there would always be a place for her in the ranks of the Home Office. The letter, now a week old, asked if she had decided whether she would investigate the dead man's list, as Mr. James's office was now calling it. If that didn't appeal to her, Mentor wrote, they had a position abroad ideally suited to her talents. She had told herself that today she would decide whether to take the job or not. But in truth, it could wait. She could always decide tomorrow. Or perhaps the next day.

Harrison had agreed to let her go. She'd received the settlement with his signature within days of leaving the abbey. She had returned it to him, at the last minute slipping into the envelope the tiger's-eye he had once stolen from her. She could have kept it, but she had enough to remember him by already, and she found she wanted him to have something of her. It was a foolish notion—that he might wish someday to have a remembrance of a murderess—but she indulged it.

Pier had insisted that they decorate the mantels and doorways with evergreen boughs, hoping it would improve her spirits. She'd pretended that it had, but, even so, each morning she found it difficult to rise at her usual time, and more than once in the past weeks she'd found herself remaining in her room, in bed, until long after light.

Pier said nothing, simply brought her a tray when she rang for it and brushed Olivia's hair as she sat listlessly at the dressing table until Joan brought her walking dress. Everyone spoke cheerfully when she was about, but more than once she'd noticed them looking at each other in concern. And she didn't even have the spirit to object.

She had thought that she had mourned his loss as fully as she needed to, after his first long absence. And she had. If he hadn't come back, she could have lived her life without this aching pit of longing in her belly. But he *had* come back, and she now was lost once more in her desire for him, aching after the scent of his skin and the strength of his embrace. When he'd held her, she'd memorized each caress, but the memories, inescapable, had turned to wormwood, bitter and corrosive.

She was fragile and even a little broken, but she would not always be this way. She would once more find her way, and one day, she would find some pleasure in living. But not today, and perhaps not tomorrow either.

A knock at the door roused her from her listlessness.

"Yes, come in." Olivia sat in her chair, a book unread open on her table.

Mrs. Pier stood at the threshold, folding a letter into her pocket, then looked at Olivia with barely concealed pity. Pier's pity should have roused Olivia's ire, but she'd used up all her anger. All that was left was resignation and longing. She loved him, heart and soul. But he didn't love her.

"Wassailers sing through the village tomorrow night, Miss Livvy. We'll need to provide some refreshments, especially for those who've come a long way. I've asked the cook to prepare some of Mr. Stanley's recipes, but she cannot decipher them."

"I suppose one has to have the proper hat to do that."

"Why, I believe that was humor, Miss Livvy, or an attempt at it!" Pier beamed. "Joan is airing your green silk. You'll need to greet the guests."

Olivia stared out the window. "Must I, Pier?"

"Oh, yes, miss. It wouldn't do not to greet them."

"As you wish, Mildred." She picked up her book, but didn't read it.

Harrison sat at the shared table in the scholars' lodge, a half-empty bottle of port at his side. He had moved his belongings into one of the spare rooms in the lodge. Olivia's ghost haunted the main house. Yesterday, he'd seen the flash of her dress out of the corner of his eye. He'd rushed after her and grabbed it, only to discover one of the maids wearing a dress Olivia had left behind. The abject fear on her face was enough to give him pause, but even so, he'd told her never to wear that dress in his sight again.

Before him sat a fat packet with his copies of the settlement papers. There was no real reason to look at them. He knew she had signed because his solicitor had told him so. But he needed to see her signature himself to know there was no future for them.

"Might I help, sir?" Otley hovered at his elbow. Otley had become his adviser, a role he knew the old man had often played for Olivia, but somehow he didn't mind. It connected him to her.

The thin old man untied the string around the packet and withdrew the contents. On the top stood a small box. Otley set the papers and the box in front of him; all Harrison had to do was reach out. But somehow he couldn't even lift his arm.

The other scholars gathered around.

"The box is addressed to you, sir, in Miss Livvy's hand." Otley held out the small package.

"Open it." Harrison refused the package.

"You should do it yourself, son."

"Open it, or I'll throw the lot of you out on your ears," he growled.

"Oh, dear, I believe he's serious." Lark fidgeted anxiously.

Otley very carefully unwrapped the thick brown paper that covered the small box.

Partlet whispered, "Do you think it's her wedding ring?"

"Ssh. Don't need to remind him that he's lost her," Lark chided.

Otley held out the box, but Harrison brushed it away. Nathan took it and lifted the lid.

"It appears to be a rock." Quinn leaned over, his large belly brushing the desk.

Martinbrook leaned in. "Ah, it's a quartz, one of the metamorphic rocks. Pretty, but it carries no antiquarian interest. It's most likely imported—from the Cape Colony, India, Australia, or perhaps even the American states."

"So, it's a rock." Quinn antagonized, genially.

The scholars crowded around to examine it.

"It's a very interesting pattern." Lark examined it through his magnifying glass.

"A pattern?" Harrison felt hope rise, then just as quickly diminish.

"Yes, it's commonly called a tiger's-eye. Miss Livvy had me find her one like this once."

Harrison held out his hand, and Martinbrook put the stone in his palm.

"It's hers, a memento of her father." Harrison turned the stone over between his fingers, welcoming the familiar comfort. "I carried it with me to the wars."

"Well, then, that's excellent news, your lordship." Otley nodded diplomatically.

"I don't see how." Harrison turned the crystal into the light, distracting himself from his sense of bone-deep hopelessness.

"Because Miss Livvy is an orphan, sir." Partlet brushed a tear from his monocle.

"It is her only memory of her father, something she has loved, and she has sent it to you." Quinn fingered his cravat. "It's a gesture, sir."

"Yes, of course." Nathan nodded. "It's like a leitmotif in a musical composition, a melody that comes up and recedes, then comes up again. Here, it's something you have both treasured. This is very good news."

"How can that be?" Harrison turned to the scholars.

"Perhaps I can explain, sir." Smithson twisted his thick mustache. "For Miss Olivia, this rock is like the cornerstone of a building. A gift from her father, but also associated with you. It's central to her sense of the world and her place in it."

"Yes, sir, it's an invitation, even if she doesn't realize it," Otley explained.

"But what can I do? I tried to find her, but she's just disappeared."

The scholars shifted nervously.

Harrison searched their faces, finding a mixture of apprehension and guilt. "What do you know?" he growled, all his frustration and sorrow captured in a single sentence.

Lark was so startled he dropped his magnifying glass, and Partlet removed and replaced his monocle without cleaning it on his shirt.

"We send her updates on our research every Wednesday," Nathan explained.

"Yes, Quinn slips the lot into your parliamentary packet to avoid the postage," Martinbrook said, rubbing one dirty hand on his belly.

"And here I thought you had all grown fond of me," Harrison muttered.

"We are fond of you, sir." Otley put his hand on Harrison's shoulder.

Smithson shrugged. "We are simply more fond of Miss Livvy."

Harrison laughed helplessly, and, if he was willing to admit it, a little desperately. "What should I do, gentlemen? I put myself at your mercy."

The scholars bent their white heads together.

"Christmas, sir. Miss Livvy always loved Christmas. We believe we should take it to her."

"Take the rock to her—as a gift?" It was hopeless. Couldn't they see? He'd ruined it. Harrison felt despair like a giant rat eating at his entrails.

"No, sir, Christmas."

"Yes, we should take her mistletoe and boughs of holly . . ."

"And a Christmas ham!" Quinn announced.

"No, a goose. She likes goose," Martinbrook said.

"We could have both," Lark suggested, then gave Harrison an abashed look.

The scholars were still a little wary, grateful that Harrison had voided their dismissals, but they clearly had not completely recovered.

"I don't understand how taking her a Christmas ham—or goose—will make any difference at all."

"But you, we . . . together, we are her family. That's what she wants."

"What she's always wanted, sir."

"Yes, yes, it's the reason she waited for you."

"She wants a family to fill the house with laughter—the family she's made over the years. Why do you think she kept such good care of your estate?" Quinn's tone was admonishing.

"We could wassail."

"Oh, yes! We will go to the door and sing, and she will be obligated to open it." Nathan almost giggled.

"But wouldn't we need a troupe?" Harrison objected weakly. "And what if we go to the trouble and she refuses to come to the door?"

"We are seven, plus you, your lordship. I'm sure Molly, her husband, and old Herder would go. And Joan and Susan—and Bertie. We might even convince Stanley to make a special Christmas biscuit—he loves creating things."

"But he'll need a new hat."

"Yes."

"Yes."

"Yes."

How could he protest? If the scholars thought there was a chance . . .

"Yes."

Chapter Thirty-Five

Olivia heard the sound of revelers gathering outside, and she dragged herself to the door. Pier had insisted on the green silk, and Joan had been equally insistent on twining a pearl and diamond strand, a gift from Sir Roderick, through Olivia's hair. Though the cottage had been bustling all morning, not a single soul appeared to be present now that the wassailers had arrived. Oh, well.

She stood listening for a moment, the sounds of Christmas tempting her to celebration. She breathed deeply, ready to pretend to be welcoming, and opened the door. But instead of the neighboring villagers singing, it was Harrison, his deep baritone caressing the notes as if they were her heart.

She was entranced, through one song after another, until at the end, Mrs. Pier had to step forward and usher them all in. Olivia embraced the Seven and greeted the abbey staff with sincere welcome. Bertie, already taller, flung himself into her arms. She was still holding the child when Harrison stepped forward.

"Might I come in as well?"

Olivia felt as if she couldn't breathe, the pain, the longing was too great. But she wouldn't let him see. "Of course.

There are refreshments in the drawing room." And then she escaped with Bertie to the center of the room, where the scholars and the staff would protect her.

Harrison followed Livvy into the center of the room. Taking Bertie out of her arms, he handed the boy to Mrs. Pier. In the next instant, all the scholars and staff had escaped to the edges of the room, where they stood whispering nervously.

Olivia tried to escape as well, but he grabbed her hand. "I've come a long way, with seven mad men and a gaggle of maids. I won't keep you long."

The look on her face was pained, but she acquiesced. "Go on."

"I've been named to the retinue of the ambassador. There are rumblings in the Crimea, and some expect war between the Greeks and the Turks within the decade. It will be important for the Home Office to have ears abroad."

Olivia stiffened. "I will not return to your estate to manage it in your absence."

"No, I've hired an estate manager for that, or rather you did. Herder's son-in-law is an able man, and with his head for figures and obsession with the commodities market, the estate will do well. I've even agreed to help fund some of his own investments. It's an arrangement that suits us both." Harrison found himself at a loss for words. As usual, when dealing with Olivia, all the sentences Harrison planned seemed to fade like fog before the sun. "It's unclear how long I will be gone—perhaps some months, perhaps some years. Otley has agreed to manage the scholars while I am gone."

She turned her face to the window, looking into the night. "Why did you come here, Harrison? To let me know that in your absence, I may go about in London without fear of encountering you on the street?"

"I came to say . . ." His hands trembled, and he hid them behind his back. At least she wasn't looking at him; perhaps he could get through this if she kept her back to him. Behind her at some distance, the Seven had clumped together, watching them. Lark raised his magnifying glass, and Partlet adjusted his monocle. Nathan and Martinbrook pushed their fingers forward in encouragement, while—as Otley looked on kindly—Quinn and Smithson mouthed, "Go on."

She looked full in his face, her lips still that inviting fullness, her eyes still the deep brown that made his stomach ache with longing.

"I've been a fool." His words came quickly, stumbling over each other as he tried to explain. The great orator reduced to dribs and drabs of speech. "For years a fool. My father was right. I needed a home. But he was wrong that I needed the estate. That was his home, his safe spot in a world gone mad."

"And you hope to find that home abroad?" Olivia's voice was sad and tired. It broke his heart.

"No, Livvy." He reached out, then stopped, unsure of her reaction. "My home isn't a place. It's you. From the moment our eyes first met. It's always been you."

"You don't mean that. I remember that night all too well. I saw anger and hatred, not love."

"I was angry. I'd been duped, drugged, and kidnapped, then told my father had found me 'the perfect wife,' one who would dutifully help me keep my estates and bear me children, all so I could begin the cycle of loss all over again." He held out his hand, but she waved it away. "But then, I met you. I stormed into that room, knowing I would hate you. I'd even considered how—without my father knowing—I might quietly throw you out on your ear. But you lifted that firm chin of yours, as if you were a princess, and smiled at me. My heart was yours from that moment, Livvy. Always yours."

She folded her arms below her bosom, as if comforting herself, shaking her head no. She didn't believe him, and he was going to lose her. He spoke more quickly then, desperate to help her see.

"I should have known then what kind of woman you were. That firm chin, that smile, should have told me, and if not those, then I should have seen your strength in your refusal to be bullied. But my father said 'perfect' and I heard drab and manageable. And even so, I found myself falling in love with my dutiful, happy-to-be-bound-to-the-estate wife, and I ran. Because I'd promised myself to marry a strong, adventurous, capable woman, and then my father gave me a governess, who was sweet and kind, and completely wrong for me."

She brought her hand to her mouth, holding back a sob, and stepped back from him, shaking her head. But she hadn't refused him yet, and he pushed ahead.

"You see, I didn't know my father—I've only recently discovered his work for the Home Office from the journal you transcribed for me. But he knew me, and when he said perfect, he meant I would find you daring and adventurous, in a way that would speak to my soul. He meant that you were strong and brave, a woman who could outwit me, but he also knew you were kind and gentle, a woman who would never let me settle for an estate, unless I could give that estate a heart."

Tears filled her eyes, as she shook her head from side to side. Her eyes never left his, daring him to come closer. He breathed deeply and let the breath go slowly.

"It took me a long enough time to see it, an embarrassingly long time for a man reputed to be the Home Office's best spy. You are the only woman I've ever desired, whether you are disguised as a governess or a gypsy or a wife or a spy. Whatever guise you wear, I will always love you."

She held out her hand to him, and he took it. And they stood for a long moment just looking into each other's eyes.

"Kiss her, boy," Martinbrook whispered loudly.

"Yes, kiss her."

"Yes."

"Yes."

"Yes."

"Yes."

And he did.

And the whole room cheered.

After a long time, after the scholars had gone to bed, and Bertie had received his new puppy, a blond hunting dog who immediately dogged his every step all the way to the nursery, Olivia and Harrison sat quietly before the fire.

Olivia nuzzled his neck. "By the way, that delegation . . ."

He stopped her mouth with a kiss. "I won't go if you don't wish me to."

"You can decide, but Mentor—I mean Joe—has offered me a position of my own."

He pulled back to look her in the eyes, but once more they were inscrutable. "Doing what?"

"He would like for me to get to know the other wives in a foreign court, become their friend, listen." She looked at her fingers, playing with the top button on his shirt.

"The other wives?"

"Of course I would have to be a wife first." She looked up once more, her eyes no longer inscrutable, but filled with love and desire.

"Of course." He slipped out of her arms, ignoring her cry of objection, and walked across the room to his waist-coat, abandoned some time ago. When he returned, her face watching him quizzically, but he slid down on one knee before her, and held out a ring of diamonds encircling a large central ruby. "I commissioned it new. The diamonds come from the ring my father bought for you, but the ruby is from me, a symbol of my heart. Olivia Fallon, will you marry me?"

She threw her arms around his neck, saying, "Yes, yes, yes, yes, yes, yes, yes!"

And he kissed her again, one kiss for each yes, and again, one kiss for each year of their not-marriage, and another ten dozen kisses, just for good measure.

Chapter Thirty-Six

"You seem to have lost interest in An Honest Gentleman."
Flute took his favorite seat before Charters's desk.

"Perhaps. We have discovered the identity of the other
writers. If we need to, we now have influence over them. I
prefer to lead those horses with a light hand," Charters
replied.

"What of Lord and Lady Walgrave? I hear he's been
named to the retinue of the ambassador."

"I'm inclined to consider that account settled. My residence as a scholar allowed me to remove my name from
Wilmot's list of traitors—or whatever that list proves to be.
Seeing the other names on it, I'm inclined to believe it was
nothing more than the addled brain of a dying man."

"That woman Calista showed up while you were gone
yesterday. She stood in the street, yelling your name. Your
anagrammatical one."

Charters blanched. "All of it."

"No, just the one word, spacing out the four syllables
like a chant. She's quite mad."

"I suppose we'll have to do something about that."
Charters picked up his pumice stone and began to scratch
it across his fingernails in sharp hard motions.

"Already done. We had a carriage of goods heading south, so I sent her—drugged, of course—to Matron. Told 'em her name was Olivia. Figure if she's not mad now, she will be within a few months of being called that every day."

Charters began to laugh, a low rolling sound that began in the depths of his belly.

"Flute, you are a worthy partner. I'll be going to the abbey periodically to ensure that no one notices any difference in my research habits, at least until the end of my fellowship. Matron's establishment is on that road—I'll check in on . . . Olivia . . . from time to time."

"What were you doing out there anyway?"

"Ah, Flute, you will be so pleased." Charters pulled out a piece of paper and began describing his plan.

Epilogue

It was the day of the wedding.

Harrison wanted no more questions about the validity of their marriage. Being—his friends at the Home Office joked—stolid and thorough, he insisted that the banns be read in the three parishes adjacent to the abbey as well as at Westminster. It was an irregular practice, but one that the ministers of each parish indulged, given the circumstances. Their friends at the *World* also published the banns, so that by the end, few people in Sussex or London, or perhaps even the whole of England, did not realize that Lord and Lady Walgrave intended to become once more Lord and Lady Walgrave. The ton briefly raised a collective eyebrow, sniffing at the possible scandal. But the presence of the Prince Regent at an engagement ball held for the couple by the Duke of Forster and his lovely fiancée, Lady Sophia Wilmot, quelled any further rumors.

As Sir Roderick would have wanted, the ceremony— officiated by Southbridge *and* the local bishop—was held in the family chapel, a situation that allowed Nathan to indulge his musical preferences, drawing inspiration from traditional church music, ballad tradition, popular opera, and the hymns of the Wesleyan revivalists.

Forster, Lady Wilmot, and her two children, and the members of the Muses' Salon took up one side of the church, along with various members of Parliament and the Home Office. The other side was filled to overflowing with those Olivia had cared for as Lady Walgrave. In the first pew, Bertie (without Kit) sat between the Piers and old Herder. The second pew was reserved for the Seven, who for three weeks had practiced a surprise wedding gift.

As Livvy walked down the aisle, unexpected music met her from every corner of the chapel as the Seven played her a processional composed by Nathan and played on a series of bowls of varying pitches. It was strange and strangely beautiful . . . a gift from her family.

In a shadowy nave at the back of the church, the well-dressed man watched the woman he'd last known as a scrawny girl of five become a countess, again. Then he slipped away, leaving the revelers to their feast.

Love the Muses?

Don't miss

JILTING THE DUKE

and

CHASING THE HEIRESS,

available now from Zebra Shout.

Dear Reader,

I thought you might like a little more information on the background to Olivia and Harrison's story.

The British Abolition Movement and Olaudah Equiano

By the last quarter of the eighteenth century, the British were heavily reliant on the slave trade for commodities such as cotton, tobacco, and sugar. But for many, those luxuries came at too high a moral price. In 1772, abolitionists tested the legal standing of slavery by bringing the case of a runaway slave before the King's Bench. Chief Justice William Murray, the first earl of Mansfield, ruled that British common law did not allow slavery in England or Wales. The ruling did nothing to stem the slave trade or to abolish slavery in the colonies.

In this context, Olaudah Equiano, a former slave living in England, published his 1789 *Narrative of the life of Olaudah Equiano, or Gustavus Vassa, The African*. Considered to be the first slave narrative, Equiano's *Narrative* was an immediate bestseller, going through at least eight editions before his death in 1797. Forcing the English to confront the cruelties of slavery, Equiano's narrative recounted his life as a slave, describing his childhood in Africa, his capture by slave traders, and his eventual purchase of his own freedom. Once free, Equiano settled in London where in 1792 he married a Cambridgeshire woman, Susannah Cullen (d. 1796). The publication of his book made Equiano—known as The African—a celebrity.

In 1807, Parliament abolished the slave trade in the British empire, meaning that no one could buy or sell slaves. But abolition of the trade did not also abolish slavery. Those holding slaves outside of England and Wales were allowed to keep their "property." The institution of slavery itself wasn't abolished until 1833. Slavery then was part of the backdrop of Regency life, even though slaves were not allowed in England itself.

I wanted a character who represented this fraught social context. So I looked to Equiano's daughters, Anna Maria (1793–97) and Charlotte (1795–1857). Left an orphan at two, Charlotte was reared by abolitionists. She inherited her father's fortune in 1816 and married a Congregationalist minister in 1821. Unwilling to interfere with her historical story, I resurrected instead the earlier daughter and renamed her Constance. Hints of her abolitionist background appear in her willingness to help a fleeing woman.

Women in the Book Trade

In *Jilting the Duke*, Lady Wilmot was an author, and in *Tempting the Earl* we see her book finally published. In *Tempting the Earl*, I wanted to represent women's importance in the book trade. What better solution than to make Equiano's daughter a bookseller? In *Tempting the Earl*, Constance also points to the complicated nature of race, fame and identity when she names her bookstore The African's Daughter.

I hope you enjoyed Olivia and Harrison's story, and that you have read the other books in the Muses' Salon series: *Jilting the Duke* (Sophia and Aidan's story) and *Chasing the Heiress* (Lucy and Colin's story).

I'm happy to hear from readers. Email me at rachael@rachaelmiles.com, or visit my website— rachaelmiles.com—for more historical notes, links to social media, and topics I can discuss with book clubs or community groups. Sign up for my mailing list to hear about new books!

Rachael Miles